Marc Vun Kannon

THE FLAME IN THE BOWL:
A WARRIOR MADE

Book Two

This is a work of fiction. Names, characters, places, and incidents are products of the author's imagination or are used fictitiously. Any resemblance to actual events, locales, organizations, or persons, living or dead, is entirely coincidental.

Echelon Press Publishing
9735 Country Meadows Lane 1-D
Laurel, MD 20723
www.echelonpress.com

ISBN: 1-59080-434-1
Library of Congress Control Number: 2005927271

Cover Art © Nathalie Moore
2005 Ariana "Best In Category" Award Winner
Editor: Kat Thompson

First Echelon Press paperback printing: March 2006

10 9 8 7 6 5 4 3 2 1

Printed in the United States of America

Other Books by
Marc Vun Kannon

The Flame in the Bowl:
Unbinding the Stone

Book One

Dedication

To my son, James Lee,

Who mowed the lawn on weekends so I could write this.

Prologue

Ardus Virlor blazed, burned, with a passion unquenchable but too long banked. He had to know.

The first few centuries had been the most enjoyable, fully occupied with his explorations, his researches into the stuff of the world. So what if his friends and relatives rejected him? They were all dead now, dust these many hundreds, if not thousands, of years. The world endured. He endured.

If only there were no people in it. The hardness of the world he could bear, the softness of people was just…mush, like swimming in oatmeal, his senses dulled, his capacities stunted. So…unknowable.

Ardus Virlor ached. He must know, the fire of his need beyond banking but in desperate need of containment. He had endured the killer frosts, the plagues, the disasters that claimed all others, he could endure this. The reward would be vaster than he had expected, the Eye of the World, through which could be seen all that was. He would see, he would know. And people wouldn't be so…changeable anymore.

He had to find it, had to learn how to use it. Had to have the lore, no matter where they hid it. They hid it, all right, carefully, tightly, worshipped it as a matter of faith instead of the record of truth, the instructions he needed. Imbeciles.

What happened to them? It was a gap in his memory that troubled him, but since he had the scroll he didn't waste very much thought on the matter. No doubt they had seen reason.

Ardus Virlor was bored. This isn't what he'd expected immortality to be. He gulped his drink, relying on the alcohol to dull his senses, or perhaps to dull his distaste for the things they reported to him. So close, so close. Terrible irony that he had to walk when they did, but this is the time. Endure, endure. It will all be over soon.

Chapter 1

Tarkas was running for his life. Again.

Well, fleeing *for my life,* his mind automatically corrected itself; *it is the watha that is running.* A watha is a beast of burden, the likes of which are to be found in nearly every realm a Hero like Tarkas might find himself in. Heroes like Tarkas avoided them, as a rule. Not that either disliked the other, but a Hero, being of Mendilorni stock, is more of a burden than any beast should be asked to bear, so Heroes don't ask, out of compassion. Besides which, a man on watha-back is a man who gets noticed. Heroes don't really want that kind of attention, but try telling that to a howling mob.

Some vacation.

Heroes don't get many vacations, either, except for the permanent kind; they attract trouble, the same way a hole in the ground allows things to fall into it. So they tend to wander, going where the gods need them to go, doing whatever the gods need them to do. The last time he'd had a break, it had lasted barely long enough for him to get back to the center of Irolla's domain. Hardly had he kissed her before an earthquake in Drakanshar called him away again. His longest respite, nearly a record-setter, had been for two whole hands of days, but that was many years in the past now.

"Drat," he grumbled to himself, although he wasn't entirely sure what 'drat' meant. (His mentor had used the expression once long ago, but had never explained it.) "What did I do wrong?" He had been so sure he had planned for every contingency, in this latest round of his game with the gods. All Heroes played it, Tarkas better, and more seriously, than most. They didn't expect to win, but playing well was more the object than actually winning, so no one minded. He'd even heard of a realm where they studied rituals and techniques of 'Free Time', but he had found a military academy instead, and quickly left.

This was a nice, stable realm, no upheavals in the recent past, no great convulsions impending. There should have been little enough for a Hero to do here. So he'd studied their customs and made his entry accordingly, sidestepping the obvious ploy of a religious holiday. He was no amateur! He'd come out of the mist in a desert as he'd expected, at the time he'd expected, walked to the nearest town (right where he expected it to be), went to the nearest tavern and ordered a flagon of their best. How could he have known about the eclipse?

Blasphemy was such an easy crime to commit.

By a fortunate coincidence, the guard who responded to the commotion had a girth that equaled his rank, and moreover, arrived at the main entrance to the establishment just as Tarkas fought his way out. A neatly-executed flying drop kick, catching the poor man under his hastily thrown up right arm, dislodged him from his perch and sent him plummeting into the mud and muck of the street. Tarkas took his seat and kicked the beast into surprised motion, adding yet more to his list of crimes.

The same religious holiday that got him into trouble also allowed him to escape it, as the gates had been left open for the entry of visiting religious pilgrims. Now they allowed the exit of escaping felonious strangers, as well as the hastily assembled posse in pursuit of him. Tarkas had been chased out of a lot of places, and knew his advantages to be only temporary. His mount would tire, his knowledge of the terrain was scant, and he was alone. If he intended to make proper use of the initiative while he possessed it, it would have to be soon.

Soon would do. Clearly this was the work of one of his many superiors, and he may as well get about it. If he refused, he would end up in even less pleasant circumstances than this. Besides, someone must be very anxious, to throw an unscheduled eclipse in his way. His research couldn't have been so far wrong! The first thing to do obviously was to lose his pursuit, and to do that he would need some help from the terrain. His arrival had been planned to occur out in the desert, in a rocky defile that had plenty of cover. Hopefully he could use that to good effect.

A good thing, also, that his destination was so close, as his watha lost speed at a great rate, stumbling and puffing. The track turned to stone and gained walls, rising high over his head, even mounted. It had been used as an ambush site many times in the past, he knew, certain that at least some of his pursuers would be directed towards the overlooks. Not that he intended to stay around long enough for them to spy him. He needed only one good corner, to block their vision for a beat or two. Up ahead, very good, a large boulder. Now to set up the timing, not hard for someone who had to practice *not* counting his own heart's beats.

Two of them later, he was ready. He removed his feet from the loops, preparatory to leaping clear. Now! He sailed through the air, landing lightly behind the boulder, the watha continuing hollowly up the defile. "All right, whoever you are, do what you will."

Nothing happened.

Thranj's Beard!

On foot, alone, surrounded by enemies in an ambush zone. Just fardling marvelous! He sped off on foot, keeping under cover wherever possible, now far more concerned about those overlooks, listening for the sound of pursuit, but not really expecting it. Even if they thought him worth chasing this far, they would not damage their mounts doing it. They would move slowly, letting their cohorts get up above first. They might even overshoot him, following the sound of his own watha's pads.

No such good fortune! His watha had stopped only a few hands of paces up the track, exhausted by its unaccustomed burden. Worse, a large boulder sat in the road, large enough that a watha could not pass it, although he himself might have been able to. Surely his pursuers had not made it so far so soon–! No. If they had just dropped this, he would have heard. It can't have been here long, blocking the main trade route through these hills; the townsfolk would want it clear. Still, he didn't like it. It reminded him of any of a number of traps he had been in over the years, even though it was not a trap.

"Of course–" Tarkas blurred into motion, the black length of his sword taking the life of a desert gnat as it sliced through the air without sound. Before the last echo of the first word had faded, the tip of the young Hero's wondrous blade was lodged under a man's chin as he sat calmly on a rock, hands on knees. "--it's a trap, you young idiot!"

He wore a long robe with a hood, so Tarkas could not see his hair; his manner suggested age, while his hands bespoke youth. He sat with the kind of preternatural stillness which usually only the undead can muster, the kind where Tarkas had to look to see if he breathed or not. He did, not that Tarkas had been concerned about it; the bright sunlight was reassuring.

"Are you finished?" asked the hooded man, rising smoothly to a standing position. Too smoothly; he wasn't so much trying to stand as allowing himself to rise, his hands hanging limp at his sides. There were not many who could move in such a fashion, not here. The stillness of the air, even his watha's pads seemed muted; they would not be disturbed. Tarkas relaxed.

"You don't know me," the cloaked man chided him.

There were a lot of gods he did not know. "I know enough."

The man smiled, humorlessly. "Do you?" he asked, but continued without waiting for an answer. "You seem to have a problem. Would you care for some assistance?"

About time! Tarkas shrugged, sheathing his sword with a deliberately nonchalant air. "Oh, only all that you may provide."

Again the man smirked. "I doubt that you will need quite so much. Proceed up the trail for thirty-nine paces. On the left you will see a boulder. Behind that there is a cave entrance to another path that will lead you to safety."

Tarkas waited, but no more seemed to be forthcoming. "And your purposes?" he prompted, wondering what need this god had of him, sure that merely saving his own life was not the reason for this manifestation.

The man's smile vanished, the sudden crashing noisiness of the world emphasizing his displeasure. "Do not question my purposes," he commanded. "Go."

An order from a god is an order from a god, no matter how

strange. Tarkas turned and went, squeezing his way with some difficulty past the stone in the crevice. The cowled one watched him leave, his stance revealing not one whit the relief he felt. The young man would accomplish all, surely, and his own intervention would be undetectable. Nor had he forgotten the details. First the large boulder blocking this path…it flickered and vanished obediently. One arm moved, flinging a vial of some oily liquid-looking substance against the rocks, where it shattered, releasing a pungent, evil-smelling stench that would have bothered even him had he not altered his own sense of smell. The watha had no such ability; it reared and fled, terror overcoming its exhaustion. The man watched it go, satisfied. The mating-musk would sow confusion among the lad's pursuers, and also convince them of his horrible demise. That it might also attract something to lair here was a negligible risk, he thought…

…and vanished, leaving only faint footprints pressed into the stone.

Tarkas sped up the track, counting his footsteps. So many boulders! How in this world would he know which one? As the counter in his head reached 'seven plus four' (a bastard expression born from two different and unrelated counting systems), he saw it, a giant rock completely out of place: the wrong color, the wrong material, wrong texture, wrong composition, it assaulted his tightly strung senses. He looked up, down, all around. Finally he scrambled up the stone wall and looked down behind the stone. Yes, a crack, a space. He pushed, his Hero's strength barely able to widen the crack enough to allow him to squirm down behind the stone, his leather jerkin protecting only his body from the rough scraping, his arms and legs scratched but not yet bleeding. Bracing his back on the rear wall, he pushed with his legs and arms to keep from being crushed, and widen the space as he descended. His head disappeared into the gap before his feet touched the lip of a hole, and now he had to fight to hold the stone back using only his arms. Ultimately he lost, but his head made it down into the space even as the boulder crunched back against the wall, trapping him in darkness.

He leaned against the wall, resting and catching his breath. His pursuers could not move that stone with a team of watha; they'd never guess where he went. He held his fingers up, running them lightly around the edges of the cave mouth. Yes, air movement. Good, time to get moving. "Light!" he commanded, and the hilt of the sword behind his head glowed, not a strong light, but enough to reassure someone who depended on his eyes.

He knelt in a tunnel, a stone tube that continued beyond the range of the sword's feeble illumination. The colors were muted, there may have been crystals but they did not glint; he'd have to be careful with his hands, lest they get all cut up as he felt his way along. With luck the tunnel would get higher soon. He crouched off, his knees taking most of the abuse. Behind him, long after he had gone and wouldn't notice, both the out-of-place boulder and the hole hiding behind it went away to wherever they had come from.

Many rest breaks later, during which he would lie flat to remind his knees how to straighten, the tunnel did widen, and narrow. It did many things, except end. There were vents, to be sure, and gaps admitting light, but high up in great vaulted chambers where they could not be reached. He alternated between annoyance and boredom, and only the thought that he was here for some reason kept him from calling up a *that*way trail and leaving entirely for parts known.

Wait.

What's that smell? It reminded him of blood, but not quite.

He stopped, not turning, his arms held out to the sides of the tunnel he could only barely see. He backed up, his fingers revealing more than his eyes. When he found the gap in the stone, he stopped, inhaling deeply. Not for the first time, he regretted Deffin's absence. The faithful beast would have found the crack fifty paces beforehand. He wondered how the nizarik fared, not moving there in the tunnel as his mind wandered. But he had other things to worry about. The smell was fainter here, and absent before the crack. He had no doubt that he'd found the reason for his coming.

The crevice ran high and narrow, forcing him to edge in sideways, his sword, naturally, in his leading hand. Here it served three purposes, lighting the way as before, but also a probe and a defense. He tapped his way through the slit, his sword ringing slightly against the walls as the smell became stronger and ever more unpleasant.

What?

He stopped and stilled, his mouth opening to make it easier for him to hear. Hear what? A faint, high-pitched whisper. He tapped his sword sharply, once.

"There is who?" a voice quavered at him.

"There is who? There is who?" the tunnel echoed on the quaverer's behalf.

He hesitated briefly, not having thought to invent an appropriate name for this realm. "Demlas Tarkas," he responded at last, and paused, but his words did not echo.

"Mortal are you?" came the next question, more strongly this time. "Mortal are you? Mortal are you?"

That stopped him. Why would–? Again he hesitated, a host of unwelcome possibilities ghosting through his mind and only one way to know. "Unmortal am I."

"Unmortal is he!"

"Praise the one!"

"Saved we are!"

Saved? *We*? Tarkas moved forward. If it was a trap, he was already trapped; if not, he wasn't going to be attacked in here. In short order his sword struck nothing. The tunnel had widened, and he could breathe again, although he didn't want to, not too deeply. The smell here was overpowering, the air still and stagnant. He did not immediately see the speakers, but only because they were lying on the floor, unmoving, surrounded by a sea of black nearly the same color as their skin, at least in the light cast by Tarkas' sword hilt. The image came to him, from his readings on this realm, one of his ancient histories. Goblins!

But the goblins had been wiped out centuries ago. At least, that is what the book had said. Tarkas had learned the hard way that some books were more hopeful than accurate, and this looked like one of those times. He sheathed his sword, aware that goblins, cowards as a rule, would have attacked him in ambush or from behind, if they were going to. His hand leaving the hilt increased the light on the scene.

The black sea was a pool of blood, goblin blood, as he had suspected. It leaked from all the cuts on the three goblin bodies, cuts that had been inflicted specifically to maim, to leave the victim cruelly immobile and utterly helpless. "You poor bastards," he sympathized, hoping that he had used the word 'bastards' correctly this time.

"Pity us don't."

"Deserve it we do."

"Stupid we were."

Ever more strange, and now the Hero had no idea what was happening. Goblins are hard to wound and harder to kill, yet these wounds had apparently stayed open for quite some time. Goblins admitting the error of their ways? The justice of their punishment? What had happened here? "What did you do, that was stupid?"

"Hero we fought."

"Captured him we did."

"Captured his woman we did."

"Hurt her we did."

"Hated us he did."

"Escaped us they did."

Tarkas broke in. "You tortured his woman and he did this to you in revenge?" It seemed odd behavior for a Hero.

"Many of us there were."

"Fled us they did."

"Pursue them we did."

Tarkas was sure that their pursuit had been unwilling. If their quarry had been strong enough to escape they should have felt well rid of it. His knowledge of the history of the goblins was scant, and he wondered who–or what–could have had the influence over them to give such orders. "You pursued him here?"

"Here it was not."

"Stupid that question is."

"Foolish you are."

The rebuke offended Tarkas not at all; he had not really thought so. "You pursued him here and then someplace else?" he amended.

"First we were."

"Magic he used."

"Portal he called."

There were not many magic-users here. One of his own reasons for coming had been the relative lack of magic, and so no real need for him or his talents, while there were others more formidable than himself when it came to physical combat. But he imagined that a Hero summoning a *that*way trail would look like magic to those with no experience.

"You fell upon him when he opened his…portal?"

"Different it was."

"Not here we were."

"Someplace else we went."

They had no idea, nor could Tarkas enlighten them.

"Foolish we were."

"Attacked him we did."

"Fought us he did."

That *was* foolish. Goblins are not great fighters, relying more on their relative invulnerability and numbers than in martial skill. But still– "How came you by these wounds?"

"Angry he was."

"Inflict them he did."

"Kill us he intended."

Tarkas could understand that. Once his Irolla had been threatened like that, and the temptation had been his. "What stayed his hand?"

"Saved us she did."

"Pleaded with him she did."

"Mercy he showed."

This? Mercy? Tarkas was almost about to vomit. He must have missed something. "How so?"

"Stayed his hand he did."

"Sent us back he did."

"Healing he intended."

The story as he understood it made no sense to Tarkas. No Hero should have acted like that, yet no conceivable accident could account for their condition. Could this be the god's purpose, to set him on the trail of a rogue Hero? After he aided the goblins, of course. What kind of aid could he provide? "Why did you not heal?"

"Know we do not."

"Know we do not."

"Know we do not."

"Masters we called."

"Come they did not."

"Help us they did not."

A surprise that was, Tarkas thought to himself, unconsciously mimicking the goblins' speech pattern in a ghastly, yet defensive, echo. None who might have mastered these would have cared overmuch about their slaves' predicament, except to laugh at it occasionally. The gods here might have been willing, perhaps, but he did not know how these poor, uh, souls would go about asking, nor were goblins at all likely to–

"Prayed we did."

"Gods we called."

"Came none did."

He received this news with remarkable calmness. In fact, the amazement Tarkas felt was a mild surprise at how surprised he was not. So many odd things–

"Then the One came."

"Aid us he promised."

"Left us he did."

To come to me, Tarkas knew, although why a god would go to such lengths–? Well, the gods did many strange things, as he knew better than any, and often trying to understand them nothing but an exercise in futility. "I have met this 'One.'" Suddenly his head exploded in pain, his skull feeling skewered with hot, dull knives, and the next moments were a blur to him.

The little chamber exploded with a high-pitched yelping, the goblins clamoring in apparent glee. But it ended soon, they were truly feeble.

"And you came."

"His promised aid you are."

"Save us you will."

That declaration was the first thing Tarkas heard that made sense, the words more than mere sounds in the maelstrom inside his head. "Save you I will," he mumbled, setting off more yelping, and he considered how he was going to accomplish that feat. His magic, in this world, was less than it usually was, and this task seemed far more than he usually tried to accomplish with it. A task of this sort seemed to call for a mira–Wait! This realm. He'd studied it, but not with this in mind. What were the rules here? If only he could think! His memory remained, and soon it delivered the information he needed.

"I must go," he told them, setting off howls of despair. "There is only one who can save you, and only I can get him to do it," he lied, with the skill of long practice. Always leave them guessing, he had been told so long ago, even when 'they' were goblins. There were some things he could never tell them, and it was not much of a lie in any event.

"Where do you go?"

"Who this one is?"

"How save us he will?"

"The one I must see is the lord of this place. He is called…" Tarkas paused, trying to remember if there was a special name he should use. "Menniver."

Again the chamber rang with yelps and echoes of yelps, but these were not of glee, nor did they fade. Tarkas clapped his hands over his ears as a pain that was painless grew inside his skull.

"Doomed we are," cried one during a brief pause for breath.

"Doomed we are," cried the second as the first resumed.

"Why?" yelled Tarkas, in the small gap between their utterances, hoping that the third would answer him, and he was not disappointed

"Menniver's curse this is!"

Chapter 2

Tarkas paused on the forest trail, to shake the ringing, painful echoes of the goblins' cries from his brain.

That had been something new, and he had no desire to remember it, much less experience it again. Some note or pitch in their voices had reached right into the middle of his head and stuck there like a thorn would in his foot. He fled the cavern and the stench, but had not even waited to get away from the tunnel, just called up a *that*way trail right on the spot and departed.

The pain and the memory of pain fled like the ghosts they had been, giving way to the pleasures of his accustomed woodlands. It was always woods, not that he minded, but the contrast with the dim stone tunnel glared, and now it occurred to him to wonder why. But that question was of little import, and he recognized its presence in his mind as an attempt to distract him from the last several beats worth of experiences. They were strange, to say the least, and almost crowded out his senses as he walked down the trail, with the questions they had raised. But only almost, since the biggest question concerned the *that*way trail he now walked. Wounded goblins! Goblins heal within beats, the book had said. Books lied, he knew, but not about these sorts of things. The goblins should have healed here as they would have in their own realm, but they hadn't. But they weren't dying either.

It couldn't be Menniver's work, no matter what the third goblin had said. Menniver had built up quite a reputation in his early days for morally righteous behavior, and his time as a Major Deity had only broadened those traits, until now most regarded him as the most insufferable, hidebound, rule-conscious…! Tarkas squelched the thought firmly, fully aware of his own failings. Nor was he a god, with all the burdens they have to bear. For all his apparent faults,

Menniver did what he did reasonably well, but Tarkas was glad he didn't dwell here.

Round and round his thoughts whirled–Menniver, goblins, trails–as his feet, lacking higher direction, carried the rest of him along the ribbon of dirt. There had to be something–Wait! Something crouched in his thoughts, something he couldn't quite remember. He cast his thoughts back, trying to seize hold of that shadowy, vital–*Argh*! A stab of pain tore through his head, and his hands flew up of their own accord, as if they could do anything.

Something large and heavy struck him in the back, shoving him forward and full-length onto the ground, even as the pain in his head vanished. "Not!" a voice reverberated in his ears, and a weight was on his back, fumbling with his scabbard. The buckles seemed to confuse the speaker, but even as Tarkas pushed himself up with his Heroic strength, the leather straps holding his sword on his back tore like leaves, and his adversary tumbled off him with the weapon in his hand.

Paw, he corrected himself, turning to see his attacker for the first time. No wonder the buckles stopped it; those fingers were claw tipped and useless for such operations. And teeth, naturally, the Hero noted, as he looked his foe over. One of the more useful traits he had received from his mentor's potion long ago, he automatically looked for the threats first: claws, teeth, knees like this, skin like that, ears pointed up, eyes forward, etc, etc. In mere beats Tarkas knew what he needed to know.

A grunt! Or whatever it might be called. There was probably a name for them somewhere, if the sorcerer who had made them had bothered to give them one. Tarkas would never know, since that particular person was long dead. But his creatures weren't, despite the stronghold being consumed by a new and active volcano. A few always got away, and much of his Hero's life was devoted to hunting them down.

Apparently this one had decided to return the favor.

"Death," it roared, stating the obvious with a muzzle ill-suited to human speaking, shaking his sword like a child's rattle. Its vocabulary was impressive.

"*Anh*," he grunted, which was all he could remember of theirs. But it was a good grunt, and the creature's howls needed no translation. Then the time for conversation passed, the grunt's clawed feet digging furrows in the packed earth as it raced forward to deliver the killing blow to its helpless prey–

–who easily sidestepped its headlong charge and tripped it into the bushes behind him. "Judge me by my teeth, will you?" But taking his weapon was really quite a clever move. Tarkas could defend himself easily, but he had no way to mount a really effective attack without something sharp to pierce its natural armor. Sooner or later even this small-minded lummox would know this, and attack more sensibly. He had to get his sword back before that happened.

The grunt clawed its way out of the bushes, unharmed, not even noticing the twigs and thorns that Tarkas' skin made sure he felt. It even used the sword like a stick, the scabbarded length pushing branches away from the grunt's delicate nose and eyes, at all times keeping its ferocity aimed at Tarkas. Then the sword, still sheathed, was also aimed at Tarkas, a long hard metal bludgeon little better than a tree branch. He caught it easily, of course, as it swung down to crush his skull, and tried to pull it from its captor's paws, but the grunt expected this and pulled instantly, drawing the Hero within range of its more personal weapons. Tarkas recovered, his other hand shooting upward to impact the snout at its most delicate point.

The creature roared with pain, flailing its arms wildly and hurling the off-balance Hero away as it retreated, its attack negated and stalemated. It patted delicately at its nose, its eyes promising an even slower and more painful death than it had already resolved to deliver. Finally it realized its advantage, its feeble wits suddenly remembering that the stick in its paw was more than that. Slowly, dramatically, it held out the sword in one paw and grasped the hilt with the other, allowing a stream of spit to drip from its fangs, its tongue curling in anticipation as its nose detected the heavenly scent of fear at last.

Tarkas tensed and moved as if to hurl himself forward in a last-ditch attempt to prevent the inevitable, and the creature reacted, flexing in the old familiar motions. But the Hero's move was a feint, and the grunt collapsed in screaming agony, as he had known it would. Only the right sort of person could draw his sword, and grunts weren't right, nor even people. But he kept triumph from his fine features as he sped forward to claim his own. A brief examination showed that the harness was useless, a dangling leather strap. "You bastard," he shouted, as the grunt ceased its whimpers and opened its eyes. Yet it lay there helpless, its wracked body unable even to twitch as the Hero drew the blade in one swift and pain-free motion. "I ought to kill you right now!"

Of course. That is what Heroes did, after all, and the grunt had known that failure would mean its own death. But pack loyalty is even stronger than that great dread, and this one was responsible for most of the deaths. And so it waited for the killing blow.

Which did not come. Shockingly, the furless, soft-skinned, toothless murderer sheathed his blade, chest heaving, and waves of conflicted scents rolling off of his slick body, his short, weak teeth bared. The creature lay confused. Surely its enemy would not attempt to use those teeth against it! But no! The furless one turned away, and the grunt felt only contempt for his weakness. That was the last thing it saw, the last thing it felt. Tarkas spun, drawing his blade with impossible hope blossoming on his face. But no! The itch that had always meant magic to him only signaled the creature's escape, not a renewed attack. It had gone by the time he turned, only a smudge in the dirt marking its one-time presence.

"Well done, Hero," a deep voice praised him.

Of course.

He turned slowly, putting his sword away as he came face to face with…someone. "And you are–?" he prompted. His visitor was obviously a god, his stance and bearing unmistakable, his sense of solidity noticeable only because Tarkas knew what to look for. His guest's appearance, however, startled him, momentarily. For some reason, he thought that this god should look different. Which was stupid, really, gods looked like whatever they wanted to look like.

"I am myself," said the god in slight reproof, "But you may call me Menniver."

"I greet you, Menniver," said Tarkas as he approached, holding out his hand in the usual way. "I am Tarkas."

The god's eyebrow rose fractionally. "Once of Kwinarish, now of Querdishan. You are known to me," he said sociably. "You're shorter than I expected."

Tarkas restrained a sigh. Everyone said that. "I am honored."

"To be short?"

"To be known to you, sir," corrected the Hero, revising his impression of this god upwards a notch. He wasn't known for banter. "And I was seeking you out, as well, so–"

"*Ah*. Business. It always intrudes, doesn't it?" The smile faded, the atmosphere of camaraderie dissipated. "Good. I prefer business. More…structured."

"That is your reputation, sir," responded Tarkas fearlessly.

The god moved his body, bringing it closer to Tarkas. "Such tolerance is welcome, especially from a Kwinarisha. Let us go."

Tarkas betrayed no emotion at the approach, spectral as it appeared, startled instead by the utterance. "'Go', sir? To where?" He looked around inanely.

If the question surprised Menniver, he did not show it. "To Mendilorn, of course," he replied, stopping at the Hero's side. "Hold out your arms, like this. That's right. We could continue this discussion here, but I'm sure you know about manifestations."

Yes, he did, but he hadn't stopped to think before he spoke, always a recipe for disaster. Besides, he had not known–"I did not know that one could get to Mendilorn from here, sir."

"Naturally not," said Menniver, not a hint of reproof in his tone. He adopted a stance similar to the Hero's, their fingertips barely touching. "Only a Major Deity would need it. Close your eyes."

Ripple.

"You may open them again." Tarkas did so, unsurprised to find the god now on his other side, fingertips still touching as if only their positions had been reversed. Yet now they stood within a room, a very bland and ordinary room, with a very bland and ordinary view coming in from its single, unadorned window. Outside he saw a street, and buildings, but no people anywhere. Tarkas would have been surprised if there had been. "I apologize for the sparseness of the furnishings," continued Menniver without seeming at all regretful, "But my house is rather beyond your, um–"

"'Mortal sensibilities'?" suggested Tarkas, recalling a phrase used by someone with a vastly greater sense of humor than Menniver. For a brief beat he recalled his home and people, wondering how they fared, but the impulse passed without even summoning an image. The past was past.

The god smirked and inclined his head. "Quite. Multidimensionality is one of my hobbies, and I have no desire to distress you." Some chairs presented themselves, and the two sat. Tarkas half-expected his host to offer refreshments, but that half was disappointed. "So. State your business."

The Hero needed but one word: "Goblins."

The god held up a hand. "You are here to plead for mercy, I hope."

Tarkas was struck dumb, but only for a beat or two. It surprised him not at all that Menniver expected a plea from him, but considering his history–"You want to release them?"

"I do. I have for centuries. They are free–and healing, I imagine–even as we speak."

Only his habitual reserve kept Tarkas from inserting another foot into his mouth as he used his wits instead of his tongue. The gods could not act without someone making the request first, at least in this realm. That was Menniver's own law, and apparently a request from a Hero met the condition. But the other information he had made no coherent Song to his ears. Centuries. Goblins. Hoping. "Are these the same–?"

Menniver nodded. "I know these creatures." How he knew them! Still he could feel the rage, the one time in his long existence when he had wanted to kill something, the shame and relief. But there were other things. "How did you find them?"

The question seemed normal enough, but somewhere between his ears and his mind it struck a glancing blow upon some obstacle and veered off into ambiguity. "They didn't look at all well–"

"No," interrupted the god, his thoughts narrowing with suspicion. "I meant, how did you happen to be in that tunnel, in that cave? It is rather removed, as I recall."

Tarkas' usual glibness ground to a halt. How *had* he come to be there? "Um–"

Menniver approached, his concentrated attention making him much more fearfully spectral. "You do not remember?" he murmured, a threatening growl. By an act of will, Tarkas held his place, forcing himself to be convinced that this apparent anger was not directed at him, even that minuscule muscle tension a shining light to the being before him.

"You fear me?" he asked, in a vastly different tone. "*Ah.* I recall now that you have a special–"

Tarkas shook his head, quite aware of that particular difficulty, somewhat embarrassed that it should be known so widely, and dismissive of both with the one gesture. "Not at all, sir," he responded politely, "I was surprised, is all."

"My apologies," replied Menniver ritualistically. Surprised? Fear? "I had in fact intended to plumb your memory, yet–"

Now Tarkas understood, or thought he did. "Do so if you must. My 'condition' afflicts me only in the depths, not at the surface." Permission granted, the god made no reply, moving briskly to place fingers in various appropriate places. Tarkas focused on the mechanical aspects of the procedure, distracting himself from what was coming, an act as common as it was personally distasteful. Memory-reading is the fastest and most accurate way for gods to learn a Hero's mind, but Tarkas at least found the experience jarring and unpleasant. It probably was his own private reaction, no other Hero he'd met had mentioned it, and certainly his first several experiences with the process had been enough to leave him scarred for life.

Strange, he mused, how the positioning of the fingers differs so much, each god choosing different points of contact. He had convinced himself that the touching was only a ritual, mostly for his own benefit, and that the god could read his memories from the other side of the realm had he wished. However, he'd never asked, certain that no god would give him a trustworthy answer, and so he always wondered.

Wondering-musing-distracting…He experienced his own feelings and actions in reverse and from a distance as Menniver sustained his present while reversing his past, scanning his activities of the last several beats for clues to the strangeness he had detected. For a Hero to not remember is not so unusual, considering the enemies they sometimes faced and the wounds they sometimes received. But Tarkas had received no wounds and did not claim to have faced any other enemies, so his Singer's memory had no excuse for failure.

…Promising-pain-yelping-PAIN! Menniver stopped instantly, his fingers springing into the air as the two portions of Tarkas' personal timestream rejoined themselves. He rubbed his fingers absently. "You said 'depths'," the god reproved his guest.

Tarkas considered the pain he had felt and forgotten. "Yes, depths," he repeated himself emphatically. "That was but a memory of pain."

Menniver looked at him oddly. "That is incorrect. I could clearly feel the tugging at your self. Your 'memory of pain' itself caused you pain, and from the same source, which is itself anomalous." Somewhere in his house, a room changed, but the Hero did not know it.

"What is a 'nomolous'?" asked the Hero in all innocence.

"It means that the problem is currently unnamed," replied the god, who declined to notice the error, since it didn't matter all that much. He had learned over eons that people didn't care for perfect correctness in all things and got upset to have it pressed upon them.

"So let us name it." Somewhere in the house, the contents of a changed room began bending themselves to that very purpose.

"That is not so easily done," responded the god, who immediately regretted it. That had been a perfect opportunity for some witty rejoinder–'I dub thee Fred'–or some such, but such repartee was alien to him. "The problem is clear, it is the source which needs resolution."

Tarkas hesitated. "Um–?"

Menniver sighed, standing upright. "Someone tried to excise a portion of your memory–"

"That cannot be done," interrupted Tarkas, whose memory of the attempts was painful and fresh. He stood also, vaguely uncomfortable.

"I know," answered the god with upsetting candor. "We all do. Only a Major Deity could have done this to you, and no one of us would without compelling reasons, none of which exist."

"For the moment," murmured Tarkas unhappily.

"At all," countered his superior, an eyebrow rising at the lack of perspicacity. "Such an act can only impair your effectiveness, as it has in this case. It cannot be countenanced."

That sounded final, and bad for someone. "What will you do?" he asked, afraid to know. He had already had a long day.

The god smiled, managing to make it look grim even so, and replied, "Whatever needs to be done, of course!"

That line was familiar; Tarkas and all the other Heroes used it to describe what they did. But gods ought not to be doing Heroes' work, he knew, and he knew also that having them do it would be bad. His face showed nothing, of course, and again he rejoiced in his partial immunity to the knowingness that gods had of their subjects. His sluggish thoughts had barely stirred before something distracted him yet again, an off-key clanging from somewhere behind him. He turned just in time to see a folded piece of paper slide through a hole in the door and almost hit the floor before flitting its way into Menniver's outstretched hand. The god didn't open it, however, and the message flared into ash immediately.

"It never rains but it pours," he murmured abstractedly.

A flood, thought Tarkas, and immediately his thoughts turned to the many things he could do to assist the victims. "Sir?" he inquired, preparing to receive whatever commands might be given.

But– "You wouldn't happen to know anything about an eclipse, would you?"

Tarkas stumbled as the dirt of the path settled slightly under the sudden and unexpected pressure of his feet, his hand fumbling blindly about him for a tree limb to steady himself as his mind stuttered with pain yet again. Surely Menniver had not meant to–! No, more likely it was the god's lack of practice with wit, his final remark, of "Forget it" as he sent Tarkas on his way, having unforeseen consequences.

Then Tarkas reconsidered the events of his too-long day, and thought that perhaps the consequences hadn't been quite so unforeseen after all. For all they do the gods' work, the little tasks which gods cannot themselves do, Heroes did not often deal with gods or get to see much of their doings. Probably all to the good, considering what gods sometimes had to do, and a certain amount of forgetfulness automatically imposed–?

Tarkas rejected the notion. Not only is mind control or altering counter-productive, as Menniver himself had pointed out, the very notion was anathema to them, as it should be to all thinking beings. In any event, there is no need to attribute sinister motives when innocent ones will do, and honest error was certainly understandable from anyone, even a Major Deity, in Menniver's circumstances. A chance at restitution to creatures long done wrong by, coupled with his own unexpected puzzle, followed almost immediately by a perturbed Demi-God wondering where his sacrifices had gone– Dizzying was hardly strong enough for such a state! He could almost feel sorry for Menniver, but truly the god's passion for order was his undoing.

Tarkas thrust the problem from his mind, focusing his attention on those that were his own. Looking around, he noted that he had re-appeared in precisely the same spot from which he had departed, as the slight smudging in the dirt made clear. His mouth quirked in a grimace, expressing his annoyance at gods, grunts, and the universe in general. Surely, he could not just kill a fallen foe, but he would have waited to dispatch the creature had Menniver not intervened. Now he had to wait for it to reveal itself again, no doubt with another surprise assault. At least now his scabbard-strap wouldn't break, Menniver had promised that much.

How *had* he met those goblins? While he did not mind doing good for someone, it bothered him not knowing why or how he had come to do so. He even imagined he could feel the tangle in his mind, where his memories pulled. But that, too, was a problem for someone else, and he put it away.

Time to be gone. Perhaps he could spend some little time with his beloved Irolla before he had to return to his family in Querdishan. So odd to think of them that way, pleasurable and painful at the same time. He would never see Kwinarish again, he knew, at least not while it was his Kwinarish, and he had heard of changes already. He regretted that, keenly aware that to do so slighted his new family and people for something not only not their fault, but beyond their comprehension. His soul divided, he treasured the divide.

He had to get going; *that*way trails had ways of showing their displeasure, when you were not walking along them, and sometimes when you were. At least there were no signposts in view. Which way, which way? Suddenly he realized that he had quite forgotten in which direction he had been walking when attacked so suddenly. That could be bad; he had never heard of anyone going the wrong way before. He scanned the ground and foliage quickly, not knowing what to look for, hoping to see some signs of his previous passage. Briefly he wished he had received 'Concentrated Elixir of Woodsman' those years ago, as his eyes discovered smudges in the dirt and broken branches elsewhere. If he remembered correctly–This way, he decided.

The trail gave way easily before him; apparently he had chosen wisely. And there before him–'Oh joy, oh bliss, oh paradise forever,' he thought tiredly. He had expected a signpost, had even told himself he wanted to see one, but still…He paused briefly, checking the various numbers and considering his options. *That*way trails collect dangers, one of their many functions; the numbers on the post indicated not only the length of the trail but also the degree of danger in taking it. Fortunately, this time the numbers were not widely separated, so he could take the longer path in good conscience. It had been a long day, and without doubt the worst vacation of his career.

Chapter 3

Humming a Song from her childhood–*The Fenrel and the Hummingbird*, Tarkas would be scandalized–Lady Elemental of Life Irolla tel Kwinarish pushed open the next door in her daily rounds. This was her favorite task, checking all the new projects in the greenhouse; her native Kwinarish being much more tropical than the realm she now lived in and cared for, so the heat and humidity made the greenhouse the homiest area of her fortress.

How odd to live in a fortress, for one of her heritage, one of the least aggressive realms in all of creation. Odder still that she would need a fortress, there being only three other people, that she knew of, in the region beyond this domain, of which she was the mistress. But the fortress did not protect those inside from those without, not at all.

She stepped inside, avoiding as always the snapping teeth of the room's oldest inhabitant, a plant-form she called Snapper, since she had to call it something. Names were for people or favored beasts, and she felt rather stupid calling a plant anything, but the inhabitants of this room and the spaces within somehow seemed to call for them. At least that one was appropriate, but some of the other biting plants weren't so fortunate. But they were here, all of them, and the spiny–Oo, that one failed after all. She let herself be saddened, momentarily, the only mourning the poor unfortunate would get. Failure was no stranger to these domains, especially not here; the successes were less common and more celebrated. She smiled even as she lifted the wilted greenish mass from its perch, remembering the joy she had felt in placing that flat spiny thing in the depths of the Blasted Lands. She would have to check and see if it had been named yet, or even discovered. She was terrible with names, she reflected ruefully as she conveyed the dead plant-form to the disposal.

THUMP! She almost jerked at the noise, lost in thought, but she knew the rhythms of life in her home too well to be surprised, even by Tusker charging the walls at the sight of her moving within. But the walls were still stone, despite being clear, and his attacks only caused mild pain, only to him. She looked out at him even as her foot searched for the root of the disposer–Tarkas had told her it was called 'garbage cane', apparently a joke she did not get–waiting to see if one of the others would…

Of course one did, but Tusker could not be so easily vanquished, even with a headache. The spurs on his rear hooves proved more than sufficient to stave off his opponent and get him space to turn. Unfortunately, the pursuit after his craven attacker took him into the foliage and beyond her sight, while the minor chore of neatly disposing of…whatever-its-name-had-been distracted her from following with her more occult senses. At the touch of her foot the plant's stubby top popped up, releasing a fetid stench from the previous failures. Rarely did the cane fully digest one before getting the next.

The room's other occupants had all survived, so her stay in the greenhouse was unfortunately brief. She would have welcomed a delay before making her next and last stop, a small stone room with no doors at the top of a flight of stairs in a tall tower with slick walls and no windows. She hated the stairs, narrow and steep and lit only by glowing moss to mask the subtly curved walls and changing heights of the steps. Even after all this time she sometimes stumbled. She hated the door, or rather the smooth and featureless wall at the top of the stairs, visible only because the moss left it darkly invisible. She reached out hesitantly, wishing that her hand would sink into the well of blackness, only to encounter the waiting stone. Her hand stung, her stomach clenched, her head swam as they always did, the Life elementals on duty in the door making sure they could allow her in before the Earth elemental parted the stone to allow her entry.

The portal split open, blinding her even with her eyes closed. Despite the lack of windows and walls thicker than her own body, the room shone with objects of great power glowing in ways that eyes could not see but her other senses could. Like a wave of stagnant sewage it poured over her, a torrent of forces decidedly unnatural in origin, the remnants of a perverted union. Her predecessor's unholy spawn. She moved her foot, ready to enter.

"My Lady?" a voice called from the base of the stairs. *The Gods be Praised!* She stepped gratefully away from the portal, but not so far the elementals would close it.

"What is it?" she said. Go away and let me get this over with, she thought with desperate clarity, Unless it is a pestilence, which I really do not want and would be terribly unfortunate for the victims but a wonderful excuse nonetheless–

"There is someone here to see you," called up a male voice. What? Only one man–then she recognized the voice, and her heart soared.

"Tarkas, my beloved, my darling," she shouted as her joy crested, with none of her elementals about to damp its rise, or slow its headlong plunge into– "As soon as I come away from here I shall be delighted to kill you." *Five minutes late you are, and me up here all alone!* Which was unfair and she knew it, but without her elementals to carry away her hurt it escaped as it would.

Tarkas bounded up the steps without a moment's delay. "Why wait?" he asked, thinking her comment mere jest. She was content to let him think that. In his presence, it was even true.

They embraced, their privacy ensured by their place, the passion of their reunion unobserved by all. Even her elementals, which would enjoy eavesdropping on human doings in any other circumstance, were absent, disliking even more than she did the contents of this room. Door duty was a punishment, and the bodiless creatures were ever so well-behaved now.

But manure is a great fertilizer for crops, not passions. They parted, embarrassed as if found unclothed by the central fire at meal time. Even Tarkas, insensitive to Natural influences, could detect something amiss, its source not hard to determine. He stepped forward, peered into the darkness, and muttered, "What else have you killed?"

The joke fell flat, but Irolla did not hold it against him. "I only wish it was so," she affirmed vehemently, stepping far enough away from the door that it would close. "But it is not living, now or ever, and its destruction is beyond my resources."

Tarkas jerked his head back before his nose became a permanent fixture, as Deffin's tail hairs had once done. He considered putting his own powers to the solution of her problem, but refrained from asking. He was no Lord, and so had no idea of her difficulties. She would ask if and when she thought it appropriate. Until then his only contribution could be to comfort her when he could. He stepped up and cautiously touched her arm, but she only stepped forward and proceeded down the stairs, forcing him to follow in silence.

Only after they left the steps behind and crossed a grassy sward, warmed by the sun and the swarms of life all around them, did he try to break her silence. "What is in there?"

She sighed, but distance did much to restore her spirits. "A…thing, not a tool or anything of use. It seems little more than a creation of evil for evil's sake, a coming together of the powers of Life and of Earth merely to see if it were possible to do. I keep it here because I found it here."

Tarkas had a sudden suspicion, born of old memory. "Is it her chair, the one made of metal?" Khan–the Demi-God Hara-Khan the Redeemer–had thought it the crucial link in their adventure together.

She burst out laughing, a little too giddy for real merriment, but a welcome sound anyway. "I gave that away long ago. It served no purpose here, but I could not see a reason to have it unmade. It was pretty, in a crude way."

She sounded so blithe about it that her lover immediately became suspicious. It could not have remained anywhere else in the Elsewhere. "You returned it to the Realm?"

She nodded, goading him. He considered this, dismayed. He had seen that throne, knew how it would be valued, and could not imagine any good outcome from giving it to any one over any other. Irolla's lack of imagination could be dangerous. "To whom did you give it?"

"To no one."

"Then where is it?"

She turned to look at him, oddly amused. "Oh, somewhere."

He gripped her arm, forced her to turn and face his unsmiling face. Some jokes went too far, and he had responsibilities. "Where?"

She looked at him, sober and composed. "I may tell you," she said oddly, as if she were constrained to some sort of silence, "That it has been deposited in one of the high halls of power in your realm, perhaps even the highest. And there it will remain until–" she stopped, but not dramatically. Tarkas knew her too well to even suspect that.

He shook her, not roughly. He knew prophecies when he heard them. "Until when?" he prompted.

She selected her words with care. "Until it is brought down by one who is more worthy to sit in it."

Tarkas released her arm, certain that he could hear quills scribing madly in yet another Book of Prophecies somewhere. He wondered if he would find his name written there as well, but he felt nothing, and shrugged. He would find out eventually. "So this is some other vile creation?"

She seemed even happy at the change of topic. "It is. I have been charged with keeping it safe, or ending its threat."

This news displeased him greatly. "You are trying to unmake it? Alone?"

"There is no one else."

True, and briefly he felt an absurd guilt at having played a part in this unhappy situation. She had her place because of him, with the Earth Lord and the Lord of the Water elementals. Only the Lady of Air was the same, but she had of necessity played no part in the other Lady's machinations and so could play no part in their resolution. "I should think the Earth Lord would have a part to play."

"As did I, at first," she replied, staring fixedly at some suddenly fascinating point in the wall of her fortress.

Tarkas, staring at his feet, failed to notice. "What occurred?" That there had been an experiment along those lines was understood.

"Nothing, as I recall," she informed him. Technically, it was the absolute truth. Most of the consequences had occurred after she had screamed and lost consciousness. What little she did know she had been told afterwards. Turning back, she took his hand. "Come. Our time is little enough, I would not waste it on my little difficulties."

He kept her hand, returning her grip, and increased his pace.

A discreet tap heralded an inaudible thump, as a tray of light snacks settled outside her door. Her servants well knew not to interrupt them during one of his rare visits. She stirred herself to get it, treating him to the sight of her in motion and herself to the sight of him in repose.

For his part, Tarkas moved himself only enough to watch, hand propped upon pillow and chin propped upon hand, as she moved with her usual grace across the floor, over to the door, which she opened with such flair. It wasn't flair, of course; he knew that she knew no one was about, but it still seemed so daring.

As she desired. She could feel his eyes, his total concentrated attention on her, and she could feel…other things as well, even from across the room. His aura fairly burned, and then, when it flared–!

She was so beautiful, so…alive. At times like these he could almost imagine what she must feel and know every day of her life in this place, and almost he envied her. Still the woman he had known in Kwinarish, the only outward changes he had noticed in all their time here were in her hair and her eyes, which had changed color slightly. Otherwise she still looked like a young woman of…how many seasons? By the Gods, he had been a Hero longer! Still so delicate, none of the calluses, the scars, the muscles that the women of their old home would have had by now. His fingers rubbed together, unseen. His calluses. And his scars. He felt so rough. She was like he used to be; being with her was like being the self he had once been and still wanted to be.

She felt it, just then, heating and cooling and prickling along her back and side as she knelt to get the tray, so she was not at all surprised when she turned back to see his needs so plain on his face beneath the careful mask. He was so soft, she knew, beneath all the hard places time had given him. She had none and mourned the lack. Without them she felt caught, trapped in an endless childhood for which she had no love. He was like she longed to be; being with him was like living the life she should have led and still hoped for.

It was all an illusion, of course, the ramblings of a tired and jealous mind. He had known nothing, so long ago, for all his learning, his prospects had been similarly barren of real accomplishment. Holding out a hand, he noticed the scars and scratches his life and labors had placed there, swords and claws and thorns leaving their traces as he had left his, in the remains of the monsters he had slain, and evil he had vanquished. In his friends in Querdishan and other cities of the realm, learning slowly to trust in him and the magic he brought. His life was hard, but good.

She took his hand, feeling the warmth surging through it and from it, balancing herself against his strength as she lowered herself and her burden to the surface of her bed. His scars were an illusion, she knew, and her lack of them equally so. His work left them, hers did not, at least, not where she could see them. Her servants were one scar, her fortress another. Her elementals flowed through her constantly, marking her soul as she marked their doings, soothed their hurts, and corrected their errors. Of the other Lords, only the Lord of Earth suffered similarly. She could well understand how their predecessors had fallen. It was a good life, but hard.

Releasing her hand, Tarkas took one of the items from the tray, as she did the same. With identical, unplanned motions, they each lifted their offerings to the other's lips.

They lay side by side in silence, unbroken for quite some time. But that had to change. "You must go," she reminded him.

"Yes," he sighed, "Founder's Day. I must be there, especially now."

His voice held a note that even she could not miss. "What is so special about this Founder's Day?"

He looked mildly surprised that she had forgotten. "Janosec is to be confirmed." But of course she did not know why it mattered to him so.

Irolla appeared to search her memory. "The…first son of Demlas Jerim. He will be Second and Heir." She wondered if he knew who the young man was. Then she thought of how much more time her beloved would have available to him, without those clan duties to tend to. Her finger moved lazily across his chest.

He reached up and gripped it, halting the teasing stroke. "I have to go," he reminded her. Swinging his legs over the edge, he left the bed a pace or more behind him in less than a beat. Irolla had been an enthusiastic lover even in her first life and even more so in her second. Here he had thought that the tall Lord of Water had been snide, in his comments regarding the previous Lady's 'proclivities', but he had decided over years of observation that whatever force or entity it is that confers an office must look for such things. The new Earth lord had been a farmer in his old life (Tarkas regretted that; he never got his promised tour of the tunnel of deathtraps the prior Lord had constructed), the new Water Lord a sailor. He supposed the Lady of Air had been a Singer or something like that, but she could not speak–not just a price of office; her painful shyness and obvious hopeless passion for him left her bright red and speechless on those occasions when they met–and her assistants would not say. And certainly his Irolla had been the most…lively. There had to be a word for it, but the Singer could not find one that expressed her love of life, and him, and her people, and children–Especially children.

She watched, sheet drawn up discreetly, as his unclad form walked over towards the closet where a new wrap–vest and leggings–waited. She always had a pair on hand; she could never tell what condition his would be in. A fleeting memory sprang up into her mind, of a time when he had arrived at her door as bare as he currently was, and much redder. His time in Querdishan had diluted such modesties, somewhat, and she kept her smile from her face, lest he turn unexpectedly.

But he did not turn, as she expected, and neither did he move to don his clothing, just standing there, his back turned and clothes in his hands. "Irolla?" he began, his tone light and his voice muffled.

She rolled over, staring at the ceiling so that she could converse without the distraction of his bare buttocks in her view. He could be so unfair sometimes. "Yes?"

He stood for another moment, silent. "Does our lack of children grieve you?" he asked, as if it were the weather he spoke of. She knew better.

It had once, but he was not speaking of the past. It might

eventually, but she dared not consider the future. And now… "Yes. No. Some."

He grimaced, a movement she could hear as he faced the far wall. "Yes, no, some. I suppose I understand."

Now she could not bring herself to look at him, buttocks or no. "Do you?" she inquired, her tone as light as his had been.

He moved then turning back to her, and she made herself look at him, despite his nakedness. His clothing held, bunched up but covering for all that, he said, "I thought I did, once. Perhaps I am wrong."

"Perhaps you are right," she answered, offering comfort, "It is a price of the office–"

"–I determined that much–"

"–but it was a price I agreed to pay and I get some compensation for it. All in the realm are my children."

He snorted, certain she was stretching the truth for his benefit. "After a fashion, no doubt."

She perceived his suspicion, but could think of no way to dispel it and so did not try. "More than you might suppose, husband," she stated. But he could not know how it felt, to feel the currents of life actually flowing through her as she did, her body, mind and spirit so attuned to life and its nurturance. She was a mother thousands of times over.

Tarkas smiled, as she knew he would, and turned away to dress himself. She did not know, and it would only hurt them both to say anything.

She felt him go, from the room, from her fortress, from the Elsewhere, back to the realm and his other family, to Querdishan and Founder's Day. He did not know, and only hurt would come of telling him.

There were two types of *that*way trails in Tarkas' experience, those that took the user somewhere else and those that did not. Those that did, transported those walking along them from one place to another within the realm more quickly than walking in the realm could have done, the speed being purchased at the cost of the great dangers lurking on the paths, waiting for walkers. Those that did not, took one from his place in the realm into the Elsewhere, and ultimately returned him to the place he had left.

Thus, when Tarkas left Irolla and the Elsewhere, he returned in short order to the place from which he had departed, standing on a ledge overlooking the fields which fed the people of his adopted home, Querdishan, visible far off on the horizon as a pair of gleaming spires. He didn't want to look at them or it, but he had little alternative; behind him, stretching off into the distance on both sides, was a vast stone wall, the lower face of a solid wedge which had been raised up under Old Querdishan years before. The Great Sorcerous War had ended then, but works such as this had left all the people of the realm with a strong distaste for magic in any form, a reticence that favored those who worked evil spells in secret. It was part of his task to reverse this, a long, slow part.

But not now. No, now his duty was there, under those spikes sticking up into the sky. He should be standing with the clanleaders, surrounded by the multitudes they led, who would ordinarily be out in the–in the–

Thranj's Beard! Those fields looked marvelous!

Deep breath, Tarkas. Raise your eyes, Tarkas.

He should be over there. Closing his eyes, he forced himself to move, focusing his mind on the thought that he should not be where he stood and let his reflexes and habits do the rest. The path his feet followed was all too familiar–every *that*way trail he ever took here seemed to end at the same spot–although untrodden by any save him. There was no useful land and too many evil thoughts here for any to come willingly. He looked at the wall, noting the wear it had taken since he had last looked. He checked the toppled tree, to see if it had finally died. His feet took him this way as his attention stayed that way.

The road, when his feet encountered it, surprised him as usual. Every season it extended farther and seemed wider. Now, with the city walls a mere smudge on the horizon, just sufficient to hide the two towers, his pride would allow him to look at the fields, so different from his first sight of them long ago. Clean, straight rows, broad, whole leaves, waving tops, and no weeds in sight. No leaves, blighted by disease, chewed by a multitude of insect mouths. The health of Querdishani crops had become famous, so famous that other cities had sent trading parties to get them for themselves. The city leaders had recently, finally, decided to start gifting them out, which Tarkas had advocated as well as Jerim, although only his clanleader's voice had weight. Their argument had been simple: if we don't give them away, others will come and take them. Lords Navak and Selter had sided with them only when he had suggested some conditions on the gifts, conditions that no city would have accepted, had not the value of the gifts been so high. Binding the cities together, pledged to each other's defense, had been a bold move for all involved. Several clanleaders had paid the price for their vision, or the lack of it, in the years since, especially when a ship, seeking faster ways to move the gifts or other goods, occasionally disappeared beyond the known currents and paths of the sea.

All because a god spat. Tarkas wondered if this had been Hara-Khan's intent, but he would never ask or know.

Eventually he came to the line of huts, a row of houses that had extended beyond the walls of the city, long ago when the number of people had grown too large. Unlike the fields, the huts had not grown in number, at least not to look at them. From here the city walls were in plain sight, but so was something else to look upon and he cast his eyes that way, across the fields. On a far hill, a second city grew, as the growing population burst the narrow bounds of the city walls. Currently a–what was the word?–satellite city, its actions under the direction of the clanleaders in Querdishan itself, Tarkas had been told that such situations rarely lasted long. Eventually, either it would seek to control its own destiny or the two cities would both get large enough to physically become one once more. From this distance he could see no evidence of towers over there.

They were much nearer to hand, the Gods' sentinels. Not only was the top of the tower of Air visible above the wall, its holy–a bad pun, and he smiled even to think it–pinnacle almost Singing in the perpetual breeze, the middle section showed plainly through the gate, its base alone blocked by the dwellings of the people. He could not see the other tower, of Water, which doubled as a lighthouse, hidden behind the bulk of Air's tower. He had been spotted, of course, and the gates opened at his approach.

The plaza beyond the gates was almost empty; this surprised him, not the emptiness, but the almostness. Tolgas Ravan waited there alone, may his family be blessed, when he should have been with his clan, busy with preparations. He could be here only because he had asked his clanleader, Tolgas Kestrel, for permission, and his sire had granted it. Tarkas walked forward, shaking his head as he worked to keep his smile from becoming a grimace. Then Ravan surprised him again, maintaining a formal posture and raising his hand in greeting. "My lord Demlas Tarkas, I greet you on behalf of my clan."

Of course. How like him. "Greetings, Tolgas Ravan," replied Tarkas with a formality the two men had not shared in years, suddenly able to feel his relief when it was so carefully shielded. "I am unworthy of this honor."

"The Lady of Air feels otherwise."

Tarkas nodded. She would, and usually did. This was a good time for her to interfere, but he wondered how she could know that. For that matter–"How do you know why you are here?"

Ravan suddenly softened, his family formality gone for at least a little while. "How could I not, my friend?" he asked, his voice soft with sympathy. "Hmm? I have known you for all the years you have been here, instructing you in our ways–"

Tarkas wagged a scolding finger at him as he approached. "Your Lord Kestrel commanded–"

"True," Ravan agreed, reaching up to place a hand on his friend's shoulder. "In the beginning, but beginnings often change. How could I teach you without learning you, coming to know you, hence changing myself? How could I not see what the events of this day will mean to you, and be here to soften the blow?"

Tarkas reached up and gripped his friend's hand in gratitude, even as his eyes turned away, drawn by the murmur from beyond the houses, from the temple square, where the people were no doubt impatiently waiting on them both. Ravan kept his eyes firmly on

Tarkas. "He's not lost to you, you know."

For a moment, Tarkas could not speak, and covered it by forcing himself into motion. "As good as," he growled.

Ravan fell into place, a pace behind and to the left. Teacher he may have been, but his student was Brother, Second, and Heir, and outranked him. Their informal relationship had to be put aside for now. "I wish," he began rather wistfully, "that I could bring to you the peace that you have brought to me."

Peace? "Peace?" The Lord Brother snorted, "What peace?"

"The peace of your unhappiness," replied Ravan with casual brutality, but before Tarkas could round on him–"What sort of place must the land of the gods be, that you should be troubled so? It's rather soothing, I think, and mere death hard to fear."

Tarkas had no reply to this remarkable statement, shocked out of his melancholy as Ravan had intended, caught between memories of his once-home in Kwinarish and his current duty as Hero. Kwinarish as the land of the gods!? He recalled it, through the filter of his years, and found it a dull and rather simple place of memory, a peaceful place in truth. But it was a peace that had never been challenged by conflict, a delicate flower that would never survive the first frost without careful gardening. Ravan craved that peace, unknowing that he would destroy it by attaining it. Nor could Tarkas the Hero ever tell him, but thinking about it, he knew that he need not. His friend could have worse dreams, and truly, he himself did not know what the afterlife would be like, if there was such a thing.

Then he heard the sigh, slightly exaggerated, from over his shoulder, and he grinned silently in the way he had learned, with only the side of his mouth that Ravan could not see actually moving. Typical. As if he would let some little details from his Hero's life slip out. They should know better.

And of course they did. Ravan did. His life was here. "You know what the Spirits say about death," he said, partly a comment, partly a question.

Ravan frowned, uncertain of his friend's meaning, suspicious of his motives. The Spirits said a lot of things about death, and somehow he doubted that Tarkas had any of them in mind. "Which saying do you refer to?" he replied, conceding defeat.

Tarkas turned a perfectly straight face to his friend. "That it is hard to fear," he said, springing his trap.

But Ravan had foreseen it. "That is true," he said with equal solemnity, "It may be inferred from their saying that the only things we need to fear are dishonorable acts, and then–"

"You mean I was correct?!" Tarkas shouted, breaking the recitation.

The perfectly faked candor finally broke through Ravan's studied demeanor, surprising him into outright laughter. Echoes of that laughter rang through the empty canyon streets of Querdishan, attracting unwanted attention. "Less mirth, if you please, Ravan, and more haste," came a directive in his clanleader's unmistakable tones.

"'More haste'?" murmured Tarkas.

"A greater degree of haste," explained Ravan, well accustomed to his student's occasional grammatical difficulties.

"Ah," replied Tarkas in acknowledgement, careful to keep his lips from moving, as they were well within view of the crowd of clansmen, and more important, their leaders. Septas Navak and Lintas Selter may not care overmuch about their propriety, but with the tone now set by Kestrel, clanleader and lorewarden for the clan NarTolgas, and unofficially for most of the city, they would nonetheless find fault.

There would be little enough of that to find; Founder's Day was a new ritual, its invention dating back to Tarkas' own arrival, and his interment of old lord Midros. Other minds had seen in that imported ceremony an opportunity, and Founder's Day emerged as the result, a ceremony of dedication to the city, above and beyond clan loyalty, as Midros had brought death upon himself in service to another clan. Unfortunately, the interment had been accomplished in unison and without speech, so the creators of the current ceremony had seen fit to make that a requirement, one of only a few.

So the clanspeople waited and watched in silence as Tarkas and his entourage of one walked to their appointed places, Ravan with his clan, Tarkas to a place to the right of the leader of his own clan, Jerim of the NarDemlas, his place as Brother. The left was the place for the

Wife, in this case Demlas Fenita, daughter of Tolgas Kestrel. Behind them were ranged their children, the sons, starting with Janosec, behind Jerim, the daughters behind Fenita. Before them, separated by a strip of earth that had no rightful place at all within the city, a strip currently covered with a cloth, the other clanleaders stood, Kestrel foremost, with Navak and Selter at his sides. He knew without checking that the priests and priestesses were looking down from their temples, representing the gods of the people.

With their arrival, the ceremony could at last begin. Normally, this would include the planting of the flags and numerous other rituals, but today these would be preempted by the ceremony of dedication, a much older rite, if seldom required. Only occasionally was the second of a clan not the eldest son, and only occasionally was a new second confirmed while the prior still lived. But the NarDemlas were a new clan, no more than the Demlas himself, Jerim, and the Wife and the Brother at its inception, only barely sufficient to qualify for clan status. Children soon followed, of course, Jerim's and Fenita's, and with the inevitable slow crawl of time the eldest had finally come into his majority.

To look at him, one would suspect that he had reached that status several seasons before, at least. Janosec overshadowed even Tarkas, who made up in mass what he lacked in size. While not larger than any of those around, there was something about the Hero that seemed somehow more…whatever it was, no one could quite name it. In Janosec's case, they could name it.

Even as Tarkas stilled in his appointed place he knew his 'nephew' moved, his mountainous shadow as silent as his feet, but more revealing. In unison, he and Jerim turned on their heels, making a passage between them artfully wide enough for the width, not of his shoulders, well above theirs, but of his elbows, which hung to that level. The young giant came between his elders and stood before his grandsire as the door behind him swung closed.

Kestrel spread his hands, and the two lords at his back moved, going to opposite ends of the covered earth. Kneeling, they took the corners of the cloth in their hands, simultaneously lifting and folding away one side to reveal the area beneath. But it was not bare, not today. Today its edges were bordered, four staffs of carved wood of equal length lying one to a side. Today it bore a robe, cowled and folded to suggest a man lying, his arms folded on his chest. Where the hands would have been, the hilt of a sword lay in its incorporeal grip, a very large sword. Only two men could have lifted that sword easily, and one of them now did, the one for whom it had been made.

Without a cue Tarkas could see, Navak, leader of the clan NarSeptas, lurched into motion himself, coming around the patch of earth with his own sword in his hand. It looked pitifully small by comparison, but Tarkas could well remember how large it had looked to him as Navak had come howling through flames to spill his blood in generous amounts. He shook his head slightly; no blood would be spilled here today. And none was. After a few ceremonial passes and exchanges, Navak yielded to Lintas Selter, who managed to move his sword in the appropriate ways without dropping it or getting it knocked from his hand by Janosec's feeble taps. Neither a warrior nor a hunter like his fierce brother, the late and unlamented Tiris, he had received the leadership of his clan through untimely death and had held it by a surpassing gift for the tedious details of administration.

His ordeal over, his duty done, he surrendered his sword to his second and returned to his place opposite Navak, as Janosec faced Kestrel yet again. The lorewarden smiled, just a little, as he raised his arms, inviting any final challenges from the onlookers as he scanned the crowd. There were none, as he'd expected, and he came down from his position on the steps of Water's temple. Crouching, he picked up the staff lining his side of the grave, a staff carved with the symbols of Water. He held it out in his hand, and Janosec took a grip on it as well, before they plunged the base of the staff into the soil below.

Turning, he marched up the side of the grave, and repeated the procedure with Navak and the staff of Earth, then again with Selter and the staff of Life. Then he rounded the grave and came up on the far side, standing next to his grandsire as he took the staff of Air from his sire's hand and planted it with him.

Tarkas felt a hand on his shoulder.

He turned, to find Ravan behind him, holding out a fifth length of wood, its head carved with a symbol rarely seen, that of Fire, which had no temples or priests. But it had its place nonetheless, and its honor, and Tarkas would pass that honor to the one who would replace him. He took the staff firmly in his grip, surprised by the weight of a merely mortal artifact. He stepped forward, to the edge of the grave, holding the staff over the place where old Midros' heart may once have been.

Janosec reached out as well, but this time he placed his hand directly over Tarkas' hand. Tarkas was startled, the true meaning of the gesture lost on him, apt student of lore though he was. But the others saw, and they knew, and if there was even a hint of distaste at the baldness of the declaration, they hid it inside the scrape of a foot on stone, or a hand scratching what did not itch. Then the staff moved up into the air and then down with the force of two unnaturally powerful arms propelling it.

The top of the staff exploded.

A column of red fire flew upwards into the air, shrieking horribly, consuming the wood of the staff and the robe beneath it in less than a heartbeat. Rather than going out as it ought, the column sank in on itself, flames spilling down its own sides like unearthly candle wax to fall on the two men, hands clasped, standing unmoving at its base. It flowed over them, coating them in red impenetrability as its nebulous mass dwindled yet further. In less than two heartbeats the column vanished into the hole in the ground, now fused and hard, where the base of the staff had been. Of the two men there no sign remained.

That day, furor reigned in the city. Kestrel took in hand the caretaking of his daughter and her husband, so suddenly bereaved by this shocking turn of events as to be witless. Selter took in hand the city, its provisions and stores, preparing them for whatever the future might bring. Navak took in hand the men of the city, mounting a defense, sending out scouts, sure that something, somewhere, lurked beyond their sight.

For the shriek of the towering flame had been no mere sound, either natural or otherwise. The more sensitive among them recognized it, the word 'Tarkas', repeated over and over at great speed. The fire had been calling his name.

And somewhere Else, so far away that distance was meaningless and time irrelevant, a furry head lifted. A keen nose attached to a keen mind tested a wind that only it could smell. The wildlife for a hundred paces around fled in terror as it growled in displeasure, its owner rising to its feet and shambling off, unafraid, into the undergrowth.

Chapter 4

Shock at the explosion.

Amazement at the red column spewing up so violently above them, and a little fear. He knew himself to be almost fireproof, but he had no such assurance concerning the other. So he moved, digging his feet in and shifting his weight to throw him clear of the inferno even now dropping onto them.

Thus Janosec discovered something he had never known about his uncle: He was heavy. Worse, Tarkas had made an identical move in the opposite direction, prepared for his nephew's weight but unprepared for his sudden shift backwards. As a result, neither man moved as the seething red nebulousness poured over them.

It tickled, a little, but before they could so much as twitch the sensation vanished. All feeling abandoned their outer senses, the touch of the air, the pressure of the earth against their feet. Only the touch of the other's hand remained to them as they hung adrift, their inner senses–queasiness, nausea–assaulting them. If they were falling, it was a long way down.

As suddenly, the red haze vanished; sight and other sensation returned with a vengeance. *Action–*

One instant, three events.

Tarkas found himself standing, his muscles still tensed to jump, in a place awash in heat, flickering light, and clouds of billowing smoke. He gagged and choked, but not on the smoke; even the vilest, thickest black cloud will not inspire a member of Mendilorn's select few to do more than cough. But the roiling mass seemed to embody the essence of evil, a palpable sense of wrongness allied with those physical sensations that had always spelled magic to him. It was not a new sensation, unfortunately, and he reacted by not reacting, allowing his body to complete its leap to left, his hand closing on air where the staff had once been and pulling free of his nephew's grasp. Even as he leapt, he called out a rhyming couplet, one of his standard attack spells culled from his complete knowledge of the Songs of his homeland.

Janosec came to himself standing, his muscles still tensed to jump, in a place awash in heat and flickering light. There a man, an old man in old robes, gesturing frantically with an expression of rage on his face, staring at no one. The meaning was not lost, and the quavering wail of his thin voice triggered the lifelong reflexes of a man raised to fear music and the magic it brought. He reacted, allowing his body to complete its spring, freeing his uncle's hand even as he reached for his own weapon.

The old man waited, his rage and hatred holding him suspended in a weird simulation of patience as his new enemies separated. He could feel the magic pouring out of the one, could see the weapon in the hand of the other, and reacted instantly, his long-ready defenses absorbing the power of Tarkas' spell as he turned to face the sword even now hurtling, javelin-like, across the space between them.

–and reaction.

Three instants, one event.

The sword, new and unblooded, flew into its own destruction, a blast of heat and flame from a ring on the old man's finger melting it into blobs that vaporized before they fell. Janosec took refuge from the heat behind a large cabinet against the wall, curiously undamaged. The fire came nowhere near it, and the old sorcerer turned his attention to Tarkas with no lost time.

But Tarkas had his sword out now, a length of blackness neither metal–so immune to heat–nor natural. If the evil one cast any other spells his way, the Hero did not notice them. He held it like a shield before him as he cast about in his mind for some charm that would kill one without killing all.

Janosec observed this temporary standoff, searching out his own advantage. The cabinet shielding him was large and heavy, its shelves laden with delicate figurines of some queer red crystal. But it was not flush to the wall. He pushed, but it didn't mo–By the Gods, it was bolted to the wall, there up at the top corner! Why would–?

Who cares! Jamming his fingers behind the cabinet, he turned and leapt, bracing his feet against the wall and pulling. The fastenings holding the brace to the cabinet were no match for his muscles, but the ones sticking into the wall were less so. Little shreds of wood flew unnoticed as the teeth biting the wood were dragged backwards by main force.

The corner under him came loose, and he almost fell, but he stretched out swiftly and held himself off the floor, until the brace on the opposite corner stopped him. But now he had the cabinet on his side, its twisted weight pulling for him, snapping the sturdy pegs like reeds. His pull now unopposed, the china closet toppled forward, the little pieces of bric-a-brac practically leaping forward to their fate with tinkles of crystalline glee.

Tarkas leapt, not at the old sorcerer trying to destroy him, but at his nephew, just landing in the middle of the room. Also coming to a halt on the floor was the cabinet, the old man's meager strength no match for its weight as it bore him down. But Tarkas ignored that, knowing what would happen and not needing to see any of it. Just needing to be in the right spot, behind his nephew–

–As the cabinet exploded, the contents of the first figurines claiming their freedom. They could not affect the other ornaments, any more than they could have affected their own, but the flame they brought with them, and the air trapped under the cabinet heated by that flame, moved some of them against the wood. The wood stubbornly refused to move, causing the delicate crystal structures to break and release their own contents, which added to the force moving yet others, until all the fire elementals trapped by the old man were freed within a heartbeat, or perhaps two.

Tarkas didn't care about all the steps involved, but he knew what they were. Just as he knew that he need not fear grisly death by impalement from the fragments of wood that had once been the cabinet, for they were being consumed faster than they could fly towards him. Just as he knew that anything in the way would get flung by the force of the explosion, including his nephew and himself. And the only thing behind them was a, perhaps, stout wall.

Not very stout, he judged, as his back burst through under their combined weight. But then, a sorcerer who spent his time capturing and abusing fire elementals had little to fear from fire, or winter's cold. The Hero tensed, ignorant of what might lay beyond the confines of the shack, except for the cold hard ground, grateful that the tough material of his vest would protect him from the sticks and stones–

Impact!

–Oh, that hurt. He rolled almost instantly, but his nephew's mass had still slammed into his belly like a large stone. Tarkas let him go, guiltily aware that he might come to some further injury. There were not too many stones, though, and the dirt track and ground cover friendly enough; at least Tarkas got no stones in his face, and his clutching hands brought him to a quick and leafy halt.

Janosec fared worse, from lack of both experience and divinely-inspired reflexes, but not much worse. His bulk was a match for his uncle's, but it took up much more space. Tarkas' back had split the wall of the shack, but his nephew's extremities, especially his shoulders and upper arms, took some minor damage from the splintered sides. His uncle's body cushioned the impact with the ground, and his guilt at the distressed noises puffed into his ear prompted him to move sideways, separating himself from Tarkas as they rolled across the ground.

The shack was isolated; a sorcerer would not long stomach or be stomached by civilized folk, so the approaches to the entrance were few and narrow, tracks made by the old man himself. Most of the ground over which Janosec rolled was covered with weeds, bracken, ivy, and similar ground cover. And corpses. Lots of corpses.

They were quite gooey, of course. Most of them had been charred just enough to leave their previous occupants a quick and painful death. Janosec, his eyes still shut against the explosion and its aftermath, didn't even know what they were, except that they felt slimy and smelled bad. He recoiled from the last, only to encounter another, and then another. Then he stopped, frozen into immobility by horror. He raised a shaking hand, reaching up to clear his eyes, but stopped, irrationally convinced that unspeakable gore coated it. He wiped it excessively on his leggings instead, before finally brushing imaginary dirt from his eyes. He looked about, only to find his uncle watching impassively from the patch of scrub in which he had brought himself to a halt.

"Good reflexes. At your age, I would have hit a few more." At that age, he had not yet even been a Hero, but why clutter the issue. Rising to his feet, Tarkas strode over to offer a hand up to the younger man.

Janosec just stared at it. "I don't think so," he said, pushing himself up after checking to make sure he wasn't leaning on any more corpses. "You're going to be in need of aid yourself soon."

Tarkas stared at him, then at his hand. Janosec gestured. "Scratchweed."

Now the Hero understood. The sorcerer had maintained a patch of vines outside his door that would make anyone touching it itch uncontrollably for days. Typical. He was immune to its effects, of course, but it would be better not to–Then again, maybe he should–*Hmm*. It would save time in many ways. "Let me clean up, then."

He turned to the ruins of the shack, still burning, and walked closer to them, fumbling in his pouch for something. Janosec watched closely, unsure what his uncle planned to do with the disc of wood he finally produced. He looked on with amazement as his uncle knelt at the very edge of the flames, thrusting the disc and the hand holding it into the fire, calling out loudly, "Trent!" He stared in shock as the smaller man stood at the sudden geyser of…shaped flame?…and calmly stepped into it.

After all the strange events of the last several moments, Janosec took this with bizarre calm, striding up to the column of heat as far as he dared. It buzzed loudly, in the cadences of someone talking quickly, a few words at a time. There was a darker patch, where he imagined Tarkas stood, and he reached out a hand tentatively.

The column of flame erupted, spitting out a ball of fire that enveloped him from head to foot before winking out. He jumped back, his reaction time pitifully slow as he shielded his eyes from the first missile in time for the second. So he had blinded himself and missed the collapse of the pillar as Tarkas stepped smoothly out of the embers of the shack, perfectly clean. "How do I look?"

Janosec blinked at him. "Clean. Um…Fire spirit?" he mumbled.

Tarkas nodded. The people of Querdishan had no dealings with elementals directly, instead dealing with the priests in their temples, receiving hints, advice, and occasional orders, making rare requests. The Lords and Ladies with whom they actually communicated were outside their experience entirely, their elemental minions also completely unnoticed. But fire elementals had no Lords, no priests; their dealings with mortals were usually direct, mostly catastrophic. An ordinary household fire was not strong enough to support one, and no ordinary mortal knew their names to call them. The last mortal Janosec had known able to summon them was the old man he had just slain. "Yes."

"A *good* fire spirit, I guess."

Tarkas froze for a long moment, at a loss to address a statement, essentially true for all the wrong reasons, when the true reasons were either complicated, or worse, untellable. "Yes, he is," he finally replied, determined to stress *that* point, at least. "But Trent is–" his hands fumbled, just like his brain "–unique. Fire spirits are not usually good *or* bad, but the people who call them are usually bad, and everyone thinks it's the spirits' fault. It is like a tree blaming the axe that splits it rather than the man wielding the axe."

"Really?" Janosec, at least, seemed willing to listen and accept.

"No, not really," said Tarkas ironically, remembering all the times he'd been on the receiving end of these only-partial explanations. "Fire spirits have more sense than an axe, of course. But really, they just don't care." Not when elementals inhabited their elements, instead of *being* their elements; the flame had to exist first, before they could come, so they had no interest in what was burning, normally. But he absolutely could not say that, not even to Janosec.

Fortunately, his nephew found something else to think about. "*Can* they care?"

Tarkas just stared at him, then pointed over his shoulder at the burnt-out hovel before he walked carefully down the path between the patches of scratchweed. "What do you think?"

* * *

Janosec caught up to him just as he came under the shadow of the trees surrounding the ruin. "Where are we?"

"Somewhere west of Querdishan, I believe," replied his uncle, not for a moment stopping restless, searching eyes. The trail was easy to spot, the other watchers that should have been there were not. Incredibly, there didn't seem to be any.

Janosec rolled his eyes, well acquainted with the older man's sense of humor. All points *east* of the 'City on the Eastern Sea' would be under water. "You don't know?" He sounded surprised, if not shocked. Tarkas wondered at his reputation, in this respect.

"I have been to many places," he said, bearing slightly left to remain in the middle of the broad swath of mashed vegetation and scuffed leaves. "But not to all places. But think. If I had been in *this* place in prior days, would that sorcerer have been there, *this* day?"

"I suppose not," Janosec mumbled, turning to follow.

The Hero continued, taking the other side of the issue, "Although he might have come since I might have last been here." That wasn't likely, given the way Heroes affected the world about them, but that wasn't why he'd made the point. Janosec would lead the clan someday.

"His charms were delicate," that worthy pointed out.

"Very true," commended his teacher. Too delicate to carry, the unspoken argument, and so at least some of them had to have been constructed here. "So you see I have not been this way recently, if at all."

"And the spirit–?"

"Would neither have known nor needed to know where he was. Only where *I* was."

"Where *we* were," amended Janosec.

"He came for me."

"Then why was I also taken?"

Tarkas shrugged, uncomfortable with the question. "You were there? I clasped your hand?" *Some other, deeper connection?*

Janosec gasped in sudden horror, stopped in his tracks. The Hero stopped instantly, alerted by the sound. "The ceremony! Mother! Father! What did they–?"

Oh, that. "My advice?" put in Tarkas, relaxing, "Don't think about it. You can if you try. And we'll have enough to do soon." He inhaled deeply, tasting the wind, trying to take his own advice.

"This happens to you all the time, I'm sure," responded Janosec, stung by the apparently casual disregard for his parents' supposed plight. He stomped forward, taking the lead in what seemed a vain attempt to get them home by simply walking on.

"Often enough," replied Tarkas mildly, only too aware of the many sudden translocations in his life, ever since he had left home so precipitously, so long before. "I will never know what my parents think of me, if they think of me at all," he finished, with the utter certainty in his voice drawing his nephew up short. "And don't ask why, either," he added hastily.

Janosec floundered in confused silence–he had indeed been about to ask why–and disguised it by walking faster, if anything. Tarkas followed, a tolerant smile on his face, wondering how long it would take for his nephew to find a safe topic and what it would be. But Janosec's thoughts spun so chaotically that he could not really be said to be thinking at all. Rather, he spun through emotions with words sometimes attached to them. Concern for his mother collided with his uncle's loss of any mother; hatred of sorcery warred with his uncle's own trafficking in spirits; pride in his accomplishment and the fear that he had exceeded his untested ability, and back again to his uncle, to Tarkas, father's adopted Brother and the man he was supposed to replace–

What?

He found himself standing, suddenly convinced he had heard something. Turning, he found Tarkas waiting quietly, just behind him. "Did you speak?" he asked.

Tarkas smiled slightly. "A little," he admitted, with a secretive air that Janosec decided to overlook.

"Why have we stopped?"

Tarkas shrugged. "I was going to ask that of you, since it was you who stopped, not I."

Checking his memory, the young not-quite-Second of his clan found this to be true. He had been somewhat ahead, when something, he wasn't sure what…Unhappy at this lapse, he inhaled deeply, and then remembered what had stopped him in the first place. The smell of smoke was unfortunately familiar, and quite present, in faint traces, on the breeze taking advantage of this natural pathway to make its presence known in unwonted places. "Do you smell that?" he asked unnecessarily.

But the question, surprisingly, was not at all rhetorical. "Smell what?" asked Tarkas, his senses quite uninfluenced.

Janosec's eyes flashed to his uncle, not quite sure that this wasn't yet another testing trap, or trapping test. But no, the inquiry was genuine. "The smoke," he said, concern edging his voice. How could any man not notice that reek?

Tarkas took a deep breath, and then another. Yes, there was something, at the very edge of his perceptions. Janosec shifted uneasily. Two breaths–?

Tarkas surged forward, distracting his nephew, only his knife drawn, not his black sword. While some trouble might yet await them, he intensely doubted it, and he didn't want to draw his blade in front of a mind already so riddled with uncertainties. Then he paused, a scrabbling sound from behind him: Janosec searching among the usual forest debris for a stick. He passed the knife to him and continued on, empty-handed.

Janosec took the knife, conflicted. Was it his duty to protect the Brother of his clan, or Tarkas' to protect the Second? But his uncle moved too quickly for him to much consider the issue, and he finally gave up. With only two of them it scarcely mattered anyway.

It was quite horrible.

Neither of the two men was a stranger to the violence that men can do to each other, sometimes quite savagely. Nor was either of them a friend to it. The warrior takes no joy in his work, the butcher no perverse pleasure in blood; these thankless tasks have other compensations. These two had done battle to protect their clan, even though Tarkas was guiltily aware that no merely mortal soldier stood a chance against him. Many times he had consoled himself with the memory of Septas Navak, years before, thanking him for the loan of his then-sword, its edge keen enough to protect him from his own bloodlust.

There had been no such edge here, nothing to save these poor people from…from the death that had befallen them.

"This was no battle," Tarkas judged, the vomiting, the shaking, the tears behind them both, if narrowly. In its way playing the detective was a solace. "No strange clothes, or hair, or anything. No real weapons, mostly things any village would have at hand." Janosec stood by, his attention focused on his uncle's calming, matter-of-fact tone. Those last words brought up a staggering vision of rocks, and children, but he as quickly thrust it down again, concentrating until even his vision seemed to–wait, what was…?

No, nothing there. It had looked for a second like a path, but now he saw no path there, only rubble.

Tarkas clapped him on the shoulder, startling him to alertness. "We must search," he said, his tone one of sympathy. Janosec groaned–hadn't they searched enough?–but even so, he knew it to be true. No battle and no bandits meant murder and–His breath caught, and his face jerked up to meet his uncle's.

"No," said Tarkas, his voice firm, his manner sad. "He came after."

The younger man's face crumpled, and lowered, but his disappointment was short-lived with so many opportunities for emotion so near at hand. All around them, death and destruction filled the scene, smoke and steam filled the air. The sight and the smell and the intensity of his own disgust made him want to retch; for a second he envied his uncle, standing there so solid and untouchable. Breathing in the stink so easily. Probably didn't even notice it. How come? Easy to be solid when you couldn't even feel it in the first place. Envy skated along the thin ice of reason, skirting barely past contempt to find itself lodged–where?

"How do you stand it?" he heard himself asking, of no one, everyone, Tarkas, anywhere some explanation might be found.

"There is a saying I heard once," Tarkas replied, not answering the question, since he knew full well it had no answer. "'Who must do the hard things?'"

Just for a moment Janosec's chaotic world resolved itself into a flash of pure hatred, but just for a moment and only a flash. He wasn't being patronized with some sing-song truism, he was being offered advice from someone who had always been special to him, and now, it seemed, was more special than he knew. So he merely cleared his throat, and responded: "Who?"

Tarkas reached up and grasped the hilt of his mysterious sword, sticking up behind his head. The drawing made a curious rasping sound, not the pure steel-on-steel ring he expected but something duller, smoother, less vibrant, but more implacable. The sound was put into words: "'He who can.'"

Suddenly Tarkas transformed in Janosec's sight, without a muscle moving or a hair stirring. He had heard stories, from his father, from his mother's father, even from the Septas, about his uncle, but they were just stories, told to impress him about someone rarely there. The truth, the savior of Querdishan, the Champion of the Gods, stood now before him, beyond the ability of any story to tell. A man untouchable by the world–no wonder he couldn't smell!–but a man nonetheless, his face twisted in pain, placid with determination. And sympathy for his unworthy nephew, unconsciously walking backwards in a half-crouch. He offered a sad little smile, and a greeting. "Welcome to my world."

Demlas Fenita knelt on the hard stone floor, her back straight, her head high. She waited. Let her father and her husband search their precious lore. Let the other lords do their futile best. She knew they would, hoped they would, but none of it would tell her what she desperately needed to know.

So she knelt on the floor of the Temple of Air, hoping beyond reason that the priestess could find that information for her, if the information existed to be found. Listening to the sound of the winds, moving through the holes in the tower, making sounds that the priestess could interpret for her. Hearing those sounds, but now from the door, from outside, winds whistling in the streets, over the walls. Pebbles tapping against the hard stone of the other temples, people crying out at the loss of clothes or the dust in their eyes.

She smiled.

The gods themselves would seek Tarkas, as was only fitting. She would seek her son, as was only right, and the gods would help, if Tarkas was with him, as he must be. She had a new idea, and rose, with a new and slightly modified goal: the Temple of Life, and its priestess. She would see what kind of reaction that brought.

In a different somewhere Else, the creature paused, weary and frustrated in its bestial way. Movement was needed, but it did not help. He moved and he hunted, but his prey got no closer and the need did not slack. And he hungered, for his rampage had driven all the smaller prey far from him.

A wind kicked up, unusual in the woods, with trees to block. The smells would be thinner, the prey harder to find. But instinct, reason and reflex drove him, and he tested the wind anyway. Smells! New smells, strong smells. Blood, blood's good. Smoke, not pleasant but he could bear it if the hunt called. He lurched into motion, heading upwind. Follow, find its source.

The hunt called to him. He could smell that too.

Chapter 5

"How may I serve you, my lord?"

The request was heartfelt, the tone firm. The stance was balanced and poised, ready to race off in any direction. The face was still, the eyes clear, the words absolutely galling. "Two things," Tarkas replied, his voice stone, "First, never call me that again. Your father is 'my lord', not me." He paused, his sword hand flexing absently, slicing bits from a nearby post without him even noticing it. One deep breath later, he continued, "Second, whatever happens, you may not plainly speak of it to anyone who was not there with us."

Janosec looked a bit confused by the latter requirement. "I must not?"

"You *may* not," Tarkas reiterated, ever conscious of the subtle distinctions of words.

"Why may I not?" he asked. *Who forbids me?*, he meant.

"I may not tell you that," Tarkas answered, accepting one responsibility and disclaiming another, "I would have to kill you. Or something."

That brought Janosec up short, for Tarkas was utterly serious. The twitching sword chopping away at the post didn't help. His uncle trapped, bound by a command he despised yet must obey, Janosec found himself wondering: "What gods do you serve, Uncle?"

Tarkas sighed gustily, his head bowed. But at least his hand stopped twitching, although the nearly disemboweled post continued to creak and groan its distress, like a dying thing. He stood for some time, immobile but not unmoving, pulled in so many directions that he traveled in none, all forces balanced. Janosec waited, unafraid, to see in which way they would resolve themselves.

Finally, his uncle looked up, a strange expression on his face. Janosec had never seen the like, and was profoundly grateful for it.

"It is not for *them*," the Hero said, half pleading, "It is for you! Well, for you, before–for them–" he amended, making a vague gesture at everywhere else and the people in it. The wounded post lost its top to the absently flailing weapon "–I do what I do so that they can live as they will."

He said no more, for he'd said enough. Either Janosec could see more of the truth than his words revealed, or he could not. The benefits and pitfalls of either alternative were too finely balanced for him to know if there was a better course, so he had to refrain from doing or saying anything that might tip the balance, settling instead for the finality of the click as he slipped his black sword back into its holding place. No doubt the lad would think of something, and anything he thought of would be far more acceptable and believed than the actual truth, while close enough to the actual truth to be useful. If nothing else, this variation on the usual ploy would be interesting to watch as it played out.

Janosec was less than wholly pleased with the answer, but he expected nothing more. Not only his uncle, but his sire and grandsire as well, held to the opinion that absolute truth and certain knowledge were fine things but in short supply, and so they schooled him not to seek them out. Even, or especially, when the answer to the obvious half-truth and evasions stood right before him. If nothing else, it would be impolite to dig into someone else's truth like that. But for form's sake, he merely replied, "Do you?"

With that acknowledgement, so pregnant with implication, Tarkas relaxed at last.

SNAP.

Seemingly without moving, Tarkas was suddenly in a new place, and only his warrior's reflexes kept the sword from his hand. Janosec jumped as well, his knife out already, but it was only the post, finally losing its battle against the inevitable. Groaning in distress, it toppled slowly, pushed to the earth by the crumpled remains of whatever structure it had been that was still attached, there on its backside. The two watched casually, Janosec stepping slightly off to his left, Tarkas dismissing it entirely, as the post came to rest at last. After a quick scan of the ruined village, Tarkas turned back to his nephew, mouth opening to speak. Janosec's mouth opened as well, an expression of surprise and, eventually, horror that Tarkas spent a crucial instant in interpreting.

"UN–!"

The Hero whirled, knowing in his potion-instilled reflexes that it was too late to draw, otherwise weaponless. Even so, his left hand went up, and the right, prepared to defend himself as best he could from whatever monstrosity his nephew had spied. A monster it was, in truth, for it had once been a man, now a thing that merely resembled its former self, in some distant way. Tall and thin, gaunt, dressed in rags, it also carried a killing rage in its mad eyes and a woodsman's axe in its hands, an axe now descending upon its hapless prey.

But the Champion of the Gods is no prey. The axe came thudding down, impacting the Hero's left hand, and staying there, held in his fingers' iron grip. His right hand, at the same time, took hold of the man-thing's left wrist and drew him down, as Tarkas pitched backward, his feet catching his foe at the waist, carrying him/it up and over. He launched it/him into the air at the other side of the roll, as his body started to uncoil, then rose and spun to confront the now-weaponless creature.

"–CLE!" Janosec's cry of warning echoed in the crashing silence, louder by far than the mere whisper that was all that showed of the Hero's exertions, louder even than the ugly, strangled croak that now bubbled from the creature, twisting and broken, soon to die. As one, they ran to it, Tarkas still carrying the axe. Janosec halted a little short, put off by the fresh blood, but that was nothing new and soon he knelt by his uncle's side as the creature gurgled obscenities at them. Or at least, Tarkas supposed they were obscenities, for he had heard plenty in his long career and these didn't sound much like those. The tone was identical, but what under the sun and stars was an 'edge' and why would he care if it took him? Certainly the list of Major Deities for Querdishan contained no mention of one called Edge. Perhaps it was a demon's name, but they tended to be harsh and blood-chilling.

Abruptly Tarkas realized that he had gotten distracted by words once more, a failing more common to his earlier years, and the creature had died while he had been away. That pleased him, in a perverse way, for the foulness that had twisted the man into a thing vanished at its death, restoring the dignity that had been taken, at least of spirit. Janosec stood, moving away from the stained, reeking corpse, and Tarkas followed suit, even his nose affected by the final bodily indignity.

Tarkas looked it over, distracting himself yet again, but more productively, until Janosec brought him back to the real world. "Uncle! Your hand!"

He had forgotten that he still held the axe-head in his hand. "Oh," he commented mildly, "Grab the handle, will you?" He held it up so the handle stuck out. Janosec stared. Tarkas waggled the handle in front of him, and he started forward, grasping it normally in his calloused hands. "Pull," commanded his uncle.

He pulled, then strained harder. His uncle must be–no, his fingers were open. The head was…it was stuck in his palm! Horrified, he let go, falling backward with his own force. "Gods Within," he cried, scrambling back.

Tarkas waited patiently, until his nephew could take his eyes away from the afflicted appendage. "I know," he said, "It is not real, and it does not hurt. So if you do not mind…?"

Janosec stood, and took the handle gingerly, half-expecting his uncle to shout in sudden pain, but Tarkas merely braced himself. This time Janosec pulled differently, harder, as if tugging the blade from a tree stump. It certainly...felt...He leaned back, propped a foot on his uncle's bent knee, and...tugged...*Oomph*! The axe sailed over his head as it pulled loose, while he fell down again into the mucky remains of the street, his eyes focused on the outstretched hand.

"Ah," Tarkas sighed in satisfaction, wiggling his fingers. He reached down, offering his hand to raise the younger man. Janosec stared, watching as the axe-carved gash across the proffered palm sealed itself slowly, bloodlessly, until it looked like an ordinary hand again. Taking it, he felt its warmth, its softness. He noted the movement of the hairs, and the play of tendons across bone as the fingers shifted. The whole arm flexed smoothly as he rose to his feet, and he wondered how far the falseness extended.

He kept his grip as they stood, tracing a finger along the length of one tendon, up past the wrist and onto the arm. Ah, there! He brought the finger down again, noting the spot. Only half the forearm, and the hand. He released it, relieved. He looked up, into his uncle's concerned eyes. "It is a long story," Tarkas said.

Janosec looked around, once more conscious of his surroundings, and what they still had left to do. "You must tell me, sometime."

Tarkas eyed him up and down, frowning. "Hmm, yes," he muttered, displeased at the sight of his muck-covered protégé, "Let me give you a hint." He glanced about, looking for something, and apparently found it. "Come," he commanded, beckoning him to follow. More smoke, errant flames, perhaps it had been a blacksmith's forge in life. In death it had become a hole in the ground filled with ashes and coals. Janosec knew what to expect when he saw his uncle fumbling in his pouch for another disk. The sudden flaring appearance of the being called Trent seemed almost normal, but his uncle's firm hand on his back caught him unawares, and he plunged forward into the scarlet mass before he knew it.

Silent redness again. Wait, not silent; it rang, it bubbled, words spinning around him, like shrill echoes of echoes: "Tarkas not-Tarkas you. Friend you." The echoes and the redness were already fading. At its dimmest edge he heard, "Stell you." Then it was gone and he was back in the wretched ruin of the smith's forge, Tarkas looking around for something he was not finding, rubbing his real hand. This was the second time he had stuck it into a fire in a short time. Janosec looked himself over, running his hands up and down, finding only ash, not the stiff stickiness he had smeared all over himself outside. Even his hair was clean.

"Wait here a bit," he heard, as his uncle left what was left of the building. Janosec waited, moving somewhat closer to one of the holes in the wall, a cooler and less smoky place. When he saw his uncle returning, a few brushy-looking stalks under his arm, he tried to leave, but Tarkas moved faster than he'd thought and entered the ruin first.

"Turn," he said, and Janosec turned obediently. The wispy fronds dragging across his back almost tickled, both his skin and his memory. The smell was pleasant, and tantalizingly familiar. He sniffed loudly, and sneezed on the ashes being swept off of him. "Flutterwort," said Tarkas, answering the unasked question, "I saw an herbman's sign before."

He knew the name. "Stomach problems, correct? You drink it?"

"You should know, you drank enough of it when you were young," Tarkas responded, as if he weren't still young. He took his nephew by the shoulder and started him turning, fronds still sweeping back and forth.

Janosec dredged up a memory, his focus aided by the heat and the motion. "Yes," he said softly, "It hurt for days. And then you brought me something–"

"Tureg-spawn."

Janosec smiled, eyes half-closed. "It was delicious," he remembered, "I can still taste it. And I ate it all, didn't even save any for anyone else."

"They did not want any," Tarkas said, dispelling an old guilt. "It was for you, not them. I would not have let them if they had, but–"

"But it didn't smell the same to them, did it?" finished his nephew, his mind wandering down unaccustomed trails.

Tarkas shrugged. "They never said, and I never asked. It did not seem important." He lowered the fronds, surveyed the younger man critically. "Do me a favor," he said, "Go outside, let the wind blow off the loose ash, and while you are about it, try to find that axe. It is the closest thing to a weapon we are likely to find." Janosec nodded, leaving the hut silently, still somewhat bemused.

"You may come out now," Tarkas said to the air, when he judged the younger man to be out of earshot.

Above and behind him, a shape not made of firelight and shadow moved, creeping down the wall on its many legs. Tarkas turned slowly, knowing that it was there only by smell, not knowing who–or what–else it might have been. When he finally caught sight of the visitor, he nearly jumped, but managed to prevent that fact from getting past his skin. He hadn't seen any creature of this type since his first, last, and only encounter with the wezin, a spider-like monstrosity he had destroyed even before becoming a Hero. That there were others, not monsters but people, he knew in an intellectual way, but he'd never met one and his emotional self had never caught up.

He moved down, into the hollow where the small fires still burned smokily, having judged that his guest's size would limit its mobility anywhere else and determined to be polite in spite of what his body told him. It was actually rather pretty, black legs supporting a black-and-gold body well suited to hiding in firelight, its movements graceful as it maneuvered its streamlined form around to face him, if that was its face. A long leg reached down, under itself, and produced a dangling loop. "Ub kluibbo," it said.

Tarkas took the loop and draped it around his own neck, having noticed a similar loop draped about the other's upper body. "You are Foobar, are you not?"

"I be Foobar am Tomo time short greetings Tarkas."

Tarkas was nothing if not adaptable, especially having spent years talking to fire elementals. "Greetings Tomo ask why."

"Tomo InterPub ProphPol," said the Foobar. Tarkas had second thoughts about matching its accelerated speech.

"Slower please what be?"

"Interworld Publishing Prophecy Police," Tomo elaborated, "Reveal direct guard prophecy fulfillment."

This Tarkas could understand. He hadn't seen a copy of the Book of Prophecies in ages, but the few he'd heard were tremendously vague, and had nearly destroyed two worlds, but for sheer good luck. Looking at the creature before him, Tarkas began to wonder if that had been the case. "Intervention?"

"Never," the Foobar replied emphatically, "Prophecy boulder headlong interfere squish. Prophecy terrain we compass."

Tarkas paused at that last, then realized it was an analogy. Interesting. "Selection revelation?"

"Try."

"Mistakes?"

"Seldom."

"Now?"

"Correct. Revelation premature misdirected selfward."

Maybe so, but there was little point in just telling him. "Mission? Purpose?"

Tomo produced a crystal from below. "Retrieval. Forgetting."

Ah. Simply remove the memory, end of problem. Unfortunately…"Impossible."

"Must."

The creature contrived to look threatening, but did a poor job. Probably a bureaucrat, if the mistakes were seldom so were the retrievals, and those would most likely be from the willing or the unconscious, and the poor Foobar had no practice. Nor is threatening a Hero a good idea.

"Cannot," the Hero in question reiterated, "Registered authorized."

"Fex." The creature drooped. No easy solution, then.

"Agreement," said Tarkas, ruefully. "Silence?"

Tomo sighed. "Non-viable. Agent."

"Fex." Tarkas drooped. The last thing he needed.

"Agreement. Mission ongoing?"

"Correct. After?"

"After," the creature agreed, and held out a claw. "Gibberator."

Tarkas took off the loop, handed it over. "See you later."

Tomo started climbing up the wall, disappearing into smoky blackness. "Blum dugo." Carefully as he watched, Tarkas could detect no difference between when he was there and when he was not. Alone once again, he allowed himself a small moment of self-pity–an agent of the Prophecy Police, by the gods–before climbing from the smith's pit to find his absent nephew.

It took longer to find the spot where he'd fallen than it did to find the axe he'd let fly, but at least he wouldn't have to fashion some kind of belt or loop. His new sword belt was not-so-easily modified, so he wouldn't have to carry the thing in his hand all the time. He emerged from the wood surrounding the village with the axe slung at his hip, feeling foolish and off-balance. Until he caught sight of the pathetic corpse, still lying as it had fallen. They had not even closed the eyes, surely the most routine of gestures.

He knelt, careful not to mar his newly clean state, to bestow that last dignity, and caught a glimpse of a thong under the neck of the robe. Jewelry, perhaps, or a pouch. Either way, probably something Uncle would want to see. He tugged at the leather. Ah, a pendant, heavy and circular. Hmm; three circles, nested. In his bones, he knew it had to have meaning, but he did not know what that meaning could have been. Perhaps even Grandfather did not, the lore was so fragmentary.

Whatever the symbol meant, it deserved better than to lie in the mud.

He pulled gently on the leather, turning it until the knot appeared, tight, and heavily grimed. Clearly the pendant was not removed, even to sleep. Unhappily, he took out Uncle's knife, and cut the leather, feeling too much like a grave robber for comfort. "Sorry, old man." He would not hide this medallion in a pouch, even if he had one. He would carry it openly. The thong was too short to fit around his neck, so he tied it onto the cord that held the axe instead. That felt right.

A quick pat about the body revealed no other objects hidden under the cloth, which relieved him no end, and he arranged the man's clothes almost as penance. Looking up, he found himself staring at the tumbled ruin that had started it all. There were many buildings around, most in far better shape. Only the burnt out blacksmith's hut was as destroyed as this building. Only this one had collapsed.

It had hidden the man, what else might it hide?

He was on his feet and halfway to the building almost before he knew it, and he would not have known even that little bit had he not kicked something hard and blocky on the way, a chunk of wood, strangely familiar. Roughly cubic, if he held it…this way, it became flat on top and the sides, but the bottom was neither straight nor rough. It had been the top of the post, struck off so easily by his uncle's blade. His fingers felt something odd, and he turned the block in his hands to look.

Three circles, nested.

The sound of his uncle's sandaled feet slogging through the muck of the street made him turn his head, but the older man strode over to the body, just as he had done. Tarkas knelt and looked the body over, fingering the material of the rags. Then he moved, checking the man's hands and feet. Finally, he moved the cloth away from the neck and turned the man's head, looking closely. Apparently dissatisfied, he put the head in its prior position and restored the cloth, just as Janosec had done.

Tarkas looked up, to where his nephew stood, still holding a wooden block in his hands but otherwise merely returning the look. Nothing seemed obviously different about the younger man, no telltale bulges, only the axe whose handle stuck out on the far side of his body. And of course the block of wood, held casually in one large hand. "What is that?" he asked, indicating the wood with a jerk of his head. There was something visible on one side, but he had to move closer before he could see it. Janosec held up the block, reorienting it so the circles faced his uncle when he handed it over. Tarkas studied it a bit, but found nothing but what Janosec had found. "Do you know what the significance of these circles is?"

His nephew shook his head, keeping the secret of the matching medallion just a little longer. "Hmm," Tarkas responded carefully not watching Janosec's face as he said, "Perhaps it has something to do with the missing necklace."

The younger man gaped, and flinched, his body telling Tarkas that his little joke was successful, without the need to shame him. Still apparently scrutinizing the wood, he continued, in a bored monotone, "I presume you took it."

Again, Janosec moved, his slight sense of guilt making him uneasy prey. "Yes, I have it here." His hand moved down towards his hip, but Tarkas wasn't looking.

"Tied by the axe, I imagine," he said, looking up at last, to meet his nephew's astonished gaze, "Good. I know no more than you what it may signify, but significance it has, and should not be left in the dirt. Care for it well."

Janosec fumbled with the heavy disc, looking down at it as if it might have been smashed while dangling at his side. Tarkas looked at it once, noting only that it held the same sign and no more, then turned his attention to the structure. "No doubt you are correct," he began, once again accurately assessing his nephew's purpose, "This…temple…almost certainly will have some answers for us."

Again Janosec started, not at the interest, but at the designation. "Temple?"

Tarkas shrugged. "Most likely." He looked up, drawn to his nephew's silence. "The old man was too finely dressed, his hands and feet too smooth. That suggests a scholar or a king or a priest, but a village this size would have no king, and the symbol is too mysterious for a scholar." His voice, which had started the litany smooth and matter-of-fact, ended sounding tentative. "What did you think it was?"

Janosec looked uncomfortable. "The most destroyed hut in the town," he almost mumbled, but Tarkas could hear it nonetheless.

Startled, Tarkas looked back at the temple, then did a quick examination of some of the surrounding structures. "You are correct," he commented in a voice of wonder, "I never even noticed."

Navak, head of the clan NarSeptas and de facto commander-in-chief of the armed forces of the city of Querdishan, stomped up the last part of the road to its gates with neither fanfare nor warning. Behind him, something heavy on an improvised litter burdened four men, while another two got a third wind before it came their turn again. The guards at the gate heard them, of course, long before they saw them, and saw them before they were within hailing distance. They recognized the lord easily, from the sword carried loose in his hand (a notoriously bad sign), to the colors at his belt. Despite his obvious hurry, still the sentry moved to bar his way.

As he by all the gods of Earth should! Navak was not so far gone from himself not to notice adherence to his own rules, nor so merciful as to give the poor watchman, of the NarLintas, any relief in his sweating misery as he returned the proper code phrases in the proper order, his voice clipped but steady. He even skipped the bowmen test in his concern over more important matters. "Send runners at once, lad," he commanded, "All the lords. Open the gates!"

Watchers above scurried to obey–*Ether take them, they should by the gods of Air know who to take their orders from!*–but Navak refrained from reprimanding them, only beckoning his squad of exhausted bearers through as soon as a large enough gap appeared. It passed close by, but the reek of whatever lay on the litter overpowered the sentry's desire to see for himself, so he only got a glimpse of something large and dark before it was past and inside, leaving only dark blackish stains in the dust. A lesser man would have looked after them, but the sentry knew his duty, and throttled his own curiosity as the gates boomed shut behind him.

The sentries behind the gates were posted there for a reason, and lost no time scurrying up their ladders to get the view from above, as lord Navak busily posted guards to keep the people on the ground from getting too close. So enthralled were they by the distorted black shape that they failed to notice that some of the guards actually looked inwards, as if a monster so thoroughly skewered could still pose a threat.

Time seemed to hang, neither long nor short, until the other lords made their appearance, dressed, armed, and clearheaded despite the late hour, their entourages somewhat less so. The watchers above divided their duties, some watching the approaches, a few the creature, but the lords were by far the most interesting, and the watchers amused themselves in the usual ways: trying to guess what they said, wagering on the origin of the thing, and other things bored men do at night to keep alert. Only after a particularly vigorous gesticulation accompanied an especially loud"–near to the Wall, by all the gods of Earth!–" did they turn, satisfied, back to their responsibilities.

Jerim, lord of the NarDemlas, since the death of old lord Midros the smallest clan in the city, twitched at this very same outburst, but the guards, and more important, the senior lords, failed to notice. Nor was he about to bring to their attention a fact that his Brother, Tarkas, had broached unto him many years ago, on condition of secrecy, that there was a place by the wall where 'the world was thin, and a man might slip through.' At the time, it had only seemed reasonable, that the Gods would give their Champion secret paths to do their work. But now it occurred to him to wonder if the Gods had made the paths or merely found them, and could things other than a man also slip through? But that puzzle was his alone. "Are you suggesting, my lord," he began tentatively, as befit his junior status, "That this creature is a visitor from Old Querdishan?" That should be sufficient, he thought, to keep them thinking about paths in the world, and not beyond it.

"I should hope not, lord Jerim," Navak replied forcefully. "This one killed three of my scouts in moments, and only the speedy arrival of reinforcements kept it from killing more. Even so the wounded–!"

Lord Selter, the least hardy of them all, shuddered visibly, and Navak refrained from lurid descriptions. Lord Kestrel, head of the NarTolgas and Jerim's father-in-law, diverted the report into a less graphic vein. "Many, my lord?"

Navak practically groaned, "Scads."

Lintas Selter paled. "Your forward units?" They were, of course, NarLintas; the best scouts always were, and as scouts their arms and armor were light.

"No, my lord," Navak assured him, and Selter sagged in relief. "They struck from the sides, forcing the thing towards my own squads and doom. The wounds it dealt were nearly as grave as the wounds it took. Your healers, lord Kestrel, will be busy far into the night." Kestrel raised his hand, and a child of his clan raced off, no doubt to fetch more healers.

"How long did you pursue it?" asked Jerim.

Lord Navak laughed at that, but without humor, only satisfaction. "The monster was as stupid as it was tough, my lord," he replied with a certain degree of contempt in his tone, "Or perhaps confused. But it made no attempt to avoid us, or flee. It just attacked until we slew it, like any evillish beast would."

He seemed so pleased with the performance of his men that Jerim felt reluctant to fly in the face of it. But he had doubts, and doubts, the Spirits said, withered in open places. "I believe you might be mistaken, my lord."

Navak's night had been bad enough, and his short temper shorter still. "In what respect, my lord?" he asked in brittle courtesy. "What aspect of my report do you believe to be false?"

"I did not say 'false', lord Navak–"

"*Mmmm*," rumbled the perturbed clanleader, accepting the distinction. "You doubt the valor of my men, perhaps?"

"Of course not–"

"Or the evidence of your own eyes?" He waved at the fetid heap on the cloth.

"If you would but be silent a moment, my lord, you might perhaps learn what it is he meant," broke in a voice at Jerim's back, in high, caustic tones. In the absence of both Tarkas and Janosec, his entourage, already small, was further reduced, until only his wife, Fenita, stood with him, and through her, the NarTolgas as well. She was not one to stand silently by, and with two clans to call on, felt no need to.

But Navak could negate *that* ploy. "My lady Demlas," he began, emphasizing the one clan and thereby removing the other from consideration. He got no farther.

The black form on the cloth, so still and lifeless, rolled and struck in the same motion, felling its two watching guards before they could inflict more than minor wounds on its no-longer-wounded body. Had slaying them been its purpose they would have died, but it was not. Its purpose was quite terribly clear.

"Demlas she is!

"Demlas she is!

"Demlas she is!" it cried in a high, thin, ghastly voice, all the while toppling the unprepared guards like straws. But Navak was ready, Navak was prepared, Navak was–

–a convenient platform, as the apparition vaulted the onlookers in its path, guards and lords, even Selter, weapons drawn, twisting impossibly in the air as if unconcerned about any damage it might do to itself, landing hard behind Jerim and in front of Fenita, who had not retreated with the others. She struck out with a short knife, but strangely Selter got in the first blow. Lagging in the back, his weapon barely clear of its scabbard, he just let his arm continue moving and opened a deep slice on the back of the creature's arm. Others did more damage then, as the monster dodged Fenita's blade, swords and even a few arrows finding their mark on its exposed and unprotected backside.

Finally, the creature disarmed the lady by the simple tactic of impaling itself on her knife and dropping to its 'knees', pulling the haft from her hand. This maneuver coincidentally put its 'shoulder' at her waist, so it scooped her up and ran, even though the swords no longer fell, nor arrows. The surrounding mob even cleared a path, as it made for the nearest structure, a barn for housing animals during the winter (or in sieges), now temporary housing for some families as homes were being built in the town on the other side of the flats. Sleeping children awoke crying, and parents reached for arms, as the walls rattled with scrabbling claws and the stench of the black thing's blood, old and new, saturated the night air.

But not for long, as the monstrosity fairly flew to the top of the building, pausing only long enough to take its bearings before charging off and leaping from roof to roof, putting some distance between itself and the noise of the pursuing mob. Lights went up, bright flares that illuminated the rooftops and left it plainly visible to the sentries on the walls. It knew they would tell their fellows where to go. It stopped, finally, at Temple Square, for lack of further roofs.

"*Ummph*!" puffed Fenita, as the beast threw her down like a bag of roots. One hand rubbed her sore belly, the other supported her as she hurriedly moved backward, but there was not much roof left, and the creature watched. Not moving or threatening, just staring and flexing its claws. Her gaze went to her own knife, sticking out of its chest and dripping with indescribable gore.

"Demlas Tarkas here is, is, is?" it screeched at her, its voice like a blade drawn across a whetstone.

But Fenita had not totally lost her wits. "Demlas who?"

It shrieked then, flexing talons ripping out shingles with ease, to go sliding noisily to fall in the streets below. "Master Tarkas smells, smells, smells," it howled, eyes twitching back and forth. "Master Tarkas wants, wants, wants. This one Master sends, sends, sends."

Fenita had to decide. The creature's master had tracked Tarkas here, but the creature didn't seem too happy to be here. "Yes, Demlas Tarkas lives here," she declared proudly. He was the God's Champion, after all, and much more. "But he is not here." Hopefully he even now hunted things like this one down, but saying that would be imprudent at best.

The creature relaxed, withdrawing slightly. "Here he is not, not, not? Today here he was, was, was," it challenged, eyes flickering more slowly. It seemed oddly relieved, in spite of the question.

"He left," she replied shortly, unwilling to tell any more, not to this…hunter. She hadn't even wanted to tell it to the priests.

Strangely, the creature seemed to accept her story without argument. "Good, good, good."

In one way, Fenita, too, relaxed, in another, she became tenser than ever. "Good?"

The thing sank back on its 'haunches', its head shaking slowly from side to side. "Master Tarkas dead wants, wants, wants," it said, raising claws to fangs like a beast whose head hurt, "Kill Tarkas this one cannot, cannot, cannot. Kill Tarkas this one must, must, must." It had two clawed hands up now, its voice once more strident.

"Tarkas here is not," said Fenita soothingly. The monster did not want to kill, which sounded very good to her.

"Tarkas here is not, not, not," it breathed, and its hands came down, one to the roof, the other to her dagger. It pulled it out, with only a slight grunt of pain. Advancing on her, crouching, it raised the blade high, slamming it down, deep into the ridgepole, between her knees. "Kill you this one should, should, should," it wheezed at her, "But this one may not, not, not."

She sagged in relief, but not for long. The beast leapt over her, coming down on the edge of the roof and striking her sharply in the back, throwing her off balance. She pitched forward and started to fall, but for the knife handle sticking up. She hung on to that with both hands, screaming for help from the approaching crowd, as the monster launched itself into the air. Its ploy, if a ploy, worked well, with a goodly portion of the crowd diverting to her rescue, leaving only a token force to pursue the creature across the open square, through the gate, and onto the cliff overlooking the Eastern Sea from which the city took its name.

The creature leapt, standing astride the great block and tackle used to raise goods from the docks far below, and turned, trapped between the raging sea and the storming, armed throng. An arrow flew out of the dark, striking it in the throat by some lucky chance, showing feathers on one side and point on the other. The creature reached up by reflex, clawed hands clutching at the arrow. But breaking it and pulling it out threw the beast off balance, and it fell, howling, to the rocks at the base of the cliff, narrowly missing the main dock.

A sentry went forward, and his garbled cheer and bright grin soon brought the lords forward to see for themselves. Only after they had satisfied themselves and stood back did the rest of the crowd, now growing with the rescue of lord Jerim's wife and the awakening of the city, take its turns gawking. When Fenita appeared, safe in the circle of her husband's arms, they parted for her, to take a look for herself. But when she looked, it was gone, the rising surf only beginning to wash away the smeared grue on the rocks.

"Good riddance," said Navak, and strutted away.

"If it stays gone," amended Fenita, shuddering at her memories.

"What do you mean, 'if'? Surely it is dead," asked her father, looking down himself, at nothing.

"Lord Navak thought the same, father, when he brought the creature where it wished to be," she answered, holding out the haft of her knife, still smeared and sticky with the monster's flowing blood. "It's escaped."

And somewhere Else, a beast rested, its stomach full for the first time in days. The fire had passed and the dead waited, of no use to themselves but of great use to him. He had traveled with men before, and did not automatically disdain cooked food, as most of his kind would have done.

Now the creature dozed, the call of the hunt abated for a time. Still it called, and still he heard it, even in his dreams. They held prey aplenty, fast prey, fierce prey, prey that fought and prey that fled and prey that died, bright blood flowing and–

–turning black and foul in his mouth, the sweet flesh gone stringy and vile on his tongue. The creature wurfled in its sleep, distressed by the sudden change. Then the prey rose up, whole again, and in his dream the beast smelled nothing, neither challenge nor fear, no delicious smell of terror, nothing but the foul, putrid ichors of prey that refused to be prey.

The beast's roar of outrage would have woken the dead, but they were otherwise occupied.

Chapter 6

Tarkas and Janosec spent entirely too much time trying to raise the slumped mass of the temple, if temple it had been. A lot of time and a lot of muscle, before they noticed that the roof was built in sections, somewhat triangular, lashed together around a circular hole in the middle, where a central support pole should have been. But the supports, like the pole Tarkas had chopped down, were outside, leaving a space. After that, they simply slit the bindings and removed the sections, letting the walls fall away.

The interior was a shambles, naturally, the furnishings smashed as much as they were smashable, and tossed about in addition. Somewhat more than the building merely falling over would accomplish, in fact. A tree stump occupied the place of honor, at the center. Not coincidentally, the circle in the roof would have been positioned directly above this stump, everything else positioned around it in the ubiquitous nested circles. It was also dressed, and this drew Tarkas' attention like a magnet.

There were marks on the top, but he decided to ignore those at the beginning, to look for the subtler signs first. He knelt before it, to bring his eyes and hands closer. But only his eyes touched it now, noting the grain, the smooth finish, the straight cut. A token worthy of the gods, even by his standards, but not for burning. His hands could feel it, a shell, a preservative for which his former people would have had no use.

Only then did he turn his attention to the top face, to examine the marks carved so firmly on that side, and the other marks, not carved but worn in by use. Worn in by what? Something hard, heavy. Have to ask Janosec. Hmm, these circles followed the rings, trenches gouged out in as nearly perfect circles as the rings allowed. And the middle, a hole. How deep? His hand felt no bottom, but the sides were as completely smooth as his own best work. The trunk tipped forward. Hmm, the hole did not go through to the bottom. What was it for? No clues.

Now then, the markings, the carved ones. There were…three? No, five. They looked like normal marks, but he didn't know any of–wait, rotate the trunk. Yes, they were marks. Maybe. That could be a 'one', that one a 'two', but what were those little pips here and there? That's a 'three', surely, but what are these other two?

His examination was interrupted by a small sound of distaste, little more than a sharp exhalation, from his young partner, somewhere behind him, searching the wreckage. "Janosec?"

"Your pardon, Uncle," requested the young clan-Second, "It was…vile. I was merely–"

"*What* was vile, nephew?"

"But a pedestal, Uncle, put to an unseemly purpose."

Tarkas considered this, staring at the stump. Pedestals held waxlights, like the sticks of his once-people, but for illumination, not for time-keeping. They were hard and heavy and his fingers traced the gouge already. "Bring it here, if you don't mind."

Janosec did mind. "It is…filthy, Uncle."

"Then cleanse it." The tone was sharp, peremptory, but the more effective for it, as the Brother of the NarDemlas was not known for such talk. A few moments of rustling, a few splashes, and the object appeared before him, slightly dented, but otherwise ungrimed. Tarkas fingered the dent, noted tiny stains, too dry to clean easily. Blood. "A truncheon?"

Janosec nodded unhappily, staring unseeing at the stump. Until Tarkas placed the base of the unlikely weapon into the groove in the wood, which fit like a glove for fingers. Startled, he moved the object, forgetting his earlier distaste, noting instead the groove it had made as well as the other gouges in which it had clearly not had a part. "*Hmmm*," was all he said as he strode purposefully off.

Tarkas waited patiently, made room as his nephew came to kneel beside him, the obscure marks plain. "What are these marks here…and here?" He pointed at the pips that confused him.

Janosec pointed at the first sign. "'First.'" Then at the second.

"'Second.'"

Tarkas pointed to the third, like but unlike the other two. "'Third?'" He didn't sound like he believed that.

Janosec shook his head, not at all surprised at his uncle's ignorance. He'd grown up with it. "More than that. This part here is 'third', but these bits here indicate finality. It's more like–" his hands moved as he fumbled for words "–'third and last'."

Tarkas rested his hand on his knee and his chin on his hand, staring unseeing at the third mark. "Third and last," he repeated, "The last of three? Three what?"

Janosec hesitated, but pointed at the trunk. "Perhaps it means the circles themselves?" At Tarkas' interest and scrutiny, he pressed on. "See? Here, this mark is on this side of the line, but here it spans it, and this one is on the other side. These symbols here, whatever they mean, are clearly placed between the lines. And the gouges–"

Tarkas recognized a dramatic pause when he heard one. "Yes, what of them?"

Janosec manipulated the pedestal back into its former place. "Obviously this is the cause of the first, and perhaps this–" he held up a flat, battered, crushed sheet of the same metal as the pedestal "–is the cause of the second." Less clearly, the sheet had a circular portion attached by a thin stalk to the main mass. The second, lighter gouge fit its curve closely.

Tarkas took the piece, examined it closely. "It is what?"

Janosec shrugged. "I have no knowledge of it. I thought we could take them with us and perhaps puzzle them out."

Tarkas froze in mid-examination, only his eyes flicking over to look upon his nephew's guileless face. "What puzzle?"

The young man turned away, fumbling with something out of Tarkas' vision as he said, "Gaze upon the pedestal from above."

Frowning, Tarkas obeyed.

Three circles, nested.

A thump as his companion placed yet another object on the top of the altar drew his attention to a cap of wood, sitting somewhat askew in the hole. Tarkas lifted it up, frowning again at the thin jagged edges underneath. Janosec scattered a handful of fragments, along with a thinner mate to the cap in his uncle's hand. Tarkas held the two larger pieces a few hands apart, in a line. "It was hollow?"

Janosec concurred. "Notice the smooth edge here." He pointed. "It looks like a hole in the wall." Tarkas noted a similar curve on the other piece and turned it to line them up as well. A cylinder with a hole cut in the side.

"Something was contained within, and secured within the stump," stated Tarkas decisively, trying to place the cap of the tube in the hole, without success. "There is a method to its removal and replacement. Without that, the contents are inviolable."

"I have found nothing that could be its contents, Uncle."

Tarkas looked out over the chaos and slaughter. They would look, of course. They were in need of supplies as well, goods that the villagers no longer needed. And keepsakes, if any remained; these people had families, surely, and lives to be remembered, not left to rot. But he knew they would not find that one thing, just as he knew where it had to be.

Janosec dawdled, dragging his feet, and he knew it, but made no effort to change. "Check the houses," Tarkas had said. He was quite happy to do just that, especially since his uncle had gone off somewhere to do something. Food, of course, dried, stored, take-it-with-them stuff, or fresh, if they ate it fast enough. The most perishable he ate on the spot, or took to the remaining fires for cooking. He didn't know what the other things were that he was supposed to be looking for, 'items of memory', Tarkas had called them, which told him nothing. A skillet could be a treasured memento, passed down for generations.

Hmm, a woodcut. Pretty girl. Idly he wondered who she had been, before putting it back on the living room shelf. Important things aren't out like that. Loved things are kept safe. Like that ring he'd found, in a bag at the bottom of a box under a bed. Nothing under this bed, though. Kneeling, he looked about him at the room, not trying to think of anything, almost like trying to…to hear it with his eyes, or smell it. Some sense that had no name. He'd felt something with it occasionally before, but he didn't know how or why it worked. He stood and made a slow circuit of the hut, not really looking at anything, and for no reason he could name he stopped at the woodcut, looking closely at the simple frame, running a finger along the surface. He slid out the cut, revealing a smaller cut underneath, a different girl, but similar-looking. A sister? Daughter? He'd never know, but the frame and its contents all went into his small bag, itself a valued item from another shack. Time to move on.

The lowering sun forced him to squint as he left the shack. How much more did they have to do, by all the Powers? His uncle seemed to have forgotten that not all men were–

"Ah, Janosec, there you are!" cried that worthy, in a bright, jovial, obscenely un-tired voice, carrying a tree trunk at a brisk pace. Janosec would have hated him, but it took too much work.

Then he saw the Hero's face. "What is the matter?"

Tarkas dropped the trunk with a thud. "Find a house, preferably one at the edge of the village. Clear a space on the floor, lie down, and go to sleep."

Janosec focused on the instructions: house, down, sleep. Wait a minute. "Where will you be?" he asked with some difficulty, yawning.

Tarkas reached behind him and pulled out a blade that Janosec had never seen before, short, heavy-spined, thick-edged. And black. Stooping, he grabbed the trunk by one end, dragging it over to a convenient stone. "Busy," he replied, "Go to sleep."

Janosec merely stood, watching blearily, until the first THUNK jolted him out of his trance, or perhaps the sparks, struck by the sword against the stone, fizzling in the muck. Tarkas had chopped clean through the trunk in one blow, chopping off a disk about a finger thick.

Janosec cast a worried look towards his uncle. Tarkas, kneeling, caught it with some magical sixth sense of his own.

"For the bodies," he explained, still chopping away. "Go to sleep, Janosec."

To his shame, itself comfortably distant, Janosec felt only a small urge to assist his uncle, and a vast relief at being offered an opportunity, even encouraged, to depart. He turned, vaguely aware that he perhaps ought not to do so, and stumbled off for a shack decently away from the polluted environs. With an effort he said, 'Smith's', fairly clearly as he went.

Tarkas kept chopping, until the trunk became a litter of disks and a short length left over. The disks went onto his improvised carryall, the short black sword again became its longer, straighter self and sheathed, the stick planted small-end down into the soft ground. Looking about unnecessarily, for only Janosec would have been there and he would have known better, Tarkas recited:

"Where the home berries are sweetest,
And the hearth fire burning."

The torch burst into flame, the only way in the world to ignite wood from the Elsewhere. Tarkas stuck a finger into the fire, saying, "Stell."

Smaller and paler by far than Trent, the fire elemental Stell appeared as he'd been bid, shortening the torch only fractionally. "Stell me. Who you?"

"Tarkas Hero me."

"Me know?" Aside from Trent, fire elementals had no memories to speak of.

"You know." Tarkas waited, as Stell spat out a fireball that washed over him without damage, a fire elemental's way of determining the truth of a statement.

"Trent-friend Tarkas me know me know me know," it burst out, skittering up and down the length of the torch with little puffs of smoke. "What want, friend good friend?"

"Consumption," he requested. Stell flared, more than happy to comply.

Tarkas smiled, gently. It took so little to make fire elementals happy. Taking up his carryall full of disks, he brought the torch to the first body, the priest, of course. A chip went onto his chest, the torch touched onto the disk. Stell took the cue, consuming the disk and the body beneath as greedily as only a fire elemental can. By the time the disk was gone the body was ashes.

By the time all the disks were gone, all the bodies were ashes.

Stell proclaimed his departure and departed. Tarkas dropped the stub of the torch and his pathetic litter of chips into the bag at his side, and walked away in the fading light, even his preternatural endurance nearing its end. In the smith's burnt out pit he found the food his nephew had left for him, some meat, some root vegetables. His canteen got filled from a nearby barrel. Janosec himself was as easy to find; he merely had to remember in which direction the young man had been pointed, then travel in a straight path to the most distant house. Alternatively, he could also follow the track of the large duffel, as the lad had dragged it along. His nephew had of course passed up the bed, reclining on the floor with a rug wadded up beneath his head, and the remains of a few leftover fruits nearby.

The borrowed packs, stuffed with someone's treasures and foodstuffs, lay side by side near the door. Tarkas automatically moved them further in, lest someone (the Gods forbid!) should sneak in and take them. The spot where he left them held no great distinction, but putting the bags there made it suddenly much more inviting, and Tarkas sat himself down with a great sigh and greater relief.

Ye gods! *Could* it have been worse? His memory flashed, in spite of years of practice at steering his thoughts elsewhere, but it gave him no definite answer, images and sensations flowing like a river. Then he noticed that he was kneading his own left hand with his right. He flexed his numb appendage, spreading its fingers, pondering kinds and degrees of badness in the abstract way of someone who had already visited his own dark places.

Janosec sat up straight, suddenly, howling incoherently. In a younger man it would have meant a nightmare, and Tarkas would have moved instantly to offer him comfort. In Janosec it was no nightmare, but reality, which moved him, and so Tarkas was comforted. Until the half-awake young man cried out, "UNCLE!" Until the sleeper turned anguished eyes on him. On his hand, still held up and spread, on display. Inside Tarkas, something went cold, and very still. Janosec sat panting, his gaze fixed, until he could gasp out, "Burning!–You–"

There was no fire near, nor any smell of smoke. But Tarkas knew what he meant nonetheless. His dead hand clenched, falling into his lap. "Yes."

His nephew's eyes shifted now, from the hand, no longer visible, to the face and the pain, equally obscured. "Trent!" he blurted out, making the connection in some roundabout way, "Why–?"

Tarkas closed his eyes, bracing against the memory those words called up. *(He does not know. He could not know.)* With a long, weary, pain-wracked sigh, he whispered, "Trent consumed my arm because I told him to."

The effect of this remarkable statement was as dramatic as the Singer in Tarkas had probably intended it should be. Near-perfect silence reigned in the darkened shack, only the sound of one man's slowing breathing disturbing the tomb-like stillness. Then Tarkas spoke again. "I have served the gods all your life," he observed, "In the beginning I had never killed a man. Oh, I had killed, of course. Beasts. For food. Perhaps the gods were favoring me, perhaps they were unsure of my willingness, but for a long time I did little but what you might call rescue work. I did many strange things, conveyed objects, delivered messages, but mostly I saved people from ruins and disasters." He breathed slowly, thinking of younger days as the dim light faded. "That was good."

"You saved Querdishan," said Janosec, stating one of the basic facts of his life.

"In a way," Tarkas admitted. "But I have been many places, other places, places where the air is hot and the ground is dead, where the air is wet and the ground soft. I have been places where the magic is weak, or where it is dead, or terribly different." His voice changed, firmed. "It was a shack, a ruin, really. I have no idea what took me there or why, only that I stood before this hovel when the screaming started."

"Who was screaming?" asked Janosec, well aware of his part in the story-telling game. He even shifted his position, sitting cross-legged, like a child.

"Children," Tarkas' voice grated out of the deepening darkness, "They were trying to cook something, a bird I think, but they didn't–"

"Where were their parents?"

"I was not told," Tarkas replied, in no way put out by the

interruption. From the tone of his voice, he might have been discussing his favorite color. "But the bird was very greasy, and they had not prepared it properly, I think. It exploded, setting the walls of the hut afire."

"Ah," breathed Janosec, "Your 'rescue work.'"

"So I thought. But the hut was small, and close, and burned very fast."

"You called Trent."

Tarkas' eyes were closed, but even so he winced. The memory was eternally fresh, the disadvantage of Conlon's curse. "It should have worked," he claimed. "It *did* work. He came. But there was something different about the place, and it could not… sustain him." His hands gestured, trying to convey some part of the explanation, but Janosec could not see them.

"'Sustain?'"

Tarkas laughed a miserable, pathetic excuse for a laugh. "A fire without sustenance goes out. The spirit goes with it."

Janosec sat up straight. His uncle did not have to see it to know it. "You had to rescue *Trent*?"

Tarkas shrugged casually. His nephew did not have to see it to know it. "He could not leave, not on his own, and he could not live–"

"Not on his own," finished Janosec. "You set your own arm afire to sustain him." He cringed at the very thought.

Tarkas was slow in answering. "It didn't hurt long."

Janosec could think of nothing to say in reply to that, so–"Did you save the children?"

Tarkas sat up straighter, his back rubbing against the wall. Even his voice became more alive. "Oh, yes. To save Trent I had to use one of the many ways in the world known only to the Gods' Champions, and so they came with us, which meant that they could never return. I suppose the people who lived nearby thought them dead anyway. I believe they were settled Elsewhere, but I cannot keep track of all whose paths I cross." He sounded wistful.

Janosec understood. He, like his uncle, was a natural storyteller. "It must be hard, to know all these stories by the middle only," he sympathized, as if the previous recounting had never happened. "Do you ever get to know the end?"

The Hero's mouthed quirked slightly, to a happier memory, eternally fresh, the advantage of Conlon's curse. "Sometimes that is all I know," he said. "I once told a band of warriors that their goals would be accomplished, and their sacrifice would not be in vain, without the slightest notion of what those goals were or why sacrificing themselves would accomplish it."

Janosec made a muffled noise, which Tarkas took to be amused sympathy. "Not exactly a happy ending, but a good one."

"Better than most," the Hero agreed, and immediately regretted it. But Janosec missed the reference, which told Tarkas volumes about his condition. Steering the conversation into simpler channels was child's play, and then he merely had to wait for the inevitable. In a short time the younger man's body had settled back onto the floor, and in a shorter time he had stopped talking. Tarkas stopped talking, too, preferring to listen to his nephew breathe.

He had not thought about the warriors for years. A giant metal box, it had seemed, full of men in strange clothing and devices that he could only assume were weapons, completely foreign to him then and not much more recognizable now. Only his later readings had enabled him to recognize it in his memories as some sort of giant weapon, improperly mounted, but he had known then why and how they had died. The memory played easily in his mind, bright and vivid: stepping forward and declaring himself, the warriors, shocked at first but quickly believing by the very impossibility of his presence, frightened but determined. He saluted their courage, stepping quickly back through the screen of Reality that would protect him even as he saw their bravery and its consequences, the bright flash and the view of stars, like the night sky, but thicker and oh so bright.

Janosec moaned in his dreams, pulling Tarkas from his memories in time to see the man flinch, raising an arm to his face and grimacing, not in pain but as if…as if seeing a bright flash. Then the moment passed, and the raised hand kept moving, Janosec rolling over in his sleep.

Tarkas sat, unmoving. Stilling the thoughts in his head with hard-won ease. Watching the sleeper, equally still.

Thinking, *What the hell is going on here?*

Demlas Fenita, Wife and mother, awoke at her usual time, unaccountably puzzled. She lay there for a time, taking stock of herself. Her memories of the previous night were unfortunately quite clear, her memories of the questioning that followed somewhat less so. Despite the trauma of the monster's assault upon her person and subsequent near-fatal fall, the lords had judged, rightly, that they needed fresh knowledge, and immediately. They had, accordingly, kept her up for a while more, repeating the tale of her ordeal several times before they were satisfied and let her get her rest. She felt certain, laying there, that Jerim had not seen his side of the bed at all, and idly reached out a hand to make sure.

In a way, she decided, they had done her a favor. Even had she been allowed to sleep immediately, she doubted that she could have, and reliving the events in her mind while awake had probably spared her any reliving of those events while asleep. She had no memory of any phantasms.

So what puzzled her was not within; it must therefore come from without. Her eyes she kept shut, exploring the house beyond the confines of the room's walls with other, more useful senses. Eyes told her of states, she had learned long ago, but unless she happened to be looking in the right direction, were useless for telling of events. For that, she relied on her ears, which had once told her when Denora, her youngest, had gotten into one of the kitchen crocks and had been spreading its contents on the floor. They had even told her which crock it had been, from two rooms away.

As if on cue, a woman's voice rose in horrified outrage, "Denoraaa!" Whose voice? Eyebrows quirked over closed eyes, until she recognized the voice as belonging to one of her cousins. No doubt Father had sent her over to help. Opening her eyes, Fenita sat up, and moved to dress. Had *that* bothered her, the sounds of the house? It seemed so, but still, it seemed like there should be more.

Like the oddly light belt, still hanging in its usual place, but lacking its usual burden. She had last seen the haft of her knife on the main table, really, on a board on the table. No one had wanted to stain an eating surface with that noisome ichor, but the board would have soon been discarded anyway. She raised her hands to her nose, sniffing daintily. But no, the smell she had managed to wash off last night had not returned to embarrass her, thank all the gods.

A sudden flurry of knocking shook the door, and she hastily scanned the room before bidding the knocker, "Enter." Her cousin, Tinisa, as expected, Denora in her arms as expected. Bloody bandage on infant fingers, not expected.

"Good, you're up," said Tinisa without preamble, as usual, her hands all aflutter and her voice with that irritating nasal tone it got whenever she was upset, "Denora's gone and cut herself. I'm going to the Tolgas for a healer." As if Fenita hadn't seen it, she tugged on the little girl's bandaged fingers.

Fenita reached up and grabbed Tinisa's fingers, as Denora started to cry and squirm. "Tinisa," she said, low and direct, "Favor me, please, with a child not as upset as your own self. Speak calmly, and she will be calm. Act like an untamed wissin, so will she. I know what I would like to see in *my* home." Either the instructions, or merely the fact that she was *being* instructed, had the desired effect: hands stilled, breathing steadied.

"Yes," continued Fenita lightly, smiling at Denora and touching her nose, "I think taking her to Father is an excellent idea. Thank you." Tinisa took the hint. Fenita frowned in her wake, not at the young woman, perhaps too young to be burdened with such a responsibility, but rather at the implication of her remarks.

As her father's daughter, Fenita knew all too well that, if far-off times and distant lands, there were clan leaders and Wives whose knowledge of their own kitchens was limited to the part of the house in which they lay, leaving the mundane and unglamorous chore of food-preparation to unprosperous clansmen, whose causes would in no way be advanced by sudden unexplained deaths at table. But not here, and not now. The floor was well known to her feet, the furnishings, and the things that should and should not be on them, equally familiar. But she took no time out to wipe up this or move that there, intent instead on one door, and the steamy warmth beyond.

"Cook," she shouted, simultaneous with the sudden slam of the door opening to her hand. She could have used the woman's name, but this was a kitchen matter, not a personal one.

"Yes, Lady?" replied the cook, wiping her hands on a towel hung from her belt, well versed in the nuances. She may be a Demlas now, but she had been a low-rank Tolgas once. A new clan gets many, small fish in big ponds moving to smaller ponds, working to increase them.

But her quizzical reply sounded a bit *too* quizzical, and Fenita modified her tone and her question. "You are aware that Denora just injured herself with a knife?"

Concern bloomed, but not guilt. "Not in my kitchen, Lady. She's been out in the main room all day. I'm surprised you slept at all, with her yelling 'Denora!' all the time."

Fenita decided that 'her' apparently meant Tinisa, not the only one to gloss over details. "Very well," she acknowledged, "I'll discuss the matter with Skander, while he is *not* improving your people's knowledge of wood care, about removing the water stains from his fine tables." Skander was a craftsman, but more important, he was also in charge of the armory. Her mild admonishment delivered, Fenita turned and left, as Cook turned and bellowed for whatever unfortunate boy was currently front and center.

The armory was not far, a short hallway and a circular stair from the ground floor, but Fenita never reached it. The rear door opened, one of the boys, her own, returning from the rear yard, where the privy stood. "Good morning, mother," he said, meaning it more today than usual.

"Good morning, my son," she replied. When it became clear that his destination was the same as hers, she asked, "Is Skander above?"

Her son paused, rolling his eyes so he wouldn't have to express himself in a manner possible to overhear. "He's had us sharpening blades since sunup," he explained, flexing his fingers dramatically. "Shall I tell–I mean–" He stopped, unsure what word to use. He was the son of the clanleader, Skander was an adult in authority.

Fenita saved him. "Do not trouble him, or yourself. You have told me that which I wanted to know." With a flick of her hand she dismissed him, back up the stair.

She pondered this, as her feet paced slowly, suddenly directionless, her quest balked. So, they had been whetting the blades all morning. Skander's idea, or Jerim's? Skander's, most likely, but with her husband's connivance. And it gave the children something to do, ended their ceaseless fretting over Janosec. But her original problem remained, even more imperative, for now it appeared that whatever naked blade had wounded her daughter wandered beyond its proper bounds. The possibility that either Cook or Armorer had somehow allowed one to slip away unnoticed remained, but that was the possibility of last resort, not worthy of extensive consideration.

Then she noticed that her ambling feet had brought her into the main room, at the front of the house, and she remembered what Cook had said. Certainly this was the proper place to begin seeking out errant cutlery. Looking about, she sighed. It was also a good place to commence demolition. That would be the easiest way to restore order to any room inhabited by Denora for any period of time. Wait, look about. Yes, the aid kit, left out by Tinisa in her haste, sitting on the table by the–

Mother's knife?

Father's most cherished item, his treasure, kept in a locked box in his own quarters. What was it doing here, by her–and the sheathe! And fresh blood, a few drops. Denora, of course, fascinated as she herself had been. Suddenly she blushed, alone in the hall, remembering why her father had put a lock on the box.

Slowly, she reached out a hand for the knife, and another for the sheathe, her eyes caressing the weapon's deadly beauty, the edge, the finish. Truly, it looked almost cut from pure metal, not folded and pounded on a mortal forge. Alone, but feeling somehow observed and self-conscious, she allowed her fingers to curve around the untarnished, wire-wrapped hilt, saw her fingers reach the dark hollows made by her mother's fingers. She had never held it before, barely ever touched it before.

Why was it here, in her hall?

Suddenly freed from the grip of memory's spell, she twisted the blade in her hand, aligning it with the sheathe and sliding it home in the stiff leather. Automatically, she raised her eyes and hands, to place the item onto the shelf above the–

A tray. A tray *full* of knives!

Well, three knives, actually, counting the one in her hand, but it was a small tray. The space in the middle was obviously meant for Mother's knife; Tinisa was NarTolgas, after all, and had known what she held. So the other blades had lofty origins as well, and she had no difficulty determining which clan leader had sent which blade. Both were well-made, naturally, one a standard woman's knife, the other a heavier, less versatile tool, more likely to be found on a skinner's belt than his wife's. Navak's sense of humor was as temperamental as the man himself, and revealed itself in unusual ways.

Tears stung in her eyes, tears she would never show, at the honor they were doing her. But it left her in a bit of a dilemma. She could not appear in public without a knife, but whose? Father's would be an easy solution, but it didn't feel right. Too much memory lived in that blade. That left lord Navak's, for lord Selter's would never do, a quandary in itself. What to do with it, in a way that would not offend him?

A problem for another day, she decided, undoing her belt, to remove her old sheathe and slip on the new one. Ye gods, it was heavy! She took a few steps, and felt absurd and unbalanced, as the longer, thicker blade slapped against her leg. She would have to get a cord, and tie the end of the sheathe down so it would not bruise her as she walked.

Easy enough to do. Gathering up the rest of the knives, she went to the front stair and climbed up to her own bedroom door, and put her Mother's blade carefully away. A check of her own clothes chest delivered what she needed, a length of cord normally used with leggings. Unfortunately, the sheathe had nothing to which to attach the cord. Skander would know what to do. At least the main armory entrance was on this floor.

A light tap on the door received an instant response, a panel sliding back to reveal a grill and a pair of eyes. The door opened.

"Skander, how fortunate you are," she said cheerily, bypassing the opener, "To have a doorman who can see through walls, and know that I have no knife at my throat." Skander spared a glance at the doorkeeper, a glance promising a number of extra duties, before returning his full attention to his Lady's presence.

"Certainly, madam," he assured her, after hearing her problem, "If you would remove the sheathe, while I get my tools?" Fenita complied, as Skander went to another part of the room, to get a box, which he placed on the center worktable. The boys left off their work to gather round, their interest whetted.

"It's very simple," the armsman explained, "First, I punch a hole in the leather with this." He held up a tool, a crosspiece for the hand with a semi-circular blade at the end of a central shaft. "Then we insert one of these–" 'These' were little metal loops, flattened on one side "–with the flat side against her leg. As I said, simple." It was so simple, in fact, that he suddenly handed the tools to the boy across the table and stood back to watch.

It was simple. It took longer for Fenita to figure out how to tie the cord properly, afterwards. The task, unfamiliar to her, occupied enough of her attention that she missed her man's silent nod to two of the young men, but could not fail to miss the sibilant hiss of steel on steel, as they drew their blades from the rack and checked their edges. Noting their preparations, she turned her eye on Skander, brow raised.

"They wanted the Brother, they got you," he stated flatly, "They'll get no more Demlas." As if a mere two blades could do anything against a beast that would not die. From the look in his eye, Skander knew this as well as she, but at least the younger Demlas could feel like they were doing something, so she acquiesced.

She felt better when she reached the Temple Square with her escort in tow, and none of the throng gathered there seemed either amused or even surprised at her companions. Many had gathered by Air, of course, fully prepared to turn any news into gossip with the greatest possible speed. Nor was she surprised to spot a detail of Tolgas and even a few Demlas bravos at the entrance to Earth; no doubt her husband and sire were within, dredging up scraps of lore from the memory of the world. And of course life went on, some ship docked below delivering goods of some sort, loading up on their famed produce and an even greater supply of no-doubt expanded stories.

Her rank sufficed to get her through the crowds, her escort more parade than protection, but rumbling carts recognized neither, and the local equivalents of watha were far stupider than watha. So the path she beat to the Temple of Life's door was not quite as straight as an arrow's flight.

Her vanguard pounded the door rather more forcefully than her mission required or his authority allowed. She made note of it, for Skander would surely want to know. The rearguard, for his part, did a marvelous job of standing there, looking intimidating. When the door opened, she strode forward, her guards falling back to either side as she entered the Temple alone.

They stood rather stiffly, there, out in the open, directly across the square from their elder brethren, who stood so casually, chatting with the Tolgas guards. Neither of her guards knew which was worse, pretending not to notice, or pretending to be as at ease as they.

These minor considerations vanished, as they both simultaneously felt the arrival of…something. Something felt wrong, somewhere, and the guards on the other side had noticed it, too. Everyone slowed, stopped. Hairs raised on the backs of uncounted necks, gooseflesh erupted, bellies tightened, breath quickened.

WHAM! The door behind the two young guards slammed open, and they both shrieked and jumped, missing each other with their swords only because they jumped in different directions. Fortunately, the one on the right was also right-handed, for it kept his left hand free to catch Fenita as she fled the doorway, heedless of direction or safety. The two Demlas guards at the door of Earth watched with pride as their two brothers stood their ground, interposing themselves between the door and the Wife in spite of the chaos now gripping the other side of the square, animals bolting and people running, apparently at random, upsetting carts and spilling goods. The rearguard was suddenly very busy, and merely looking intimidating no longer helped.

As suddenly as blinking an eye, the tumult ceased, panic giving way to confusion as people wondered what had frightened them so. Confusion gave way to relief, to joy, to exhilaration, and a hilarity in its way more unnerving than the fear had been.

Then the door opened again.

A wave rolled out, an invisible wave that carried with it a thousand longings, a hundred desires. The priestess of Life strode forth, and knees buckled all over the square, even up to the steps at the temple of Earth. The guards there would have panicked even as they abased themselves, had they been capable of it, but the swirling of life in them upset their thoughts. Only one, in the door of Earth and safe, watched and tried to understand, the two hastily summoned clan leaders beside him doing the same.

The priestess stood just outside the door, tall and imposing, a complete turnabout from her usual self. She looked upon the square and its writhing occupants, and made a curious gesture with her hand, as if beckoning. In response, the people fell prone, panting and weak, and near-complete silence reigned.

"Fenita!" In the quiet her voice seemed enormous, and tremulous. Her body began to shake, the forces that had overwhelmed the townsfolk coming home to roost. "I am coming. Await me."

Then she collapsed, a marionette with its strings cut.

And somewhere Else, the beast cringed, whining in pain and distress and covering its sensitive nose as best it could, with moldy leaves and vegetation. But even these were only partly able to cut the piercing stink that had exploded around him, the combined effluvia of hundreds of species going into full mating rut simultaneously. It didn't affect him directly; his kind was solitary, and he had never yet seen or smelled a…

Suddenly he spasmed, some especially choice bit of mildew overwhelming his control. His head shook as he sneezed, dislodging the protective debris and forcing him to breathe deeply of the–*hmm!*

FEMALE!

Purpose warred with instinct, and lost.

Chapter 7

Janosec awoke the next morning feeling remarkably refreshed. The previous day's exertions had fatigued him greatly but not strained him unduly; his mind and soul that had been most stressed, and he'd expected to carry that burden with him a while longer. He still remembered the face of the first man he'd ever had to kill, and he supposed–hoped, in a way–that he always would. But yesterday's horror had already settled in him, fallen in a thousand memories, like leaves to the forest floor, trampled and faded and matted into indistinguishability. Even as he awoke he could feel them fading, the images that had seemed so bright: mountains of fire, bizarre creatures by the dozens, large and small, natural and otherwise, places of wonder and of terror. All gone before he could think to try to hold them. Only two remained, anchored by last night's talking, and he didn't care to think about those.

So he opened his eyes instead, sitting up to look about the strangeness of the hut where he had lain. Many of his last waking moments were blurred as well, and he had no memory of coming to this place, or doing any of the things he must have done. He found his uncle, the Savior of Querdishan, Champion of the gods, by following the snoring to where he sat sleeping, propped up against the wall, and felt oddly pleased at the simple human-ness of the sight. The Brother had seemed so much…larger… yesterday.

Now everything seemed so much smaller, and he almost felt a twinge of vertigo as he stood, but it soon passed. Almost everything was almost normal again, almost. Even this house, now merely abandoned. Except the privy wasn't where it should have been, forcing him to consider his options, painfully. Fewer scruples would be really helpful right now, but he had them anyway, so he searched, with as much haste as he could muster. Afterwards, his relief multiplied when he rejoined his uncle. "Ah, Janosec, there you are. You wouldn't happen to have found a privy, by any chance?"

Janosec pointed, and smothered a laugh as Tarkas hobbled off in the indicated direction, before returning to the hut to retrieve the abandoned packs. When he left the little shack, he found his uncle standing in the middle of the street, looking rather perplexed.

"You have a problem?" he inquired, walking closer, with one hand on the ax-head and the other steadying the large bag on his shoulder. The small bag and a number of water bottles had been looped around his torso, their weight, combined with the axe's, balancing the weight of the duffel. Janosec barely noticed the burden.

Tarkas gestured vaguely at the spread of the street. "We must give chase," he stated. Janosec agreed, waiting for something that wasn't obvious. "You have spent more time among the NarLintas than I," Tarkas reminded him.

Janosec knew enough from that time to know himself not up to the task. The outskirts of the village were too extensive and overgrown, the road too hard packed, for useful tracks to be gleaned by only himself. Perhaps the entire clan NarLintas might have accomplished something, had they been there. Dismayed, he dropped his head, shamed that he had failed his uncle in so important a task.

Tarkas took it philosophically, already aware that the task was too great, but it was courteous to ask. "I thought as much." The casual tone lifted the younger man's head, gratified. It was not his failure to be overmatched; after all, Tarkas himself must have been, he realized, else why ask the question.

But Tarkas was not looking at him, or at anything especially interesting, as far as Janosec could tell. He just stared into the distance, at a bush. "What are you looking at?"

Startled, Tarkas just looked at him. "Nothing," he replied dismissively. His mind had just been wandering, that's all. Reminded of his purpose, he strode off intently, determined to wreak a miracle out of his bare hands and leaves, if necessary. Of that, Janosec had no doubt. He waited, eager to see what it would be.

As Tarkas walked, his eyes searched, his mind searched, for some divinely inspired idea to arrive between his ears. Being the

Gods' Champion did not bestow great tracking prowess, nor had he ever needed it. He had somehow never needed to look very far for his employments, and deliberate pursuit was a rarity. Only in the Elsewhere did it differ, and even there they were usually trying to– *Hmm.* A *that*way trail? He paused, considering.

Janosec saw his uncle stop, obviously deep in thought, but once again looking, now over his own shoulder, at the bush he had stared at before. Had his uncle heard something? Certainly *he* had not. "What is it?"

Once again, Tarkas looked surprised, and just a little annoyed. "What is what?"

The young man gestured at the outskirts of the village with his free hand. "What did you hear?"

Tarkas practically ran back to his nephew, reprieved by the Gods themselves, yes! "You heard something? What?"

Janosec retreated, confused. "I heard nothing," he said, "What did *you* hear?"

Tarkas stopped, dismayed. Fex, no easy solution after all. He turned away, paused, then turned back. "Why do you think *I* heard anything?"

Again Janosec pointed. "You keep looking that way."

Tarkas followed his finger, noticing for the first time the spot he had stared at so often. "I do?" he said, but the rising tone was not of the questioning sort, and Janosec did not try to answer. He stared at the bush, even went over to it, peering around and through it, finding nothing. So he backed up, returning to the place in which he had stood before, but the bush appeared no more remarkable from this vantage. *Drat*, he cursed silently. He pondered the problem, once more staring, unseeing.

"Uncle!"

This time Tarkas thought to keep his head still as his eyes and attention focused. *Hmm.* "Once is chance," he said, softly.

Janosec had sharp ears, but not sharp enough. "What?" he asked, moving closer.

Tarkas became aware of himself as he stood thoughtfully, one arm braced against the other across his chest, his hand up under his chin in a pensive pose. He dropped his arms into a less defensive posture. "A saying I heard once. 'Once is chance, twice is coincidence–'" he frowned at the offending bush "–three times is conspiracy."

Janosec considered, his gaze flicking back and forth between the one and the other. "What draws at you?"

"I do not know," replied Tarkas more briskly, his eyes scanning the two of them, and their appurtenances, assuring himself of their completeness. "Let's go find out," he stated decisively, punctuated by a growling in his own Heroic belly. "After breakfast."

Breakfast was a bit of a compromise. They ate on the road, Tarkas hefting the enormous duffel of preserved and fresh foods, the two snacking as they walked. Coincidentally (or perhaps not), one of the roads out of the ruined village seemed to lead very much in the direction they wished to go, wide enough that they could walk nearly abreast with their shoulders touching no leaves. Neither of them turned for a last, nostalgic look. So neither of them noticed the soft stealthy feet treading out of the shadows, leaving tracks made by no man in the ashes blowing everywhere.

The mood got progressively lighter as they got farther away from the village of death. The duffel followed suit, the young, big, and still growing man replenishing his body and refreshing his spirits with food that would clearly not go to waste today. Tarkas also consumed at a steady pace, his ordinary size disguising his superhuman vitality, as hard to restore as it was to expend.

Janosec, taller, unburdened by things and burdened by experiences, took a quick lead, eager to get to some other place. He was in front, he was forward, he was on point. He was the scout, even his uncle admitted that, and scouts watched, searching for signs and traces. Broken twigs, bits of fur, tracks–he struggled to recall the NarLintas lore, but so little of it applied to trails in the forest. The NarSeptas teachings should be of more use, but they were for dealing with known enemies and their traces. He had to reconcile the two bodies of lore, a welcome exercise and diversion from the other things he could have thought about.

Tarkas followed, fast enough to keep his advance guard in sight but no more, secure in the knowledge that he carried the food. Janosec returned often, ostensibly to retrieve yet another fruit or piece of not-quite-stale bread. But the frequency and the timing put Tarkas in mind of his former home and some of his former fellows, who had kept a pair of beasts of a type he could not name (a side-effect of having passed through Mendilorn to a Realm where those words did not apply), the younger of which had the habit of racing about and then racing back to touch noses with its dam before racing off again.

After the umpteenth such return, Tarkas called a halt as they passed near a fallen tree, to rest their feet. Sitting on the bole, he pulled off his vest and undervest as Janosec rather perfunctorily consumed another fruit. After swallowing in mid-fruit, he asked, "Do you see so much battle?"

Tarkas looked up, then down at the undervest he'd just folded, trying to make the connection. "Oh," he said, finally making it, "No. I am just cold." A native of a much warmer Realm, he used the quilted garment, normally used to cushion blows in combat, as insulation against a Realm that had grown less bearably chill as he had grown older. "In fact," he continued, answering his nephew's real question, "My life is much like this, walking a lot until something decides to attack me." He paused, as if expecting something to take his words as an invitation, but nothing occurred to disturb the moment.

Janosec finished his fruit, Tarkas waiting until he did so. "You said last night that those children could not return. Why could they not?"

Tarkas paused, and then busied himself putting his folded underclothing in the duffel, considering the import of the question and how he might answer. "We who serve the gods are bound by certain rules," he finally said, reminding the youth of past events, "Those children were not bound by those rules, so they had to be placed where that freedom would cause no harm."

"Then why do I remain with you?"

The question crystallized the dilemma in Tarkas' own mind, and an answer popped in from thin ether. "Because it is not my way to put my companions in danger of their lives."

Janosec considered this, absently rocking back and forth. "The journey would be so dangerous, then?"

A trip of unknown length, at a full run, every step of the way beset by monsters of every conceivable kind. "Oh no," replied Tarkas innocently, "But you can imagine your mother's reaction. Give me some of those bottles."

Janosec could indeed. Abandoning his uncle, and forcing the Gods' Champion to divert from the Gods' purpose to assist him in doing so, with no guarantee that the Gods' Champion could return to take up the threads of this mission afterward. She'd put him on privy duty for a month, while she thought up a suitable punishment. "I, uh, I suppose I could put my duty to my clan to one side," he said, divesting himself of some of his burden.

Tarkas kept his expression deadpan. "Oh, would you?" he asked wistfully, taking the jugs. "I thank you, on behalf of the gods." He stood, swinging the depleted duffel on to his shoulder with deceptive ease. "And I will be sure to inform them as well, that you are in my service, so perhaps you will be returned, with life and memory intact."

"You are most gracious, my lord," Janosec replied, the excessive formality making his words a jest.

Tarkas extended a hand to assist his nephew to his feet. "Don't thank me yet."

As Janosec took a step forward, Tarkas reached up to adjust the strap around his shoulder, so it wouldn't interfere with his sword. Something large and heavy struck him in the back, shoving him forward and full-length onto the ground. "Not!" a voice reverberated in his ears, and a weight was on his back, fumbling with his scabbard.

But this time it pulled at a scabbard made by a god, which would not break, and the grunt wasted precious seconds pulling futilely. Tarkas, overburdened by the weight of both duffel and creature, made little progress in his attempts to stand, but Janosec suffered from no such hindrance. His headlong rush took the thing by surprise, removing it completely from his uncle's back and several paces down the trail. Tarkas raised himself to one knee and watched as his nephew engaged the grunt hand to…paw.

He did well, all things considered. His youthful strength was phenomenal, his courage undeniable. But the grunt was built for hand-to-paw combat, and had all the advantages of a creature from Elsewhere. Janosec won free with a simple ploy: striking the creature sharply in the nose, in his experience the most sensitive part of an animal's body. Sure enough, the thing practically threw him away, patting delicately at its snout while its soon-to-be-devoured enemy pulled out his knife.

Tarkas watched these developments with a certain unease. The grunt had a knife of its own. But he also knew that grunts wore knives the way they wore clothes, grudgingly, at the whim of their maker and master, and in all likelihood had already forgotten it, in favor of its own natural rippers and renders. Even so, Janosec was overmatched and probably didn't know it, and the teachings in the lore about learning an enemy may not work with a foe so bestial and random as this. The trick would be saving his life without killing his pride. Hmm, yes. His divinely perfect memory had numerous images in it, Janosec's tutors in the arts of combat. Deliberately, he mimicked their stance.

Janosec spared his uncle only a glance as he moved, but Tarkas was not going to embarrass him with a rescue. He was merely shifting around–Hey!

The creature roared and charged, and Janosec dropped and rolled, keeping his distance from a stronger enemy as his instructors had taught him, watching without wasted movement in what had to be a contest of endurance, not strength. *The strong are often unsubtle*, he recalled. And this beast even more so, he hoped.

The beast turned and attacked again, and again Janosec dodged, his knife flicking in and scoring a deep wound along the creatures ribs and side. *Make the first cut count.* Yes, the beast kept its distance now, circling cautiously, whining slightly through its bruised nose. The young man circled also, puzzled. Surely the creature should attack even more fiercely, before it lost the advantage of strength.

A branch cracked.

Pack! Janosec had no time for more thought than that, flinching automatically around to face the rest of his imagined opponents. But there were none there, and the grunt took advantage of his lapse to lash out and strike the knife from his hand. The wound in its side slowed it enough that Janosec escaped with no more than scratches. Except for his hip, something was–his fumbling hand fell on the head of his ax, tied with a vine to the swordbelt around his waist.

The vine was not a problem.

The ax was. Querdishan had no tradition of warfare with axes, and what the man had learned of the beast gave him no hope of using such a slow and clumsy weapon against it. Nonetheless he swung it, hoping the mere appearance of a threat would keep his enemy at bay.

It didn't. The axhead dragged his arm along with it and the creature dashed in, forcing Janosec to turn away with a set a parallel slashes on his own ribs. He stood, panting, one hand touching the burning lines on his chest as his thoughts whirled frantically. Speed! He needed speed! The beast lunged, sure of his victim's helplessness. Janosec moved, swinging the ax up in a pitifully slow arc.

A stone flew out of the trees, smacking with some force against the beast's head, distracting it at a crucial second. Janosec watched as it charged headlong past him, and pivoted, using the axe's momentum to bring the head down faster and with power behind the blow. Yes! That was it!

Crunch!

The creature toppled like an honest man would have, the scattered blood and brains no viler. It was disappointing, in a way. Janosec expected black blood and a hideous stench, anything but a normal death. Fiends should die…fiendishly.

He recognized the rhythmic pounding from behind him as applause. "Thank you," he said, formally, stiffly. The axhead slipped closer to the ground as his fingers loosened.

Tarkas stopped slapping his hands together. "For what?"

Janosec nudged the stone, fallen from the beast's temple into the dirt of the path. "Your thrown rock was timely."

Tarkas walked over slowly, crouching to pick up the stone as Janosec suddenly whipped his head around. Hadn't the stone come from–? "You did not," he realized.

"No, I did not." The two men turned together to face the hole in the vegetation from which the stone had emerged. "Friend or foe?" Tarkas called out in the traditional challenge.

"Neither," replied a voice from further up the path. Looking over, they found themselves staring at a young woman with a knife–Janosec's knife–in one hand and a sling whirling in the other. Neither were aimed just yet, but both men assumed that that could change faster than they could reach her. "The NarZirtas greet you, in Mirani."

The two men looked at each other, then at her. "Where is Mirani?" asked Janosec.

The woman seemed perplexed by the question, but finally replied, "*I* am Mirani."

"Ah," said Janosec, embarrassed. He stumbled a bit, trying to rephrase the usual greeting. "I am Jano–the, um, the NarDemlas greet you, in Janosec."

Tarkas was a bit quicker. "The NarDemlas greet you, in Tarkas." He tossed the rock to her feet.

The woman stood quite still for a few beats. "Demlas, eh?" She tossed the little silver knife at the ground before them. "Take your blade, Demlas. The NarZirtas use no blades." Janosec stooped to pick up the knife, flipping it underhand to Tarkas. The Hero, however, refused the offer, batting the blade back in its arc to the Second, where it ceased its gyrations, inserted into its usual place in his belt. The stone, for its part, ceased its whirling, tumbling into her hand and into her pouch, clacking softly on what were no doubt other stones.

Tucking the sling into her belt, she turned her attention to the grisly piece of debris they would be leaving behind them. "That one's new. Any more?"

Tarkas sighed, even though the delay of answering the question offered a welcome excuse to delay his next, noisome task. It never occurred to him to try to lie outright, but shading the truth properly was second nature at this point. "Some," he breathed out gustily, reaching down to hook the corpse by its belt, "They are scattered, though." 'Probably no more for us to worry about' being the implication, emphasis on 'probably'.

She watched his practiced motions, gripping it here and there on the parts that were least sticky, as he prepared to drag the body away. "You scattered them."

"*Hmmm*!" was all Tarkas replied, as he hefted the dead weight, trying to keep the icky parts from dripping on or near him. Janosec and Mirani watched as he trudged off into the woods, presumably to dispose of his burden. Janosec knew better than to ask, Mirani took her lead from him, only a little dubious.

"What will he do with it?" she asked, to fill the silence after the crashing through the underbrush and leaves had faded.

"I do not wish to know, and my wish is granted," he replied, in total honesty. He had spent less than a day in his uncle's world, and already he yearned for the quiet simplicity of open warfare. "Do you get many creatures like that here?"

She shrugged. "Often enough. We are close to the Eye of the World. The strange is commonplace."

Her words resonated with such an air of pride that Janosec refrained from asking what the Eye of the World might be. But it sounded far from the City on the Eastern Sea, long considered the very edge of the world, and he shivered in sudden aloneness. Not even Tarkas was here, just this woman, neither friend nor foe. His rapidly weakening knees carried him back over to the bole with every appearance of casual ease, as he considered that little nugget. "You said 'neither.' A flung stone hardly bespeaks neutrality."

She shifted around to face him. "A duty, only."

He stared up at her, a total stranger. "What duty?"

"Honor to those who give honor."

Now that made Janosec even more confused, as he had never done this lady a service in his life. Belatedly, he offered her an item from the half-filled duffel.

But–"I'll not eat tainted food."

Janosec stared at the item in his hand, a fruit, with sudden suspicion, but it looked no different from any of the others he had eaten that morning. "Do you mean poisoned?"

"She means tainted by association, nephew," came Tarkas' voice from the forest behind him. Then the man himself vaulted the bole to stand in the path once again, facing the lady. "Are you from the village, then?" he inquired, not even breathing hard.

She looked down, then up again. "No," she claimed, "But I had dealings with them, good, honorable people who deserve better than whatever befell them."

Tarkas looked at her oddly. "Do you know what befell them?"

"Don't you?" she asked in return, "I saw the two of you strolling about this morn, with not another soul in sight."

Janosec folded his arms, stung by the thought that anyone might suspect him of that–"How do you know we were not the villains, then?"

Now *she* was embarrassed. "Ug oogum niffy," she said to the ground at her feet.

"What did you say?" choked out Tarkas, laughter in his voice.

"You used the PRIVY!" she shouted, glaring at both men equally.

She turned her back on them and commenced walking. Janosec stood and hefted his gruesome ax, discovering to his surprise that the vine no longer circled his waist. Tarkas found it, and the attached medallion, lying in the dirt, along with the dropped water jugs. He didn't bother to untangle the mess, just tore the medallion free and left the foliage behind. Janosec re-rigged the loop his sword had been in, fitting it to hold the ax, while the medallion found itself where the whetstone should have gone.

The sun was warm, the day pleasant, the temptation to amble and admire the scenery great, once the axe was properly secured. But they had a purpose, and the view of her backside was nothing compared to the possibility of an alliance with a woman of such skill and apparent determination, not to mention any knowledge at all of the local environs. After Tarkas passed on his thoughts concerning combat with axes they made some slight effort to draw even with her.

"That creature, what is it called?" she asked while they were still somewhat behind.

"You mean its name?" replied Janosec. He looked over to his uncle in confusion. "Why would a monster like that need a name?"

Tarkas shook his head negatively. "She means its kind,

nephew," he clarified, and projected his next comment forward, "It was called a grunt."

She snorted. "Appropriate."

Tarkas continued, for Janosec's benefit now, "Nor was it a monster. Monstrous, perhaps, but all of the true monsters I've had to deal with had names."

She snorted, dismissing the point. "Monster or monstrosity, I wager the distinction never stayed your sword."

"You have already lost," the Hero said quietly, but she heard it nonetheless, and stopped, turning on her heel to face him.

"You were unable to kill the grunt, so you allowed your nephew to do it for you?" she asked, shocked, "I thought you were a man of honor."

Janosec would not allow this slur on his uncle's reputation to go unchallenged. "Of course he is," the younger man declared, not bothering to speak to her face. "Perhaps if you had wit, you could understand his actions, and so refrain from dishonoring yourself with slanders. Failing that, silence is the first rule of wisdom, and will no doubt suffice."

Tarkas watched her face flame, watched impressed as she held it impassive. She turned slightly to face her accuser, disguising the motion by running a hand through her hair, and he wondered which horn of the dilemma she would seize. The mere fact that they outnumbered her would not necessarily stop her, but he did not think his nephew's words quite insulting enough for that. Nor were they. "Very well then, most honorable Demlas," she began, either surrendering or sneering, "Perhaps you would be good enough to explain."

She stared at him, but Janosec had never claimed to have wit. "Uncle?"

Tarkas decided to start walking, mindful that they were, after all, in hot pursuit, while trying to think of an explanation he could offer. As they fell in behind him–slightly–he thought of it, an episode not from his life, but his nephew's. "Janosec, tell her about Lintas Nurler's dak."

She frowned at him, as Janosec frowned himself, unable to see the relevance of that –"Yapping. Yapping white ball of fur," his first words, a sign of the trauma it had inflicted, "There were some who felt it a greater trial than the Desolation of the generation before. It was never quiet unless Nurler was around."

To judge from her expression, she was familiar with daks.

"Why was it not killed?" prompted Tarkas.

Now Janosec was confused. "For that? You don't kill something just because it's annoying, the city would be emptied in no time."

That got a smothered laugh from both of the others. Mirani had a sense of the purpose of this exposition. "It *was* killed, though, wasn't it?"

"Yes," replied Janosec thoughtfully, remembering the event and relating it to the recent past, "Eventually it attacked a child, a Septas child, about the only person around smaller than it. Not that the boy wasn't a pest in his own right–"

"Nurler sacrificed it himself," Tarkas broke in.

"Naturally," she accepted, "Because it had moved from an annoyance to an actual threat, as had the grunt just now. An annoyance to you, but a threat to him. Us."

"*Perhaps* a threat to you," Tarkas amended, apologetically. "I had to see, but I would have stepped in if necessary. Fortunately–"

"It wasn't," finished the man who had actually slain the beast.

"Would you have slain it?" She made a guess. "This time?"

Tarkas smiled, pleased with her cleverness, but all she could see from behind was the shrug of his shoulders. "As opposed to the other six? Probably."

Silent for a time, she pondered the kind of strength–or patience, a product of strength–that allowed him to let the thing live, even to continue attacking him, however fruitlessly. But there are some questions one should not ask, so–"And the boy? How did he fare?"

"He was healed," replied Tarkas, in an *of course* sort of voice, but not one that invited further comments.

Janosec supplied them anyway. "Miraculously. The Gods themselves aided him." His hand orbited quickly, taking in the whole of the woods and the sky and the earth. Mirani watched with less than total credulity, her eyes almost immediately going to the olde man's back.

Tarkas sighed. "*I* healed him, nephew."

Now, Janosec shrugged. "It is the same thing."

Tarkas paused, turning slightly to stare at his nephew. "Yo knew?" he asked, one eyebrow up.

Janosec caught up and kept on, forcing Tarkas to continue Mirani, looking about them, walked around to the pair's far side, no that either of them noticed. "Father knew, and Grandfather. I hear them speaking of it one night, debating whether to keep silent."

"Obviously they did," concluded Tarkas. "And Fenita?"

Janosec smirked. "I believe Mother told them."

Tarkas smiled nostalgically. He could readily believe that.

"If I may interrupt?" asked Mirani, shattering his mood. Bot men afforded her some slight measure of their attention, and Tarka made a slight growling in his throat, apparently an invitation t continue. "If you are so skilled a healer, Demlas, why are thes slashes still untreated?"

Tarkas looked over, startled, following her gaze to the long angry lines drawn serially along his nephew's ribs, old enough to hav crusted over but too recent to be showing signs of infection. Grunt being what they were, he had no doubt some would soon appear if h did nothing. "Nephew?"

Janosec looked down at himself as his hand came up with the a in it, flexing and using the muscles on that side, as if merely bearin such wounds was insufficient reason to seek treatment. To no one' surprise, he grunted at about the halfway point, and lowered th weapon, passing the small duffel to Mirani as he shifted the weapo to that hand.

Tarkas dropped his own duffel to the dirt of the path, freeing u his hands as he raised the tips of two fingers and placed them on th ends of one tear. Singing so softly it sounded like humming, h brought his fingers together along the line of the wound, rejoining th flesh seamlessly.

Janosec looked mildly disappointed. "No scar?"

Mirani rolled her eyes, no words necessary.

Tarkas, quite focused on his Songcraft, appeared not to have heard, but the remaining slashes left little pink lines behind, proof of Janosec's prowess. "Is that better?"

The patient glared at his healer. "I earned these," he protested, stung by some imagined criticism, "They mean something."

"Indeed they do, woodcutter," retorted Mirani, not at all impressed, "They mean you think with your testicles." She strode off in a huff.

Janosec was all set to follow, but Tarkas' hand on his chest brought him up short. "She does not need to know, nephew," he cautioned him, his voice soft, "Either she would not believe you or she would, which could in some ways be worse, as we are without guards save each other."

"But Uncle–"

"The political and dynastic considerations are irrelevant, anyway," Tarkas continued, "Your instincts were right and you did the honorable thing. Don't make it dishonorable just to impress a girl." He paused, a slight smile on his face. "You would just prove her right."

Tarkas hefted his pack and followed, with Janosec in the rear, scrutinizing his scars and moving the ax experimentally. Mirani, despite her strong start, had not gotten very far ahead in fact, and it took them little time to catch up. "You are going to tell me," she predicted as they approached, "That I was overly harsh. That there are overriding considerations about which I know nothing." Her singsong delivery left no doubt of her opinion of such a patronizing attitude.

Tarkas grinned. "Actually, you were right. He *was* thinking with his testicles." The choking next to him was perhaps louder than the offended "Hey!" from behind, but it was a near thing. "He *is* a man, after all, and men have testicles, just as women have wombs. Most men *do* think with them and very little else, and will judge those scars accordingly." He shrugged eloquently. "It is not as if they were the *only* things he thought with."

She looked away, considering this as she paced rhythmically forward. The Singer in Tarkas found her normal beat quite acceptable, not slow like some people's are. He naturally thought of several Songs with a walking beat, and as naturally refrained from actually Singing any of them, unsure of what side effects they might have. Janosec wanted to speak in his own defense, the gap seemed a natural place to do it, but it didn't feel like a good time, so he refrained, trusting to his uncle's words instead. Funny, though, how Tarkas wasn't looking down the path anymore, but off to one side. Did that mean–?

Suddenly Mirani stopped dead in her tracks, an arm raising. "Oh, the Gods–" she began, but her own fingers entering her mouth cut off the rest of the oath.

The two men both looked at her, but the sound of pain-filled squealing drew their eyes away, and all three were soon looking at the same thing: a beast, scrabbling frantically and feebly at the dirt of the path, its body held to the ground by a cruelly sharpened and barbed stake. The stake wasn't straight up; rather, it impaled the ground at an angle, the far end pointing, coincidentally enough, into the mouth of a dark, overgrown path.

Which, coincidentally enough, had been the way Tarkas' eyes had been looking, mere moments ago.

The two men went to the beast, their own capacities for horror still somewhat overwhelmed from the previous day's experiences. Mirani had been spared that, and so approached the grisly…sacrifice…more slowly. "It was impaled first," she heard Tarkas say, repulsed and amazed by his ability to speak at all. "Too hard to do it at an angle and force it through the ribs like this. It will die soon."

"Not soon enough," said Janosec, pulling out the knife. Mirani silently applauded, falling to her knees by his side, her hands going to hold the poor beast still, so the man could at least end its suffering cleanly. Tarkas stood, carefully stepping over them all, no doubt to pull the stake once the beast could no longer feel the pain, and they could rid the world of the obscenity. She again marveled, happily this time, at being with such men who would do the right thing so easily and quickly.

With only the slightest hesitation, Janosec plunged his blade into the beast's neck, pulling it forward, allowing the dark blood to gush out, and the life with it. The poor creature quivered and died in mere moments, and they drew back, giving Tarkas room to pull the stake from the ground without spraying them all with gore.

Nothing happened. They looked up.

Tarkas, the top of the stake, and the dark path into which he had stepped, had all vanished.

Lady Elemental of Life Irolla tel Kwinarish was not happy.

A creature that would not die when killed! After her man, who had saved similar creatures mere days before. Who was missing!

Doors couldn't slam hard enough.

Normally they didn't slam at all, since they opened as she approached and closed after she was out of arm's reach. But the thought was there. In fact, the doors themselves were moved by Earth elementals, beyond her direct control, working in tandem with those of Life.

Then she thought of her poor priestess–! Wheeling, she shouted, "SLAM!" at the doors just behind her.

They flew into their jambs so hard the inner parts kept going, fragments flying in all directions as the edges, unsupported, fell in a line, marking where the panels should have been. It didn't help. In the absence of her lover, only the constant flow of her elementals through her kept the grief and rage from overwhelming her completely, each one taking little bits away, spreading them far and wide. The world would feel her mourning.

The world would feel a lot more than that.

Tarkas.

Her mind echoed with the name. Her pulse beat with it. He had the knowledge, he was the focus. They had to find Tarkas.

Unfortunately, they couldn't. He wasn't from Querdishan, his life wasn't from here, his water and other elements weren't native to this realm. To the elementals he was mostly invisible, and they had no other direct means available. They did have another method, which they had used only once before–during the disgraceful Affair of the Seven Virgins–but that had depended on them having Janosec available.

Fex.

Tarkas had so many strange curses lately.

Very well, then they needed a link to Janosec. And fortunately she had bid Fenita wait upon her. Excellent! Now she needed the cooperation of the others.

"Kolo!" she spoke aloud, to no one, "We need to borrow someone." No one replied, as she expected. Kolo would hear (she heard everything), and Kolo would do. Exceptionally shy, she kept herself carefully hidden behind her winds, elementals, and priestesses, and masked to boot. She had only once ever revealed any part of her inner self to another, after Tarkas had rescued her from captivity many years ago, and her crush on him had only grown with time. She would scour the Realm bare if allowed, so Irolla gladly provided a useful alternative.

Using her other media, a bowl of water and a block of crystal, she called upon the other two lords, before setting out to the place where the borrowing would take place, if it took place at all: the center of the Lords' Domain, a flat, roundish mesa in the middle of nowhere, the spot where all four domains came together. Technically speaking, since Life was an immaterial element, she should have started walking, but there were in fact many beasts of air and ground more than willing to provide her with transport. Her current steed was a murf, large enough to carry her but too large to fly, without the special assistance of some air elementals loaned her by Kolo to provide continual updrafts.

She met the other Lady on the way as she flew, so they arrived together, while Earth emerged from a bubble in the rock and Water literally washed up only a few beats later. Irolla had called them together, but Earth looked to Air, as senior, to open the proceedings. She did, but only to slough off her unwanted responsibility on Irolla, the actual instigator, who was more than happy to take the lead.

"The world is other than it was," she said formally, to the bafflement of the other lords. All the ritual statement meant–most of the time–was that some thing or some one had entered from outside, as Tarkas did. It happened often enough, surely a more standard notification would have sufficed. Then she clarified, "Unsanctioned."

Water started more noticeably than Earth, as one might expect. "I thought that such a thing was impossible. That's what we were told."

Earth looked vacant for a moment, as Kolo looked at all three in confusion, her hands fluttering in agitation. "You are incorrect," said the former farmer, his recollection quite accurate, "We were not told that it was impossible, but that it was not possible."

Irolla started to shout, "What diff–I'm sorry, Kolo." The Lady of Air took back control of the meeting, her hands moving rapidly through the signs by which she expressed herself, the others following easily as she expressed her ignorance.

Earth replied, as expected. "My apologies. When we three were installed, the powers that be informed us of our responsibilities together, and we forget that we may use some terms that have meaning only to ourselves. We were told the only way in should be from the center, the only way out of the center should be by going into and through the center, which requires the sanction of its guardian. Without that, it should not be possible to pass." But his voice trailed off uncertainly at the end.

"If one takes that route," concluded Irolla thoughtfully. "Might there be others?"

"The person to ask is your paramour, not one of us," suggested Water.

Exactly the track that Irolla wanted the discussion to take. "That will be hard to do, as Tarkas is still missing," she replied worriedly. "We can trace him, as you recall we did once before."

Two male heads nodded, understanding her request for a borrowing now, they thought. But Kolo's hands moved again.

"Yes, that's true," replied Irolla, "But since Janosec is with Tarkas, a link to the youth will serve as well as a link to the man. Fenita awaits."

Fenita waited, too nervous to be bored and too bored to be nervous, held in an unpleasant suspension. The hardbacked chair in which she sat had few comforts beyond the fact that someone had thought to fetch it for her, and the hands of her husband, Jerim, gently pressing on her shoulders as he stood behind her. Around them, a discreet distance away, the few NarDemlas still able to stand, around them a ring of NarTolgas, and around them–

No one. The square was strangely empty considering that a goddess had announced her imminent appearance. But as Fenita squirmed in her chair she realized that it was not so strange after all. Had she not been specifically named, she would have dragged Jerim home herself and...*Don't think about that*, she commanded herself silently, forcing her libido back into its place with cold, hard words.

Instead she looked at the place where the body of the fallen priestess had been. For a moment she had hoped for the lady's recovery, but those hopes died as her elements were recovered. Now the temple sat empty, for no one would dare go in there without her, and she sat staring at the closed door, trying to recall whatever she might have known about the lady who once dwelt within. Not much, for she and Jerim had had all of their children without once needing her good offices, nor was there much room for conversation at the rituals. The times she had seen her these last few days were the most she could recall ever speaking to her.

She felt vaguely guilty, presumptuous, to even be mourning her, but she knew of no one else who would.

Suddenly, unaccountably, she trembled, little quivers starting from somewhere within and swiftly moving into the muscles of her arms and legs, and from there into her husband's fingers. "My wife?" he asked, crouching low to speak softly.

Her fingers reached up, clutched his as tightly as decorum permitted. "I don't know, I don't know," she whispered.

Within moments, though, it ended, the last vestiges of foreign lust and imported sorrow yielding easily as her mind reclaimed its territory. Free at last, her body slumped in relief, and now she was grateful for the rigidity of the chair as it kept her from flopping about gracelessly. "Oh my," she breathed, her hand going to her mouth, "I feel–" she belched delicately, under cover "–unwell."

Her husband's hand went to her cheek, caressing her gently, lovingly, and she leaned into the warmth of it. "Neither clammy nor hot," he judged, shattering her mood, "Merely symptoms, I would say. There is lore–"

She whacked at him. "You beast," she yelled at him, laughing, and then reclaimed the assaulted hand, kissing his fingers. Around them, their clansmen shifted more easily, standing taller next to their NarTolgas friends.

Moments later, messengers arrived, the other lords as surprised by the effects of the visitation as any, struggling to determine their causes ahead of their clans. Around them, the city began to stir, the tiny noises of new life ringing loud in their ears.

FENITA.

The tiny noises blanked out instantly, the voice in her head pushing out mere sound. Deep, yet strangely feminine, it did not roll, it did not thunder, nor did it echo; it simply *was*, and other sounds were not. The summoned woman leaped to her feet, knocking the chair over and nearly her husband as well, but she didn't see. Her eyes were aimed upward, at the temple and beyond. The steps were empty, the doorway closed.

The Goddess of Life stood on the roof of her temple. As did Air. And Earth, and Water.

Cloth red as blood draped the flagrantly womanly figure of the goddess. Was it cloth? Looked like cloth, had to be, although it flowed so liquidly and dripped like blood over the eaves and down the columns. Was it blood? Looked like blood, had to be.

Jerim first righted the chair, having heard no voice, only then hearing the groaning sound emanating from the temple of Earth behind him. Only then did he notice the figure upon it, and the others, gazing down upon his wife with expressions so serenely beautiful as to be completely uninterpretable. In addition to Life's red, Air wore white, practically a cloud upon her own roof. Water, in blue, seemed to flow up from his temple as Life seemed to be flowing down, and Earth, solid, massive Earth, was garbed in yellow, the primary color closest to brown. Kestrel would be sure to ask.

"As you command, my Lady," said Fenita, the only half of the conversation he would to be allowed to hear, apparently.

"You will take me to my son?" No, she can't be making

conditions. Her question was too breathless, imploring. He saw no obvious change in the Lady's form, yet somehow the clan leader sensed amusement, not sternness, or offense. During the pause that followed Jerim wondered what they said, only to his wife.

"Yes, yes I will," Fenita shouted into the air, apparently an answer to some question from the Lady of Life.

Jerim closed his eyes, knowing what was to come through some fatalistic foreknowledge, not any lore. Sure enough, the blinding flash elicited shouts of pain and surprise from all but him. Equally surely, Fenita was gone when he opened his eyes.

In a different somewhere Else, a beast fled down one forest path after another, blood streaming from innumerable gashes and scratches. All females of its kind attack the males immediately after mating, not so much to kill them as to drive them very far away in order to prevent inbreeding, but this one's recent mate was taking the practice to unheard of extremes.

For all its strength and ferocity, the beast was near exhaustion as it–he–plodded down one track after another, leaving a trail of blood spots behind him to reveal his every move. All males of its kind would have fled, as surely as all females would pursue, for a time at least. Few of those females would pursue this far, fewer of those males would have the strength to continue fleeing, and would have been slaughtered long since. So he was probably the first to ever feel anything remotely akin to fear, that would even begin to feel the need for any kind of…safety. A guardian. A protector.

Just as well, really. His kind only ever knew one protector, one nurturing presence in all their long lives. And mothers are female.

This beast, however, *this* beast had lost his mother at a very young age. This beast had been protected by another, not female, not even its own species. In its stupor, its gaze focused on its own feet, its mind focused on its memory of its protector…what is that smell?

A path, off to one side! The very air was ripe, laden with the smell of blood and the aroma of slaughter and decay. Furiously he tried to stop his feet, his reflexes too slow at even this weary speed, and he tumbled, his back and legs twisting as he kept his nose focused on his bestial paradise, heedless of the scruff and mess he left behind him. Only the deep claw marks in the ground remained to point out his way as he gallumphed without thought or hesitation up the trail, off that way somewhere.

Behind him, an enraged female came charging up, pursuing at a pace not much greater than a man's slow walk but still greater than that of her intended victim. Here was the blood, and she paused over a few remaining odors. There were the claw marks, and the way he had–!

She sprang through the bushes with renewed vigor, knocking herself quite senseless against the bole of a large tree directly in the way.

Her erstwhile victim, on the other hand, picked up speed, the scents of combat stimulating him, driving away the chilling effects of fear from his usually powerful and ready muscles. He roared with the joy of it, the thrill, and was nearly overwhelmed by the response, a confusing gust of fresh input, strangely devoid of the fear to which he was accustomed. So much challenge, nothing pulled him to one side or the other... newness struck him, something he had never slaughtered before, and off he went, into the undergrowth that lined the trail.

Progress was slow after that.

It would have been slower had not so many of the losers tasted quite foul. And eventually his reputation preceded him, the various bloods and ichors contributing to a mélange that heralded the approach of death on four feet. He shook his muzzle, spraying droplets of foul-tasting gore far and wide, shocking a number of flying killers into the–leap! *Snap! Crunch!* A final swallow without losing a stride or slowing his pace. Victims became fewer as they started to run earlier.

But alas–! All good things must come to an end: A stone too large to leap atop forced a turn in the path and in his progress. On the other side he found the nasal equivalent of a darkened room after bright sunshine, cold but dry, the poor beast temporarily blinded by the lack of sensory input. Nasal input at least; his ears were useful, somewhat, but his eyes were far superior to those of most of his kind, almost as useful in dim light as his nose. And the light was dim, the air warmer than he had thought and clammier than it had seemed at first.

But he could still detect no challenge, none of the scents of blood and power that made a beast's life worth living.

His ears could detect things, rustles in the brush, the crackling of very small branches. His eyes could see, even in the dark, the movement of leaves as something hidden disturbed a bush or leapt to a branch.

But no challenge.

He stood, confused and indecisive as only a very intelligent beast could be by the lack of spoor. A lesser beast would have taken the absence of signs of striving as a sign of peace, and safety, and proceeded on its way to live. But to this beast such complete peace was as dangerous as wood smoke, and less traceable. Into his furry mind came a memory, an unpleasant memory of a dream. A creature that tasted foul and didn't die when killed.

The world must fear him. Or challenge him. Anything else was abomination.

He roared his own challenge into the vacuum, to be swallowed and digested. Nothing took flight, nothing took wing. Something slithered, but towards him, and he didn't notice it until it looped around his forepaw. He reacted instantly, pulling and biting, but the severed end of the tentacle merely whipped back, out of sight, and made no further attempt.

The beast prowled forward, mainly because it faced that way. The track made by the whipping end of the tentacle had disturbed some leaves, but the smell was only decay. The thing had left no trace of itself in the–something struck him in the back! It clung to him, and now he had pain in his ear! He rolled, his head spinning faster and paws reaching. He grabbed and pulled, the tearing in his ear a mere trifle as he tore his diminutive attacker into little scaly bits. The blood didn't appeal to him, so he urinated on the remains and loped off.

Progress was slow after that.

Many attacks were made. Many attacks were defeated, the

attackers slain and slaughtered with increasing fury. Other attackers watched, unmoving and unmoved, from underneath rocks and behind leaves, as he dispatched their lesser fellows. They merely waited for their own turns. Eventually one would succeed, the death accomplished, and existence would return to its proper pattern, waiting for interlopers to slay.

And the beast would begin to tire, of course. Wanton slaughter could only do so much to make up for the exertions of mating and flight, while butchery did nothing at all. Even his mighty strength began to give out, and the fact that his destruction would require the participation of those who almost never participated was little comfort and no restorative.

So now, as thick, scaly, muscular tentacles wrapped his limbs, the little suckers on the underside even now nourishing themselves off his own blood, leaking from innumerable cuts and other wounds, his living body drawn inexorably towards the clacking, beaklike jaws, ready and waiting to tear him apart, it began to occur to him that he might at last have met his match. He roared yet again, somewhat frustrated that he was having trouble killing this one. A thin stalk whipped around, wrapping itself around his muzzle, forcing silence upon him.

Suddenly his head came up, in spite of the thin tentacle holding it down. Challenge! It resonated in his nostrils like perfume, water after long thirst. He reared up, pulling the clinging lines taut, no longer interested in merely rending yet another abomination.

Something struck him on the back, scaling his massive body by climbing the tentacles wrapped around it in so many places. A paw stood upon his shoulder, but the challenger failed to attack. Instead, it leaped into the air, spinning and diving into the maze of lines holding him still, its talons flailing. The tentacles jerked, and the beast swung back on one side as some of them parted, his forepaw and snout free. He leaped himself, not at the challenger but into the maw of the thing that knew neither fear nor lust, his arm free and claws ready.

The beaked horror was unprepared, its snapping mouthparts closed when they should have been open. Then the beast stood atop its mouth, perched dangerously within range of its–

With one swipe of his free arm, the beast blinded all three of the monster's glittering, multifaceted eyes.

Despite the wound, the creature held on, as uninterested in its own pain as it had been in that of the others, the lesser abominations that had to have been slain in order for its current victims to have gotten this far. Its tentacles still held, the victim even closer to its grinding, snapping beak.

But it could no longer see, and the tentacles, which held its current victim, were unable to tell it of the other in the vicinity, unless they should happen to touch it, an event the other was eager to avoid. The flailing of the arms had a pattern, of course, a sequence, but some of the arms were missing, and the pattern had gaps. In only a few beats the other had seen the steps of the monster's dance, and stood ready to exploit those gaps.

Now! As a trunklike limb swung past, it leapt forward, roll, roll, left and spring!

The other had inserted itself almost directly under the abomination's 'chin', and leaping upward, had driven its dark claw into the thin armor under its beak, between the joints of its carapace and directly into the vicinity of its brain. When the monster wrapped a limb around the other's legs, it sealed its own doom by pulling him up. The imbedded talon jerked, slicing through the creature's flesh and severing the controlling organ it had initially missed.

In dying, the monster could very nearly have accomplished its objective, dropping the massive body of its first prey onto the second, just as the second pulled out its talon, ready to impale the first.

But it didn't.

The second was small, lithe, and most important, knew that there was a great heavy beast falling down on top of it. Rather than risk getting squashed trying to impale that beast, it chose to throw itself to one side, letting the beast fall safely atop the cushioning coils of its former adversary's tentacles. But as the beast struggled to escape the coils, the smaller one did not attack, in fact it retreated, its great black claw held ready.

It was well that it did, for the beast was quite ready to answer the challenge, now that the minor detail of the ravening giant vampire land squid had been dealt with. Only the black claw slowed it, not from fear, of course, but from memory. The beast had seen it, fought alongside it and its bearer. Even now he could feel it, nearly humming with a love to cut, to slice, to do what it had been made to do that characterizes all Great Swords.

Yet its bearer merely stood there, drilling the point of that magnificent blade into the dusty, lifeless, challengeless earth. The beast approached, memory churning mightily, striving to place the familiar challenge of this one. It seemed so–

Allowing for the passage of many years, it was.

The beast rose up on its hind legs, suddenly towering over the smaller funny-smelling upright one, and put its forepaws on the other's shoulders. The other fell backward, remarkably undisturbed as the beast's snout came in close, all jagged teeth and poisonous breath. It didn't even try to push that ghastly muzzle away until the beast started licking his face and neck.

"*Gah*," shouted Tarkas hoarsely, coughing theatrically, "Enough, Deffin! I am glad to see you too!"

Chapter 8

To Mirani's surprise, she had help extracting the body of the murdered animal from its death and giving it peace. Janosec's search of the bushes beyond had been cursory, at best. "Aren't you going to look for him?" she asked, when he returned quickly and grasped the stake as Tarkas ought to have done. "Aren't you worried?"

Janosec was too nervous and upset to even snort at the absurdity of the suggestion. "This is his life, what he does," he replied, pulling mightily, "We were in pursuit before, and no doubt he is in pursuit still." The stake pulled out slowly, her hands steadying its burden so it would not shake gory bits everywhere.

It was a grisly job, and talking to him was a welcome distraction from it. "If there is anything to pursue."

His mind, focused on pulling the stake slowly and evenly, could handle even this thought with relative equanimity. "You think that…this is…a trap?" On the last word the stake pulled free of the ground with the slightest of jerks.

"You think not?" she asked, shifting her hands, "Push."

"What?" he asked, then noticed how she'd positioned her hands, "Oh, yes." He rearranged himself, his hands on the stick and his feet on the ground, determinedly kicking aside some annoyingly persistent twigs that interfered with his footing. He shoved, careful to aim the barbed, noisome end between her knees and above the ground as her hands held the body still. Slowly the stake passed through the sacrificed beast's corpse to freedom on the other side.

Mirani stood quickly, standing away from both objects, shaking her hands with disgust. Lacking water, she stooped and rubbed them in the dirt of the path, trusting in the clean elemental earth to carry the filth away.

"It was not very effective," said the man, standing there

watching her.

"What, the dirt?" she responded, giving her merely dirty fingers another wipe.

"No, the trap," he explained, pointing at the place where Tarkas wasn't. "If it was a trap. It only got one of us."

"The fiend–or fiends–improvised," she said, defending her theory. "Perhaps there are others further along, to splinter us more."

He turned to look at her. "How many?" he challenged, mildly. "For how many pursuers? How could they know?" He shook his head. "Getting Uncle was sheer accident. Had I killed the beast first…" He shrugged.

"Whereas a few moments delay on our part would have allowed the beast to perish on its own, thus closing off the path before we could follow," finished Mirani, giving Janosec's side of the argument.

He grimaced slightly. "Not a certain method, I admit, but with fewer things left to chance."

She nodded, accepting his reasoning, her eyes dropping to the…things…in the path. "We must dispose of these, the staff especially."

He looked too, but felt no inclination to touch either thing. "How? Burial?" Not a common method, when priests directed the recall of elements from the dead, but it happened occasionally. Midros had been buried, sort of; his earth and his robes interred in a strip of earth that had no rightful place at all within the city.

"Gods, no," she actually shuddered. "An anchor for the other side, however temporary? I dare not think of what might take root and grow from such seed."

"Burn it, then," replied Janosec. There's one sure way to stop seed from sprouting.

She nodded again, and looked around. "Let us build a fire."

But the fire did nothing, not to the staff and not even to the beast, as if it refused to pollute itself. Piling on the twigs rewarded them with the smell of scorched fur, but no more. Janosec fingered one of their last, thicker branches. "Perhaps I should try some of my Uncle's magic," he suggested, unhappily.

She nodded, dubious. Magic was a weapon that cut both ways,

like a knife, and the NarZirtas used no blades. Like all her clan, she had heard many times the nightmare tales of spells that would not start and misfired, or worse, those that would not stop. They could accept that others might use them, but they preferred that the wielders be as competent as possible, and Janosec looked too hesitant for her taste. "A simple spell, I hope. He taught it to you?"

Janosec looked down. "I saw him perform it."

She hid, behind a large, *thick* tree.

After a few seconds, she heard: "Trent! OW!" But nothing else. Sticking her head around, she saw him squatting there, sucking on a finger, the fire extinct, but for the coal she had saved in a pot by her feet. As she approached she noticed the corpse was gone but not the staff, so at least something had been done right. "Did it work?"

Looking stupid with his finger in his mouth, he nodded as his eyes rolled. It worked *a little*. "Fire Spirit," he explained, removing it. "A very strong fire spirit." He stared at his thumb, and the first burn he could recall.

She stirred the ashes, but not even bones remained, although the stake had been merely polished. "Too strong, it seems."

Janosec nudged the stake thoughtfully, with the end of his stick. "Perhaps not. Had it been able to consume this it might have stayed longer. It took what it could, and that little was not enough." Remembering his uncle's tale, he was glad the spirit could leave on its own.

She rubbed her hands on her leggings, and looked away. "We must take it with us." Merely breaking it was a possibility not worthy of consideration.

"I know," he answered, and reached out before she could stop him and grasped it. And as quickly dropped it, his face screwing up around a cry of "Yuck!"

"What?" she cried out, afraid for him.

He wiped his hand on his vest. "Have you ever stepped on a slug, cold and slimy, first thing in the morning?"

Her face screwed up around a cry of "Yuck."

He stopped wiping and looked at his hand, but of course it wasn't slimy and never had been, then looked down at the stake.

"Another vine?" he mused, "Tie it, like my ax?"

"And have it bump against your legs, or mine? I think not," she decided. "We shall have to wrap it."

"With what?" he asked.

She nodded in the direction of their abandoned bags. "Do you have any spare cloth in those?"

He followed her glance, and levered himself up. "In the small bag," he grunted, "No. The large bag so far as I know is food. But I shall–" His voice stopped as he bent over to heft the named bag. "Ha!"

"What?" she asked, rising herself.

"I had forgotten," he started to say, "My uncle's vest." He lifted his prize to her view.

"We can't use that."

He stared at its folded bulk. "My mother would kill me."

She folded her arms, staring at him sadly. "I meant, it's too short."

He tried a few possible folds, but none of them would cover the length of the stick. "No," he agreed, "But perhaps we can use it to simply carry the thing."

She took the folded cloth from him, flipped it into the arrangement she favored, and moved to crouch next to the stake. With the stick Janosec had held, she moved the stake out of the ashes so the cloth wouldn't become more sullied than necessary. "It's heavy," she commented, hefting it experimentally.

"We'll have go rounds bearing it."

"Yesss," she drew out the word absently, sliding the cloth along the length of the stake, looking for its balance. "Already my hand begins to tire."

"Shall I–"

"You shall walk, Demlas," she stated flatly, but not harsh.

Janosec wisely shut up, decked himself out with the two bags, and started walking. Mirani took the side opposite the ax on his hip, the pointed end of the stake held ready for some good use, should the need arise. Her other hand was empty, as he discovered when he attempted to dip his own hand into the large bag between them and found her arm already in the way. He said nothing, merely lifted his arm until she removed her own, and proceeded.

The level of food in the bag dropped steadily, for some time.

"I have discovered a new concept of taint," she said with her voice. *I need not apologize to you,* she said with her manner.

He shrugged. "It seemed a waste, to us," he remarked, likewise looking forward, "Their time and effort, and our own as well. This seemed more fitting." *No you don't,* his attitude said, *but the ones to whom you must apologize are not here and never will be again.*

Suddenly she made sounds, sounds he recognized, and he coughed discreetly and turned his head slightly away, as she stalked a few paces forward for all the privacy her own quivering back could give her. He watched her from behind, of course, restraining himself from offering even so much as a cloth, as her nose snuffled and her hands scrubbed at her eyes, the stake switching sides with great speed. At last she gave up the pretense, dropping the stake but keeping the cloth as she fled the path entirely. Eventually he could not hear her sobs.

Even so, he moved to the far side of the path, carefully circling the stake, and began to sit on a nearby, convenient stone. But midway through the seating process, he looked down at himself with an expression of mild surprise and annoyance, stood up again and turned, relieving himself into the sheltering trees. He sat back down on the rock and stared at the stake, the only item left that could present a reasonable case for serious scrutiny. For a long time he sat there in a contemplative pose, looking sternly thoughtful, his mind awash with crass ideas of stakes and proper places for peeing.

His mind snapped back into place with the sound of approaching feet, most likely hers. Two-legged, at least. Four-legs make a different sound, scuffling through the leaves. He raised his head to the spot where she had gone in, and sure enough, she came out again there, eyes red, streaks of dirt on her cheek, and dangling cloth liberally soiled. But her voice was quietly steady when she said, "I had an idea."

"About what?" he croaked, and cleared his throat.

"About carrying that thing," she said, pointing at the object, still lying where she had dropped it. "You thought about it, too, did you not?"

He hesitated before answering, just a little. "Yes I did," he agreed, eyes not meeting hers. "What is your idea?"

She'd found a tube, really a piece of bark without the wood inside, the remains of a branch, rotted from within and fallen from the tree. The bark was still sound, and with some of the ever-present vines they fashioned a crude sheath. It even slung upon her back as a sword might. Janosec offered to carry it, but the vines were too short to go all the way around his chest, and really, he was carrying enough stuff already.

She looped the thing across her shoulders several different ways, trying to find some position that she could tolerate for any length of time. Finally she allowed it to hang across her back, the strap passing between her breasts. "Stop staring."

Janosec looked away, whether through gallantry or fear of the rock in her sling will never be known. "So that's why women don't use swords."

She snorted. "Don't flatter yourself, woodcutter," she sneered, "We just use the men who do. So if you're done ogling, we must hurry a bit." She strode forward quickly.

He left off ogling a tree of a kind he did not recognize, surprised by her words and her pace. He hurried, just a bit, to catch up. "I was not aware we had a destination, much less one to which we had to hurry."

"*We* don't," she said firmly, her words already measured by her breaths, "*I* do, and a number of other responsibilities besides. I will allow you to accompany me, unless you prefer to stay in wait for your uncle."

"What responsibilities?" he puffed, and silently vowed to speak no more until he no longer puffed. Silence in the presence of his betters had left him unskilled in the art of walking conversation.

"I must report that beast–the grunt–to the authorities in the city, so that they may add it to their lists. I must report you, for that matter. I must report the death of the village. I must report–"

Janosec held up his hands. "I understand," he exclaimed, and he meant it. The loremasters at home did much the same thing, although as a junior he had never had to witness the event. Home–"What city?"

Her foot came down. "Querd."

"Querd what?"

Her other foot came down. "Just Querd."

He considered this, but decided against pressing the matter. "Why do we rush?"

"Hmm?"

He shrugged. "None of the things you must do need be done at a particular time, so far as I can tell. What time is so special?"

She hesitated, not sure how to violate this particular trust, if she was violating it at all. "We must arrive in Querd by next God's Day, if not before."

"Umm…"

"You would call it Fireday."

"A week from yesterday?" he confirmed, his voice going up in a strangely querying note, his eyes glazing over.

She sighed. He saw it, he would think about it, he probably would not ask about it. "It's a ritual," she explained, as minimally as possible.

"Not your own," he stated with great certainty.

She almost said something, not quite obviously nonplussed. Then she tried again. "How–did you know?"

He smirked. "You did not say it was *your* ritual."

"Ah," she accepted her defeat with good grace, at least. "I had friends. In the village. It was their turn to take their walk. I planned to accompany them." Her voice firmed, her chin came up, her eyes hardened. "Now I am going to walk *for* them."

The gods of the Querdishani are not at all the same as the Gods of Querdishan, if Gods there were. They accomplished the kind of transition effected by Menniver upon Tarkas with far more than a mere ripple, just as casting the voice Mirani heard in her head had taken far more effort than it would have cost one of the true unmortals. This is as it should be, for what the Lords Elemental were doing was actually contrary to their purpose, and could only be accomplished because the Gods of this place had not ever thought to make it impossible.

Fenita experienced the transition as immensely painful, utterly peaceful, of long duration and of short, full of sensations and devoid of any. Her elements had been taken in hand, the lords straining to the utmost to keep them in place so the pattern of her could be restored at the other side. But the self of her, the thing which removed the elements from the world of Nature while it lasted and she lived, was an element without a lord. It had to make the transition on its own, its connection to the elements of its body tenuous and fractured.

Which is why the first thing Fenita did when she arrived at the plateau was scream in the face of the goddess of Life and fall, kneeling, at her feet. This didn't help Irolla, who had developed a sudden splitting headache, along with her fellows. The last time they had had to use a focus, she had simply gone to Janosec's cribside and done what needed to be done. Clearly this method needed some improvement. But the lords recovered quickly, elemental assistance and supernatural endurance proving their worth. Soon after, Fenita showed clear signs of recovery from her own brush with Eternity.

The borrowed mortal looked up, the figure of Irolla instantly recognizable through her tears, despite the totally different character she presented here on the plateau. "We thought you might find these forms less…imposing," the Lady of Life explained, in subtle misdirection.

Fenita rose, staring at the Lady curiously. There was something…strange about her, different, but a difference she had seen somewhere before. Belatedly, she gazed about her, at the circle of her gods. A crash and rumble drew her first to Water on her left, pale, tall and thin, broad-shouldered and narrow-hipped, with the surf behind him coming up to lap his feet. Earth, again to her left, stolid and immovable, eyes like crystal, hair like granite, but skin the color of summer soil. And Air! Air was a cloud, yes, but a cloud with a tornado inside, a feeling bolstered by the swirling and moaning of air from behind her. She could feel her strength as if the Lady's long yellow hair were thinly disguised lightning. Her eyes were quite sober, and on her mouth–

"Few have heard her speak and lived to tell of it," said Irolla, drawing her attention around, full-circle. "The Voice of Air is Death."

Fenita knew exactly of whom she spoke. "Tarkas."

Life nodded. "He is one. He said she has a fine voice."

Air moved suddenly, her hands twisting and fluttering.

Irolla grinned, looking almost human. "You should be," she said, as if the Lady of Air had spoken, "It is a very high compliment, for him."

Air's hands moved again.

"Yes, she is the woman," Life confirmed. At Air's signed request (although the emphasis moaning in the chasm behind her made it more of a demand), Irolla said, "Go to her, Fenita."

Fenita would rather have jumped off the cliff. The wind behind Air had begun to billow, her gown rippling, her hair flying, a storm come to life. Suddenly a gust of wind caught the hapless mortal woman in the back and sent her stumbling to her doom, if doom it was. She stopped herself in time, less than an arm length away from the Lady in white, and waited. The Lady did not move, but Fenita was clearly being examined, scrutinized, for what she could not know or tell.

Air reached up, touching her lightly in the throat, once. Irolla looked over to the lord of Earth, unnoticed by Fenita, and he rolled his eyes. He and the lord of Water shared a glance, and he nodded. He remembered what they had done to her to bring her here. "She gives you her gift, little one," he stated, in hard, bass tones. "She gives you the power to speak in her voice, one time, at need."

Fenita reached up a hand to her own throat, her eyes questioning, afraid to ask. "Fear not, Fenita," Irolla assured her, "It must be invoked, with her name. She is Kolo."

"Come to me, Fenita," said Earth suddenly. She turned and moved slowly, but he seemed as patient as the mountains behind him. He held up his hands, and she took them in the natural response. "I am Strom," he said, clasping her hands firmly. "I give you leave to use my hands, one time, at need."

He released her, and dropped his hands, as a voice to her left said "Fenita" in a rather low tenor. The lord of Water waited as patiently as Earth had, although his hair undulated in the slight breeze, as Earth's had not. Fenita went, and stood before him, but he did not reach out to her. Suddenly her feet were wet, and cold. Looking down, she saw that a wave had come up, lapping over his feet and her own. "I am Targon, and I give you leave to use my feet, one time, at need." *Gods do not bend to mortals*, she thought, not daring to shake the water and sand off her sandals. The leather would be ruined.

"And I, sister," came Life's low voice. *Sister?* Fenita strode up to her, and searched her over, but could see no family resemblance. "I am Irolla, and my blood shall be yours, one time, at need. Now come with me, for this search is ours." And truly, the others had already disappeared, or were clouding her senses, or hid behind rocks, or something.

Fenita followed, the edge of the plateau dropping off suddenly as they approached. She gasped in surprise, not at the vast expanse of greenery below them, but at the size of the murf waiting only a short distance below. Trying not to think of a lirrik, act like a lirrik, or smell like a lirrik, she followed the Lady's lead in climbing upon the predator's great back. The murf leaped off the ledge, and for a heartbeat or two her heart stopped beating, until the updraft caught it. Then she felt like she sailed, a raft of feathers on a sea of air. Surely they were not going to search for her son like this!

No. The flight was more direct, and too fast, not a searching pattern at all. Looking down she saw that a search from above would be futile anyway, with nothing but the forest's leafy roof to be seen. How odd that something so open when seen from below should look so solid from above. She might as well look for a dak in the fields while perched on cliffside, and as successfully.

The layer of green got closer, and she realized that the murf didn't really fly at all, just used its great wings to hold the air as it...slid down the wind. Towards what? Something had to be on the bottom.

She dared a peek over the Lady's shoulder, and saw their destination, a stump, a gigantic stump of a gigantic tree, ringed in stone. Yes, now the beast used its wings, for they moved too fast, too high to be able to stop when they reached it. They slowed, dropping, circling around the target and…oomph! The Lady's back was firm and steady as Irolla pitched forward, nearly thrown as the beast caught the stump with its talons.

"Don't ruffle its feathers," warned Life as she slid expertly back, shoulder and wing forming a sort of a slide down to the wood below. Fenita moved far more hesitantly, and nearly got thrown off and eaten as the murf twitched to remove her irritating presence. She only fell a short way, to land near the Lady on the top step of a stair, cut into the inside of the tree stump. The slightly blunted edges of the wood were clear signs that the tree had been much higher in life, and the stair had continued its ascent, but both had fallen many years ago.

It was an uncertain perch at best; had she not been landed at the top she would not have stood there, regardless of her company. Strangely, the Lady seemed just as eager to leave, no doubt to do what needed to be done, and Fenita felt vaguely guilty at imposing upon her time as she followed down the spiraling stair.

At the bottom she stopped, held back by Life's imperious hand, in this case a menagerie of creatures ranging from the dangerous to the grotesque, sometimes both. The Lady paused, letting her get a good look, and then she barely moved her own imperious hand. Beasts large and small fled in elemental-inspired terror from the way she had indicated, a route that ended at a black door set into the wall of a short tunnel. And within the door–

A pedestal, a large pedestal bearing a tray, upon which sat no more than a clear goblet of water, and a hallway beyond. The Lady lifted the glass and took a sip, and said, "I greet you, Demlas Fenita. I am Irolla tel Kwinarish, the Lady of Life. Welcome to my home." She held out the glass.

Fenita took the water, but just held it. "You take a sip, and say 'Thank you'," coached the Lady, cognizant of her guest's ignorance. Fenita did as instructed, not entirely happy about drinking from a vessel someone else had just drunk from, but less happy about offending a goddess. Perhaps it was a way of guarding against poisons, like the handclasping at home warded against weapons.

Irolla nodded, and replaced the glass upon its stand. Then she led the way further into the palace she called home, her back straight, her face composed, absolutely terrified. *What* was she doing, dealing directly with a Querdishani woman?! She knew nothing of their customs, nor their rituals, it wasn't her job. That's what priests were for. That's what Tarkas–

Her own arguments steadied her, the links strong. Tarkas and Janosec, Janosec and Fenita. Tarkas and Fenita? No, that was too long ago, too fleeting.

"It is nice to meet you at last." Having her guest at her back, following as they walked the hall, comforted her. She did not have to see her face.

Fenita jerked. A goddess knew of her? Wanted to see her? Why would a goddess *need* to see anyone? Surely she can know what she wants to know.

Habit carried her through her puzzlement. "I am honored, my Lady."

"I wanted to see what kind or woman managed to turn our Champion's head at last," Irolla explained.

Fenita replied without thinking, "I had not noticed that it took all that much to turn a man's head."

Irolla laughed out loud, a merry sound ringing from the smooth stone. "Too true, and busy does it keep me," she remarked, "But not of him."

Now Fenita was even more confused. Was she being congratulated or condemned? "I…would not know," she replied, trying to be diplomatic, "He spends so much time away from us. I do not think he has spent more than seven nights, not even so much as a week at once, within the city walls."

Irolla heard the bitterness in her voice with complete understanding. She hit the door before her with unnecessary force, evidencing her own displeasure. It refused to slam, but she got her point across. She stalked the grassy area beyond like a tigress, not speaking until she got to her favorite sitting place, and turned, to find her guest standing hesitantly a few paces away. She gestured at the place before her. "Sit."

Fenita obeyed, not daring to even look about her at the fantastic sights the room revealed.

"Were Tarkas to spend 'even so much as a week at once' in the city walls," Irolla explained, or tried to, "He would almost certainly destroy all you have worked to build these last twenty and more years, by the end of that week. He would stay if he could." At least relieve her guest's mind on that score.

Fenita was appalled. *The loneliness...* "Is he that powerful?" She had seen his strength first hand.

Irolla felt her guest's reaction and hid even that truth from her, that it was worse for Tarkas, who came from a people far less nomadic than her own. "No. But…he does not seek his enemies, not entirely. They are too cowardly and too numerous for him to spend his time in endless search," she explained as best she could, without hinting at the true nature of the Hero's handicap, "It is part of his nature that they come to him."

Fenita gasped, memory slamming her with full force. "Last night's creature."

Irolla nodded. "And worse." No need to mention that its appearance had been far too soon for any effect of Tarkas' to have been the cause.

Fenita stared at her hostess, a strange look on her face. "Worse than a creature that will not die?"

Irolla stared back. "I was being polite," she retorted, in a brittle voice. "We need to find Tarkas."

"Why? To kill it?"

Irolla looked away. Talk of killing could not be pleasant for the Lady of Life, but death was a part of it, or should be. "If he must. Not long ago, as you measure time, he encountered creatures similar to these, and aided them."

Fenita nodded slowly, her eyes glazed over in memory and thought. "It said it had to kill him and did not want to," she said softly, but that did not last long. "If they are the same, it has betrayed him, however unwilling it might be. There can be only one response to such…treason."

Irolla grasped her one feeble straw. "If they are the same. Only Tarkas would know."

"You need me for that? You said you would–that *I* would lead *you* to my son!"

Irolla relaxed. This was a much better topic. "We do, and you will," she said, smiling, and cocked her head slightly to one side. "You will lead us to your son, and your son will lead us to his father."

And somewhere Else, the nizarik called Deffin by only one man gorged himself on dead creature flesh (bite-rip-swallow, bite-rip-swallow), while his smelly, upright, two-legged parent sat on a rock. Life was good again; Tarkas supplied the challenge while the prey supplied the blood and the death. Had Tarkas been aware of the situation he would have agreed with the allotment.

But he was not. The two of them together were more of a threat than this place –wherever it was–had ever seen, and some pretty arcane things had crawled from the deepest shadows. They displayed no great creativity; brute force, in terms of size and speed, seemed to be the order of the day, while the things getting larger and faster were little more than variations on the claws and tentacles they had already dispatched. But Heroes, unlike nizariks, do not find slaughter more pleasant than sex and more restful than sleep, and this Hero was getting tired.

Suddenly Deffin jumped and ran, a sensible move even for a beast of his sort, when faced with a new and unknown threat. Tarkas stood wearily, sword ready, to face whatever new threat apparently hid just behind the mounded corpse of their latest kill. Whatever it was, it was noisy, chattering loudly as the body–moved! Falling away from them!

He leapt back onto his rock, the only smart thing to do when faced with what seems to be an underground threat. But no! It wasn't underground, it ate the corpse, so fast that the rest of the body fell backwards. But the thing advanced even more swiftly, and Tarkas saw it first, a great black tide.

Bugs! Flesh eating devourers!

And him without a swamp to stamp them back into.

Deffin scrambled up onto the rock with him, and now he needed a bigger rock. Fortunately, this rock was part of a jumbled heap of boulders, many of which were larger and higher off the ground, so they went there. Next thing, how to wipe out a horde of flesh-eating bugs. Easy enough, he'd done so at least three times before. A simple fire spell should do the–

But it didn't. He could feel the words as they left his lips, the dead sound falling powerless. A leg or two shriveled, but the injured bugs fell, and were immediately consumed by their brethren. Now they were leaving the corpse, a heap of bones in their wake, looking for new prey to feed their collective, ravenous appetite. The rock stumped them for a little while, but the scent and feel of new prey drew more and more of them, until eventually they piled up and spilled over the top of the lowest stone.

By that time the two prey had clambered to the top of the highest stone, and Tarkas, at least, looked about for some means off. The swarm may not be great enough for them to climb all the way to the top, but it would be foolish to trust to that defense. Since it seemed that they had no interest in trees, the obvious thing to do was somehow get themselves up into those low branches.

Hmm. Can't jump that high. Maybe–watch the teeth! Okay, standing on Deffin's back is no option. Could use a rope right now, or a vine. A whipsnake even. Wait, yes, of course! He slipped his scabbard off his shoulders, feeling for the buckle that held it at one end or the other and undoing it. The strap itself was too short, but with the sword to extend his reach–

Yes! The strap wrapped around. Now if only it stays wrapped long enough to climb up. A quick hand-over-hand to the top and…Safe!

Well, *he* was safe. Probably. Deffin remained down on the rock, and he wasn't going to climb on the strap, no matter how human his hands looked. Okay, then secure the sword at least, buckling it around the branch so it wouldn't fall down. Now, get Deffin. Up into the tree? Probably not, in spite of the beast's early life as a climber. Off the rock at least, those bugs have almost reached the top. Have to give him something he can grab on to.

Tarkas dangled himself upside down from the branch, his legs crooked as firmly over the branch as he could get them, reaching down for the nizarik. "Deffin. Shake." That was something the beast could understand, an old game from long ago. He reared up, slipping one paw into the man's hand. Tarkas grabbed it tightly, and the Deffin reached up the other one to get the first free, as the Hero expected. He grabbed that one too, and pulled for all he was worth, lifting the beast's feet off the stone just as the first insect crawled over the edge.

Ye gods, he was heavy! For a moment, Tarkas could see only the inside of his own eyelids, as he grimaced at the strain. Finally, he opened them, to see what the bugs were doing. Fex, they could sense Deffin above them, and not far above them at that. They were piling themselves up again, trying to reach his furry nizarik butt and stumpy nizarik tail. Tarkas couldn't lift any further, he could barely hold on now, and his knees or the branch would break eventually.

He pulled his eyes back up, and found himself staring at the heap of bones. The swarm wasn't infinite, and pulling every member up onto the rock had left their path clear! Flexing his knees, he started to swing, slowly at first, but faster each time. The bugs sensed this and worked even harder to reach the beast. Then the Hero let go.

Deffin almost ruined the plan by trying to hang on, dragging his parent off the tree and into the waiting mandibles below. But his hands were beast's hands, horny and dry, and he couldn't keep a grip that Tarkas didn't want him to keep. He fell as much as flew, far enough to grab onto a large rib bone when he slammed into it bodily. It toppled under him, and he had to scramble madly to avoid being crushed or impaled by jagged, calcic splinters. In the end he emerged relatively unscathed, atop a pile of bones and bone fragments.

Tarkas waited and watched, but the bugs appeared uninterested in the tumult and the actual reachability of their prey. As he expected; bugs of this sort never, in his experience, went back over their own track, since it had to have already been cleared out for them to be where they were. Deffin was safer than Tarkas himself.

The Hero merely sat in his tree and waited, far beyond the range of the bugs' senses. It felt strange, sitting up there and watching, but it took him some time to recognize the sensation of nostalgia, or reminiscence. Conlon's gift had left his memory completely available in its entirety, but only from the moment it had been given to him. The events before that day were only as available as any man's, and that included the memories of his trip, arduous and ugly, through the swamp that surrounded the land of the gods, with all its denizens. Little red things that ate whatever they swarmed over. Sleeping in trees. Strange creatures that ate to live and lived to eat, an endless contest for dominance. The work involved in remembering was notable, and noticed.

Why would he think of such things now? He had seen many voracious bugs over the years, yet the first thought in his head this time had been of his days in the swamp. This place was as far removed from the swamp as he could imagine anyplace being, in almost every respect. Dry rather than wetlands, dusty, its life given over to a cold, orderly, systematic death-dealing that made him yearn for the chaotic turmoil of the swamp's daily routine. A place less like the swamp couldn't be found even if someone went and–

built

–one.

Chapter 9

Janosec's head spun, bits and pieces of strange lore careening wildly as he struggled to make sense of it all. "But Fireday is the *last* day of the week!"

"To you," she replied, "To the Upwellers, it's the first day, in accordance with their lore. 'On the First Day, the Eye of God opened, and it saw the Light, and the Light was.'"

"Why do they call it 'Gods-day'?" he asked, absently pushing yet another clump of leaves away from his face. This path may be well traveled, but not by people as tall as he.

"I don't know." She shrugged, causing the tube on her back to shift. He enjoyed the motion of her, just as glad he saw it from behind and so could not be distracted by the movements of her front. He had no desire to know how skilled she was with her sling firsthand. "Certainly it is the only day they have taken the trouble to name."

"What, do they call Lifeday, *umm...*" he paused briefly, counting on his fingers, "Seventh-day?"

"Of course," she agreed, sure that it was no more than a lucky, if logical, guess on his part. "They know only the one god, and they don't count the elements themselves as worthy of name-bearing–"

"No elements!?" Janosec was scandalized.

"Oh, they have them," she responded somewhat absently, fishing in her pouch for a stone, her eyes raised to the branches ahead, "'On the Second Day, the Eye of God opened, and it saw the earth, and the earth was', and so forth."

The lorewarden in Janosec could hear the lack of a capital on the name of Earth when she said it that way, obviously distracted. He looked himself, but his angle of vision was too different, as usual, and could see nothing beyond the leaves hanging low. Then the soft whirring sound of her sling drew his attention down, and the sound of the stone cracking drew it back up, in time to see a large body falling limply, with no attempt to break its fall.

"A lirrik?" he asked, smothering a groan. Only stewing could make the strong meat even remotely tolerable, in his opinion, and stewing was obviously not an option.

"With speed, if you please, Demlas," she urged, "My stone could not have finished it."

Nor had it. The little arboreal rodent could be seen twitching in the dead leaves, like but unlike the earlier sacrifice, but with the same ultimate fate. Idly it occurred to him to wonder what she would have done without him to wield a knife, but surely she would have used a larger stone for the finishing blow.

He upended the beast so the blood would flow out more quickly, incidentally keeping it out of its own wastes. "Surely we do not stop now?" he inquired, not so much asking a question as requesting her plan.

She knelt, pulling out a length of thong from a different part of her belt, and tied one end smoothly around the beast's ear, tying it off to the tail so the wound gaped open. "Surely not," she agreed, testing the portability of the cadaver, "But the supply in your bag will not see us to our destination, by any means, even if you had found and collected all the stocks of waybread to be had." Not that anyone would eat waybread except as a last resort.

Janosec half-turned, patting the bottom of the sack, but the leather was too thick for him to be able to tell much. It was a surprising ignorance, considering that he had been the one to fill the bag, but his memory of the previous day was thankfully spotty. There were some large lumpy shapes in there, too large for the fruits and other things he had put in it, so he shrugged the bag off his shoulder to the ground at her feet. She rummaged in there very shortly, drawing out a few large parcels from the very bottom.

"It smells like you found the herbist's hut," she commented, laying aside one package, a roll, with lumpy shapes within. The second package, more squarish, she peeked into briefly, announcing, "This seems to be all the bread stocks." Her interest focused on the roll that smelled of herbs and she undid the package completely.

It was a large cloth, but it had been rolled around a large assortment of smaller containers, crocks, leather bags in some cases, or some long items gathered together and secured with a string. For a time she just sat back and stared at the collection, before finally stating, "A most…varied assortment, Demlas."

Something in her voice made him squirm, just a little, there inside his skin. "My uncle is an unusual man," he said, passing the responsibility.

"He must be," she agreed, shaking her head slightly, "To put the bay leaf next to a jar of unguent for numpus rash–" she held up one jar "–with the rest of the cooking herbs over there, beside the emetics!"

"He was in a hurry," defended Janosec weakly.

She squared her shoulders, propped hands on knees, and glared at him. "He certainly would have been after *that* meal!" She didn't bother waiting for a response, just set to work reordering the pile, a few things here, a lot more there, and the jars in the middle as before. With lots of breathy sighs thrown in, for emphasis.

"Why do you put that there?" he asked suddenly.

"What, this?" she answered, her fingers resting on a bunch of stalks.

"Indeed," he agreed, "Should they not be over there, with the emetics?"

"Is that what they are?"

He shrugged, but she didn't see as she lifted them up again, learning their taste and smell and other sensible properties. "For stomach ailments," he accepted, "But flutterwort is for minor discomforts, not poisonings or the like."

"Ah," she said, laying the stalks in their proper place, "Tell me if you see any more." And he did, once or twice.

At the end, she demanded his knife.

"I thought you did not use blades," he questioned, handing it over.

"For killing," she clarified, taking the hilt, "Hard to prepare the food afterward without them, though." She started slitting the lirrik skin carefully. "Besides, you'd probably just cut your own fingers off if I asked you to do it."

He just watched, her baiting sarcasm not calling for a response.

She handed his knife back. "Thank you."

"You are welcome," he replied soberly. When she began inserting some of the leaves into the slits, he asked, "What do you do?"

"Flavoring the meat, absorbing some of the oils," she explained, holding up a leaf, "There are some who find fresh lirrik too strong."

"I am one," he said, despite her implied criticism. "I hate it, except in stew."

"Then you will soon starve," she told him, deadpan, and rose, the body dangling. "Every inn between here and there has lirrik among its offerings. Every wife has an old family recipe."

"I love lirrik," he declared stoutly, as if the gods were listening, and knelt to put the two packs back in the large duffel.

She grimaced. He rose and fell in close behind her as she started walking. "And I, too. At least the Upwellers won't–wouldn't eat it."

"Why not?"

She held the body aloft so he could see better, and touched one of the dangling limbs. "They won't eat the flesh of any beast with hands."

As she lowered the beast, he asked, "Why in the name of Earth not?"

"God's Within!" she exploded suddenly, turning her head to glare at him over her shoulder, "Why should I know? Do *you* know every littlest detail of your own lore?!"

"Well, most of it," he replied casually, as if her question had been seriously meant. "The Divine Dicta are the easiest, I suppose. 'The Gods said so' is good enough reason for most of us."

She half turned and looked up at him, to see if he was joking or mocking at her, but he was staring sort of absently at the trees as they passed by. "The Ancestral Dicta are pretty easy too," he continued, "Usually *somebody* remembers why some great aunt or grandmother said 'make the food this way'–"

She turned away then, her own memory triggered, of a kitchen tyranny two generations in the unmaking. "I had a great aunt, Zirtas Namutha–"

He snorted. "No doubt your stories would be like the others I've heard," he acknowledged sympathetically, and continued his prior discourse. "It's understanding the Spirits that makes a problem, they don't really say anything, but the gods help you if you don't do what they want."

"I could say the same of Zirtas Namutha," countered Mirani, with no small degree of bitterness, "The Elders themselves kept their distance if she had a spoon in her hand, but those of us doing our kitchen duty weren't so lucky." Her pace increased, stomping out her inner agitation. The lirrik sprayed little drops of blood in a much wider arc.

He looked down, pulled from his recollections into matching her new speed, as he wiped a hard-flung droplet from his cheek. "Surely she told you what she wanted done."

She shrugged. "While you were rubbing the bruise." Her hand reached up and stroked her own arm, as she slowed down. "I was actually relieved to be selected for weapons instruction."

He pondered that, frowning. "Released from kitchen duty?" he guessed uncertainly. *He* hadn't been.

She shook her head. "No, but the weaponsmasters wanted us uninjured," she explained. "And they were nicer to us."

He couldn't help it; he laughed, loud and explosive. "Your weaponsmaster's best friend!"

She stopped dead in her tracks, and he slammed into her back. "You can't be thinking–?"

"Gods within," he remembered to murmur, as he bent down past her ear to pick up the lirrik she'd dropped, "How should *I* know? Deliberate or not I cannot say, but it all seems to have worked out well for you."

A smile ghosted across her face, but only because he could not see it. "Oh," she said, coolly, taking their dinner back, "You think so much of yourself, do you, you're so fit to judge my ability? All I've seen you do so far is brain a creature with an ax after I distracted it for you." Which was unfair and she knew it.

"I'd like to see you even try to move this axe," he countered, a poor response and he knew it.

"So now muscle equals prowess?"

"Of course not," he replied irritably. Did she think him a fool? "But if muscle is needed, there can be no prowess without it. I doubt I could ever learn to wield a sling as you do, or fight as my uncle did–does."

There was a moment of silence at his slip. That moment gave way to another, and the silence gave way to anything else, the sound of leaves rustling far overhead and small animals scurrying, suddenly loud as they walked by. The wind whistling in their ears almost drowned out their own cacophonous footsteps.

Finally–"Do you fear for him?" she asked softly.

"Yes. No," he replied, not at all sure. "He's been doing things of this sort for as long as I've been alive. It seems more dangerous, perhaps, now that I have some notion of what he goes through. And I have seen him at weapon's training, over the years."

"He is good," she was sure.

"Unbelievably so," he expanded her praise, "With every weapon, or even with no weapon. With weapons I had never before seen, that he brought with him and showed us how to use."

"Slings?" she asked, her own area of interest.

He considered the question. "*Hmmp.* I don't believe I ever saw him use one," he finally concluded, his tone much subdued, then continued brightly, "But I have no doubt that, should you put one in his hand, he would be able to hit any finger after only a few practice throws." He held up his hand, fingers outspread.

"Oh, *really*," she protested, a little exasperated at the, in her opinion, overblown estimation of his uncle's probable skills, and held up just one particular finger of her own. "How about this one?"

He looked at it, considering.

"He'd probably need a few more practice throws for just the one."

She threw up her hands and turned away, snarling her frustration. Janosec had better sense than to ask her why. Instead, he cast about for a safer topic, and actually found one. "We'd better find a place to camp, it's getting a bit late."

"I know," she snapped. "I was hoping we could get to one of the usual spots on this road, but you and your monsters have delayed us tremendously."

He returned to scanning the trees, wondering which of the creatures they had seen thus far were supposed to be his, pleased with the realization that all his purposeless scanning of the woods about them had had a purpose after all.

He saw it first.

The lirrik tasted pretty good.

"The trees are laughing at me," he murmured in the dark, trying to pretend that the rock under his head was as soft as his pillow at home.

She shifted a little, wishing as always that she could have as many blankets above her as below. "Hmm?" she said in reply, not really wanting to bestir herself too much.

He paused before he replied, for he didn't want to bestir himself either, and had to wait until he drew breath again. "My littlest sister said that," he began, then paused again for breath, "The first time she was close enough to the trees to hear them moving in the wind."

"Mmm," she could barely manage in reply, her attempts at repose successful.

Nor did he say anything further, just lay there listening to the sounds of leaves in motion high above as the darkness closed in.

In motion high above, the elementals of Air heard nothing as they carried on their mistress' search for her favorite man, not interested in mumbled nothings from the mouths of anyone else.

Fenita closed the door quietly, shuddering slightly. The goddess may have called it a privy, but still–! Surely there should be more between the privy and the field than that! The short walk through the cold stone corridors was barely enough to allow her to settle her stomach.

The Lady had not left the room when she returned, although she had shifted her position. Now she stood by a stumpy block of wood that stuck up out of the ground, very much like the…thing she had just left. But there the resemblance ended, Fenita noted with relief. Closer inspection revealed that it was barely more than a tree stump, if a little oddly shaped. It actually looked like a short–

"Be seated, please," the Lady invited, graciously, gesturing at the stump as if it were the chair it mimicked. Fenita sat, fumbling a little as her normal motions of sitting were disrupted by the strangeness of the seat. In the end she fell into it rather than seating herself.

The Lady, too polite or focused on other things to draw attention to this, moved behind her guest and dropped closer to the ground, actually kneeling behind Fenita. This explained the strange shape of the stump, as her knees fit comfortably into the notches below the seat. "Do not fear," said the goddess as her hands went around Fenita's waist.

Fear? What was to fear? For a second her heart throbbed, until Irolla's hands clasped and settled upon her belly, tightening and pressing Fenita's body close to her own. Nothing seemed to be happening. For a moment she was insulted that the goddess seemed to be think her afraid. "Are you doing anything?" she asked, a little rudely, considering her position.

Irolla's voice, when she finally replied, was a little distant. "I'm trying not to destroy you utterly, blast your mind into a million whirling fragments of screaming emotion, or leave you evermore barren. This is delicate work, on a woman. But we have begun."

According to Elder Holan, Tarkas' instructor and mentor in all subjects Song-related, the principle of contrast was most effective when incomplete. The parts of the Song that were the same made it easier for the listeners to perceive those parts that were not, which in turn–Tarkas shut off that train of thought before it got any further advanced. The relevance of the principles of evocation to landscaping was not hard to see, especially considering the high degree of creativity so far displayed.

Not that it meant…anything at all, really. But it gave him something to think about as they walked the track left behind by the bugs, the one place in this territory where they could have some feeling of security, however fleeting. As soon as he saw one living thing other than themselves, they would leave. Or as soon as they were attacked again, if there should be a difference between the two.

The real question was in which direction to go once they departed the track. So far the terrain had been pretty uniform, as the swamp had been, but in the swamp there had been a view of the mountains high over the trees to inspire him. Here there were trees, but no mountain, and certainly no inspiration. Or, for that matter, water, although there had to be some, he supposed, to sustain these miserable excuses for trees. His collection of jugs would run out eventually. Deffin did not seem to be suffering, and Tarkas supposed he slaked his thirst with blood and other fluids, but that might perhaps not be the best thing.

Eventually, Deffin lifted a leg against a boulder, and Tarkas watched the flow as it drained off straight in one direction. Drinking salty liquids like blood actually drained water, leaving the drinker thirstier than before. If Deffin was loosing more than he seemed to have drunk–

But he didn't seem to be, and what he did loose was quite rank. Which inspired Tarkas to wash it away and he decided to relieve himself on the same spot. He loosed quite a bit more, and the track Deffin had started was considerably extended. Mostly straight, except for the usual ridges and hollows.

Always in one direction.

After he finished, he turned to look along the damp little track they had made, but there was precious little to see, on the face of it. The slope was too gradual to merit the name of slope, and so he declined to use it. The trees were thin, but thick enough in their numbers to foil his vision. He looked up, but saw above the trees only more gloom, a darker patch of monotonously gray sky that normally would herald the coming of night.

It might be the same here. It might not. He would know soon enough, and this was still the safest place to be, while sitting and waiting. In the open they had little to fear but rain, and rain had not fallen for some time, apparently. He and Deffin were fortunate that he'd brought so many jugs with him. He'd salvaged a bone fragment in which to give the beast water; blood should not be his only drink.

He had no faith in the ground, but the larger stones seemed a good defense against something from below. He lit no fire, of course, and had no one with whom to converse. His meal precluded both; a strip of flesh, sliced from the flank of some beast or other long since consumed. Chewy, much like fresh slib, and it did in fact taste like a freshly cooked slib, perhaps sautéed, some onions, garlic. It was too bad, since freshly cooked slib tastes terrible, although it does have its merits in hand-to-hand combat.

The memory of that singular event carried him through the twilight, as he settled against Deffin's warmth and prepared to try to survive this first night.

Chapter 10

She awoke first, but only by a few seconds. She couldn't really take credit for it; a bird dropped something hard onto a rock and the crack disturbed them both. They headed off in different directions, of course, hands rubbing and mouths yawning, but when they returned she was frowning and he was smiling.

"What?" she grumped, stooping to root through the big duffel for something edible.

"Good morrow to you, too," he replied, checking the firepit for useful coals, his smile a bit less broad, but determined to be cheerful.

"No morrow is good," she complained, fierce and low, "The Eye of God never saw one, someone made them, and I will see him executed."

For some reason he laughed out loud. "Sorry," he replied, not sounding very sorry, when she glared at him for the outburst, "I was reminded of a dream." He started dropping a few small twigs and leaves, encouraging the coals to a fire.

She bit into a spotted fruit, but that didn't stop her from commenting, "Executions amuse you?"

He cast an acerbic glance her way, since the twigs needed no further help bursting into flames. "It wasn't an execution, thank you," he responded primly, then grinned again, "My uncle killed an assassin with a fish."

She spat her fruit out explosively, and started coughing. He ignored this unseemly outburst and continued preparing breakfast.

With an air of defeat, she asked, "Very well, perhaps you would care to tell me how your uncle slew an assassin with a fish."

"Are you sure you want to know?" he asked with mock-solicitude.

"It will pass the time," she replied casually, as she passed yet another tree, stepped over another root, rounded yet another bend in the trail they followed. It was reasonably clear, the bushes keeping their distance, although the branches had not yet learned to lift from the passage of exceptionally tall people. Fortunately Janosec had good reflexes and ducked frequently.

"I must see if I remember it all," he temporized. He had, in fact, been pondering the dream, studying it, memorizing it for fear of losing a detail. Not that it showed sign of fading as most dreams do.

She smirked, not at him. "Continue, I pray you. I am becoming fascinated by this barely memorable dream."

He frowned, mostly but not entirely at her. "I suppose it must have been a dream," he began, thoughtfully, "But it did not...*feel* like a dream. It felt real, very real, but it wasn't mine, if that makes any sense to you."

"No," she replied, refusing to admit the beginnings of interest on her own part. "But it's certainly a better start to your tale than the first one."

"Thank you," he responded, so properly as to be reproachful. "So. This is what happened: I was walking on a–"

"*You* walked? I thought this a story about your uncle?"

He shrugged, almost entranced by the inner vision. "It is, but I was him, I was walking and I knew my name was Tarkas, as one does in dreams. And then I was standing in the sea, near the shore, hunting slib."

"What are slib?"

His voice came soft, low, "They are long, thin, slimy. Hard to catch, just like the–the–something I once hunted in my youth–"

His uncle's youth*,* she thought

"–but they come to the sea every year, and every year I hunt them, catching them in my bare hands."

"That sounds hard to do," she supplied dutifully.

"Oh it is," he agreed emphatically. "It takes–it takes–the gods' own patience to do. And it's either that or catch–catch–some kind of insect."

She snorted. "'Some kind of insect'? Is that the best you can do?"

His face twisted, as if in pain. "I–know what he wanted, what he saw, but the words aren't there, like I hear them and they're just noise, think them and they're just confusion–"

"The insect confuses you?" she inquired, incredulous, "Simply its name, the word for it?"

He shook his head, his attempts to grasp the ungraspable merely increasing his distress. "I do not know," he groaned softly, "There are no words in me–"

She looked at him for the first time, and did not like what she saw. "Continue with the assassin," she directed.

Like magic, his face cleared, became peaceful once again. "A large man, all in black–"

Naturally, she thought.

"–his weapon out and ready, my own far from me. I had not even my sandals on. He challenged me–"

"What about?" she asked, and almost regretted the interruption, but he didn't really notice.

"I do not know, exactly," Janosec admitted, his face twisting slightly again. "His employer had, I think, been a man of power and means beforehand."

"Before what? Before your uncle arrived in the town?"

"Indeed, and ill-gotten, as well, otherwise–"

"Otherwise he would not have bothered?"

"He probably would not even have been there," he corrected, "My uncle goes where he goes for a reason, even if he himself does not know what it may be. In this case it was the assassin's employer, I imagine, and perhaps others, and they sought revenge."

"Foolish of them," she declared.

"Of course," he agreed, "But they could not know that. Nor did it look that way, at first. The assassin was clever, hidden by night, and my uncle unarmed and nearly defenseless."

"The situation you describe looks grim, hopeless even."

"You would think so," he responded, the words flowing more easily now, "But I am–he is no man's victim. He merely looked at the man, and heard his words, and then turned his back, and proceeded to make dinner. He even invited the killer to share his meal!"

"Such boldness!" she exclaimed in almost-mock enthusiasm, "This tale of yours has merit. Surely the killer lost his temper and attacked, and Tarkas bested him easily."

"Not at all," Janosec countered, dismissing the notion. "My uncle had no grudge against the hireling, and was giving the fellow the chance to depart peacefully. The killer knew this, having been informed of my uncle's strength and courage, and took this gambit at face value. But he declined, and my uncle cooked only enough slib for himself."

She considered it only a moment. "The killer feared being poisoned?"

Janosec shrugged. "Perhaps. Perhaps it was the rather unappetizing appearance of slib when uncooked–"

"Does it look better cooked?" she asked in honest inquiry, never having seen a slib before.

"Not really," he muttered in an aside, "It sort of…twists, writhes as it bakes. Or fries. Or broils, for that matter."

"You make it sound so pleasant."

"And then there is the smell–!"

"Please," she held up a hand, "Desist, if you would be so kind."

He paused, gathering the threads of his tale before taking it up again. "The assassin, of course, fancied himself the equal of an honest warrior, and so felt no fear or hesitation in approaching my poor, helpless uncle. He even went so far as to sheathe one of his own blades, since he stood between his victim–my uncle–and my uncle's own sword."

"He thought so little of Demlas Tarkas, then?"

Janosec snorted his contempt. "He was but an assassin, my lady. What could such a man know of honor, or insult. He was not even aware that he had walked blindly into my uncle's trap."

Mirani frowned. "A trap?" she asked, "That sounds less than honorable."

He shrugged. "So was the assassin. Stupid, as well. He asked his victim–" here Janosec affected a high, sneering tone "–'You actually eat these things?' To which my uncle replied–"

"'Of course not'," Mirani finished for him, her voice comically low, hollow, and deep in the throat, sure that Tarkas would have said nothing less than the truth.

"Ah, you know him so well," agreed Janosec, beginning to gasp a little, so he had a little trouble talking, "Then the assassin has the effrontery to ask him 'Then–then what do you do with–them?'" At this point, his self-control broke down, and he laughed so hard he could not tell any more of the story.

She, however, had enough imagination that she could guess how the story proceeded, and the humor of the story's last sentence brought a smile to her face, also. "He killed the man with it, of course."

"Of course," agreed Janosec, hiccupping slightly. He paused to swallow a few times before continuing, "I said he killed him with a fish, didn't I? Wrapped it around his throat and only the kicking remained. But it had to be cooked first. Raw slib stretches too much to do that, and nobody ever cooks it, so the killer didn't know."

She frowned suddenly at the inconsistency. "Then how did your uncle know?"

That brought him up short, and his face went blank again as he went over the dream again in his mind, searching for the detail that would make sense of it all. But in the end, he had to admit defeat. "How he knew it, I cannot tell you," he conceded, "Although he seemed pleased by all the twisting in the fire. But the best–"

"How could twist–? Sorry."

He completely overlooked the interruption. "The best part was the last thing he said to the man. He said, 'I would have killed you with my own hands, but I just washed them in the nice clean sea and would hate to get them dirty.'"

She laughed at the comment, so she must have known what seas were, and how clean they really weren't, even if she did not know what slib were. "A fine last line," she judged, clapping once. Then she looked up, and back. "Or is there more?"

Janosec was a little taken aback by her praise. Certainly the story he'd just told her was amusing, he'd found it so himself, but it was not his story, just a dream he'd recounted. He had no business taking credit for powers of invention that were not his, only for powers of storytelling that he didn't think were his either. "I know of no more," he said, determined to distance himself from the tale as thoroughly as he should. "No doubt there was more, but my recollection of the dream fails…"

She seemed relieved that she had not actually spoken too soon, and dismissed his modesty with a casual wave. "No matter," she stated firmly, "it ended well as it did."

She still seemed to think it a story he'd made up. "Of course, the *telling* of the tale needs a great deal of work before you will see even one copper in your bowl."

A copper in his bowl!? The outrageousness of the suggestion cut right through his pride, weakened as it was by undeserved praise, and he stopped in the middle of the path. "You think me some sort of wandering performer–?"

Not that he was wandering just then, and she disdained to respond over the distance increasing between them as she continued. Only when she felt his familiar presence at her back did she reply, "I have no doubt that you are a lord from a faraway land, this man you call uncle most likely no more than a bodyguard with a fortunate resemblance. You were spirited away by powerful, obscene, dark magics, and only managed to find yourselves here, rather than well beyond the Edge, due to the miraculous intervention of these gods of yours. Am I close?"

Uncomfortably so. "You forgot to mention the betrothed waiting in tears and the mother dying of a wasting disease."

She erupted into laughter, which swiftly gave way to coughs and choking gasps. "A true storyteller," she managed at last, "How could I have forgotten those."

"Probably spending too much time at weapons training," he offered, blandly.

She strove for, and achieved, an equally bland, "Probably." No need to encourage him, after all, and besides, he was almost certainly right.

The silence that fell satisfied them both, near total strangers with little in common except a high degree of respect for each others talents, and imperfectly matching goals. For Mirani this was a duty, self-imposed, but then, duties always are. In addition she was burdened with this NarDemlas, so ignorant in the ways of the world, but who might, with proper coaching, become something of an asset, especially in the more civilized areas they would soon be reaching.

Janosec's worries were more concrete, and numerous. A storyteller's bowl. A clanleader's son with a storyteller's bowl! But Uncle was quite right, a clanleader without a clan was no more than a target, or perhaps a hostage, and now they did not even have each other for guards. It would be to his advantage to not be one, then, and his pride could accept the role of storyteller much more easily than that of beggar. In addition, he had no coin, or a pouch to put it in, Mirani may or may not have had any, and he would not ask her. Directly. "The Eye. Is it far from here?"

Her answer was disheartening. "I do not know, never having been there."

"Then…you do not know how long it will take for us to arrive."

"No-o." The word was simple, the way she drawled it out less so.

"The ones who walk every year, are they told? How are they to live these days?"

"In accordance with the lore, of course," was the easy answer, the tossed off answer, but that only bought her time to think about the question. "They do need to eat and sleep, don't they."

"For eighteen days," he added. "I find myself doubting that they carry that much with them, at least not in goods."

"Nor in coin, even had the village been older and stronger than it was," she commented, inadvertently telling him what he wanted to know. "That would not have been in accordance with the lore, anyway. In 'The Betrayal and the Sorrow', they are told 'work shall be your lot, for the rest your days.'"

"So they will be expected to work their way," he concluded, a little dubious.

"A group working together for a short time can get enough for the group to survive," she noted, and finished her argument with, "Simplicity is ease, luxury is hardship.'"

Janosec noted the lore, as his various male relatives would have expected, but only for thinking about later. "Are two people a group?" He didn't have to wait for her negative reply, and sighed. "Perhaps you would be so kind as to tell me what the flaws were in my storytelling, then?"

Fenita awoke, neither rested nor refreshed, her bed a twisted mass of damp sheets. Her reasons for waking were the usual ones, raised to the point of pain by her strange lethargy, which prevented her from seeing to their demands at a lower point. Even the bizarre and unnaturally natural privy didn't disturb her as much as the surprise appearance of Life outside the door when she emerged.

"You slept poorly," the Goddess stated, a bare fact. "Come with me for food."

Fenita followed as Irolla led the way down some corridor, her interest reserved for the promised breakfast. It turned out to be the same room in which she had passed the night, and apparently much of the day, if the light didn't lie. A table just large enough for her meal had been placed before her bed, with a small chair. Fenita sat much more gracefully than she had the previous day, and fell to, reducing the tray's contents to mere scraps in unseemly haste.

Irolla waited until her guest had almost finished before she tried to speak. "I must apologize." To have a goddess express remorse was enough to interrupt the steady stream of food into mouth, and Fenita stared as Irolla continued. "What we are doing together is straining you terribly, but there is no more I can do to ease your part of the burden."

Fenita recalled yesterday's session, finding little straining about it, except the struggle not to fall asleep from boredom. "What burden?"

Irolla looked askance for a moment, just like a mortal woman would, who had something to say and doubted how to say it. Eventually she looked back. "Life…is not a child, to do as it is bid or asked. It just is. I take this thing called life and do things with it as you would use a cup, or a stick," she tried to explain. "Finding Janosec is not as easy as finding Tarkas, who is so different from you all, and there is nothing connecting him to you. I…use you, your body, looking for the other bodies in the world that are most like yours."

Fenita waited politely, but her hostess paused a bit too long. "And?"

"And…you are in some small way touching the world even as the world touches you. It…tires you, drains you, unduly."

Fenita stared with new appreciation at the empty tray before her, the windows with afternoon light shining into them. "I did not–feel it," she murmured, shocked and bewildered.

"You should not have," agreed Irolla, "It was a great part of my labors yesterday that you would not. But your mind and body know what was done, and your sleep suffered because of it. This time." She stared hard at Fenita, almost as if trying to will understanding into her. "It may get worse. It will not get better."

Fenita did not hesitate. "Is there any other course we can take, to find my son?"

Clearly Irolla did not want to speak. "No."

Fenita stood, far bolder in her ignorance than Irolla. "As the Spirits say, 'The necessary takes precedence over the possible'." She didn't pretend to be unafraid. "We will do what we must."

Tarkas awoke quite suddenly, to a stinging pain in his foot. At the same time, he jerked his foot up and his body forward, somehow in the back of his Hero's mind yet aware that he perched on a rock, so he did not fall as he had in his youth.

Something small, white, and obscenely wiggly had attached itself to his heel, a grub, swollen to grotesque size. Now it hung by large pincers as he held his foot up for inspection, pincers large enough that he could grip them and pry them from his foot with little difficulty. The squirming larva got a rock dropped on it unceremoniously, while Tarkas examined his foot for wounds, fearful that the bug had injected some kind of poison. Not that anything yet encountered had used anything so subtle as venom, but he trusted that observation about as much as he trusted anything in this bizarre realm.

It appeared that Heroic skin was more resistant to buggish mandibles than whatever covered its normal prey, so he quickly turned his attention to other things. Like the squirming line of icky white grubs crawling around in the dirt at the base of the rock on which he had slept. The track of wetness from the night before had long since dissipated, but his memory had no trouble remembering where it had been, or letting him know that the bugs squirmed along that very track.

For a moment he considered smashing them all simply because they were disgusting, because they would probably grow to replace the monstrosities he had spent the previous day slaughtering, but ultimately decided not to bother. They were no threat to him at the moment, nor would it really help. If spilled water prompted this spawning, be it urine or blood or whatever flowed in the other beasts, they had already left so much behind them that smashing this bunch would be too little too late. And would probably call up more, to boot.

Instead, he simply jumped from his rock at a different place and skirted the creatures entirely, Deffin trailing filially, completely uninterested in bugs for breakfast. Tarkas took a few sips of water to break his own fast, sure that something would offer itself as a meal before too long. The drink prompted his body to remind him of certain other basic needs, somewhat lower down, but he refrained for the time being. What with dodging around trees and possible combats, he might need to find his direction again fairly soon.

Chapter 11

"What?!"

The reaction was almost the one they expected. They had left the forest behind long before, in favor of more settled regions, and so they found settlers and settlements.

From the very start, they had met with a mixture of shock, fear, and bewilderment when they told the suitably abbreviated tale of their discoveries at the ruined village. For those closest to the area, most isolated and farthest from the help of their fellows, fear was by far the most prominent element, as they could and did expect. They spent a great deal of time reassuring anxious farmers that the danger, if any, either wasn't coming or had already passed them by. Probably wasn't coming, since the only person seen recently had been a lone traveler, an old scholar of some kind, who had reported the village intact just the day before.

From one village they had received directions to other villages, almost always harder to understand than to follow–knowing what a fork was, but not having any idea which one was marked by 'old Dinnas Flister's shed, fore it burnt down'–but in the direction they needed to go, even as sons were diverted from other tasks to send word in other directions. The wives at the cots expressed great sorrow, even as they pulled out grandsire's old sword and stone for one of the girls to sharpen as another went out the door. Of course they thanked the couple politely for their reassurances about the probable non-appearance of any threat, before curtly nodding at their daughters to continue whetting the blade. Not much was left from dinner, the midday meal, and supper would not be for a while, yet there were some breads and cold sausages available to help them on their way.

"You mean they aren't coming?"

To the town, where they encountered the first reaction other than shock, sorrow, and fear, namely anger. Neither of them could tell if it was directed at them or not, perhaps in their roles as the bearers of bad news. Although why the non-arrival of a bunch of Upwellers on their annual Walk should arouse such hostility they couldn't understand.

The unhappy person turned away without another word and stomped his way back into the building he'd come out of when they'd first arrived. Janosec and Mirani waited a bit, but no one came out again, so at least they *seemed* safe enough. Just a heartbeat or so before he would have gone himself, Mirani strode forward to see what, if anything, would result from the news they brought.

The door flew open and a man came out in a great hurry, startling her into falling backward into Janosec's broad chest, which was far better than the alternative. After the first man came another, then more, and the two retreated a little until the stream seemed to be over. Finally the door began to close, and then Janosec reached out and caught it again, so that they could enter.

It was a brewhouse, as he'd expected, although why so many men would be in it at this time of day puzzled him. There were only two now, the man who served the brews, now collecting cups–only cups–on a tray, and an old man in a corner, hands wrapped around something. Both watched him as he–they–entered, Mirani ducking only slightly to pass underneath his arm.

The server stared as she did, that Janosec was tall enough for her to do that. With their eyes blinded in the sudden dimness, neither of them noticed his slight pallor, or nervous twitch. But he gathered himself in no time at all, and asked with a certain amount of ease, "Serve you, sir? Lady?" as he set the tray down.

Mirani forestalled answering the question with one of her own "Those men who left–?"

He snorted and turned, bending to pick up his tray again "Farmers," he said, over his shoulder as he walked away, "Waiting for the Walkers, like usual." He carried it behind his bench and set it down carefully.

"Why?" asked Janosec.

"Chores," said the server, his arms in motion behind the counter, "Little ones, mostly. They need the work and there's always something to be done. Usually a good trade, but not this time, with them not coming."

"We know," said Janosec, letting the door swing shut behind them, sure that the man knew they knew. His voice sounded too flat for anything else.

"You the two they saw up the hill? They thought you was them, coming at last."

Mirani thought she detected a note of censure in his manner. "Sorry."

He snorted again. "Nothing to be sorry about, little girl. Not *your* fault. They would've left anyway, *some*one has to do them chores." He watched them a bit more carefully. "It true, what he said you said?"

Mirani nodded. "And more."

Janosec began the story yet again, prior tellings and Mirani's coaching having turned it into a quite creditable story, one that their last audience hadn't waited to hear. The counterman had nothing better to do, however, and seemed willing to hear every detail they decided to throw in, even when they were making them up. There seemed no point in confusing the issue by mentioning Tarkas and then having to explain why he wasn't there, so they improvised their way around those parts.

When he finally finished, the server said simply, "A fine tale. Sad, but fine, even those parts where I'm sure you were lying." He held up a hand against their protests. "No, no, I've yet to meet a teller who told all the God's truth. Probably be a boring story if he did." He put out two cups, and pumped them full. "You really taking their Walk for them?"

"Y-Yes," Mirani stammered, unexpectedly interested in the foaming dark brew below.

He placed the cups before them with practiced hands. "My gift. For your words, sir. And your honor, lady." Abruptly he smiled. "A joke. Words? Honor?" He didn't wait to hear their half-hearted pretences of amusement. Just as well.

They took their cups, gratefully, over to a table with chairs, wonderful chairs, and tried to see if their legs remembered how to sit. *Ahh, ooh.* And brew, too. Stout enough to be a meal itself, not that they needed one after all the farmhouses. The real value was in its 'restorative properties', all too welcome after the last nightmarish days. The world could shrink for a time, nothing more to think of than a good brew, a trusty comrade, and–

Thump!

Two sets of eyes automatically flew up, hands flying down to sling and knife, but it was only an old man. He stood on the far side of the table, hands still clasped around his mug in plain sight, shifting a little backward after stamping all his weight down on one foot like that. He waited patiently, until their wide eyes narrowed and their hands came away from their weapons, and said, "The NarMiskas greet you, in Fornet."

With much grunting and groaning, carefully stifled, of course, for politeness' sake, they forced themselves to their feet again and completed introductions. "I greet you, honored Zirtas, a name of much esteem in these parts," replied Fornet, once they had done him the honor of giving him their names, "But Demlas, I'm afraid, is unknown to me, and I consider myself a well-traveled man." He stomped forward and sat, as did they. He frowned at Janosec, as if his ignorance was somehow the young man's fault

For some reason Janosec felt moved to respond to the old man's unspoken accusation. "It is a new clan, sir, larger in numbers than in years," he said, stealing one of his uncle's turns of phrase.

"And largest in honor, surely," finished Fornet politely, "Yet surely it is not so far as to be unknown to me?"

Now Mirani turned to stare at him as well, but he could face them easily, over this question. "I do not know," he said, taking a restorative sip. "I was brought–"

"By a spirit of Fire, yes, I heard," interrupted the old man, grumbling, "Surely you know as well as I that such a claim is a standard one in the wilder tales. But the tellers of those tales are speaking of great heroes of antiquity, not themselves. Forgive me, but somehow I do not see in you the sort of heroism that would attract the notice of the spirits in such a grandiose way."

"You are forgiven, sir," replied Janosec easily. "I do not understand it mysel–"

"You mean that part of the story is *true?*" interjected Mirani. She had heard the story several times lately and had assumed it was the usual storyteller's device.

The old man chuckled. "So you were not there with him?" he noted, "That is one of the lies the server was sure you were telling? And even you did not believe his claim." For some reason this seemed to amuse him enormously.

"In all truth, sir," she started to say, and paused, thinking of Tarkas, and grunts, and beasts with stakes and paths that vanished. "In all truth, sir, I had not even considered the matter before this. But if he were to disappear now in a burst of flame I would consider that one of the more normal experiences I've had since I met him."

"When was that happy event?" inquired Fornet.

"I believe it was shortly after we met, sir," replied Janosec, not *quite* willing to be as rude as the newest member of their group. The old man turned his head to look at him, a slight smile upon his lips.

"If my curiosity seems excessive, that's because it was fed quite a rich and varied diet over the course of my life, young warri–storyteller," replied Fornet easily, not obviously bothered at effectively being called a busybody by some young warri–storyteller. "I'm afraid it has long since outgrown the bounds of this poor flesh, and I must make it do with a starvation diet of tales of those lands beyond my knowledge, when I can get them."

Both Janosec and Mirani burst out laughing, but she kept her silence as her companion spoke. "Then we are not only chance met, we are well met," he exclaimed, surprising her with both his sudden animation as well as his curious turns of phrase, "For I am descended from a long line of tellers of tales and keepers of that lore which is all that raises us above the level of the beasts of the field."

Mirani tried to match this impressive description with her own memories, and failed, perhaps because of the way he kept laughing at his own stories, no matter how often he repeated them in their lonely trek to civilization. This failure was all to the good, in its way, for her own reaction of surprise and interest was now genuine, and thus far more effective than a mere pretense.

"Tellers and keepers both, you say?" replied Fornet, playing the part of the skeptic so well that that she could not to tell if he played a part at all. "That sounds like a powerful joining, if the truth of the keeper does not overwhelm the fancy of the teller, or allow itself to be so overwhelmed." A sip from his cup emphasized his point, at least to his own satisfaction.

"A man of wisdom and vision you are, to be sure," answered Janosec heartily, so much so that Mirani wondered if another being lived within his skin. "For you have noticed in an instant the sword's edge on which I walk daily. Yet fear not, for it is broader than you suspect, when the power of truth is brought to bear. The certain tread of knowledge and experience makes even the sharpest edge a broad path for the honest walker."

The *thunk* of the old man's cup on the tabletop drew Mirani's eyes back to him as if she watched a child's game of bats. "Truly, sir, I do feel within me a stirring of hope once more," said Fornet with a broad grin on his face, and she realized that she *was* watching a game, although not bats. "Many have I met, who confuse a certain facility with words and imagery with the substance of which you speak, and think to satisfy me with vapors." A grimace accompanied his peevish, dispelling gesture. "I can only pray to whatever gods there are that the truth matches the promise you hold."

Now Janosec glanced her way, but it was not the sort of look she expected. He was not nervous, nor seeking reassurance from her. He wasn't looking especially triumphant, not that there had been a contest between them in any case. He merely seemed somehow satisfied that she was there, but she had never been used as any sort of touchstone before and so wasn't certain of that interpretation.

"I'm afraid you must be the judge of that, sir," he said, startling her from her thoughts. He spread his arms. "Allow me to begin with a small tale, one truly trivial, for your amusement. A tale of my uncle, the great Demlas Tarkas, and how he slew an assassin."

Fornet snorted in disdain at the choice of topic, disappointment plain upon his face. "He had a great sword, no doubt, laced with enchantments, eh?"

Janosec wasted no time in pretended considerations, to Mirani's unvoiced approval. "Indeed he did, sir, and still does," he replied, and took a sip of his rapidly dwindling supply of brew, "But it plays no part of this event, being out of his reach at the time."

The old man's face cleared somewhat, an eyebrow lifting at the remark. "Another might cheat, and substitute a knife, or a club, in the place of the sword, but I doubt that you would be so crass," he stated, either approving or warning. "Perhaps an enchantment of some sort, a spell–"

Janosec shook his head sadly. "I would be lying to you if I said there was. He had not even enough to give him warning." Mirani, remembering her own attempts to unravel the story untold, covered her smile with another sip from her own cup, only to discover that at some point she had drunk it to nothing.

Fornet looked over as she set it down on the table, his face a study in humor. He knew he was being set up to stand them to a round, and expected it from a teller as one of their usual ploys. But she wasn't the teller, and her cup really was empty. And the young man's, if his annoyed look down was honest. Apparently resigned, he signaled to the server. "Two cups of the mild, please." He handed the man some small coin. Then he turned a fierce eye on Janosec. "I admit you have aroused some little curiosity in me, sir," he said, grudgingly, "My knowledge of empty-handed combat is–"

But Janosec shook his head at even this small inquiry, forcing the old man's eyebrows higher still. "He was but an assassin, sir, the lowest form of man, if *man* he could be called. My uncle disdained even to touch him." Here he paused, for the server had returned with his cup, and Mirani's, and all three of them took a sip together. "Shall I begin?"

"Do, I beg you," implored Fornet, "I am greatly interested to hear how a man may slay without weapon, spell, or hand."

"Very well then," agreed Janosec, and he took a deep breath. "This is what happened…"

As it was his first public performance, Mirani found herself listening closely, in spite of the many dreary times she had heard the tale before. She was quickly rewarded, for some force seemed to have taken possession of her companion since their guest had arrived, Janosec's strange speech and manner during their chat erupting full-blown in the actual tale. She even found herself laughing with the others at his description of the assassin's clothes–"Black they were, black as night, black as the darkness of an Edge-borne demon's heart, when it's being very, *very* naughty"–although in her case it was more like choking, for she alone had dared to drink.

But Fornet seemed not to notice that his dampness, merely wiping the drops of sprayed brew off absently, caught up in the bizarre tale. She noted that for all the details and embellishments he wove into his telling, Janosec added no new dialog from what he had earlier recounted. Granted, he talked about it a great deal, how Tarkas felt about it, but his refusal to change it, even to improve it, made it feel more…solid to her. She wondered how it felt to the old man, with his claim of vast experience with tales.

When the tale ended she knew, for both the old man and the server, who had busily polished every table within earshot for some time now, laughed heartily at the tale's final joke. The server bustled off to the room behind the curtain, muttering, "The sea. Dirty," under his breath and chuckling anew each time, while the old man praised Janosec for a tale he hadn't heard before, a treasure beyond the mere pittances, which were all he had for a reward. Not that he didn't offer the younger man a coin, and not that Janosec didn't accept it.

But it was a silver, and the value of the coin overwhelmed the recipient's scruples about taking coin for a tale not of his own invention, and he insisted on offering the man another tale. This generosity earned him another pair of raised eyebrows, but the old man was not going to refuse the offer, although, "The light goes, the day goes, and I go as well, before the eaters and drinkers come to make any tale a trial. A short telling will be the best."

This gave Janosec some occasion to pause, for none of the tales he had prepared himself to tell were notably short, except…"I could perhaps amuse you with the tale of how my Uncle Tarkas had a hand in the creation of the most deadly, horrifying, fabulous beasts in the entire lifetime of the world." The magnitude of this announcement was disrupted, unfortunately, by the arrival of two bowls, filled with stew from the server's pot. With spoons. Payment for a story well told.

Fornet looked dubious. "That doesn't sound like a short subject."

Janosec shrugged. "That part of the event in which my uncle's contribution is so crucial, is rather small. But if you would rather I chose another…?" His eyes began to glaze over once more, although the smell of the stew might have had something to do with that.

The old man's iron grip dragged him back from his inner vista with great strength. "Be not so hasty, if it would please you," he admonished his host. "I merely fell prey to an entirely understandable doubt, forgetting in my haste that great events may sometimes follow the smallest of changes. So please continue. What are these fell beasts, of such ill omen as you would claim?"

"They are called–Dirkins."

The server rolled his eyes and wandered away, while Fornet's cup hit the table with a thud. "They need a better name than that, son."

Janosec spread his hands apologetically. "I only tell what happened, and that is what they were called."

Fornet only snorted, while Mirani asked, "By who?" For not even she had heard this tale before.

The young teller's mouth flapped on silently as his eyes glazed over again. She had time to take a small taste of her stew before her comrade replied, "The one who made them, a sorceress of great power and ill intent."

"Before or after your uncle's intervention?" she queried.

He jerked, as if woken from sleep, and spooned up some stew. "Oh, before, of course. There wasn't much left of her to be naming anything, after." He stuck the spoon in his mouth.

Now the old man asked, "And did your uncle give them a new name, himself?"

At that Janosec brightened, and swallowed hurriedly. "No, he didn't. So I guess that means I can give them a new name, doesn't it?!"

"Later, if you please, young Demlas," suggested Fornet, after a glance at the light. Without further ado, Janosec began his tale, his words and images not quite so powerful as before, yet the strength of the experience resonating in every word. Unfortunately. Fornet left the room shortly after, still howling. "Squish, ha, ha, ha," he roared. "Gods! Burned his foot!"

Mirani watched him go, grateful for the silver piece, regretful that the coming dark cost them any more. But he left laughing, an excellent first performance for her com–Janosec slumped backwards, spoon falling from limp fingers, only prevented from toppling to the floor by the presence of the wall at his back. "Janosec!" she called, concerned, her own spoon falling to the table as she leapt to keep him from falling sideways. "God's Within, what ails you?"

"*Ummph*," he said, his posture forcing his mouth shut, not that he had anything coherent to say at the moment. His shoulders worked, he trembled, he finally sat forward, just barely bracing himself upright with his arms before inserting his face into his bowl of stew. "Feel terr'ble," he added, unnecessarily.

But he was at least marginally upright, and Mirani was reluctant to push her assistance on him more than he needed. She moved away slowly, and sat, not eating until he did, but not trying to keep up with his ravenous scrapings. Whatever force had possessed him all during his telling had left him empty and weak, she realized, or perhaps it was simply two brews without much food under them. When he finished his she switched her barely touched bowl with the one under his face, and he continued without pause while she went back for a smaller portion for herself.

And returned, unhappy. She had hoped, expected, that the silver piece would carry through the next few days, if they ate sparingly. It had not occurred to her that storytelling would be such hard work, yet he was eating like five woodcutters born. And prices were higher than she remembered. At least now he ate more slowly, not like a starved targ, she observed, and she matched him as best she could so they both finished together.

With a weary, grunting sort of sigh, he pushed himself back up into a normal human sitting posture, to find her already waiting there for him. "That was…strange," she said mildly.

"Urgh," he replied, his once-mobile tongue limp with fatigue, his voice a monotone buzz in its lowest register. She tried again, but met with an equal lack of success. Apparently his first exercise as a storyteller had left him wordless.

The server watched them covertly, but they did little beyond sit there. It wasn't a busy part of the day, although it soon would be, and he was rather kindly disposed to them, so he merely requested that they perhaps give him some custom, rather than suggest that they find lodgings in an establishment more suited to the purpose. The woman held up a finger, then added a second, and he poured two more for them, of the mild, and went back to polishing what was already clean. A peaceful time, for all concerned.

Naturally it couldn't last. At first the server thought the noises from the front meant his regular patrons were arriving, but when he turned and looked he found a small group of youths had invaded his establishment. He should have known it from the noise they'd made, but at least he knew what his immediate future had in store for him. Nor was he disappointed.

"Server!" the leader practically yelled, "A round for me and mine!" An expansive swing of his arm, as if the older man couldn't see what he claimed as his. His other hand, meanwhile, dropped a silver onto the counter, where it settled itself with a proper and true ring.

The server nudged it back towards its owner. "Water costs little enough, Dragel," he pointed out to the smirking young man, "I'll charge it towards your sire when I see him in, oh, a quarter hour or so."

But the implied threat didn't move the leader, except forward, to answer this challenge in front of those that were his. "My sire is still hard at his labors, server, as you well know," he responded impudently, "Or should. With no Walkers coming there's no end of little tasks he finds himself doing."

The server snorted his contempt. "No doubt because he couldn't find *you*, at all."

Dragel shrugged arrogantly. "He released me. It's not my fault if the Walkers decided not to come this time." He pointed to the coin. "We're all the custom you'll get for some time, I ima…gine…" He slowed to a halt as a shadow fell over him. It fell over the counter, and over the two friends nearest him on either side. He turned, looking up. And then up more.

Janosec loomed over him, tall, grim, and silent. He was good at that. "The first rule of wisdom," he intoned solemnly, his voice soft and low, "is silence." He placed a hand companionably on Dragel's rounded shoulder. "The second rule," he began, squeezing just enough, "Is respect." His hand fell from Dragel's shoulder to the head of the axe, still at his hip. "Those about whom you are speaking, who do not come today or any other, are not present, and never will be again. They deserve your silence, if respect is beyond you."

Silence echoed throughout the brewhouse. Dragel's mouth worked, but his voice didn't seem to, or those of his erstwhile followers either. Janosec also became quite silent, and quite still, but only Mirani recognized it for what it was. "My lord," she broke in, gripping her frozen comrade's arm tightly, "You are distraught." He allowed himself to be led away. The cringing youths fled, Dragel in the rear for once.

A little later, the server came up, as Janosec practiced the first rule. "Your victory, 'my lord'," he said, placing Dragel's abandoned coin before his guest.

Janosec had a use for the coin, but he didn't want the coin, didn't even like the coin. Yet Fornet's coin was already sorely reduced, and storytellers couldn't afford to be picky. "Take it," he commanded. "Hold onto it. When someone else is in need, I will pay for them." The server looked shocked, and almost didn't do as he was bid. But eventually his hand remembered how to function and the coin left the table.

Mirani contained herself until the coin had vanished back behind the bar. "Well done, lordling," she snapped. "I hope your honor keeps you full and warm tonight in the ditch we'll be sleeping in." She almost threw back the remainder of her brew but decided not to. Who knew how long it would have to last, until the next one?

The deed accomplished, Janosec began to feel qualms about the wisdom of his act. "It was the right thing to do," he said, but not forcefully. He was supposed to be a storyteller, get them to Querd and wherever she walked to, get his uncle, get home. Somehow. Weren't they the right things to do, too? Was it proper to sacrifice them? *Perhaps* sacrifice them? Just because this right thing was here and now and those other right things were there and then? If they ever came to be? Maybe mere rightness wasn't enough.

Or maybe it was. Mirani sighed. "I know," she said wistfully, then decided she didn't like the sensation. Instead she reminded herself that a silver wouldn't buy *that* much stew, no matter how hungry she suddenly felt. The sound of approaching footsteps caught her attention, drawing her from her unhappy contemplations.

"Teller," said the server, as he walked over to them yet again, "My lord, I have a proposition for you."

"Tell me about your son," the goddess directed suddenly. Her hands were centered once again on Fenita's belly, the work to be done much easier now that she had had some practice in the doing of it.

–Her last sight of him, standing with the father who could not be his father, owning him anyway with a clasped hand. A small 'eep!' of dismay had escaped her throat but failed at her tongue. And then the flame–

Fenita was startled no little amount. "Why do you ask?" The *Surely you know all, being a goddess* remained unspoken, yet plainly evident to her inquisitor.

–so busy, he has to be ready, he is *ready, he has to look ready and perfect, the whole city will see him today as he takes his place–*

Irolla considered the question soberly, on both of its levels of meaning. The secret aspect had no clear answer–why *had* she asked the question? She hadn't meant to–but she left it to ponder in the background of her thoughts while she addressed the question her guest had actually asked. "There is neither need or desire for us to so closely monitor your doings as you think," she said, in her slightly pompous *I am a goddess* voice, "At this time I dare not, for your sake. But speaking of him will ease your heart, perhaps, and strengthen those thoughts and feelings I can use to conduct my search, along with your physical self." All of which, she realized with a start, was true. How odd; glibness wasn't her forte. Nor did any of those reasons have anything to do with why she had really asked.

–swaddling clothes–

Fenita hesitated, the sudden sensation of being on the floor leaving her strangely speechless.

–first steps, jumping from stairs–

It was not as if she hadn't been on it before, but those times had been to present family issues for action, or the examination some nights before, after the beast's attack.

–that damned dak!–

But not as some kind of…performer.

–that horrible time when he broke the little girl's nose by accident, unaware of his own strength. No boy should have to learn that much control so soon. The fear that they had succeeded too well, as he turned to the lore and away from the active life for which he was so admirably suited–

And to describe Janosec! Where to start, how to proceed?

–the man who bounced off him at a collision in the street, and Janosec helped him up, absentmindedly pondering some question of the lore–

What an impossible task, to reduce a life to a few sentences.

–the first time he had to kill, and she consoled him–

"Ah! That's very good," said Life enthusiastically.

What? "What?"

"Your sense of him," Irolla explained, "It's very strong."

I am his mother.

Tarkas sat on the bole of a large fallen tree, stumped.

Something was under him, under the tree, under the ground itself, waiting. Clever enough to wait until he had entered this cleared area, and sat down to rest in the one place he'd seen where he could sit off of the ground. At least the blood had stopped flowing, from the gouges where the creature had tried to grab him and pull him down. Only his lightning reflexes and Deffin's support had saved him there.

From that time they had been in something of a standoff, since the creature below had made a similar grab for Deffin himself. The faithful nizarik had not managed to pull the creature out of the ground, although it had been a close thing. It required no special brilliance to know that the creature would simply wait below until they grew weak enough to conquer.

His options were limited. There were no trees nearby to swing from, probably because the roots would interfere with its movement. Or perhaps it had simply discovered the place, found it to be a useful lair, and settled in. The more he thought about it the more he believed that notion; it didn't look unnatural, the way the wezin's lair had so long ago. He had no great hope that another victim would come along, to distract this creature, or mask his own escape. These hell-beasts had not yet attacked in tandem and he saw no reason for them to start now.

His only real chance lay in the plan he'd been following for the last few hours, to sit there and wait until the creature moved in closer to where he sat. The encounter with Deffin's claws had apparently scared it off, sending it circling about their refuge from an unbridgeable distance. But Deffin had gone to sleep, and he himself had been unmoving for some time, his eyes watching, his mind wandering, musing for no particular reason about dirkins, and how stupid the name sounded now, given what they were growing into. For a while he sat, grateful for the opportunity to rest, throwing little bits of wood into the loose dirt surrounding them. But the thing seemed to be resting, not reacting to his little provocations, as the ground had ceased to ripple in any noticeable way.

He stirred, bringing himself up with smooth grace, rolling forward onto his feet with a minimum of noise. His hand moved up to his sword's hilt, drawing to the beat of his own footsteps on the wood, Deffin stirring at the faint sound. Ah, there it was! One of his little sticks, planted in the ground over the course of several hours, moved and fell, its feeble implantation disrupted by the passage of the creature beneath. It approached slowly, waiting to pounce–sort of–on the foolish prey trying so quietly to escape.

Except that the prey was not trying to escape but to attack, as soon as the enemy came within range. Deffin reared up as Tarkas leapt, his sword pointed down with all of his Heroic mass above it, his left hand clenched with all of its unliving strength. The sword plunged into the ground, burying itself almost up the hilt, and the creature screamed–an underground monster sort of scream–as he stabbed it in the back. It jerked into furious motion, its squeal of pain sounding like the rending of metal. The hilt pulled along with it, and only his numb hand kept its grip, dragging him along as the beast fled. Deffin pursued as his littermate moved away. The creature was forced by its own nature to move in a nearly straight line, approaching the edge of its clearing at great speed.

Which was the point. The creature used the clearing as a trap, but it had also trapped itself, unable to move freely beyond its bounds. It had to turn before the trees, and the Hero awaited that proper moment, before rolling away, into the trees and the safety of their deep roots. Deffin nearly stayed behind, but the creature's fluids were foul, the stench of them in no way like challenge. But they were liquids, feeding into the dry soil, bringing out of it such life as was possible.

The pair left, quite willing to let the inevitable grubs and the creature determine the proper ownership of the clearing without them.

Chapter 12

Which came first, the kicking or the nag? Janosec would never know, for the sharp impact of her foot into his leg was as nearly simultaneous with her cry of "Up, Demlas!" as makes no difference, far too little for his sleep-clouded mind to discern. Fortunately he had neither the hair-trigger reflexes to slay her where she stood nor had he seen much value in developing any, so she left able to walk away to the privy as he fumbled his way out of the hay in the loft where the server had let them spend the night.

Hmm, yes, the server. Wouldn't do to let the man encounter Mirani first thing in the morning, or even the second. That could easily cost them the breakfast he'd promised them in the arrangement they'd made the night before. If they hadn't already lost it; he couldn't recall doing anything at all last night to 'keep a friendly tone about the place', as he'd been requested to do. The people seemed friendly enough already, and somehow he'd gotten it into his head to make a better name for the dirkins.

Not that he'd been able to do that, though. Fabrications of that sort were just beyond him. Yet the effort had left him quite oblivious; a duel could have been fought in his lap and he'd have missed it, most likely. But he could have told quite a pleasant tale when it was done. Not like the bugs and wugglies he'd thought of last night, surely, those were much more standard Hero-fodder. Maybe he should try to dream of a name.

Oh, dung beetles. It had happened again. Like a stupid field beast, he'd been ruminating over yesterday's thoughts while his treacherous feet had carried him to the door of the brewhouse. For the best, probably, get the embarrassment over with. The door creaked. "Server Marlik?"

The noises came first, naturally, sounds from the back rooms where someone worked at or on something. He'd done his share of kitchen duty as a child and knew something of what had to be done to prepare for the day, although perhaps it was different in a business place like this. Then the door in the back opened and Marlik's wife came out. Oh, of course, he'd been up all night serving the brews, but the kitchen had closed earlier in the evening. Naturally it would be she who got up first.

"Janosec, is it?" she asked, wiping her hands on a towel at her waist. She held out her empty hand. "We were not introduced last night, I know, but Marlik told me much."

Janosec froze, his own hand partly extended. His own training as a youth had included cautions against speaking of people who were not present, and so could not defend themselves from defamation at his hands. Clanleaders in the old days had fought duels over such acts, although not lately.

"Oh now," she laughed, reaching forward to grab the unmoving hand, "He said nothing ill! With the Walkers not coming and them being put to so many sudden chores I'm sure they all must have been no little bit put out. I merely asked him why so many ate and so few fought!" She rested a hand lightly on his arm and peered myopically into his face with a smile.

For a second he was again struck mute, this time by the minor intimacy of her touch, but she looked too much like his NarTolgas aunts for him to be offended. *Not a lord's son,* he reminded himself, belatedly, and then it was all right again. He smiled. "And he said–?"

She laughed as she used her grip to maneuver him farther into the room. "He said that they didn't dare, there was this fierce-looking young warrior in the corner, disguised as a teller of tales! Well, I'm sure you know his humor by now, so I didn't believe a word of it, naturally, but I snuck a peek through the door and I must say…"

Janosec allowed himself to be shepherded, her rambling discourse not allowing him to get a word in edgewise, but it didn't look as if she needed any help to have a conversation. He merely inserted the appropriate 'hmm', 'really', or 'of course' as the context demanded, comments which degenerated into mumbles as he started sticking great quantities of breakfast into his mouth.

"–nice to see a fine young appetite, you know, Mar and I had no kilder of our own so we sort of adopted everyone else's and no one can eat like kilder, surely the Eye's seen that often enough, although with prices the way they are–"

Mirani came in after a bit and had her share as well, the continuing monolog not allowing any morning-tainted unpleasantness to join them at the table.

"–really wish you both could stay with us longer, although I certainly understand about your Walk, but still you both need feeding up, and of course those traveling leathers need looking after as well, and your hair, you have such beautiful hair–"

Mirani endured the woman's hands stroking her head with ill grace, concealed by the chewing. But when the woman started grabbing at her hand, talking about her callouses, she rudely pulled it away, masking the intent somewhat by reaching for a nearby spice shaker. Which was empty.

"–you want some spindles, dear, I'm afraid we just ran out, yesterday it was, that old man used up the last ones, never would have thought him the type, a learned man like that, it's usually you big husky types eat them down to the ground and–"

Suddenly Janosec choked, spraying half-eaten food all over the clean surface. He gasped for air, ignoring the concerned looks and overtures of the ladies blessing his existence. Finally he could speak. "Old man? A scholar?"

"Oh, yes a very–well, not a *nice* old man," the hostess started up again, wiping the table with her ever-present towel to cover the residual embarrassment, speaking ill of him behind his back. She got over it. "Came from over-hill, just like you, not–" she paused, flicking her fingers "–just the day before you, in the morning though, walked right in, didn't even give his name, and ordered zuffla with toast, plain as day, as if anybody's had zuffla for, oh, I don't know how many–"

Janosec stood up, and she stared at him in shocked silence. There was still a slice of sellit-pie on his plate! "We must go," he said, apologetically. Mirani made a questioning sound. "We need to speak with that old man," he said, trying not to be too specific. She didn't seem to get it. "He went to Querd?" he asked the hostess, a brief diversion. The lady, for once, only mumbled something affirmative and pointed. He turned back to his partner at crime. "You know," he reminded her, "The one who left the village just before we did?"

That she understood. She forced a swallow and shoveled the remainder in as fast as she could, while he picked up his slice of pie and crammed the whole thing into his mouth. He couldn't speak his thanks anymore, but his hand moved in the classic pattern, and her hand responded absently, not nearly as talkative. Only after they had gathered their things and left did she recall the meaning of the sign, and her reply. She would spend the rest of the morning congratulating herself.

"I would understand your thoughts, Demlas," requested Mirani. She picked a good time to do so, after they had finally extricated themselves from the usual morning crush of traders coming in and traders going out, caravans, convoys, excited daks and small children, local guards trying to look obviously inconspicuous, messengers, bakers and sellers of all sorts, the stuff of a town waking up for a new day of life. It was also a perfect opportunity for someone evil-minded enough to kill a village to stage an attack on those pursuing him, as they navigated the crowds towards the road to Querd. Had either of them been experienced guards or pursuers, they would have been looking for that and quite a bit more besides, and probably gotten themselves arrested for suspicious behavior. This way they were just two more walkers trying not to get crushed under large hooves and heavy wagons as they made their way to wherever they were going.

"I would understand them myself," he responded normally, the noise and jostle a better cover than privacy and whispering would have been. "They seemed so clear to me, in there. 'How many old wandering scholars could there be?' I thought, 'Moving faster than we were? In the same direction.'" He paused, taking the passage of a cart as a good opportunity to gather his scattered thoughts.

"I don't recall seeing many scholars back home," supplied Mirani, waiting for him to continue, "Of any age. And certainly not wandering ones. They were usually going somewhere."

"Very much what I thought," agreed Janosec, whose knowledge of scholars was limited to his sire and grandsire, but whose knowledge of the difference between wandering and traveling was great and getting greater. "This person has been called a wandering scholar by two people very far apart, so something about him must give them that impression." *Yuck, don't step in* that.

"His clothing?" she suggested, staring at the passers-by. The feel of his hand, impacting her arm, drew her attention back to her immediate surroundings, and she took a step to the side as well.

He stared at the people for a moment as well. "Perhaps," he agreed dubiously, looking back to take in her appearance. Certainly she, and therefore he, looked like she had been wandering in the wilds. "It could also have been his manner."

Mirani was as doubtful of that as he was. "They are going somewhere," she said, looking at the backs of a group they had somehow fallen in behind, as they rapidly closed the distance. "They walk with purpose. And this old man had a purpose, at least yesterday."

Janosec considered that in silence, as they overtook that group and moved out before them. "How bad, how unkempt, must he look?" he mused aloud.

She had not given any thought to the matter. "Why do you ask?"

He gestured at themselves. "We pursue, with speed," he noted, puffing a little from it, "He is pursued, and draws away from us. How bad must he look, that they can see him walk and still think him a wanderer?"

Suddenly she laughed. "Perhaps we may track him by his smell."

He gusted out a small chuckle in return, but their haste robbed him of breath to reply. It was too much to maintain, really, even more so for Mirani, and they settled to a much slower, more maintainable speed before too long. Slow by his standards, anyway; in a straight march his long legs had a decided advantage. They were now, too, in a different way. Since the pace was no strain on him, he had wind enough to talk, which meant he could tell tales.

He told them, short tales, long tales, epic tales, comic tales. Not all were suitable for an audience, of course, being neither uplifting nor wholesome, but with her assistance he refined those he could tell into a form worthy of the feat. "Are all of your tales about your uncle?" she asked eventually.

He looked away at the question, finding the vista, flat lands bounded by the dark tangled masses of trees in the distance, oddly fascinating. "He has been much on my mind lately."

"And mine," she admitted. "You realize that, if we pursue the villain, then–"

"Then my uncle has been trapped," he concluded, miserable at the thought, "I would that you had been wrong."

"And I. I only hope–pray–that these tales of yours are a sign. A sign that he still lives. Why else would you dream of him so much?"

He shrugged. It had not seemed odd to him that he should dream so vividly of such a character as the Savior of Querdishan. "Perhaps it *is* a sign," he agreed, trying to force a brighter mood upon them, "A sign that the gods want me to tell tales, by making me dream of the greatest possible hero for them."

Nor was she averse to a change of topic herself. "You'll need more than that."

"What!?" Janosec was scandalized by this…treason.

"It's not that I mind," she hastened to assure him, "For I know your uncle and can well believe all the incredible claims you make for him. But the others may not, and truly, a little variety is sometimes welcome."

"He has variety!" exclaimed Janosec.

"I know that well," agreed Mirani, the mere thought of the tale of the Seven Virgins bringing a renewed blush to her face. "I meant a little variety of characters. Do you have no tales of others doing remarkable things?"

Now he began to panic, for he knew his tales were a sham, even if she did not. "I don't know what you mean by remarkable," he stalled.

Her answer, no doubt a long and detailed statement outlining the concept, was cut off before it had truly begun. Someone was whimpering, someone high-pitched and barely audible over the wind blowing over the grass, saying "Ow, ow" in a repetitive, almost ritualistic fashion. He looked at her, she looked at him. Together they looked over to the place from which the sounds came and strode through the tall grass towards it, weapons at the ready in case it was a ploy.

But no. It was what it sounded like, a child, crying with the pain of her blistered feet, sitting on a rock as a woman collected water or something from a stream a little way off. She was completely invisible from the road, even from two paces away, in a hollow with a smokeless fire nearby, a small pan steaming. They approached only enough to see her, and stopped, lest they either scare the girl or provoke an attack from some unseen defender. "Hello," said Mirani. She wanted to ask if she was all right, but obviously she was not, which left the warrior-woman with nothing else to say.

The girl suffered no such lack. "Mommy!"

Mommy came charging up the hill, knife in one gloved hand and a blob dripping water in the other. No one moved as she examined her uninvited guests. "What do you want?"

"To help, if we could," replied Janosec, easily. "We heard her crying from the road." He pointed back the way they came, but of course the road was equally invisible from where they now stood. The world was empty grass and trees, not even the wind seemed to be stirring anymore.

The woman looked down at the child, who looked down at her sore feet. "I told you to be quiet." Sensible; their chief defense would lay in being unnoticed.

"Sorry," the girl whispered.

"You would've been," suggested the woman coldly, eyeing them with equal frost. Then she relented. "But these two don't seem like bandits." She put her knife away decisively. "God's Within, if you're gonna be here at all, at least come on down so they can't see you from the next town."

The hastened to step down into the little pit, especially Janosec. "We have herbs–" he began, fumbling with the large duffel.

She eyed the bag doubtfully. "Thank you, but no. I have fresher right here," and she held up her damp bag. "Most of the ones I need are common enough." With that, she sat by the fire and took some of the herbs from the bag, tearing the leaves into little pieces and dropping them into the hot water.

Mirani watched her preparations with interest. "Isn't that scratchweed?"

The woman grunted an affirmative. "That's why I boil it," she explained absently, as if hearing the doubt in the younger woman's mind. "The juices get the skin healing faster if they're weak enough. Drain the sores with those–" she pointed to the untouched stalks "–soak the feet with a cloth soaked in that–" pointing at the brewing leaves "–and she'll be good as new by tomorrow."

"It'll hurt," the girl pouted.

"Yes it will," the woman agreed pitilessly, "And next time you might think to tell me your sandal's undone, eh?"

Exactly what his mother would have said. The only reason she hadn't ever actually said such a thing was because none of her children had ever gone on journeys so long as to raise blisters until after they had learned to do up their own sandals. That reminded him…"Don't you know how to do your own laces?" he asked the girl curiously.

Mutely she shook her head. The mother was more expressive. "Not for lack of trying."

He nodded sadly, silent commiseration. "I once knew a little boy, with the same problem." Her face came up again, even though she still wasn't talking.

"No, it wasn't me," he chided, reading her eyes, "I was the one showed him how to do it right. Can you show me how you do it?" Slowly, the girl went through the motions, lacing up the sandal on her good foot. Janosec watched carefully, and instantly spotted her error. Fortunately her mother's attention was on her poultice preparations, since she really should have spotted the problem herself, and he didn't want to seem to be slighting her. But he merely pointed out the flaw, and suggested a simpler way of doing the same task that she grasped immediately.

"I'm glad to help," he told her as she smiled up at him, one lace tied, however loosely. "You remind me of my sister," he added a trifle wistfully.

"I do?"

He smiled. "Oh, yes. I have a lot of sisters, too, but Denora's the most…"

"The most what?"

"I don't know," he gestured vaguely, "Smart. Fun. Clever, maybe. She was always doing something. Most of the time it was something naughty, but it was a smart, fun, clever sort of naughty, so it was hard to get *too* mad. I remember this one time, I was talking to my mother, and she just looked up, and my father looked up, and they said something adults say a lot and he left real fast. Mom looked at me and said 'Your sister's in the kitchen spreading salt all over the floor.' A few minutes later Father came back and said it was Denora, taking salt from a crock and making designs all over the kitchen floor."

She looked up at him, eyes wide. "How did she know it was salt?"

He gestured extravagantly, playing up to his audience. His voice changed, stretching out syllables with special emphasis. "I don't know, maybe it's some special parent magic. You know," he lowered his voice, practically whispering conspiratorially, "Adults can even see behind them."

She leaned in close, and whispered back, "Yeah, I know."

"I heard that," her mother said loudly, filling in Janosec's tale with perfect timing.

Teller and audience shared 'that look' together, and giggled their way into the next in a series of tales about Denora and her doings, the little girl so entranced that she barely noticed as the steaming pad was applied. Janosec, somewhat fatigued, kept her company as mother and Mirani took the pan to the little creek, to wash out the taint of scratchweed juice. They came back with a full pan of water and a mipsi–not alive–product of Mirani's skill with her sling. The woman politely invited them to share and they as politely declined. The food was small, the water cold, and their quarry no closer, so they took their leave as quickly as possible.

"Now *that* was remarkable," commented Mirani, as soon as they were out of earshot.

"True," he replied absently, not following her reference to their talk prior to the meeting. Before she could chastise him for his apparent rudeness, he continued, "A mother and her daughter, traveling alone. No food, no goods–"

"No shelter," she continued, her mind resuming its accustomed functioning as well, "Yet they could not possibly have left the town behind us just this morning. A daughter who blisters easily. Only a knife."

Janosec turned around in his tracks, his feet planted while he reversed himself on them. "Waiting for us." The timing of the event had become suspicious in his mind. "Very remarkable indeed." The grass clearly showed the way they had walked as he went back over it. Even in those places where it had not been growing before.

They were gone, of course. No fire burned, no fire had ever burned. Only the stone was the same, that and the little creek, and the grass grew close up to both. Mirani raised a hand, three fingers extended, and made a circle over her breast. "God's Within!"

A moment later, a trembling Janosec got his once-mobile mouth working again. "Yeah."

This was not a tale to be told in public.

Not that they needed to, the public seemed quite pleased with his more traditional, non-occult offerings, in the town they came to that night and also the night after. Like Fornet, the people were eager for new stories, even strange stories, just not *too* new or strange. Janosec told many tales those days, some of them repeatedly, developing in him a capacity for judging which tales were popular and why.

But without Mirani it would all have come to very little, for Janosec was a lord's son, no matter what he seemed, and he had little grasp of the value of coin, beyond that of having some instead of none. It was she who arranged their board, bought their supplies, criticized his tales in private, and suggested some in public when the audience faltered. She who roused him in the morning, never bruising the same spot twice. She who inquired about their quarry–discreetly–and told the tale of death left behind, the only tale he did not tell. It occurred to Janosec, to wonder why she stayed with him. She seemed so capable on her own and surely the coin he brought in was not such a great thing.

Until he saw the way men's eyes followed her, shying away whenever she drew near him. To confirm this, and, it must be admitted, for his own amusement, he took her hand the next time she brought him a brew and brushed a light kiss across it, his eyes half on her and half on them. It was hard to say who flinched more, but he had a grip on her hand and hers did not show. She leaned in close. "Bastard," she whispered lovingly. "Thank you."

"Perhaps later," he replied, knowing his lips could be watched. They both laughed, and nobody bothered her that night, least of all Janosec, who preferred the various parts of his body just where they were.

Querd, when they got there, took Janosec by surprise. He had assumed that anything called a city would have a wall around it, and of course a tower for the temple of Air. But as they approached, the rather low towers rose above the horizon without fanfare, the sounds that such a temple would make.

Even had they been there, it's doubtful he could or would have heard them. The roads had changed lately, more of them, wider. The foot traffic was great, but the paving indicated something more damaging to roads than mere feet, wagon wheels, perhaps, or shod animal feet, although there were none of those to be seen. The Walk neared its end, or *an* end. Many Walkers from many villages were coming together with the roads, and they used no rides or vehicles. With them came names, villagers identifying their homes to others, with names that meant nothing to Janosec.

But Mirani held the names of the dead village and its children, and they spread with the tale, jubilation giving way to grief and shock. Details were sought, and Janosec found himself giving some, grisly no matter how he tried to soften the tale. It seemed never to end, new faces replacing the old, only the questions the same. At some point they must have passed over some invisible border into the city proper, but he missed it, only noticing the closer quarters, higher walls, and strange echoes long after they had entered.

The Walk was expected, naturally, quartering for the pilgrims already arranged and ready, with city officials in place to direct them. Janosec and Mirani were swiftly strained from this flowing stream of people, washing up in the office of a minor functionary who rather quickly determined that this wasn't within his jurisdiction. In fact it belonged to a wholly different office. Yes, that was it. Send them to the palace.

Off they went, as fast as an honor guard could be collected.

Technically speaking, the city of Querd is supposed to be a republic, governed by the heads of the families for the good of all. In fact, most of the families had little real wealth. Some of those that did had even less interest in the tedious details of governance, a sordid business with little to recommend it in their eyes. Thus power had devolved, as it usually does, upon that small group of people who had a passion to match their influence.

Which meant that Mirani and her comrade did not have to continue telling the story to anonymous hordes, or career-minded officials, or uncaring plutocrats, but rather to a select few, whose interests may have held innumerable facets but at least was interest. The ruling council held five members, older men and women whose wooden expressions revealed nothing, at least not to outsiders. Perhaps not to each other, either, thought Janosec, comparing this lot to the elders of Querdishan. It didn't seem natural, that people who worked so closely together should be so closed to each other.

His tale, in all its glory, waited ready in his mind, as he waited for the council to gather, for messages to be passed, initial conclusions drawn and questions formulated. It's what his father and the others had done, during those rare occasions in the later part of his minority when they had to meet. The appearance of control, his sire had called it. They had to seem aware of, and ahead of, events, to reassure those watching. But this meeting was private, he noticed, with only the lords, themselves, and one scribe in the corner. Even the person who led them into the room, giving their names formally, left immediately upon doing her duty.

The five sitting at the table were ranged equally, none advanced over the others, yet Janosec turned his attention to the man in the middle, a natural position for the leader of an odd number of persons. "We have become aware," that person said gravely, "Of certain ill events in the Outmarches, of a village destroyed from within, in its entirety." He paused there, looking blandly at Janosec, who stared blandly back.

"This event is beyond our jurisdiction," the leader declared calmly, sending a small chill into Janosec's belly. They had come to Querd as part of Mirani's Walk, not as part of their pursuit. "We are therefore wondering about your presence within our city, and indeed, within this very chamber, on what should be a day of celebration."

Janosec paused to consider his words, aware that some or all of these people might have a grudge to bear, if he had pulled them from their revels. Not that this man seemed to care one way or the other. "We are here," he said at last, "Because your men from the streets sent us here." Which was true, as far as it went.

Which was not very far. "You temporize, young man," the councilman pointed out. "Either you had a reason for appearing in our streets or you did not. You have come *here*, we wish to know *why* you have come here. There are many possible reasons why and while none of them bode well for us, some are less ill than others. We will not ask again."

It was a more even-handed approach than Janosec had expected. It solidified the logic of the story in his mind, giving him a format in which to present his explanation. "If you will allow me, I will tell the tale of it, as it happened."

"Tales!" broke in another on the council, second, on the right. "I did not come away from my sacred duties to be entertained with fancies!"

Well, that's two. Janosec turned his head to address the man directly. "I do not spin fancies, sir," he stated, as if speaking to Navak, also full of bluster, "I am Demlas Janosec, son of tellers and keepers of lore, and I do not waste my time with anything less than what is true. Nor is it my purpose to entertain, not with this tale."

"I would think not," said the leader, easily resuming control of the meeting. "Page." He did not yell, but the force of his voice washed over Janosec and the whole room, through the back wall and into the waiting ears of the summoned person, who stuck his head in at once. "A seat for our teller, and his companion." He looked at them with a certain dry humor in his eye. "I imagine it will be some time in the telling."

The door opening again, two pages bringing well-padded chairs for the travelers. They must have kept them waiting nearby. They sank into them with some relief–even the benches in the hall where they had waited had been bare wood–but Janosec did not make the mistake of relaxing in it. Instead, he sat upright, his back not touching the back of the chair. The chairman nodded appreciatively. "Begin, if you please."

"Very well, sir," said the teller, girding himself up to tell the whole story, in its gruesome fullness, something not even Mirani had heard. "This is what happened…"

The chairman was partly right. The story would have been some time in the telling, had he been allowed to tell it. The first part of it, the interrupted Founder's Day ritual, drew a sniff from one woman, second on the left. "Mirani, you did not know?"

Janosec turned, to find his companion staring at him in surprise. "I thought you were joking," she accused him, quietly.

"I know," he replied, as quietly, "We thought it safest not to noise it about."

She sat back, frowning fiercely. He turned back to the council, trying to pick up the tangled threads of his tale, but the councilwoman wasn't done. "Noise what about, young man?" she asked derisively, "That you are the Second of a clan smaller than my immediate family? Mirani has more breeding than you! No one in our family has changed their name in over 10 generations–"

"Grandmother!" Janosec heard with great surprise, for the voice was Mirani's.

"Fractious child," said the Zirtas representative. "A disgrace to your lineage, just as well you were in the Outmarches. And when you finally choose to display some proper respect, it is on behalf of some Upwellers, outrageous–"

The chairman held up a hand, and she stopped her tirade instantly. Janosec was impressed despite himself. *That's three.*

"Such comments have no place at this table, Zirtas Tamara," the leader said, warningly, "We would not want the Upwellers among us to feel slighted, when your true complaint is with the acts of a rebellious child. Isn't that so?"

"It is so, chairman," she replied, in a much lower voice.

"*Mmm.* Then perhaps we can get on with the young man's tale?" Janosec took this as an instruction, and began anew, with the events at the sorcerer's shack and afterwards. Focused as he was on the chairman's reactions, Janosec missed those of the lady Tamara, but Mirani didn't.

"My lords," she interrupted loudly, standing, "I beg leave to address the council!"

The chairman looked up, startled. The lady Tamara looked away, furious that protocol trapped her in silence, as Mirani no doubt had planned. Let the child do what she would, the judgement of the chair would fall upon her. She herself would then be free to do what duty required of her. It was not safe to startle the chairman. "I trust it will be a matter of greater urgency than this," he stated, making it quite clear that very little could be.

Tamara half hoped that her wayward child would recant her request, avoiding a scandal, but didn't expect that to happen, not from Mirani. "It is, chairman," the young lady said, killing even that feeble hope. "I wish to prefer charges of arrest against my companion, Janosec of the NarDemlas."

The lady Tamara was easily the most surprised of all, even more so than the one named. She had intended to do the same! Was this some new disobedience, or could she actually be doing her duty for once? "*On what charge, girl?*" she demanded, usurping the chairman's prerogative.

Mirani turned a stony face away from Janosec's shock, towards her clanleader's. "Murder."

"Thranj's damned Beard!"

Fortunately this exclamation was made in an empty room. Fenita did hear something, but muffled by at least one door, and so she could not clearly make out an invocation of a deity who no longer existed, and never had, in this Realm. The tone, on the other hand, was quite clear.

"You sound…vexed," she said in a low comment as Irolla came stalking through the opening door.

"'Vexed', is it?" the goddess snarled back. "Searching for days, without result. Stressing your body and mine to the limits, fruitlessly. Only to find myself undercut by my own colleagues!" The patch of grass Fenita sat on withered under her legs.

She stirred, irritated by the sudden stiffness underneath, and moved to brush the dust off. "What have they done?" she asked, glad it was only the grass.

The Lady of Life turned away, toward a clear panel on one of the menageries. "Kolo," began the Lady, a specification that told Fenita a great deal already, "Is so…enamored of your Savior that she has spent the last several days looking for him!"

"I thought you said that that couldn't be done, that you couldn't find him directly?"

"Oh, it *could* be done, really," Irolla admitted off-hand, "If one of us happened to be looking in just the right place to notice something happening to the things we can perceive that had to be caused by something we can't." Her voice rose with incremental step, the violence in the preserve similarly escalating.

Fenita took her meaning. "That…sounds unlikely."

"Yes!" Irolla agreed instantly, grateful that *some*one grasped this basic point. "For all this time she's been looking for Tarkas when she should have been looking for people talking about Tarkas. To Tarkas. *With* Tarkas." Her tantrum stopped abruptly when one of her smaller beasts flew from the menagerie's wooded area and slammed into her window, leaving a trail of blood and drool as it slid slowly down to settle on the ground.

She stiffened, taking control of herself with visible effort, turning from the quieting wood. "I corrected her error."

Fenita looked away, at the window on the far side of the enclosure. "That would account for the whirlwind."

Irolla looked at it, and shrugged. "It won't last long," she stated definitively. "That way lies the *aviary*, and my *hatchery*."

In a few seconds she was proved right, as the cyclone lurched and dissipated with shocking speed. Irolla looked smugly at her guest. "The limits may be loose," she said, keeping the triumph out of her voice, where Kolo would find it, "But the balance of Nature does have limits."

Finally!

Tarkas rarely cast his thoughts into words in the privacy of his own head, but on this occasion he indulged himself. Days and days of trekking through dry, withered forest. Slipping and sliding down a dry and dusty slope, as steep and treacherous in its way as the mountain it mocked. All to wash up at last on the shore of a lake.

Sort of a lake. Inky black, and smooth, it did not…move like water should, or sound like it either. Completely opaque, it rippled constantly in the windless air of the valley, and he wondered what variety of beasts waited below. He tossed a stone, right into the dark mass, which actually bounced once before being swallowed by the black. It neither sank nor submerged, but was swallowed, rolled over, and consumed.

Obviously, whatever entities lived in the grim and dark piles of stone in the middle of the lake needed some conveyance, or perhaps a bridge. That there were such entities he did not doubt, and he strongly suspected that he knew what they were, as well. He considered going in search of a landing, but decided not to. It wasn't as if the spot he was in would not serve as one already, and no bridge showed over the parts of the lake he could see.

Oops. The lake was moving, the ripples moving consistently in his direction. Deffin tensed as well, alerted by his partner's change in smell more than anything. Then even his eyes were able to perceive the change, as the lake started to swell upwards, something huge pushing the…glop…before it as it came to land. There was nothing else, just the glop, mounting higher and higher, like a tidal wave with purpose, intent on smashing and devouring.

So Tarkas moved, and the wave came crashing down on empty beach and retracted. Not very smart, it rebuilt itself opposite his new position and tried again, with the same results. But it was smart enough to adapt, slowly, and it made itself larger, too large to be casually dodged. Going backward was not an option either, the dry soil allowing no purchase to scale the walls of this trap.

The wave crashed down again, and once again he escaped its clutch, but only because it had oriented itself on Deffin's bulk, snaring a back paw. For a second the nizarik went strangely limp, but then he exploded into frenzied motion, shrieking, snapping, and clawing.

At nothing.

The paw held by the sludge was still limp, and the glop advanced slowly up his leg as the rest of Deffin fought phantoms. Tarkas moved closer, trying to see what he should do, but at the sound the beast turned on him, a focus for the prey on his mind. Only the disability of his hindquarters preserved Tarkas from the ability of his front quarters, and the Hero leapt high over his companion's prostrated form. Landing lightly behind, he slashed easily through the thick strand of goo with his sword, hoping that it had the same effect against this as it had against everything else. It did, mostly, although this glop bent a little before parting, like a vine made of molten glass.

But it parted, which was the important thing, the one side retracting into the lake, the other sort of…shriveling, drying and desiccating into something both more solid and less glassy. With the tip of his sword he pushed the little lump away from his friend, who lay twitching. "Don't!" came a shout from behind him.

He spun in a flash, even as the echoes of the shout bounced off the surface of the substance in the lake. It was a…person, a man perhaps, draped and cowled into obscurity, standing confidently in a boat gliding upon the surface. In its hands it held a pole, which it used to push the boat closer to where Tarkas waited. "'Don't' what?" asked the Hero, his head clutched in sudden pain from an enormous and unexplainable feeling that this had happened to him before. The memory was there, it had to be, but such pain was involved in bringing it out that his automatic defenses kicked in, and he just didn't think about it anymore.

The boatman waited until his vessel came as close to shore as it could before replying, "Don't flick the lump away. It's very valuable stuff."

"Really?" asked Tarkas, his head clearing. He took a step backward so that both lump and poler were in front of him, and crouched down to look at it more closely. "What is it?"

"The same stuff as the lake," the other pointed out, unnecessarily. "The stuff that dreams are made of."

"Dreams? Looks like roofing tar."

"I didn't say they were good dreams, did I?" said the boatman reasonably, leaning on his pole. "Although, to be honest, I don't know that there's such a difference. I suppose there might be some kind of wash-with-soap-and-water variety somewhere, but I've only ever seen this pave-the-road-to-hell stuff."

Tarkas looked at Deffin, trying to get to all four of his feet. Exactly the sort of thing a nizarik would dream of. "I suppose it could be what you do with it, and not the dream itself," he pondered.

"*Hmm*, could be," said the boatman, without the slightest trace of interest in his voice, "Look, are you going to get in my boat or not?"

Tarkas looked back, frowning mightily. "Why should I do that, Charon?"

The boatman turned to look behind him, but no one was there. "Who the hell is Charon?"

Tarkas was a little surprised. "Aren't *you*?" he asked, standing. "Charon, ferryman, carries the souls across to the Land of the Dead, two coins and all that?"

"Is *that* the image? Impressive," he exclaimed, pleased, looking down at his own drapings. "I cared, once," he claimed, looking back at his prospective passenger. "What do I need the coins for?"

"You don't," Tarkas replied, a little confused, "The souls bring them, to pay their way. If they don't have them they don't go."

Not-Charon looked as confused as a cowled faceless man can look. "What would I do with 'em?"

Tarkas assumed–hoped–he meant the coins, and shrugged, trying for an air of nonchalance. "Throw them into the lake, make a wish?"

The boatman laughed weakly. "Yeah. Right. You've seen what

lives down there. I've got no use for coins."

"Then why do you want to take us across the lake?"

"I'm bored, and you're a Hero. A few explosions will liven the place up a little."

Chapter 13

Janosec would have paced his cell, a caged, angry beast, tail lashing in pent-up, undealable fury. But he hit his head if he stood straight and hurt his back if he stooped, so he didn't. Instead he sat.

So this was prison. How strange. So familiar, from his dreams. Tarkas often got arrested, held in prisons like this, some better, some much worse, until freedom or punishment. Sometimes prison *was* the punishment, which struck Janosec as odd. Why would a city burden itself like that? Not that it mattered, in his uncle's case, freedom was just–*Hmm.* Why that image? His thumb? Why his thumb?

Well, that's why he wasn't in prison anymore and Janosec was. Thanks to Mirani. At least she hadn't betrayed them bo–! *Wait!* The trap, the staked beast, could that have been–? No. No, the sequence was wrong. He was surprised by his own sense of relief. Why would he care about saving her honor now? Surely one betrayal is enough!

Even the thought repulsed him. The accusation of betrayal is itself a betrayal, only worse, for the accuser is self-confessed where the accused may be innocent. How could *she* be innocent, though?

CLANK.

Someone had opened the window to his cell, but he didn't bother to look up. "Wallowing, are we?" said a voice like Mirani's.

He kept his face down by an act of will. "Giving honor to those who do honor."

He heard her shift, could imagine the most likely expression on her face, he'd seen most of them. "And so you shun me?"

Now he looked up, for her voice was not the voice he expected. "I try to find a tale to tell of this event in which you have done me a service."

Her face rearranged itself again. Interesting. Not outraged, but prim, and disapproving. "You confessed in front of us both."

"I told the tale of how I participated in the death of a sorcerer as he was trying to kill us by fire. I did not murder him, certainly not because he was NarZirtas."

"You dropped a sideboard full of explosive baubles on him while he was attacking someone else!" she exclaimed, "And he was deranged, by your own account."

Janosec stood in sudden fury, not comprehending the defense she presented. "And when is it murder to put down a mad dak?"

"When my grandmother would have it so," Mirani replied, getting to the point at last. "She would defend a snake, were it a proper NarZirtas."

He knew better than to believe her stony exterior. "Unlike you."

Strangely, she smiled. "Unlike me. Although I was at least proper enough to denounce you."

"Is that why you did it?" he asked, head tilted, "To curry favor with your grandmother?"

"No," she replied, tilting her head the opposite way, in subtle mockery, "That's just an unfortunate side-effect."

"Unfortunate?"

Mirani made a face. "She's trying to arrange a marriage for me now, while she sees an opportunity." Her eyes rolled. "Even if I wanted to marry, I wouldn't marry someone *she* would approve of. The things I have to deal with for your sake."

Janosec stood straighter, trying to relieve a pain in his back, from the stooped posture so he could see through the door. He stared blankly at a stone, thinking about what she'd said. She'd saved him from her grandmother, and therefore from her grandmother's champion, in a dueling circle. Fine. "Thank you."

"You are welcome," she replied automatically, at his chest.

"So what is next?" he asked, "In Qu–in my city, the issue would be between you and me, in the same circle."

"Yes," she agreed, a drawn-out sigh that brought his face back down to the window, "And to the death, as well, although I do not want to kill you."

He chuckled. "You think you could?"

Her voice hardened. "I know I could. I saw you with that axe, don't forget, and my sling is faster by far!"

Perhaps not, but Janosec had no desire to press the issue when they had more important work to be done. There was only one way to prove her wrong. "Are there any other possibilities? 'To the death' sounds a little extreme."

"It is meant to be," she commented, "To prevent the sort of thing I am trying to do. Friends would be forced to fight, and ultimately kill, unless the accused surrendered."

Perhaps that was the alternative he sought. "What happens if I surrender to you?"

She swallowed hard. "It means you accept the charge," she murmured. "You give yourself without reserve to the accuser, which means to the accuser's whole clan, and they can do anything they want with you short of killing you."

"*Hmm,*" he pretended to consider, "I'm beginning to think the single combat is the best chance I've got."

"It's meant to be."

"Then why did you go to the trouble of charging me yourself?"

For once he heard her familiar snort of exasperation. "Don't be stupid, Demlas. Obviously, you should surrender to me, I keep you by me, we continue our hunt together when the Walk leaves tomorrow. Do you think I will let my family have its way with you?"

Well, no, but…that wasn't the issue. "Do you think I would accept the label of murderer when I am not one?"

Of course she'd known he wouldn't, he wouldn't even change the dialog in a tale. But she'd hoped he would not think of it, he could tell that from her silence. "When will the combat take place?" he asked, already determined that there would be one.

For a moment she said nothing, making only a strange sound that might have been an expletive except that her teeth were clenched. It escaped through her nose, instead, and came out sounding like 'sncrg'. "It will have to be tomorrow morning, first thing," she declared with the icy pronunciation of true rage. "I must be there, and I will leave with the Walk right after."

He smiled grimly. "Mourning the stupid waste?"

"Can you doubt it?" she almost shouted, but that would have

brought the jailer. "You've never seen anyone as big and strong as our clan champion."

She didn't know that Tarkas was clan champion, although she probably would have judged him by his size anyway, and the connection between him and Tarkas was not nearly as indirect as she had been told. "Has he seen anyone as big and strong as *me*?"

For a moment she said nothing, merely stared at him with pursed lips and frowning eyes. "Only when he looks into a glass." Then she slammed the window, leaving him to deduce her exit by the sound of her stamping footsteps.

Tomorrow came too soon, a night of shadow-practice in a too-small cell, followed by a few hours of sleeping in a too-smelly cot with a too-small blanket, awakened too early to eat too little food. Fortunately, it was eight-day, not two-day, else Janosec would have begun to suspect a conspiracy.

Mirani was quite right, the combat would be early. The jailer watched him eat his meal and took the food back himself. Another officer retrieved Janosec's gear and passed it to yet another for the short walk to the NarZirtas compound and their clan dueling grounds. A few people ogled him as they walked by, but there were not many, for most attended the invocation ceremonies in the city arena.

But not the NarZirtas. Their compound was quite full, as full as Zirtas Tamara's authority could make it. Janosec's escort was itself escorted, a living cage that held him as much as protected him, not that the NarZirtas seemed terribly rowdy in that respect. Perhaps it was the early hour, more likely the great distance and circumstances of the crime. But the city official, making his announcement, and even the clinks of the coins as the city received its payment for holding and transporting the prisoner, could be heard clearly by all.

The explosion of booing as Janosec came forward took him by surprise, the great cheers as the champion stepped forward less so. By all the gods of Earth, he *was* big. And his sword bigger. Obviously not a NarZirtas. Janosec felt vastly exposed out there, with nothing but an axe available to him, but that's the way they wanted him to feel. The champion embodied clan honor, only a step or two removed from the Fist of Earth itself, and the accused was supposed to feel puny and mortal before him.

It took a lot to make Janosec feel puny.

He looked upon Mirani, clad in Walker's garb for her immediate departure after his bloody death, her face closed to him and all others. The old grandmother sat next to her, naturally, staging this spectacle for no greater reason than to appease her own sense of honor. And perhaps as a torment for the rebellious one sitting at her side, or a test of her newfound appreciation of clan duty.

He removed his axe, and stepped forward to the jeers of the crowd.

The champion knew better than that, but not enough. An axe is a formidable weapon against a tree, but trees do not move. Trees are not armored. But he still moved forward more slowly than he would have had his opponent held a sword. Soon this person would be dead, Mirani would be his, and properly respectful. If not then, eventually. Tamara had promised.

Janosec swung, and again. Yes, the bucket in his cell had been about as heavy as this. The momentum as great, the timing almost the same.

The champion watched the practice swings, and relaxed a little, confident in his own abilities. The axe was slow and dangerous only when moving fast. The axe pulled the wielder's arms after it, leaving him hopelessly vulnerable. One more swing and the victim–pardon, the accused–would be in range and ready for spitting. Honor, especially his rather elastic notion of honor, one of the reasons Tamara had chosen him to be champion, would be satisfied.

Janosec took one more step, and began. The axe came up in a wide arc, his two hands working on the handle to allow it to spin while still keeping control. The first rule his uncle had told him about fighting with an axe was *Always keep it moving!* The axe's strength lay in its momentum and it must never stop, even when it pulled his hands away from his chest. Yes, the champion was waiting, ready to lunge just as the grunt had, but he knew better now.

Now! thought the clansman, beginning his own sweep. His sword moved up towards the top of its arc and– "*YAAAAAAAAHHHHHHH,*" Janosec screamed into his face, shocking him tremendously and completely throwing off his timing. Then the axe was coming down and it still had its power and–*God's Within!* He jumped back, trying to regain his composure and get some distance to use his blade properly.

Keep attacking! His uncle's second rule and the advice about screaming certainly worked. Who would scream like that at a duel? The champion's experience could not help him if the duel was like nothing he'd ever seen before. Certainly Janosec had never seen it before. He made it up as he went along, charging like a mad nosk at a weapon that could spit him if its bearer could aim it properly.

It takes proper footwork to use a sword effectively, and with his feet constantly moving backward the champion had no chance to display any, not to aim it, and certainly not to impale anyone. Finally he turned and ran, trying to get some distance, but Janosec merely ran after him, less encumbered by armor and still howling like one moonstruck.

This was something of a mistake, though, robbing the axe to pay his feet, and he soon came to regret it. The champion at some point came into sight of Tamara, her expression ferocious, and decided to take his chances against the axe. He turned, swinging the sword wide, and Janosec found himself running towards the impaling blade. Surprised, with no time to think, he lost his concentration on the movements of his axe. Uncontrolled, it kept swinging in its arc, dragging his arms around and his body with them, pivoting him around. He miraculously avoided the sword's point, came in close behind his opponent's hand, and hit the back of the champion's padded helm with a resounding *clang!* before tripping over his own feet and falling facedown into the dirt, victorious. The champion fell next to him, very like a tree toppling, but only the one who felled him rose.

The arena was deathly silent as he clambered to his feet, spitting dirt and blood. He rolled his armored opponent over, checking his pulse and breath, sagging in relief that he had not killed the man. Then the applause erupted, one pair of hands praising him, only one pair needed, since they were the right pair. Mirani looked enthusiastic, ecstatic, and utterly adorable with her hair all done up and proper pilgrim clothes on, hands pumping furiously and a ridiculous grin on her face.

He stumbled forward, to the granite-faced grandmother, and formally said, "I claim the victory." Mirani wasted no time seconding the claim, merely grabbed her gear in one hand and him in the other, towing her companion through the ring of stunned guards and out of the compound. His last sight was of a man, hopefully a doctor, keeling down beside his former opponent, while Tamara dealt coldly with the city man.

The streets were empty now, and the echoes of their sandaled feet came loud to them as they navigated the narrow streets to the public arena. Wait, those were not their feet–from behind, city guards grouped around them on all sides, but they had no time or reason to fear. They were comrades now, fellow warriors, and where did you learn to fight like that?

For a time Janosec tried to avoid their questions, but they were as good as trapped, and the guardsmen had no place to go and no greater concerns. In the end he had to give them most of the tips he had received himself only a few days before, only without the proper attribution. Immediately they started critiquing his performance, a task that kept them fully occupied right up to the moment when they came out at the head of a flight of steps.

The invocation of the Walk was held, as all of them had ever been, on a stage facing a steep drop, at the edge of another steep drop. The Walk, strangely, sat for the invocation, on steps cut into the side of the wall of the first slope, a half-circular notch in the wall of a vast valley, looking out over open space as the ground fell away once again just behind the stage. Against this backdrop the chairman stood, not so much invoking the glory of the God's world spread out behind him as channeling it into a form suitable for thought and speech.

For a moment Janosec stood gaping, the speaker's words just so much sound against his ears as his eyes roamed the vista before him. In particular he focused on the huge, black spot set into the ground of the valley floor, so far away, and far below. Around it, two concentric bands marked, between them, a great green swath ringing the spot. Beyond that the ground rose ever more sharply, through forested waste, to become the wall of the valley.

Three rings, nested. The Eye of the World.

Blue in the distance, on the far side of the valley, he could see a switching stair much like the cliff steps of Querdishan, becoming a path when the slope permitted it. Ah! There by the stage, the head of what was no doubt another such stair. When the invocation ended, the pilgrims would go down those steps to complete the Walk.

"–you have no doubt heard the horrific tale of the deaths of our brothers and sisters, and the destruction of their village in the Outmarches, a place which many of you call home." The crowd had fallen completely silent for these words, which thus carried up clearly to the group on the wall. "Some of you have been fortunate to receive some remnants of those lives, treasures of family and memory, rescued from oblivion by those who brought the tale. Now we honor those who give honor.

"Zirtas Mirani is not one of us, not of our faith, does not follow our ways. But she knows our ways, and respects our faith. Today, in this Walk, she walks for some of us. She walks for all of us."

He raised his arm, gesturing to where she stood, plainly visible at the head of the stairs. Heads turned, and a generally approving murmur washed up and over them. Pointed out, she paused only long enough to drape her burden over her shoulder–that long tube she had been carrying for days–before moving forward into full view.

The speaker, naturally, took advantage of this spontaneous gesture. "Zirtas Mirani, we, the Upwellers of Querd, offer you our thanks."

After a second, unprepared for a spectacle, she found her tongue. "I accept your thanks, and offer my own for the honor you show me now."

He bowed slightly, then continued on a different subject. "Most of you are young, making this Walk as the lore requires of us all. But the lore does not require us to make the Walk in our youth, or in our prime. The lore only requires us to make the Walk at some time in our lives.

"Today we have with us a man making his Walk for the first

time, in a life longer than three of yours put together." Down at the front of the crowd, an old man smiled grimly to himself at the understatement, as the chairman received an item from one of his aides by the stage. "A long life, a scholar's life, full of learning and accomplishment, a life soon to be crowned by the greatest of the God's wonders at the Eye of the World. In token thereof, we present this crown to you. Ardus Virlor, come forth."

Ardus Virlor didn't want to come forth, had better things to do than come forth, wanted nothing more than for this whole farcical ritual to terminate. But protest would mean delay, compliance would not, so he complied as the outcome of a chain of logic. Striding stiffly forward, he mounted the stage with a vigor that belied his claimed age, stood waiting for the chairman to place the absurd crown upon his head, refusing even to tilt it forward to ease the task. The speaker took him by the elbow and forced him to face the crowd, a move he couldn't resist without a display of untoward strength. The speaker opened his mouth to make yet another fatuous comment, hopefully the last.

"YOU!"

The one word echoed and re-echoed over the heads of the crowd, cutting off the speaker. Virlor looked up suspiciously, and saw some young giant standing upon the lip of the cleft, pointing down at him! "You are the man! The man we have sought all these days!"

For a second all was quiet; this interruption at an invocation unheard of. Then the chairman found his voice. "Demlas Janosec, I congratulate you on your success! The God smiles upon you! Are you now the accuser, rather than the accused?"

Now Janosec came forward, projecting his voice as Tarkas and experience had taught him to do. The room was simply larger. "I accuse no one, sir. I condemn no one. But we have passed through many towns these last several days, as you know, hearing always of an old man and scholar ahead of us. We have passed through many crossroads, met other Walkers, and none of them had encountered old men in their travels, ahead or behind. I submit to you that *this* man is the last man to come from that village before its death, and I would like to hear his account of its latter days."

He spoke slowly, letting the echoes fade and his listeners think, knowing already the tale of its last day. As the sounds of his last words rolled down over the cliff towards the Eye they too wanted to hear that tale. The chairman knew it, too, no matter how irregular it might be, and he knew better than to try to argue with popular sentiment. He turned to Ardus Virlor and asked, "Would you care to speak? If you have aught to say it would best be heard now."

If Ardus Virlor had anything to say that would be best heard at *any* time it was beyond his own ken what it might have been. Certainly the scroll and his ownership of it must never be known, these hidebound barbarian ritualists would mob him if they got wind of that! How had he gotten it–No, the memory still wasn't there. But the scroll was the key, the scroll was everything. Always fearful in the face of the unknown, assailed by an even stronger sudden doubt, he reached into his Walker's togs to feel the stiff parchment, masking the act by folding his arms dramatically. *Yes*, he breathed, relieved as he grasped his last, holiest, rede. "No," he said aloud, "I've nothing to say. The world is full of old men! Let them trace this fiendish sorcerer of theirs to the ends of the world, over the Edge and beyond!"

For a moment the issue was in doubt, Janosec above and Virlor below seemed poised on the uncertainty of the crowd. Then the chairman spoke very quietly, although he was heard nonetheless. "No one said anything of sorcery, sir." He signaled to some of the city men at the head of the stair, and they made their way up onto the stage even as the old man blustered his way through the shreds of a defense. As he grew steadily more strident they finally decided to lay hands on him, lest he break out into open violence.

"Release me!" he yelled furiously, breaking their grip with fantastic ease and hurling himself across the stage. The crowd gasped in shock, but not at his display of unnatural strength, or his youthful speed and vigor.

His hand held the scroll, clutched in a death grip. Even Janosec could see he held something, only his lack of familiarity with the Upweller's holy objects made him ignorant. But he could hear the crowd's reaction and knew what it had to be. "'Something was contained within'," he murmured, "'The contents are inviolable.'"

Something grabbed his hair, and pulled hard.

His head went back sharply, and he yelled in sudden pain. Then a hand fell on his side and pushed sharply, sending him sprawling away from the stair, away from cover of any sort. "You!" roared a voice, like a beast given speech. The fallen champion, smaller without his armor but swollen with rage, towered over his foe-turned-victim. "You will die, and your stupid axe won't save you! You will die and she will be mine and I will be champion again!"

"Well, at least you know what you want," Janosec mumbled, as he got to his feet.

The champion made no move to stop him, certain of his superiority, unwilling to squash a fallen bug. Let it stand, *then* squash it. Death isn't enough, he has to hurt! Hurting isn't enough, he has to be beaten! His sword swung restlessly, thirsty for blood, unwilling to wait. He knew his mistake, letting his victim get the axe moving. No more waiting, just cutting and killing, a quick death and a slow wedding. Or perhaps the other way around.

In seconds it was Janosec on the run, his weapon slow and crude against his enemy's expert swordsmanship. Nothing could save him now. "Nothing can save you now, treacherous dog!"

That sort of remark in itself requires no answer, although fallen heroes usually say something anyway, if only for the sake of bravado. But Janosec had run out of bravado some time before, and was stoically silent–another heroic favorite in the face of death–as his executioner slowly stalked him, savoring his triumph. His brief life passed before eyes, too short to be more than a bright flash.

"By the Gods!" shouted a man's voice from behind, one of the city guards, until now refusing to insert himself into a private quarrel. The champion paused, expecting an attack from behind, but all that came were more shouts. "By all the gods of Air!" "The God's Within!" "Gods Within!"

"Janosec!" shrieked Mirani, dropping the stone she had been about to hurl at the killer's head. She was back at the stairs, looking down in horror. "Janosec, finish him quickly! He's doing it again!

The old man, he's killing them all, just like before!"

An unexpected surge caught Irolla by surprise, and some of it leaked through her control to reach Fenita.

The blast of pain to her midsection took Fenita by surprise, bending her double and springing her from her perch headfirst into the grass.

The sudden motion caught Irolla unprepared, her arm caught as Fenita doubled over, dragging her forward and over the stump, where she banged her chin and split her lip. She recovered quickly and easily. Fenita did not, although she would later bear triplets. "What the *Hell* was that?"

The worst thing about nizariks and boats, Tarkas reflected, staring at the image of himself in the polished side of the vessel, *is getting them into one.* Especially when touching the fluid in which the vessel sits means an explosion of violence. Not-Charon was all for leaving the beast, but then decided that watching Tarkas do it himself was almost as much fun as the destruction of the city would be.

After a few false starts Tarkas spoiled his fun, grounding the boat so Deffin would climb aboard, and then pushing it out with a display of Heroic strength and gymnastics that the boatman could not have expected. At least the glop was thicker than water, so it jiggled the boat less, even if the vessel was slow.

Not that Tarkas was in any rush. The leaden gray sky changed as they approached, becoming more leaden and grayer, a virtual reflection of the dark sink beneath them. The city, as they approached it, looked strangely regular, gray stone layered in perfect straight lines, geometrically perfect. For a while this puzzled him, such order, but then he looked within himself and found that it had a depressing effect. Order on this scale left no room for spirit, creativity, growth. There was no self here, and none would be allowed, not for long.

The boat impacted the rocks with a dull thud, by far the most vital sound to be heard. Tarkas jumped out instantly, followed by

Deffin, the force of his leap pushing the boat well out onto the lake. "Wait until I get clear, Hero. I'll get some popcorn, some hot chocolate, set myself up nicely about halfway across. Don't forget."

Tarkas forgot about him instantly, far more important things on his mind than some entity's desire to be entertained. He had to navigate the city quickly. He could not expect to have a being waiting here for him. Even if there was, the preservation of his life would not be high on its list of priorities. If this place had an exit, it would be on the far side of this city, and he had to reach it before the city itself killed him.

Fortunately for that ambition, the roads of this city were all straight, as he had expected them to be, and he sped down the nearest one with all speed, Deffin galumphing along in his wake. No time for sightseeing here, or desire, just a quick–*Hmm, that's interesting, a bubble-shield here as well*! *That* he skirted very carefully, quite certain he wanted to avoid anything *this* realm wanted contained! Okay, pick an exit, any one should–

Another bubble ahead? He stopped, panting, looked back over his shoulder. Odd, that looked like the way back to the lake, there behind him. He turned around, loping more slowly back to the end of the–

Another bubble? And the lake again behind him. Tarkas drew his sword, and struck hard at the smooth gray stone of the alley, making a small crater. Then he replaced his sword, and sped off once more down the alley.

Ahead, a bubble; at his feet, a hole.

Okay. All roads lead to the bubble. So then we have to go to the bubble.

At least it had no house in it. He held up a hand, momentarily suspecting that the relentless opposition of this place might mean the bubble was impervious, but no, it was as immaterial to him as the other one was. In fact, it pulled on him, drawing him–

Inside, the bubble looked quite different, the surface now an opaque gray, and a man motionless in the center. Deffin popped through a moment later, and his soft growl alerted the other to their presence. He turned, bestowing a fierce glare upon the two. "Ah," he bellowed, without welcome, "New fish! Come to displace me, no doubt?"

"Uh, no."

The big man sniffed mightily. "Then you do not know where you are, or what will become of you," he commented off-hand, unlimbering his sword. "They only want one in here. They kill the rest."

Tarkas, not surprisingly, drew his own sword, finding the man's words unpleasantly ominous. "Who are 'they'?"

The man lifted his blade into first position. "Why, the demons, of course." He lunged, his form perfect, but easily parried. That was the end of their duel. Deffin, starved for challenge, his need only partly palliated by Tarkas' presence, took the man's attack as a gift from the Gods, and took full advantage.

"Coward!" cried the man, "To hide behind a beast!" He had no time to say more, for Deffin had many teeth and claws, while he had only the one sword.

"Not usually," replied Tarkas, aware of the man's predicament and trying not to distract him overmuch. "But he's so happy it's hard to deny him." Indeed the man could understand that, he was having trouble denying the beast as well.

Abruptly the demons arrived, dark blobs excreted from the side of the dome to resume their normal fanged, hideous appearance. Given the man's earlier comment, Tarkas expected them to go after him, but instead they came for Tarkas himself. "Get out of the way, runt," one grated at him, "You're spoiling the view!"

It reached for him, not at all concerned about his sword's presence in his hand. That was a mistake, since Tarkas held no ordinary sword, but the legendary Sword of Brill, recently owned by the Demi-God Hara-Khan the Redeemer and passed on to him. "Ouch!" the demon shouted, when Tarkas sliced him open with it. It ceased its attack momentarily, to examine the wound, probe it, even-*yuck!*-licked it. "Well," it said, perversely pleased at the taste of its own blood, leering toothily at him, "Pain's better than nothing."

Tarkas gave it a lot better. The demon wasn't much of a challenge, really; like most impervious sorts, it had never learned to fight, relying on its perfect defenses to protect it while it just pushed on through. And it was slow, and getting slower, as its tendons and ligaments separated. Unlike goblins, demons didn't heal instantly, they'd never needed to before.

In short order, the first demon fell, a twitching jumble of bleeding stony flesh, but Tarkas had no time to rest, when another came in for him. And another.

Chapter 14

Finish him? How was he supposed to do that?

"Finish *me!?*" The not-Zirtas champion was outraged. With lightning speed he backed up and grabbed at her arm, twisting her around. "Look at your hero, now, bleeding in defeat, about to die." Her hand was fast but his was faster, and she wasn't quite able to dig his eye out of its socket. He pushed her up against one of the pillars edging the semi-circular pit, his hands busy where Janosec could not see them, although he had no doubt what the scum was doing.

He pulled her in close, practically spitting into her face. "When I'm done with him, you and I shall be wed, as your grandmother promised me. With him dead and your Upweller friends even now killing themselves off, you'll learn to keep a proper Zirtas tongue in your head." The beast paused, looking down at her front. "What is this?" he demanded, his fingers pulling at the dried strands holding the tube at her back.

Her hands pushed, but he kept his fingers running up and down between her breasts. "It's a relic, oaf."

"A relic," he repeated, as if he cared, then his voice hardened, "From your Upweller friends, no doubt." His hand bunched up around the cords, and tore the whole package from her back, flinging it across the courtyard dismissively. "So much for that, so much for him." Back to business. "So much for you."

"Hey, oaf!"

Another niggling interruption. He was molesting here! "*What!?*" Then the voice registered.

"Catch!"

The oaf spun, his reflexes in no way hampered by his manners. His sword caught the axe Janosec had thrown, diverting it against another pillar several paces away. This meant, however, that that same sword was hopelessly out of position to stop the stake as it flew out of the tube, swung with all strength from Janosec's other hand at his fully exposed body.

The barbed point of the stake pierced his belly as easily as it had pierced the ribcage of the poor beast at the side of the road, and with the same effect. Even Mirani, hardened warrior that she was, fled shamelessly from the aura of evil that burst from the grisly missile as it absorbed the life force, the vitality, of its latest victim, siphoning off that essence to do what it had been made to do.

But the hell it opened onto now was not the hell it had opened onto before. On the road, it had been trees and silence. Now it showed a dismal gray, echoing with horrible growls, shrieks of agony, and the occasional clash of steel.

Tarkas noticed the hole in space immediately, a source of light and fresh air completely foreign to this place. "Deffin! Go!" he shouted, not really caring where the hole went. 'Here' had no options left, surely the most dismal thing about the place.

"By the Gods!" shrieked a city guard, as this great huge monstrous…thing erupted from the hole, all teeth and claws and foul, matted fur, stinking of carrion. For a second it turned its wild eyes on them, and they all paled at the bloodlust living there, but something drew it towards the pillars instead. No one dared hinder it as it stalked forward, even knowing what it would undoubtedly do to the people below, already being slaughtered. At the top of the stairs it stopped, sniffing mightily, and reared up, roaring out its challenge to the unfortunates below.

"Deffin!" cried a voice from the hole, as a man stepped through, also reeking of death, "Not!" The beast, miraculously, obeyed him, which led them to wonder if this seeming hero was what he seemed. "Thranj's Beard!" he said, staring at the twitching almost-corpse of the former champion.

From behind him came the massed roar of great beings, frustrated and angry. Without further delay, the stranger grabbed the stake in one hand and the villain's belt in the other, hefting the whole bloody package without apparent strain and heaving it into the hole.

"Wow!" thought not-Charon, munching contentedly on his popcorn. "Now *that's* an explosion! Looks just like a giant mushro–"

Then the shockwave hit, distributing him and the contents of the lake of dreams all over Hell.

For a second, barely long enough to see it, the hole twisted in upon itself, in a multidimensional frenzy the sight of which would have done Menniver's heart good. Fortunately it wasn't there long enough for any of the watchers to go irretrievably insane, although one of the guards started talking to himself some months later. It may not have been related.

"Uncle!"

"Demlas Tarkas! Help!" It takes no more to get a Hero moving than that one word, especially when uttered by Mirani, who would never say it without reason. "The old man! We found him, but he did something to them–!" Which old man, and what he did, were but passing thoughts in Tarkas' head, for the people below were killing each other, in exactly the same hideously determined way he imagined the village had destroyed itself. But now he was here, and it would not happen this time.

First, stop the killing, preferably in a way that wouldn't need him to be here all the time to maintain. That's what sleep spells are for.

Janosec started, but not too badly, when his uncle began to Sing, not because of the singing itself, but the manner of it, harsh and loud, more like tuneful yelling than music. Then he thought about it, and realized that the area and size of the crowd called for just that, power rather than fine control, just as he had done when speaking to the chairman just a short while ago. Slowly they stopped, and Janosec wondered what the song was supposed to do, since he could only recognize some of the words and they seemed rather ordinary. Wait! Those words, 'sweet dreams', they repeated, surely they did. He's trying to put them to sleep!

It was hard, much harder than it should have been, but Janosec couldn't have known it. Tarkas had used the spell before, but never beyond the second line. Maybe it was the graceless delivery, but he doubted that. It *had* worked, after all. Maybe the words? But then why would repeating the one phrase have any more effect? Perhaps it has something to do with this old man's spell, no dreams, or at least no sweet ones. Hmm, no dreams? "Bring me some water," he directed, cutting short the praise of those who did not know the problem.

The city guards were less than pleased to be so rebuffed, and Janosec had no knowledge of where he might find some, but Mirani turned immediately to bring what he required, only a dipperful from a nearby watering-trough, but sufficient for his current needs. Not thirst. While she was gone he retrieved a small block of ugly black stuff from his pouch, holding it carefully with a scrap of cloth, and shaved off a sliver with a dagger just as black. Then he cut the block into parts, for no obvious reason. When she presented the water he put the sliver into it, where it dissolved, foaming, turning the water into a black goo that threatened to overflow the dipper.

But it didn't, although he walked very carefully down the steps to the nearest of the old man's victims. A pair, naturally, a youth locked in mortal combat with a woman, perhaps his own mother. Janosec and Mirani disentangled them, rolling them over at his direction, and he dripped a little of his sludge into each open mouth. Yes! Both people sighed softly, bodies slumping just a little.

Tarkas stood, careful not to spill any of the liquid, and turned to the city guard staring over his shoulder. "Take this," he said, handing the dipper to the astonished man, "And have your men prepare the rest of these people. You saw how much I used?" Dumbly, the man nodded. "Good, take this–" and he handed over the largest part of the block he had cut "–and make more when you need to. Don't ever touch it directly, it's dangerous in the extreme and there is no more."

"My lord?" queried the man, unconsciously using the honorific.

"We must go," said Tarkas, answering the man's unasked question, "This glop is at best a stop-gap. It keeps them under the spell I used, and perhaps, alleviates some of their distress, but I refuse to experiment with their lives when there are other measures available. Also, the old man, you will notice, is not down there. I would imagine that he is even now continuing his evil work elsewhere, and I, we, must give chase."

"Down the steps, my lord," suggested the guard, pointing, "With this lot in the way on all stairs there's nowhere else he could have gone."

Tarkas nodded appreciatively. "Except over the cliff, which would make him easy to find," he added. "Good man." He looked at his companions. "Are you two ready?"

They nodded vigorously, but the city guard was more attentive. "No." He called back up. "Terla, you and Verion come down here and give them your trail packs. And a sword." He turned back to Janosec, and said, "You used an axe before, my lord, but you'll have a good city blade against this villain."

Janosec thanked him gravely, and the man trundled off, eyes on the dipper, calling out instructions. "'A good city blade'," echoed Mirani, after he was out of earshot. "What a popinjay. And a toad. You should not have praised him, 'my lord.'"

Tarkas held off replying, until after the other guards, bringing down their supplies and weapons, had left. They hastened down, not up, but Tarkas doubted it was merely fear of Deffin, which directed them. The palliative they distributed would go to the important people first, naturally, and they were down below, if not already over the cliff. "I did not praise him for being a popinjay, or a toad," he replied, distributing things about his body, "I praised him for having a good idea. Praise him for that reason, and he will become a man who has good ideas, rather than a man who toadies."

Mirani looked at Janosec's new blade and belt with deep longing, but she was NarZirtas and a pilgrim, doubly bound. "By that logic," she snapped, "I should be a scullery maid." She led the way, stamping down the stairs. Janosec followed, as usual, and Tarkas brought up the rear with Deffin in tow.

"Not at all," replied Tarkas amiably, grateful for someone to talk to after so long. Not-Charon didn't really count, in his mind. "It depends on who you listened to, and what you heard them saying. One man's criticism is another man's praise." For a while, all were silent, making their cautious way down unfamiliar steps over fallen bodies, Tarkas additionally, and fruitlessly, watching how his two comrades interacted. "So tell me," he finally burst in frustration, when they reached the bottom, "Who is this old man?"

For some odd reason, the two younger people both burst out laughing, and Mirani made an odd gesture, casual, dismissive, yet permissive as well. Janosec seemed to take it as *Go ahead* or *You do it*, for he started talking. "Well, Uncle, this is what happened…"

Janosec's tale, long, detailed, and complete, occupied them down the steps and onto the rocky trail at the bottom, where the valley wall had leveled out enough to be climbed using only feet. At Mirani's suggestion he included the event of the mother and daughter, but Tarkas understood that no more than they did. Her version of events differed only trivially, regarding the nights in the various inns, diverging only after Janosec had been hauled off to jail and she had been hauled off to the clan NarZirtas.

"A true nightmare that was, let me tell you," she said fiercely, teeth clenched, "You speak of criticism as praise. Well, you never heard such praise in your life, and all it did was make me want to walk out of there and go over the cliff alone! Ye Gods! And the things she wanted to do to him! Then to speak of marriage, as if there was a lackwit in the whole city-bred bunch I wouldn't spit on–!"

"Mirani," said Tarkas gently, interrupting her tirade, "Calm down, watch your feet."

Janosec waited until she got her breathing under control, before asking, "And the oaf? Is that where he fit in?"

She laughed, short, bitter, dark. "Grandmother promised me to the man who would be her champion. He was the only man stupid enough to accept." She kicked a rock off the edge of the trail they followed.

"What did he get out of it?" asked Janosec innocently, and then hastily added, "Aside from you, that is."

She snorted. "He got the honor of being a NarZirtas," she supplied, affecting the sort of tones her grandmother would have used, telling Tarkas volumes about the unmet lady. "Whether I survived the wedding night or not."

Both men knew the answer to *that* one. "And you would be in his clan, no longer a NarZirtas, whether he survived or not?" Tarkas added.

"Hey, that's right!" she suddenly cried, stopping in the path for a second, and turned back to look at them. "As a NarBorgas, I could have used a blade, couldn't I?"

They all laughed, imagining in their various ways the scene that would have ensued, dispelling the horror of the prospective nuptials. "I regret my victory, then," added Janosec, when they resumed, "Think what a fortune I could have made, betting on the outcome!"

Praise indeed, but–

"I'm just as glad you're still alive to collect it, nephew, and not a slave to some troll." Not to mention his own predicament at the time. "Did you see what the old man did, Mirani, that made the people go mad?"

For a time she was silent, trying to remember, as the path got more and more level. Janosec took advantage of her silence to say, "A bright flash is all I saw. Then she said that he was killing them."

"I didn't see anything either," she added hastily, "At least not the flash. I was watching that Borgas swine trying to kill you, like everyone else. But when the flash came I looked." She shuddered at the memory. "It looked like…colored…slime, streams of it, in the air, oozing, flowing, from them to him. When they were gone, all flowed away, everyone went mad."

Tarkas considered this. "Colored slime? Flowing *from* them?"

"Yes, lots of colors, all different," she added, not sure what details might matter.

"So he took something from them, as I thought," muttered Tarkas.

Janosec waited, but nothing more was forthcoming. "What, Uncle? That black sludge?"

"No," replied Tarkas' immediately, but the next was a bit more thoughtful. "Something related, I should think. The black sludge, as you call it, is concentrated dream-stuff that I picked up on the side trip your old friend arranged for me. My spell worked on dreams and almost failed, which is why I thought of it. Whatever he took from them, it had something to do with their dreaming." He stopped in his tracks. "That reminds me–"

They stopped as well, and came back as he fumbled with something. "Do either of you have a cord? I need one more. Ah, Mirani, very good–" When he finished, he held out two amulets to them, little bags tied to cords, ready to be draped over their heads. They did so. "I had some of that dream-stuff left. Hopefully this will protect you from a dream thief."

Janosec fingered his bag with wonder, then looked at his uncle, not seeing any bag around *his* neck. "What will protect you?"

Tarkas laughed, with something that was not quite amusement. "I can only hope that this villain uses his foul magicks against me." Why he would hope for such a thing, he did not explain, nor did either of them dare to ask. As the trail smoothed out, their speed increased, and opportunities for speech came fewer and farther between. By all logic they should catch up to the man in short order, even Mirani should be able to keep up a Hero's pace for the short run like this.

But the run got longer and longer, blatantly defying logic, and eventually Mirani began to tire, and they had to slow their pace. Then they left the open trail, and slowed even more, for Janosec's sake. Tarkas would have been justified in not believing in the man's existence, if his eyes and experience did not see traces of him as they loped through the expanse of forest ringing the valley. The trail was maintained for pilgrims, but pilgrims only came down once a year. The overgrowth caught at the old man's clothes, even though they were much like Mirani's and close to the body. From the placement of the fragments and the length of the space between footprints and the degree of the smudging, Tarkas guessed that the man raced like one possessed to some incomprehensible finish line, and feared he might have to abandon his comrades after all.

But the woods gave out first, and they could all see the figure far in the distance, obscured by the cloud of dust his pounding feet kicked up. Surely this would be the fastest pilgrimage on record, although Tarkas doubted that such was the man's purpose. Even they could spare only a moment for a token observance at a little shrine set up right at the boundary (Mirani insisted, touching the symbol and whispering 'The Living' as she did), and he couldn't imagine that their quarry had spared even that much. They raced forward, and if Tarkas pulled ahead of the others no one faulted him for it.

What was that? Something had changed.

No dust! The old man wasn't running anymore! As they drew closer they could tell he wasn't even moving anymore. He had stopped at the last crossroad, just before the great black expanse of the Eye itself. He was even reading, apparently ignoring them as they approached, full of apprehension. When they were a few paces away, he suddenly turned on them. "You fools!" he screamed, "Idiots! It's too SOON!"

Now was the time, and Tarkas narrowed his eyes in preparation. The man was trapped, as he had been before, and Tarkas expected he would free himself now as he had then. He didn't fear the magic, but the flash, not wanting to lose their quarry while blinded. He *was* blinded, not by any light of any color but by a wave of terror, washing over him as…something…emerged from the man. A demon, probably. He'd faced demons before, of course, although not often. Without the black sword it would not have been more than twice, and the first one didn't count. He could handle a demon, although his comrades would probably be no aid to him.

But it was no demon, it was…nothing. It had no form, no body, not even a blur on the air. He knew where it was as a man knows that death awaits, as a place where his eyes refuse to look.

Then it attacked, the brilliant flash he expected, and he braced himself for–

Memory?

For more than half his life, since almost before he'd become a Hero, Tarkas had been gifted–or cursed–with an uncanny memory, the side effect of a drastic procedure performed on him at that time, an operation on his mind to restore it from near-total dissolution. With perfect ease, he could recall any event from his life since then. With the usual effort, he could recall the events from before then. What he could not do was recall them all at once. Nor could he now, although something else tried very hard to make him.

He was the battlefield in a war of wills, a power from beyond him against the power that had made him. His mind had been healed by a god, insane, but a god nonetheless, his identity fixed in place and the parts made adherent to that identity. Now the events of his life tried to erupt out of sequence, under the pull of a force beyond his ability to resist, and the will of the Mad God was the only thing holding him together.

It didn't hurt, not in the way he had known before, when other gods had read his memory too far. This force was not that powerful. But it was disorienting, and only his own long experience with suppressing the march of time in his own mind kept him on his feet. The old man wavered in his vision, but he could not advance on the villain. His ears reported shouts of alarm from his companions, but he could not turn to aid them. His own sense of self overwhelmed him, the world mere pictures in his mind.

And then it was gone. Not his self, of course, but the sense of it, the world rushing back in to fill his senses. The man still stood there, trembling in some kind of shock. A failed spell can do that, Tarkas knew. Janosec! He spun, but they were still there, a little blank but otherwise unharmed, certainly not insane with rage. What sort of spell was that? Nothing he'd ever performed had challenged the strength of a god like that, and the old man hadn't even said anything!

"Uncle? Are you well?"

Tarkas realized he had been staring at Janosec a little fixedly. "Nephew?"

Mirani stepped forward. "You…*glowed*! The colored light, it glowed around you and then went away again!"

"We thought you were about to attack us," Janosec added, a little shamefaced.

"Oh," said Tarkas, reinterpreting their previous blank looks. "Oh!" He spun towards the old man again, but he had not moved. In fact, he looked distinctly–

BAM!

Something exploded right in front of them all. Tarkas felt it, even saw it, but experienced little of it, a soundless detonation of something immaterial that washed over him and beyond. Janosec and Mirani, behind him and safe from any physical attack, apparently experienced something from the event, something positive, if the laughter was any indication.

But the old man held his interest. He hadn't moved since the whole strange attack began. He changed, instead, his flesh filling out, his hair shading back to a younger brown color, as if he was regaining youth. Not much youth, granted. It was strange to see, like he was coming back to li–

Life again.

Gaining life? His spell failed! Doubly impossible!

Therefore it was not a spell. No matter what caused those two to moan back there. Hurriedly he cast a sleep spell behind him, not wanting to be distracted right now.

"Murderer!" shrieked the old man, snapping out of his trance, shocking Tarkas a little. Sure, he had killed others before, but murder was one of those not-nice things he refused to do. But he was used to the accusation, people usually let their personal preferences get in the way of what they knew ought to be done. "You killed it! The last of its kind!"

"If its kind lived by sucking the life out of others, good riddance."

Amazingly, the old man stalked forward, waving a fist at his nose. "You're as ignorant as you are stupid," he proclaimed. "Anyone with any sense could see that it did no such thing, nor would it want to."

Tarkas watched him come, amused, but not so much so as to forget all caution. "And why not?"

"Aagh!" shouted the old man incoherently, outraged at such obtuseness. "Do fish consume water?! Do birds eat the air, or worms the ground? Of course not! They eat the things which live in the water or the air, as they do." He turned away, stamping about, literally tearing at his own hair.

What lived in the element of Life? "What happened to the life after those things living in it were strained out and eaten?"

The old man waved his arms negligently. "It gets released sooner or later, as usual." Long after those from whom it had been stolen had destroyed themselves for lack of it. "Fish don't explode, do they?"

No, but Tarkas was about to. "How did you discover this…creature?"

The old man turned about, excited. "I wasn't trying to find it, I was trying to find the creatures it feeds upon."

Good Luck. "Why would you even bother looking?"

"They had to be there, didn't they?" replied the man as he approached, as if to a very dim student. "How else to explain all the strange things I saw all about me? So I tried to catch one, but I later realized they were far too small for any net I could cast." He sounded terribly bitter, as if personally affronted by the universe, and he turned away again.

"But not this one?" Tarkas guessed.

"No, not this one," said the old man wearily, looking up at the sun. "Caught it easily enough. Holding it that was the problem, taming it next to impossible."

"You seem to have managed it, though," Tarkas complimented him.

"Ha!" the old man barked, "That wasn't me, that was…them."

Tarkas didn't like the sound of that. "Them who?"

"Them!" He spun about, animated with sudden fury, "Those who seem to plague this world, who appear wherever we go and interfere with my work. They poke and they prod, sniff and snoop, harass and harangue–"

"And eventually attack?"

"We showed them, didn't we!?"

Tarkas thought he knew who *we* were. "What did you do?"

"We–I–" his triumphant grin faded a little, "I…don't know exactly. But I could feel it afterward, there inside me, hiding. I had to protect it, you see. That was only fair; it had protected me. Those worthless peasants with their torches and spells were no match for it! Nobody was a match for us–!"

Tarkas could easily see how an anti-life elemental would bond with this man.

"–Not time, not age. No hunger or thirst. We would be forever, and we would *know*!"

"Know what?"

"Why, everything," said the man, surprised. Perhaps he had forgotten that he had an audience.

"Don't be silly," Tarkas admonished him, "Not even the gods know everything."

"HE DOESN'T WANT TO!" Virlor roared, racing up to seize Tarkas by the collar. "He could have; he did at the beginning. 'On the First Day, the Eye of God opened, and it saw the Light, and the Light was.' The Light *was*! The God saw it, and it was, and he knew!"

"So?"

"So the God stopped!" he shrieked in despair, and slumped, pulling on the Hero's vest. "After nine days, he stopped looking, the Eye ceased to open! He hides Himself. Only those things he saw *are,* but everything else *isn't*, it…changes." How vile that word tasted, in his mouth. "That is the whole purpose of this…vigil."

Tarkas *had* been wondering. "To pray for the Eye to open again?"

Virlor looked at him, astounded. Then he began to laugh. "No, you fool," he sneered, when he could breathe again, "To pray that it stays shut!" He approached the edge of the great black spot, and profaned it for the first time in countless centuries, placing his foot upon the stones and walking boldly to the center. "This 'holy place' is a monument to ignorance, an ignorance that we will correct this very day!"

Tarkas also approached, but refused to tread upon the stones without cause. "You think your prayers will be so much more powerful, then, that you will open in a day what so many others have prayed to keep shut for so long?"

The old man looked at him pityingly. "You *are* dense, aren't you?" He plucked his pilfered scroll from within his vest. "We studied this world in great detail, turning to the study of men only when no better subjects could be found. We found the Upweller lore, a vast treasure from the old days, scandalously perverted and neglected." He held up the parchment, shaking it in his clenched fist. "We liberated this hoarded knowledge from those ignorant simpletons when they denied it to us, refusing to let us put it to its proper use!"

Tarkas began to get angry, especially at words like 'liberated.' "Which is?"

The man spread his arms, to encompass the whole scene. "To bring it to this place, at this time, and force the Hidden God to open His Eye!"

Tarkas looked about them, noting the stones in their careful patterns and the grass blowing in the wind and the birds singing in the trees and…Did all those people die, and die that way, because of this man's farcical plot?! "Force a God to do something he doesn't want to do? At a shrine?"

"Dolt!" said Virlor, "No greater fool than thou! You do not stand before a shrine. *This* is the Eye of God! We will open it, if He will not, we will see, and we will know!"

The itching began, sudden and fierce, but Tarkas didn't wait to see where the magic came from or what it would do. He leaped, but the man had timed it too well. As he spoke the sun shone down becoming a palpable presence in the Eye, a wall of light that kept Tarkas out. Brighter and brighter it grew, dazzling, solid–

When it was gone, so was the old man.

Fex.

First things first: rouse the sleepers. He turned back to them and paused, shocked, a little, by what he saw.

No, wait, first things second. *Dress* the sleepers, then rouse them. Thranj's Beard, Mirani's top is filthy. Look at the *size* of those handprints. Janosec! No, don't be stupid, Janosec's hands are too clean to make those marks, must have been that creep up above. Let's just clean that right up.

Now wake them. Counterspell? No, there it is, in the back of his head like they usually are, a hold-and-release sort. That's weird didn't know I could do that with a sleep spell. Let's just release it great. Still asleep? Well, they had a busy day already, no rest last night, I'm sure. Do I even *have* a wake spell? No matter, a light tap to the bottom of the foot works just as well.

"Hey!" Tarkas shouted, when Mirani's foot made a wild swipe at him.

"Well, move your foot!" she snarled, and slapped at Janosec's shoulder. "God's Within, no one should have to wake up twice in the same day!" She completely ignored the Hero's offered hand, leaving it for Janosec while she struggled, with much grunting and cursing, to her feet.

"Where is the old man?" asked Janosec, the soul of reason, as always.

Tarkas looked askance at Mirani, and said, "Well, I discovered that he was also the inventor of mornings, and fried him where he stood. His ashes blew off that way." He pointed off in some direction or other.

Mirani immediately brightened, but dimmed when she realized it probably wasn't true. "He escaped, didn't he?" she said in a sulk. Unhappily, Tarkas admitted that he had, although the precise method escaped him, as he described its appearance.

"But Uncle–!"

"He *WHAT?!*" she cried, utter horror on her face. She ran and grabbed his vest, much as the old man himself had done. "And you stand about here? He could kill us all, kill everything from in there! You must follow, you must stop him!"

"How?" demanded Tarkas, "How am I to follow, except by opening the Eye myself?"

"But Uncle–!"

"You can't!"

He gestured expansively. "I know I can't!" he practically shouted, "I have no spell, no idea how–"

She tugged on his vest again, bringing her face directly into his. "You can't–open–the Eye," she said, with special emphasis.

"But Mirani–"

"Why not?" asked Tarkas.

She sighed gustily, annoyed at his obtuseness. "The Eye can only open twice a year," she explained, as if to a child, "If the sun is not directly overhead, if the Eye is not looking into the light which it has already seen, it will see something else."

"That would be bad," Tarkas guessed.

"That would be bad," she agreed.

"But Mirani–!"

"*WHAT!?* I mean, Yes, Janosec?" She released Tarkas' vest, looking sheepish.

Janosec looked blank. "I forgot my question," he said, puzzled. "No, wait. Why, um, if the Eye opens on its own, why did he need the scroll?"

"Perhaps the spell–" began Tarkas.

"For the timing, I would think," answered Mirani at the same time. "It's part of the lore, when vigil would be held, and by which city. He needed to know that." Then she turned to Tarkas. "What were you about to say, O font of wisdom?"

"Nothing," said Tarkas, waving a hand as if to dispel his own thought, "I was just thinking he would find the spell in there, to open the Eye."

Now she looked confused. "But, why would he? I mean, he would need that spell just to get the scroll, he couldn't–"

"Uncle, the scroll was the thing in the tree stump!" shouted Janosec excitedly. "He must have used the spell to open it–"

"And the priest, or others, caught him," finished Tarkas. "We've seen how he defends himself."

Mirani folded her arms and scowled at them both. "If you are both quite finished speculating about Upweller customs, I'll tell you." She waited until both men looked properly abashed, which wasn't much. "The scroll is contained in the altar, yes, but only the priest can open it. The spell is useless without the key."

"So he must have either interrupted a sacred ceremony, or else gotten the priest to remove it privately," Tarkas concluded.

"Ceremony," she confirmed. "Some copies are used for instruction, but the scroll is only used for worship."

"Uncle," started Janosec, "Would this spell be enough to open the Eye?"

"You can't open the Eye," she repeated tiredly, "Not without the key, which is several days travel back that way, and not without killing me first."

"Oh, piffle," dismissed Tarkas, turning to stare at the great black circle in the ground. Hmm. "I doubt a human sacrifice will be necessary. Mirani?"

"Yes?" she asked, coming to stand behind him.

"What is the meaning of this symbol here?" he inquired, indicating a second little shrine, set at the edge of the crossroad. As he expected, once her attention had been drawn to it, she moved up to the shrine and repeated her earlier observance, only this time she said 'The Word' under her breath.

Tarkas copied her, his fingers moving over the symbol's lines. "'The Word'?" She set her lips shut, and left them to stand by the side of the Eye.

"Uncle?" inquired Janosec, recognizing the tone of Tarkas' voice.

"These are the symbols from the tree stump," said the Hero firmly, "The ones we could not recognize. 'The Living' and 'The Word'."

"You have an idea," said the nephew.

"Yes indeed," breathed the senior. "We don't know the spell the priest would have used–"

"I do," said Mirani from the side.

"I know you do," said Tarkas, "And I'll not ask you to do what you think is wrong by telling it to us." He turned back to his male companion. "But I am the Champion of the Gods, even the hidden ones, and I think I have a way. You, gather some tinder on the Eye while I fetch some appropriate materials. We will give the Eye something to see!"

When Tarkas returned, carrying his burden–a tree trunk bigger around than he was–he found his nephew standing by a great pile of dried grass, next to the Eye, looking ashamed for his dereliction. "It…seemed wrong, somehow," was his only explanation. Deffin didn't apparently think so, finding the place where the old man had stood to be of great interest.

"I know," sympathized his uncle, "But we do what we must. It is more than a holy place, though, it is an object of great power, and if we do not do what needs to be done quickly, that power will be used for a far more profane purpose than our footsteps will ever be." Having steeled his own resolve, he took his burden, far more than just a tree trunk, stepped into the area of black stones, and placed it near the center of the Eye. When Janosec came up, arms full of hay, he indicated a place in the stones.

"Do you still have the priest's amulet?"

Janosec jerked and dropped his load, patting his body anxiously. Then his mind and his memory caught up with him, and he found it where he had placed it so long ago, in the pocket of his sword belt. Tarkas took it from him and knelt, placing the disk carefully in a hole among the stones, exactly the right size. He stood, lifting the wood as Janosec shifted the grass over the disk, and set the trunk in place. Then he lifted his eyes, to Mirani, a marvelous sight, clad in her pilgrim's robes and her virtue.

"Will you come?" he asked gently, "The gods know we could use your strength there as here."

"I will n–" she started to say, but stopped as his eyes shifted away from her, and her ears caught the sound of many men approaching, with gear. She turned, eyes lighting on the guard captain and his men.

"My lord," said the leader, managing to ignore Mirani and her smoldering eyes, "I have been commanded to arrest you and your comrades, for your role in the deaths of the pilgrims, and the disappearance of the Champion NarZirtas." His flat tone gave away his joy at the task.

"The story of my life," replied Tarkas, his amiable tone giving away his dread at the prospect.

"Who commands you?" asked Mirani. "Has the chairman revived?"

The officer shook his head. "We found his body at the base of the cliff," he informed her sadly. "And mourn his loss. I am commanded in this by his replacement, however temporary, Zirtas Tamara."

Mirani turned instantly and leapt into the black stones. "I go with you." Tarkas placed her at Janosec's left, while he took the right, and they clasped hands. Deffin sat with them, Tarkas hand stroking his fur.

The captain, surprisingly, made no attempt to stop her, him, or even set foot upon the stones himself. "My lord, will you come with us?"

"Sorry," said Tarkas with great cheer, "Would you mind if I escaped instead?"

"Please," responded the man, as if granting a request, and waved his men back. "What are you going to do?"

Tarkas responded with a rhyme, one of his favorite couplets, and ignited the grass at their feet. "We are going to save the world," he told the man. After a moment's pause, he continued, "And add a new day to the week."

He took a deep breath, preparing the timing in his mind. It had to be very precise. He looked at the men ringing the Eye, the only pilgrims, now. "Be true to yourselves." Advice or instructions, who could say.

He began.

"First is to Second
As Second is to Third.
The First is for the Living
The Second for the Word."

The exact words of the spell didn't matter, really. They don't, in matters of magic, where the will and purpose of the caster is the driving force. The spell represents his will, channels it, shapes it into a form the world can recognize.

Some of the words mattered, the carved ones, the ones Tarkas had made sure to fit into his couplet. The ones that seemed to come from someplace deep within or beyond himself, almost substantial in their meaning and significance. They fell like stones onto the key, casting echoes of other sounds and other words, all meaning the same thing.

The disk beneath the fire was a talisman, a tool, primed to respond to a will properly focused by the words of power embedded into the spell, transforming it into something else entirely.

The Eye began to open.

Tarkas felt it, his feet itching incredibly, but he had no time or attention to spare for that now. A second spell was needed, and he placed a foot into the fire.

"Life of flame,
I summon thee,
Come to me, to me, to me–"

…taking a deep breath…

"TRENT!"

One instant, three events.

Trent exploded, as he rarely gets the opportunity to do, the fire below clothing him, the wood within feeding him, the magic, doggerel though it was, enhancing him. A second sun rose in the valley, the only thing the Eye would see when it opened.

The Eye opened, blinded by the Light, which it had already seen.

Tarkas and his companions vanished from the sight of men and gods alike.

Chapter 15

Mirani was screaming. That's what she thought, but she couldn't hear herself, so she wasn't sure. Her hand hurt.

Janosec was paralyzed, only his firm grips on the hands of his companions reassuring him that he had any body at all.

Tarkas returned his nephew's grip, glad for the pressure, counting his heartbeats in it and waiting until he should happen to feel one. At least he wasn't seeing things this time around.

The blankness went away as fast as it had come, the return of the world both sudden and thunderous. Wait, that wasn't thunder, that was…waves crashing? No, it was winds howling. No, it was both, one on either side. Tarkas moved, dragging his companions with him towards a nearby rock wall, wanting to have at least one reasonably dependable surface at his back.

Bonk! The rock wall hit him.

Oh, that's all right then. He liked Earth elementals. They were…Earthy.

A face, ill-formed but a face nonetheless, appeared on the face of the stone. "Who are you?"

"Demlas Tarkas."

"De–" The face stopped in mid-syllable, a clear sign that the entity using it had left. Tarkas pinched its nose.

"That went well," he judged, and turned to face his comrades. They stood there staring at him. "Um, that was–"

A blast of wind caught him behind the back, a localized hurricane that lifted him off the ground, twisting and spinning in the air, to drop on the far side of the plateau. He rose, dusting himself off. Now they were staring with their mouths open. "Uh, that was–"

A wave crashed up and over him, drenching his companions with salt spray as it flattened him against the ground. "*Urk!*" he coughed, spitting out seawater as he struggled to rise. Now they were on their knees as well. "That, *hack, choke, spit*, that is–"

"That is Targon," echoed a voice all around him.

Tarkas moved, suddenly dry and clean, spinning to face the god called Targon, arising in all his majesty from the sea, his domain. It kept the smirk on his face from showing to his comrades, as they lowered their eyes in the divine presence.

"My lord."

"Honored Tarkas," said Water, "You have led Us a merry chase all these days, only to wash up on Our very doorstep."

"'The feet of Water swim fast and far'," Tarkas intoned, abasing himself. "It was not of my choosing, lord. My current foe is a man of great cunning and guile, and he diverted me to where the elements are not, with only my companions to carry on the pursuit in my place."

The gaze of Water washed over the companions, and they trembled but did not cry out at its touch. "They are worthy," said Water, keeping his face straight, and voice level with difficulty, "And honored, as you are."

"My lord is gracious." With their heads bowed, neither Janosec nor Mirani could see as Tarkas made urgent gestures towards the domain of Life.

"I am also curious," said Targon, taking the hint, "But I sense that your pursuit is not yet ended, although the end is in sight. If I am not mistaken, here is the last of Us come to welcome you home."

These last words took even Tarkas by surprise, and he scrambled to the mouth of the pass opening onto the valley that was the domain of Life. Deffin followed, of course, knocking the two upright companions over in his haste to get closer to the challenge wafting up from below. By the time they had righted themselves, the Lord of Water was gone, and they trotted over to the pass mouth themselves.

"What is that?" breathed Janosec, staring at the creature in the air.

"That," said Tarkas, "Is the largest bird you will ever see and live to speak of."

For a few moments no one spoke, absorbed in the creature's smooth, gliding flight. Then Mirani snorted. "That's a murf! They're not that big, I've held one on my arm!"

The Hero chuckled. "This one can hold you on its back."

Mirani gasped as the true size of the beast became apparent, the human figure riding it looking ridiculously small by comparison. It was also much farther away than she thought, and approaching very, very fast.

Then it was the Hero's turn to be surprised, for the figure astride the giant bird was not Irolla. Janosec was astonished as well. "Mother?"

Fenita waved, but said nothing until after the bird had settled in its previous place and she had speedily removed her irritating presence from its back. "Janosec!" she yelled, racing up the path to greet her first-born, laughing and crying.

Tarkas and Mirani both retreated, allowing them a few moments of relative privacy on the plateau, the only moments available. Fortunately, Janosec and Fenita knew this as well, so it was only a short while before Tarkas heard a judiciously loud, "I had to stay, Mother. He needed me."

"He still does," he interrupted, walking over. Mirani came over as well, and introductions were made.

"You are quite right," said Fenita, all business. "There's something very nasty roaming around down there and the Lady wants you to take care of it."

All three companions looked at each other.

"Nasty how?" asked Mirani.

Fenita looked a little worried, as well. "She doesn't know. However she knows what she knows, whatever means she has, this thing is repellant to them all."

"Good," said Tarkas, surprising most of them, "Then she can lead us right to it." He looked at all the staring faces. "What? It is easy, just look at everything, whatever you cannot see has to be it." He'd used that method before. "Then get everything between us and it out of the way."

Fenita stopped nodding stupidly. "Okay, fine. You do that. Mirani, come with me."

"Why?" she asked, not wanting to be parted at what promised to be the climax of their long chase.

If Fenita was annoyed that she was being questioned, it didn't show. "Because Tarkas is right again. This thing, whatever it is, is heading straight for the Lady's palace, some of us should be there in case it gets through, and you are the only person small enough for the murf to carry with me. Now, we go."

Mirani sat behind Fenita as the murf slid down the wind, trying to adjust for the shifts in the wind but consistently smacking forward into Fenita's stiffened back. She rode poorly, eyes blinking but unseeing, and Mirani thought she knew why. "You shouldn't have called it a pet, you know," she yelled over the wind.

"I know!" Her comrade's mother shrieked, for reasons that had nothing to do with the sound of air.

"It really is quite fearsome–" she added.

"I *know*!"

"–But it was rather poorly done of him to tell it to 'kill' at just that moment, I thought."

"I doubt," protested Fenita, moved to defend the Brother of her clan, "That he had any idea what would happen. The murf is much larger and can fly, after all. Nor do I think he intended that the beast roar so frightfully just when we were taking off."

"You're right, of course," agreed Mirani easily, now that Fenita was past her initial shock, "He's a very honorable man, even the gods say so."

"*We* say so," emphasized Fenita. "That's why he is the Champion NarDemlas."

Mirani sat silent for a while, as the walls of Irolla's fortress came into view. Finally she said, as if embarrassed, "I should like to change my name." No one of the clan NarZirtas has changed their name in over ten generations.

Fenita stiffened again. "How?" she asked at last.

Mirani gasped in comprehension, pulling away from the Wife. "Not *that* way," she protested, "I mean, your son is a wonderful man, but…"

Fenita waited but nothing followed. "But what?"

"I don't…want him," she continued tentatively, well aware that this was her companion's mother, "I don't want anyone, I never have." At least, she never had, but ever since they had collapsed before the Eye, there was something…different.

"I do hope there were some worthy men to choose from, where you came from," said Fenita. Bad for her homeland if there were none, but perhaps good for Jano–

"There were many," countered Mirani, "Our villages are not so stunted as that. But I knew most of them from the guards or the militia. It never felt…right." Which was a lie, the usual one, although a small one. But no one she had yet met understood the lack of such feelings at all, and she had long ago grown tired of trying to explain. The lack of that lack, the sudden filling of the void she was so accustomed to, she had only begun to experience, and couldn't begin to explain, even to herself.

"Ah," said Fenita, understanding. It could be indeed difficult for two who form a relationship in one shape to reshape it, after. "*Do* you want to change your name?"

"Yes, of course I do," answered Mirani, with none of her former hesitation. This woman had made no snide comments about her being among the guards. This woman understood her in moments, as her grandmother never had, had never tried to. A momentary vision, of the old woman's annoyance at her act, brought a quick smile to her face.

"Very well, when we meet Tarkas again later, I will ask him. But I do not think he will object."

Mirani's stomach dropped into her sandals, and it had nothing to do with the murf's sudden dive. "Why?" she asked, suddenly nervous.

Fenita delayed responding until after the bird had settled on the great stump. "He *is* the Brother, you know," she said sliding easily down behind the wing. A little sound told her that her new clansman had *not* known. "And I *am* the Wife," she continued, rubbing it in a little, to her fellow's continued and increasing dismay. "In the absence of the clanleader–" She left the last part unsaid.

"You might have told me," Mirani scolded, as she slid down to the step.

"You wouldn't have spoken, then," Fenita replied, not mentioning that there had been no time or need to do so before, anyway. She gave her fellow guest no time to reply, afraid of either being eaten by the murf or killed when the rotting wood collapsed under them. At the bottom of the stair she paused, feeling the same sort of glee she imagined Irolla must have felt, as Mirani saw the inhabitants of the menagerie for the first time. "Lady!" she called.

Instantly the many and various denizens in the undergrowth made way, even the insects revealing themselves in their fleeing hordes. The two ladies promptly crossed the enclosure, heading for a door as clearly labeled by the fleeing life as if it had a wide colored stripe painted up to it. They understood clearly now, how the absence of something can be as reliable a pointer as its presence.

"Wait, wait," said Fenita, when the door closed behind them. She went to the pedestal and lifted the goblet waiting there, performing the welcoming ritual of a people not her own, however unhappy she was about it.

"I am?" said Mirani in same mild disgust she herself felt, when told she was supposed to take a sip from the same cup.

"Yes," said Fenita, "A vile custom, I know." Mirani took a very small sip, from the opposite side, and practically threw the cup onto the pedestal. As they walked down the corridor she let the water leak from her mouth and wiped it away on the back of her hand.

They found Irolla in the usual room, only this time she sat on the specially shaped stump that Fenita had occupied for so many days. Her eyes were shut, her breathing deep and regular, her concentration absolute. Fenita settled herself to wait, and Mirani copied the motion, staring, as curious about her host as Fenita had been. "If you don't like it, say so," Life said abruptly. "Don't expect me to tailor my doings for you if you cannot even be bothered to express yourself."

They shared a guilty glance and blushed, but the Lady was not reprimanding them, merely stating her case. "You will be guided to a room. You will find some weapons there. Do with them what you will."

They waited politely for more, but none was forthcoming, so

they got up and left as they had come. "Does she even know I am here?"

"Of course," said Fenita, not really paying attention to where she walked. "But she is much concerned at the moment with a major catastrophe somewhere in the world, and has little attention to spare. When she sent me to you she said only 'Tarkas, murf, go.' I had to figure the rest out for myself."

"It would take more than that to get me astride that beast," said Mirani, amazed at Fenita's courage, trying to follow in her footsteps, "Your faith is greater than mine. I kept thinking of lirrik."

Fenita laughed. "I, too," she agreed. Then her face grew still. "But it was not faith. It was Tarkas. Wherever he was, my son had to be."

Mirani's face fell. "Not always," she said, unhappy to be telling a mother this but unwilling to deny her the truth. Instead, she told the whole story.

Fenita was grateful for it. "Yes," she agreed, rendering the thought in words, since the picture was too painful, "It would have been bad, but only if you had lost both. Janosec would have led to Tarkas as easily. That's why I'm here. Irolla was searching for Tarkas, through him, through me."

Mirani was no fool. "Tarkas is Janosec's father, isn't he? How?"

For a second Fenita considered answering that with *The usual way* or some equally glib comment, but chose not to. "Pellik's Rule."

"My condolences," said Mirani.

Fenita laughed again. "My husband lives," she replied, and took pity on her guest's confusion, "Nor is Tarkas his brother. It was a very…unusual invocation of Pellik's Rule."

"I'm…sure it was," said Mirani, trying to figure out how it could possibly have happened and failing. "You must tell me how it happened, some day."

"I will, but…here we are."

Mirani looked about, completely at a loss as to how they had gotten wherever they were. "Where are we?"

Fenita opened the door. "At the armory," she breathed appreciatively.

Mirani stepped forward, not nearly as appreciative. "No, it's only a storeroom. A real armory would smell much more of leather and such."

Fenita realized with dismay that the other woman was right, apprehensive at the thought of facing something 'very nasty' with dull, corroded weapons. Still, even a blunt edge can strike true if luck is with the wielder. Best to check, and quickly, among all these racks.

Well! This edge was sharp! And this one. Ow! How could this be? "We're better outfitted than I expected," she said happily, looking for a weapon she could use. Fortunately there were many, as if these blades had all been crafted for women. So she now faced the pleasant prospect of choosing the best one from among many. From behind she heard a rather random clanging. "Have you found one yet?"

Mirani seemed disappointed. "No. Just blades," she said dully, "The NarZirtas use no blades."

Fenita turned to her. "You are Demlas now."

But Mirani shook her head. "I will be, if the Brother agrees, or the clanleader," she admitted, "But they have not yet, and so I am Zirtas."

You will be Demlas, if I have to beat Tarkas with sticks to make it so. But that was for the future, and Tarkas was on the far side of whatever was coming, and even he did not really know what it was. The thought actually cheered her. *Maybe a blade would be of no help, and Mirani's skill with other weapons a boon. Who could know? But then she must have weapons. Let's see what we can find.*

Deffin found the first one, which surprised no one. A carcass, ripped and torn, its throat gone, but strangely, no blood anywhere. Tarkas thought immediately of the wezin and shook, even though the other signs of that particular creature's attack were absent, even though Death himself had said there had only ever been the one. A hurried scan revealed nothing, and Deffin certainly felt completely at ease. They continued, the two men, while the beast prevented food waste behind them.

Thus Janosec and not Deffin found the second one, like the first, a different beast but in similar condition, only smellier from the fight it had put up. The third was different, since it still lived, although its death was certain. Tarkas finished it, getting his hands all sticky with its dark bluish blood. "Blue?" asked the nephew, less well traveled in certain respects.

"Yes, blue," acknowledged the uncle, certifying the younger man's senses. "What color was the blood of the other two?"

"Red," stated Janosec firmly, certifying his uncle's mental acuity. "Is that a pattern?"

"Could be," said Tarkas tentatively, "Wait until the fourth one." That there would be a fourth seemed almost a certainty.

Deffin found the fourth, again, larger like the second but clean like the first. The drinker was desperate, perhaps, after the failed third attack, much less willing to take 'no' for an answer. In any event, they found no more with blood that was not red.

"Why does he drink?" wondered Tarkas, crouching over the latest kill. "He said he had no hunger, no thirst."

"Who said this?" asked Janosec, standing above, on watch.

Tarkas looked sharply up at him. "The old man, of course," he said, with some mild surprise, "Surely you don't think this is any other?"

The nephew shrugged. "I would not know," he apologized, "My memory failed after he stole the dream stuff from us."

"He did?" asked Tarkas, standing. "You never mentioned this."

"We didn't?" Janosec thought back with some effort. "You're right, we didn't. Mirani merely said that you glowed, she did not say what happened to us. But yes, whatever struck at you struck at us, and the bags you gave us did what you intended, I guess, great streams of black draining out of them."

Immediately thereafter the creature exploded, releasing whatever positive life forces it still had, and the man called him a murderer. What killed it? He shook his head at the notion. A question for another day, surely. Instead, he swiftly relayed to Janosec the events that followed, and the man's words, in the teller's style that the younger man envied and imitated.

"A feeder on the powers of life," marveled the man, "By the gods of Air, what a notion. And we killed it." Suddenly he turned and stared at his uncle in horror. "Is that what he does now, the man himself, feed on the powers of life?!"

"Or he thinks he does." Tarkas was all too aware of the power of belief.

Janosec waved a hand back over the long and bloody trail they had followed. "I don't think he merely 'thinks' he does. So many drained, so fast, so powerfully? I'd say he does."

The notion seemed plausible to Tarkas. "A life predator, bonded to him," he mused. "Suddenly it dies. We know, or at least hope we know, what became of the life it stole, but what of its other possessions, and powers?"

"Why blood?" asked Janosec, continuing the line of thought, "The creature didn't consume blood."

"He seeks Life," answered Tarkas immediately, the reply bubbling up from some not entirely conscious place in his soul, "Blood carries Life, but the blood is not the Life. That's why he kills so often. The blood he gets doesn't have enough Life in it, yet he runs far and fast."

"Towards the Lady's palace," continued Janosec. "Why there?"

Tarkas shifted his sword to a more comfortable position. "Let's go ask him."

The fact that Mirani and Fenita were there essentially alone, against a foe with powers they could not imagine or prepare for, was not lost on either man. Neither was it mentioned. Both ran as if the demons of hell were after them and they both knew why. Deffin followed eagerly, the scent of their challenge much more compelling to him than the effluvia of mere animals.

It was faster this way. The old man's kills were rather widely scattered, since his very presence drove them away and he had to chase them down. But now they weren't looking for the kills, and they knew the destination, so it was a much simpler task of getting there first.

They almost did.

Mirani got in the first strike, throwing something with her sling, very hard, very fast. Hard and fast enough to stop the creature the old man had become, to stagger something that had broken creatures as large as Deffin. But it wasn't enough. The man-thing came on, and Fenita stepped forward with something long and shiny in her hand. Two somethings, one in each hand. Excellent! He didn't often get to see the two-handed style done well. Mirani put the sling away, and took up instead something long and brown, a staff, for someone who would not use a blade.

Fortunately for Janosec, the approach to the fortress was very well kept, so he only had to maintain an awareness of Tarkas' position to keep moving forward, the rest of his attention on the battle. While it pleased him to see both ladies make such a good showing of themselves, he noted with dismay that they were unable to cooperate. Both were trained in combat, but not in the same techniques, and so they held off rather than interfere with the other's efforts.

Not that his mother needed much help at the moment. The creature was still man enough to fear her blades, and creature enough to have no other weapons than strength and speed. Nonetheless, his mother lost ground steadily, although she did not turn and flee as the Zirtas champion had. There really was little to be done against someone–some*thing* like him.

The noise of their approach must have startled it, for it paused a moment, and Fenita threw her knife, more like a skinner's blade than a knife, Janosec saw, and not really suited for throwing. But the distance was small and the blade lodged where she meant it to, in the chest of the beast.

It grabbed the hilt and fell, yelling, and eventually became still.

Tarkas and his companion ran up as she turned the body over with the tip of her blade. Strangely, she stuck the corpse, only turning away when the wound failed to bleed, as living men do and corpses usually don't. Tarkas was ready with a "Well done!" on his lips when a shout from Mirani silenced him. "My lady, watch–!"

But it was far too late. With its usual, nearly blinding speed, the monster that had been Virlor struck, kicking out at Fenita's legs and bringing her down. The knife, her own blade, was suddenly at her own throat, the creature crouched over her, pinning her lower body to the ground. The feet of her rescuers were just visible, but her captor was closer, speaking almost directly into her ear with rank, foul breath. "Drop the blade," it instructed, "It would not hurt me, but pulling it out again would be a nuisance."

"Next time I'll cut your head off," she snapped, but she complied, and he–it snatched the weapon up with its free hand and threw it at the two men. Tarkas parried the flying blade easily, but it was just a ploy to allow the man-thing to stand, and it succeeded, the creature dragging his shield up with him.

"You!" it snarled at them, at Tarkas, "Look what you've done to us!"

Janosec looked in disgust, for the man's face was rimmed around, almost dripping with gore, his fingers red with dried blood. Of course, it must have used its teeth as weapons, to tear so many beasts. But the blood was coated over with dirt, hair, and the usual forest debris, until he looked the bestial caricature of a man that he in fact was.

Tarkas looked on calmly, and Janosec knew he'd seen worse. "You did it to yourself."

"We were a scholar!" it would have sobbed, but there was no water in it for tears, "Now look upon us, feasting on blood! Like any of a number of insects we could describe to you in exquisite detail, ignorant oaf."

"Undoubtedly you could, having taken and spent the lives of countless others to extend your own," the Hero replied, unmoved. "As my mentor told me long ago, there are always costs. You have forced others to pay on your behalf for far too long."

Virlor spat, or tried to. "Lies! We killed no one."

Mirani started reciting names, starting with the priest's, and all of her friends in the village, and all their families. Tarkas remained silent, hoping even now for some sign of remorse from the man. In vain. "They attacked us!" protested Virlor, "We defended ourselves. Their supposed deaths are not our fault!"

"Hairsplitting!" exploded Janosec, killing the Hero's hopes of at least keeping the man-thing distracted. "Obscene details! They will not save you here, monster!"

"We are beyond saving!" the creature sneered, more correctly than he knew, or would admit. "We are one now, the power is ours, the will is ours, everything is ours, and you are nothing! We are forever! If this is a monster then this is what we are!"

WHAM!

A great block of wood, swung with no small degree of force by a lady trained in the use of such things, impacted with the monster just above his left ear. To everyone's surprise, not least its own, that piece of dead tree did more damage and caused more pain than either stone projectiles or a piece of solid metal shoved through its chest. Not enough, unfortunately, but the thought was there.

Fenita pushed its arm, and the knife, away from her throat and scrambled away, to her son and her sword, not that either was likely to be of much help at the moment. The monster made no effort to recapture its shield, now unafraid of swords. Indeed, it turned its back on them all, focusing its fury and fear upon the one who had hurt it.

Initially, Tarkas and especially Janosec were moved to come to her defense, however weak their aid might have been. But her explosion of violence persuaded them otherwise, and they actually retreated, for fear of being caught in the melee and injured themselves. The monster followed suit, as much as it could, unable to attack for itself, the pain of each strike showing in its howls and reduced speed. The three at its back merely stood, admiring her skill, entranced by its deadly beauty. They fenced it in, and the wood of its enemy scored many the occasional blow, despite its frantic dodging.

"She wants to be Demlas," Fenita breathed, excitedly.

"She has my vote," replied Tarkas, watching Janosec's face as the other man watched her.

"Yes!" shouted Janosec, perhaps at some well-executed maneuver, perhaps not. "Beautiful!"

But Mirani was tiring as well, and Tarkas thought to aid her, striking with his Great Sword at an opportune moment. The shriek of agony the thing made at the touch of his blade startled her into stillness, her staff extended in its last thrust. Instantly the man-thing seized her weapon despite the pain that such an act must have caused it, and pulled savagely. She stumbled forward, unable to let go in time, and the beast swept her up, flinging away the staff as soon it could be twisted out of her grip.

Again it was a stalemate, but now the beast was wounded and much weaker, no closer to whatever goal it pursued. The blood feebly trickling from its own wound was valueless to it, already stripped of whatever life it may have carried. It had to have more.

Mirani's neck was quite literally ready to hand.

Chapter 16

Janosec howled in horror as Mirani's neck streamed red, the beast's face nuzzling it obscenely, and they all pushed forward as one. But the beast was smarter than it looked, still a man, however fallen, with a man's cunning. At Tarkas' first step forward, it pushed its victim away, his teeth tearing at her throat, and widening what could only have been a fatal wound.

Were it not for Tarkas. By the time he reached her he was already partway through a spell, hand extended to seal her wound and buy him time to heal her. Fenita started forward, then thought better of it and raced to retrieve the quarterstaff, not that she felt herself in any way up to Mirani's level of skill. Janosec alone stood paralyzed, eyes riveted on the sight of the drying blood, the hand fixed so firmly on her throat, the head rolling semi-conscious from the sudden shock. "You will save her, Uncle?" he said, both demanding and pleading. Fenita spared him a glance, but kept going, into the fortress.

Tarkas had little attention to spare for social graces. "I will if you shut up and let me work. Take my sword and go with your mother, don't let it get away."

The sword? Yes, the sword! The city blade he carried would be useless, but not the black sword! He dropped the one and snatched up the other, mind already dancing with images of the monster's grisly death by his hand.

OW, his hand! "It hurts, Uncle!" he shouted, dropping it like a coal.

"I know," replied Tarkas, distractedly, more concerned with her pain than his. "It is a price to be paid."

"Pay?!" the young man shouted in outrage, "We do not pay! We collect!"

"Only the gods can seek fairness and justice at once," murmured his uncle, skipping over the parts where even the gods had to pay. "Now go, do what you must."

Janosec stared at the treasure, the burden, being pressed upon him with fearful unease. "I…am not like you, Uncle," he claimed, miserably.

"As long as you are like yourself I should be satisfied, my son. Best hurry, before your mother kills it first."

Janosec took up the black sword again, this time stifling his outcry. "I go, father."

Tarkas merely smiled, where no one could see it but Mirani, when she opened her eyes. "I didn't know he cared," she whispered.

"Neither did he," the Hero whispered back.

Janosec was back in only a few minutes, the black sword sheathed at his hip, hand flexing. "He has walled himself up, fa– Uncle, with a hostage."

"Your mother?"

Janosec shook his head. "No, there was another woman within. Somehow the beast located her and captured her without struggle, and is now barricaded in a tower room."

The news was surprising, to say the least, but Tarkas hid it with ease. "I have done what I may," he distracted his young protégé, "Give me my sword, and I will see what may be seen. Perhaps I could impose upon you to stay with this young lady for a while–?"

He'd picked flowers with more difficulty.

As he ran, his thoughts raced. The woman? Irolla, certainly. Hostage? Don't see how, she can't be harmed or killed by anything the monster could do. But she is with the beast, in the tower room. Luck or forethought, to capture her before going to the tower? Luck; it couldn't have known it would need her presence just to get in. Captured without struggle? Hmm, perhaps they saw it, but more likely he said that because there were no signs of a struggle. But her favorite room is the open one, not much there to show any such signs. Would sounds, fighting or yelling, carry far? Not sure about that.

Why the tower room?

There was something vile up there. 'A creation of evil for evil's sake', he knew that much, Life and Earth together, but he'd never bothered to see what it was and she had never told him. He had no doubt that the beast had sensed it from afar and come here because of it. It should have been shielded, not merely contained in a sealed room, but he could see how this circumstance would surprise even a Lord.

He heard a voice. "Janosec?" Well, then, apparently sounds carry very well here.

"No," he shouted up the stair, not that he needed to, since he even now mounted the uneven steps, but to announce himself. "He decided to stay with Mirani for some reason."

Fenita smiled to match the grin on his face, but both expressions were short-lived. "Can you get us in?" she asked quietly, "I have only one way, and I would hate to waste it?"

"Strom's Fist?"

She jerked back, stunned and…well, maybe not stunned. "You knew? You expected it?"

He shrugged. "It had to be something, and only the Fist would suffice here. But I admit I am surprised. I would have said Blood, if asked."

"I have that as well."

Now he *was* surprised, and quite impressed. "And the Feet? The Voice, too?" Thranj's Beard! How did she contrive to make that happen?

Fenita pointed at the door. "Perhaps you should ask *her*."

Tarkas took the hint, unlimbered his sword.

"I should have asked Janosec," she scolded herself mildly.

Tarkas tested the edge of the sword against the wall, measured the scar. "No," he said, defending her first choice, "It wouldn't have worked, but it might have killed him trying." He raised his sword overhead, two handed.

"I'm glad I didn't ask Janosec. You do it, then."

"As you wish."

It should have been simple, four slashes to make a squarish sort of block, balanced on one point, and then it falls out. Except it didn't fall, Edge take it. The mass of stone settled on the lower two cuts and sat there, mocking him in front of his sister-in-law. He growled in the back of his throat and made a quick slash at the top of the diamond, a hole he could stick his hand into, pulling the huge stone block out with as much casual grace as he could manage. It came, falling out of its hole, overbalanced, and tipped forward against the opposite wall. Which wasn't nearly as sturdy. The block crashed right through and fell to the ground far below, despite the fact that there was a roof and two floors in between.

Fenita *stared* at him.

Tarkas nearly winced at his mistake, not the one with the stone block. "Oops." He tried to defuse his Heroic faux pas with a courtly 'after you' gesture, but the joke fell quite flat. "You go first, Champion," she said. She did not mean Champion NarDemlas.

He went first.

The room stank, but that was just the monster. In addition to that, a miasma not perceived by the nose, he remembered its shadow from the day he had last stood outside this very room.

The beast was upright; Irolla was not, although that probably didn't mean much. A look at her and his degree of tension reduced itself a notch. She looked just like she had after that disaster in Drakanshar, when she went into a coma for several hours. Directing the affairs of so many elementals at once required so much concentration that even the minimal effort of sitting upright was beyond her. Presumably whatever the catastrophe was that Fenita had mentioned took the same effort.

The beast was getting frantic, torn between his captive and his goal. Is that all it is? A chunk of stone? Don't be silly, he chided himself, of course it's stone, whatever else it may be, and the former Lord of Earth had never been a very creative person. If it had been himself, he would have at least had it shaped like a flower or something.

The monster, sensing his interest, pounced on the stone possessively. And leaped off again, like a man burned. Interesting, the block hadn't even shifted. Could it be part of the pedestal? No, the stand was wood.

He stepped away from the door, certain that the monster would not avail itself of that as a means of escape until it reached its goal, which seemed to be possession of the block, which seemed to be impossible. For now. But the creature seemed even more powerful, however unhealthy its appearance, and Tarkas knew that just letting it be was not an option. The block must be having some effect, and he moved closer to see what it might be, and what he might do about it. The beast moved back, towards Irolla as if that would help it, and away from the black sword.

Experimentally, Tarkas touched the finger of his right hand to the stone, jerking it back as the beast had done. There was power there, surely, but evil as well, and a palpable sense of wrongness. Touching it was like…well, no, not like walking over corpses, he'd done that, and this was much worse. This was like a…a living corpse, life trapped in a dead shell. No, even more grotesque, an unliving, undead state that was a filthy gray area between the two much cleaner alternatives. A mockery of life, an attempt to fuse the powers of the various elements to create a living thing, the way his hand was a simulation of life.

His hand?

No, his hand was a replica of the hand he'd had, created to do what his hand had done, but with no claim that it was somehow *his hand*.

Hmm. His hand.

Fenita entered the room, attracting the interest of both…males, and Tarkas moved back to the hole, lest the beast try to take yet another hostage. With a flick of his wrist he transformed his sword, reducing its size, its effectiveness, and its price, all in one motion. How long since he held this little black knife? How long since it had been all he needed? But it should still be more than enough to hold off this monster, in Fenita's hands.

That done, he walked back over to the pedestal, attracting far more of the beast's interest since he was now unarmed. Or seemed to be. About the stone, the beast seemed to have lost its fear. Perhaps, it believed Tarkas to be as unable to take the damned thing as itself. Slaughter him, kill her, take the block at its leisure.

Tarkas reached out with his left hand and grabbed the block.

It was stuck. He twisted, gripping the horrific thing without any obvious reaction, and twisted again, harder. With a ripping, splintering sound, the block came loose from the stand, with little chunks of the pedestal still clinging to the bottom. Tarkas looked at it and burst out laughing.

"It's just glu–aggh!" The beast leaped, insane with lust and rage, and toppled both pedestal and man, scrabbling for the prize, screaming when it finally touched the edge of the block. Tarkas could actually feel the beast's weight increase, on top of him, and he kicked it away before it got worse. The block somehow…fed it!

The beast came at him again, instantly, and he had to fend it off one-handed, in a ludicrously hideous game of Keep-It-Away. In a new wrinkle, the beast started circling when Fenita entered the fray.

"Fenita, no!" shouted Tarkas. She looked at him, shocked that he would end her pursuit when the beast was clearly outnumbered. He jerked his head towards the door and she understood-the monster would think to flee eventually. Until one of the others appeared she had to block the exit. Perhaps even after, unless one of them thought to bring wood with them.

What to do? There must be some way to overpower this thing with one hand tied behind his–

Overpower. An interesting word, that.

He eyed the monster critically. Bigger, stronger, heavier, it was also far slower than it had been. Yes, that would work. "Fenita, strike when you may!"

The beast glanced at her, and Tarkas pounced. He swept the repellant thing up in a close two-handed grip, the block in his left hand pressed firmly against its back, his right hand holding his left in place. The monster screamed. The monster struggled. The monster grew.

Fenita moved, black knife in hand, she approached her only target, the creature's broad and growing back. Suppressing her distaste for the dishonorable tactic, she swung hard–

The knife moved, dragging her hands with it. Unable to stop herself, she watched in horror as the black blade stabbed straight through both of the Hero's hands, through the stone block, and into the monster's back! In shock she let go, just in time to save her own life.

The hilt, the only part of the knife she could still see, was changing! It got longer, thicker, like a sword's hilt, but larger than any sword she had ever–it turned white! The knob and guard stayed black, but the grip practically glowed. She averted her eyes. There was something terrible about that grip.

Tarkas and the beast shrieked together, and she fled, hands over her ears. What had she done?! By sheer chance she missed the hole in the outer wall and a plunge to her death, although she might have considered that a blessing then. She worked blindly to get as far away as she could get, stopping only when she could go no farther. The stone walls muffled the shrieking significantly, releasing her from the grip of horror into the hands of sorrow and remorse, stricken with guilt.

Eventually, the screaming stopped.

Eventually, she noticed.

How long she stayed there she did not know. Indeed she did not even know where she was. She found herself crouching somewhere, kneeling, her face pressed into her knees, hands on her ears. With a bit of effort, she took her hands away and lifted her head, and found she knelt face first in the farthest corner, like some misbehaving child. Her knees ached, and her feet, when she rose, were marked along the tops with the pattern of the stones in the floor. She stood, tottering like one crippled, and made her way to the door, now issuing only an ominous silence.

And light. She almost couldn't see it, her eyes blurry from the light streaming in from outside, but there was a light from inside the room as well. It pulsed, yes, that's what she saw, light growing and fading with a steady rhythm.

With one hand on the edge of the hole, she peeked in.

Tarkas lay alone, in almost the same position as when she had seen him last, his hands clasped and pinned together by the blade–a white, gleaming, long blade–of what had been his knife. Now the hands were resting against his own belly, also run through by the sword, making him look, but for that one addition, overwhelmingly like a body laid out for viewing. He was covered with dust, mounded up on his chest and groin, spilling over onto the floor, pouring out of the shreds of a pilgrim's outfit that had been the beast's final clothing.

He glowed with the same white light as that which emanated from his sword, both of them pulsing together. Truly, he looked like the God's Champion. A *dead* God's Champion. And all her fault.

Almost, she didn't go into the room, but in the end she did what she had to do, clambering through the hole to stand by the side of her fallen Hero. Remembering him, as one did at funerals, was easy, his visits infrequent and colorful. In particular she thought of his first appearance, their one time together. He had left bruises, then, even though she could tell he was being gentle, as though he hadn't known his own strength. Then to find out that he hadn't…!

The bruises faded, in time, but the pride didn't, pride when he saved them, saved them all, the townsfolk who'd fled, the men who'd vanished. He'd saved Jerim, not knowing what he was doing or what it would mean. And Jerim had rewarded him, made him part of the foundations of their little clan, and later its Champion.

And she had rejected him over a little bit of stone, called him 'Champion', as if he hadn't been the Gods' Champion before, as if he was somehow different! Gods within, how petty she'd been!

That sword had to go. It ruined the display, the perfection of his outer body finally reflecting the beauty of his inner self. At least the Gods know how to do funerals properly. She reached out a hand to take the hilt, a strange dread slowing her.

"DON'T…touch that," a voice shouted, the first word stopping her hand in mid-reach. Irolla's voice. The Lady of Life was awake at last.

"What the Hell am I doing on the floor?" she demanded, and struggled to her feet with very un-divine awkwardness. Then she caught sight of the sword's main support, when she could see over the fallen pedestal. "What happened to him?"

Fenita understood the tone perfectly, although it wasn't the sort of tone one would expect a goddess to take. That was a question for another day, however, and she hastily shoved it far out of her mind, focusing instead on relating the whole bizarre tale to her hostess, finishing it with: "Why am I not to touch it?"

"A Great Sword in its most active mode?" asked Irolla. "Death could collect the remains of your soul in a pouch!"

Fenita blanched, not quite as white as the sword, and backed away. "Is he… consumed, then?"

"Oh, no," Irolla breathed, gazing down fondly upon the Hero's radiant face, "He is not even dead. He will never be dead again." Fenita looked up sharply at that, but decided not to ask what that particular comment meant. Irolla reached out and took the sword by its hilt, tugging it easily from Tarkas' prone form. The white light dimmed immediately, the sword merely white, the body merely human. No blood spurted, giving the lie to the goddess' comment, until Fenita checked and discovered that there was no wound. Tarkas' clothes weren't even cut. He could merely have been sleeping.

"When will he…awaken?" she asked.

The sword made a strange, not-quite-metal sound as the goddess laid it down on the stone next to its wielder. "I do not know," she admitted, unbuckling the harness for the scabbard, "The only other wielder I know of, well, the second, actually–" she paused, rolling him over onto one shoulder "–hold him. One of the wielders was a Champion called Brill, but it wasn't his real name. His real name, if I recall correctly, was Ergon." She finally succeeded in pulling the scabbard out, and they let his body roll back onto the stone. She didn't rise, though, continuing, "But after he was pierced by the sword, he fell into a sleep so deep that none who knew him as Ergon were alive when he awoke. The people in the later time had tales of a great hero named Brill, and when they saw his many wondrous deeds they started calling him that."

That didn't please Fenita at all. "He may not awaken while we live? His son may never see him again?"

Irolla shrugged, kneeling there. "I do not know. In any event, it is done and all we may do is wait, for a lifetime or even longer if need be." Fenita reminded herself that this woman could be waiting for long after her own life had ended, and wondered which of them had the advantage.

Irolla took the sword in hand again and touched it to the scabbard. The leather, already god-touched, changed yet more, coloring and lengthening, becoming suitable to house the Great Sword. When it finished, the goddess slid the blade in and strapped it down. "Done," she sighed, and picked up the package, standing. "It is safe now."

"What is safe?" asked a masculine voice. Janosec and Mirani stood outside the door, looking in.

Irolla cast her eyes over to the hole in the wall. "Who is that?" she asked her guest.

Fenita looked at her oddly. "*They* are Demlas Janosec, my son, and his fellow companion, Demlas Mirani."

"Two?" murmured Irolla, and blinked her eyes a few times. "Ah, my apologies. It must have been a…trick of the light. I greet you, Demlas Janosec, Demlas Mirani."

"Shall we enter?" asked Janosec, looking unhappily at the little hole, and the size of the space beyond.

Irolla strode over, remembering that only her presence would open the–What in the name of Earth!? The walls were…dripping! Flowing. The lines of the door were melting and running like hot wax. Then the hole was gone, sealed by melting rock, the shouts of alarm from the two outside cut off. The roof of the tower split open, sunlight poured in, the shouts of alarm from the two outside renewed. Fenita dove for Tarkas' limp body and his wondrous sword, fearing that they would be drowned in liquid rock, but the floor was not 'flooding', nor was it even soft.

In moments the walls of rock had run down between them, and they were all left on a pedestal of rock in the open air, the rushing winds clearing the stench and dust left behind by the beast. Irolla stared and gasped, seeing the hole in the roof of her palace for the first time. And still the rock flowed, the floor dropping beneath them as the tower itself seemed to sink into the ground. Only the strange feeling in their bellies told them that it was they who moved down, not the world that moved up.

The walls rising up on two sides were a bit of a surprise, but then they were forewarned about the others, and the roof, suddenly rolling across the sky, leaving them in a new room. "Good," said Irolla when her fortress had settled down, not bothering to explain what had happened or why it was good. "Janosec, please take your…uncle, and carry him to a place where he may rest. You will be guided. Mirani, please carry this sword, and go with him."

If either of them were at all disgruntled about such brusque treatment, they did not reveal it, merely coming forward to take on their respective burdens, before leaving the room. "You people never talk!" whispered Irolla.

"What?" asked Fenita.

"I said, 'I really hope you like her'," replied Irolla.

Fenita grinned, for the first time in what seemed like days, and said in a voice filled with pride, "Oh, yes. Yes, indeed. She was not *born* Demlas, you know."

Irolla relaxed a bit. "Good. She would have become Demlas anyway, you know. Those two are so wrapped around with Life I couldn't even see them, earlier."

"Of course I knew–" Fenita pretended to sound shocked.

"–You are his mother, after all." Irolla finished, laughing. Then she grew more sober. "I envy you that." She led the way from the room, to the accompaniment of her guest's silence. The hall echoed with the tread of their sandaled feet, the youngsters nowhere to be found. As private as need be. "Soon you must leave us."

"Yes." She had found her son. She had found a new, highly suitable Demlas. And perhaps (*perhaps,* she minded herself, *they are not wed yet)* a proper wife for the Second and Heir. But among the joyful tidings, some sad. It pained her to leave the Lady here alone, goddess though she was. A silly notion, she knew, but she was only a woman, not a goddess, and could only judge things according to her own measure.

And Tarkas, as well, for the lady had said 'us', not 'me'. Would she see him again, or would he sleep her life away? How long would Irolla sit waiting, pining? How strange, a goddess, to be so stricken, but that was the only name she could put to the tone in the Lady's voice, a mortal tone.

"You will know, I think," said Irolla, and Fenita blushed, reminded that her hostess was indeed a goddess. There was no need for sorrow, especially when she could see it in you.

The room, when they came to it, was quite familiar. Tarkas now lay in the bed she had so often used, hands at his side, his sword hanging like a banner on the wall. Someone had taken the time to brush his hair and arrange his clothing neatly, but when they entered, the only possible culprits were standing together away from the bed, Janosec behind her, his arms encircling her as they both watched the comatose hero.

"He has not changed?" Fenita had to ask, however needlessly. All of them had the same expression to accompany their negative replies.

"He will, though," the Lady promised them, the only assurance they could get until it happened.

There was little else for them to do after that, except prepare to depart, and that took no time at all, since none of them had brought anything with them. Irolla allowed them to take the weapons they had used in her service, even going so far as to bestow an unused sword on Janosec, for symmetry's sake.

Getting into the mortal part of the world is very much easier than trying to get out of it, just as climbing a mountain is so much more difficult than falling off of one. There was the rub. Elementals, being bodiless spirits, don't really notice when they slam into the ground at high rates of speed, unless, of course, they're Earth elementals, and even then, they would only pass through, perhaps cursing the organic stuff polluting their nice clean silica and granite and whatnot.

That method really doesn't work for people, who generally do their cursing before they hit the ground, and not afterwards.

The problem was that there wasn't any method worked out for returning multiple people after they'd been borrowed, for the simple reason that it had never happened before. They could, to be sure, return them one at a time, but that offended the godly sense of aesthetics, not to mention violating several of the Basic Principles of Divine Agency (Latest Revision). Irolla, and of course her fellows, had been straining to come up with a viable alternative ever since Tarkas' party had so miraculously arrived, while she did what she could to delay them without being obvious about it. But there was only so much she could do; she didn't even have a kitchen, so offering them lunch was out of the question.

Besides, Irolla had heard about elemental cooking from Tarkas. At length.

Suddenly the Lady of Life stopped, her mind so clearly elsewhere that the others stopped talking in the middle of words. "The period of rightness has ended," she said to them, and turned, leading them imperiously towards a door somewhere, and the bird that would carry them back home. With all of them at her back, she grinned grimly at the curiosity she felt boiling in each mortal soul. If they couldn't be bothered to ask what a 'period of rightness' was, though, that was their problem.

Once outside the door, she stopped, so abruptly that Janosec, eyes on Mirani next to him, actually bumped into the Divine back, close enough to hear the Divine breath hissing, and see the Divine smoke issuing from the Divine ears. "Who…left… the *door* open?!" asked the Lady of life in a dangerously calm voice.

The menagerie had been wrecked, the plants destroyed, the beasts fled or smashed. From beyond the tree, where the great murf should have watched with majestic dispassion, came the sound of the destruction still in progress. And swiftly upon the sound came the destroyers, Deffin and Tusker rolling and chasing and leaping with great abandon and vitality as they tore each other into little bloody bits.

Irolla raised a hand, trembling with rage, her own fury fueled by the joyful slaughter in the bestial hearts, and Tusker leaped away from Deffin as fast as his legs could carry him. Deffin was made of stronger stuff, and pursued in spite of the Lady and all–nearly all–she could do to him. The best she could do was to keep him moving away from her as she advanced on him. "You!" she roared, and he cringed, "Get out!" He whirled and fled, not bothering to rip the three people in the passageway to shreds. She relaxed her guard, but not so much that she couldn't feel Tusker make his first move to attack her, or stop it. "You too," she said, "Out."

Tusker paused, turning to the passage as if he didn't understand. The wind came in–*Thank you, Kolo!*–and he could smell upon it the ripe and heady scent of challenge. Then his eyes noted the three–

"Not!"

–uninteresting shapes and slid over them, much more interested in what lay beyond, out in the world he had proved himself ready for. Gradually picking up speed, he loped out of the ruined park.

"We go," said the Lady. They noted the shadows first, birds all, outsized like the murf but smaller, all of them capable of carrying a man on its back. For a moment the great flying beasts resisted, but in the end each gave up its perch for a lesser spot on the fortress itself, to have a passenger safely installed on its back. When the three were all aboard, the murf came back down, to receive the Lady herself, and then they were off, in formation, for the plateau.

There were three other figures there when they arrived, persons known to only two of those newly arrived, but no introductions were made or needed. "To return you in the normal way would be dangerous to you," said Irolla, and she nodded at Fenita, "As well as extremely unpleasant. So we have chosen a different way. I would request that you close your eyes, lest the sight of the forces we manipulate here today do you harm." To enforce her ban she redirected the flow of Life in them away from their eyes, so they were temporarily blinded anyway. But the three were honorable, none tried to look and none found they could not. None noticed that the gods' eyes were closed as well.

"You may look again, now."

When Janosec opened his eyes, he wondered briefly what the fuss had been about, since there was no–what was that? Had there not been a blank stone wall there before? Now there was a wooded path, leading off who knew where. "Arm yourselves," said Irolla, and they complied. "We have striven to make this way as hazardless as may be, but true safety is not to be found this side of the grave, and you may have to fight your way through to your home. Speed is best."

Their ready acceptance pleased her, their complete lack of desire was even better. After all that they had done this day, no doubt they all looked forward to a bed. Not necessarily one each.

Only when the last of them had disappeared around the first bend did any of the lords relax their regal postures. "By all the *real* gods, I'm glad that's over with," expostulated Targon.

"But it isn't, my lord," Irolla reminded him. "Tarkas was sought for a reason, the creatures here illicitly, and that reason yet remains. Where is he? He should only have remained invisible until they left."

Kolo's hands moved.

"Ah," said Irolla. "That's no doubt wise. Those trails of his behave oddly at the best of times. He'll be back soon enough."

Tarkas moved down the trail after his adopted family, as unnoticed as his Songs could make him. While his main reason for being here was to make sure the trail went where he wanted it to–*that*way trails aren't meant to be used by ordinary mortals–he was just as glad for the chance to see them together, one last time. And an extra sword at the right time would come in handy, but so far they hadn't needed him. That gormoth hadn't known what hit it.

He didn't think they were happy. By the Edge, he *knew* they were unhappy, *he* certainly was. Mostly. Tarkas was a son of Kwinarish, even after more than half his life lived in another village, in another Realm entirely, and no Kwinarisha could ever feel happy about separation, even if only a separation in space. He would be in their thoughts, he knew, their hearts, and that was what really mattered to him. The fact that he might not, probably would not, ever see them again was nothing by comparison. Mostly.

At least they weren't talking about him. Janosec, apparently, had gotten a little extreme with his security precautions, and so hadn't told his bride anything about the city and clan she was so precipitously joining. For some reason she seemed to think it funny that Fenita wasn't dying of a wasting disease! But it was just as well, she seemed a little taken aback at the thought of a city so small it only had four clans. And the name confused her greatly also. Directional names were pretty normal, but in reference to the Eye, not to a sea! It was very subtly disorienting, not knowing where in the world she was. But Janosec was here, so she stayed close to him, and then it was as all right as it ever would be.

Fenita kept silent, far more concerned about other things than a description of Querdishan's internal relationships, although she had to admit he did an excellent job of describing the main actors in city affairs. Even Selter cut a…well, not a *dramatic* figure, she supposed, but certainly an effective one.

Tarkas was ready to explode, not only with a nagging itch, but with barely contained mirth. Janosec's portrayal of Navak couldn't be accurate, could it? Thranj's Beard! He never did that when Tarkas was around! Perhaps he was exaggerating for Mirani's benefit. Selter had even been drawn in a color other than gray. Tarkas expected a rather more honest portrayal of Kestrel, Fenita's father, and was not disappointed. About Jerim he refrained from speaking, naturally.

Tarkas paid great attention to every word, chiseling them all into his perfect recall, astonished at the city he lived in but somehow never knew. Not that he minded, people always act differently with different people, and Janosec's tale brought him a vision of those ways that he had never seen before. Even Selter's nature, so…retiring when confronted with the daunting presence of other, more powerful personalities, became vibrant in its own proper sphere. How could Tarkas have ever known, without Janosec to tell him? Even Fenita, who had known these men all her life, was listening spellbou–

Tarkas suddenly noticed that he was scratching, still scratching, at an itch that never quite went away. That meant magic, and that meant…

Janosec.

The young man was working magic, all unconsciously, weaving spells with his tales the way Tarkas did with his Songs. Tarkas listened again, but with different ears this time, Holan's ears, listening to the way the words were being put together, as he had so often been instructed to do by his old master. The words were familiar, very familiar. They were his, or could have been. His son was making Songs without music.

When the trail made its usual abrupt *this*way turn, even Tarkas was surprised, shaking off the charm with a bit of a start, and found himself sinking! The earth, the soil, the ground beneath his feet was giving way! He leaped, clutching frantically at his you-don't-see-me spell as he scrambled onto a much more solid stone, long ago cast up with the raising of the great stone wall at their backs. No one else noticed, of course; Janosec's spell, or the distant view of their home, monopolized all attention.

They took their time about leaving, not that he was at all impatient for them to be gone. But the rock was getting suspiciously soft when they finally took themselves off, heading over the ledge to the spot by the path, clearly marked from all the times he had used it himself. He didn't follow, just watched as their forms faded into the dimming light. The wind picked up, he supposed the Tower of Air was telling of their arrival, but he couldn't hear it. He could feel it though, like a wave of heat in the air, a long-pent-up sense of relief and celebration. Jerim hadn't doubted, not at all.

It was pleasant, in a way, but soon enough the intensity faded, and the glory of the world seemed far less than he remembered it being. Even the rock didn't want him where he was. This part of his life was over, and another beginning. Time to go. *That*way.

Chapter 17

Soft, white light. Puffy clouds. Music, wordless, but still music. Pleasant aromas and a general, pervasive sense of well-being.

"Where the Hell am I?" asked Tarkas loudly.

The music stopped, screeching. The machine in the corner stopped spewing out clouds of water vapor, which rapidly evaporated under the glare of the white lights hanging from long black cables. "Kill the mood, why don't you?" suggested a rough, sarcastic voice from (where else?) behind him.

Tarkas turned. "Sorry about that," he said.

The speaker, a man to all appearances, chuckled cynically. "I'll bet. You don't look like the sort to regret much."

Tarkas shrugged. "It seems a waste of time, to me," he explained, coming closer to the crotchety geezer, "Would you like to know why?"

"No," snapped the man, knocking wadded up balls of fluff from some chairs. He pushed one closer to the ex-Hero and settled into the other himself. "I don't reveal myself much, certainly not to get lectured in applied ethics by some wet-behind-the-ears new Legend."

Tarkas made no great show of surprise, seating himself comfortably with his Great Sword across his legs. "You are The Hidden One, then?"

The man laughed. "You call this hidden?" he asked, waving at all the scenery and gadgets, "This is nothing! The Hidden One would have used all this just to hide the stuff that disguised the reality he was concealed in." He placed a hand on his own chest, in a gesture of modesty. "I, on the other hand, am out there in the world, each and every day. If the people I meet are unable to penetrate this simple shell to the underlying reality that's not my problem. I was surprised by Janosec, he'll do very well by you."

Tarkas was silent for several moments, but not because he wanted to be. It's hard to blaspheme when the god whose name you're taking in vain is sitting in front of you, while profanity is just not proper, somehow. So Tarkas froze, his tongue holding back a flood of variations on the 'What (*insert profanity here*) are you talking about?' theme, until, "I hope you are willing to…explain your meaning?"

The not-so-hidden one rolled his eyes. "Didn't anyone explain to you about Legends?"

"No," said Tarkas, recalling the scene easily. "My mentor, Hara-Khan the Merciful, said that I would only be able to understand when I got there, so there was no point. I believe they have to die, but I don't even really know that."

"*Hmm*," mused the god, "Well, there's death, and then there's Death. I always thought of it this way: Imagine yourself as a puddle, a small body of water. Eventually that puddle dries up." Tarkas nodded. "Unless a stream comes along, refilling the puddle as it dries, in which case the puddle can theoretically continue forever." Again Tarkas nodded, although the 'theoretically' part gave him reason to pause. "Now a puddle that continues forever is called a pond, and ponds are useful things. Like for watering crops, and other things, from which the water makes its way into the stream, and from there back into the pond."

Tarkas rather appreciated the aesthetics of the circular process but–"And Janosec's role in all this?"

"Janosec's the farmer," explained the god. "You can't be a Legend without legends, after all. Someone has to tell the stories about you, spread the word of your exploits far and wide, watering the spiritual fields with the holy liquid of wonder and mystery–"

"And if he fails?" Tarkas interrupted the rhapsodizing. Leave poetry to the professionals.

"You'd fade," answered the god straightforwardly. "The pond would go away, not the way the puddle would have, but gone just the same. The water of life that flows through you would subside, and you would subside with it. Not 'dead', exactly, but so dispersed as to be effectively non-existent."

"Please stop," implored the Legend, "You're not making it sound any better."

"Sorry."

Tarkas snorted cynically. "I'll bet." Then he thought back, considering all the things that had been said, and those that hadn't. "How did he surprise you?"

The god raised his brows. "Don't forget much, do you?"

"No."

The room spun madly, taking Tarkas by surprise. When it stopped he was sitting at a low table, a mug in front of his place, filled with a nice serving of delightfully aromatic brew in a spacious tavern. An old man, a different old man, dressed now in well-worn traveling leathers, sat opposite him, sipping from his own cup. "When we first met he fairly reeked."

"That was sweat."

"It was history!" snapped the traveler, thumping his cup so hard on the table it sloshed brew everywhere. "A heady elixir, only brewed in the souls of those with a true awareness, and him filled to overflowing. By the Source, it was fabulous." He took a deep slurp of his full mug.

The one-time Singer was impressed. "That was very well said."

"Ah, such praise, from such a noble mind and keen sense, can only warm the heart and fill the–"

"You can stop now."

The god subsided, not without a mild frown. "Thank the gods it was late," he continued. "Otherwise I might have hurt him in my thirst for those stories."

"And what part of this surprised you?"

"I've met lots of Rememberers in my day, young Legend," said the traveler with great force, "You might even say I collect them. But never one with such a powerful connection, such a strong sense of the experiences he related. Tell me, did you really do that thing with the dirkins?"

Tarkas had the grace to look embarrassed. "Yeah," he mumbled, hiding his discomfiture with a sip from his continually-full mug. "Although recently I've been thinking that 'dirkins' really isn't the best na–"

"Ha!" yelled the traveler, smacking his mug down again. "I said the very same thing!" But not to Tarkas. "Interesting coincidence, eh?"

"Perhaps a blood bond would–?"

The old man waved the suggestion aside. "Yes, yes, of course," he agreed, as Tarkas took a sip of his neglected brew. "And if it were anyone else I'd accept that. But you're a Hero, or you were, and Heroes don't have–"

"He's my son."

"That's impossible. How'd it happen?"

Tarkas leaned back, spreading his hands. "Timing, they think," he explained. "No one really knows. It's not supposed to happen."

"It's not supposed to be able to happen." The god sipped his mug again. "It explains a lot, though." He thought about it a bit more. "Why does he call you Uncle?"

Tarkas made a face, hid it behind his mug as he tried to empty the thing. "Pellik's Rule."

"You're not even *from* this Realm! How can you be anyone's brother?!"

"I was adopted after the fact," snapped Tarkas, adding, "For services rendered."

"To *whom*?" He spluttered, either with rage or laughter, it was hard to tell.

"To him, of course," replied Tarkas innocently. "I saved his life, as things turned out."

"Tell me."

Tarkas complied. It was a legitimate command, and even if it wasn't, one doesn't argue with gods, so he told again the tale of his very first adventure in their service.

"And how does that involve Pellik's Rule?" asked the old man when he finished.

"Well, it didn't," admitted the new Legend, soothing his throat after his tale with a swig of brew. "Not directly, but as matters progressed…"

"'Matters'?"

"Size. Strength. Stomach problems, other minor disorders."

"*Hmm*, yes. And by then, Pellik's Rule would have been the best rug to sweep everything under." Suddenly the traveler grinned. "It'll be interesting to see what kind of Legend you become, with such a 'heroic' Rememberer to start you off."

"Don't you know the future?" asked Tarkas, astonished. "You are a god."

The room spun again, but only a little, and Tarkas found himself sitting on a rock, in the middle of a field. Before him on another rock sat a woman with a child on her lap.

"What of it? You're a Legend, not one of my own," said mommy. "And the day I can see the future here is the day I pop off like the Hidden One, and leave the Realm to someone who can't."

"Janosec's nice," said the little girl, "He told me lots of nice stories, and showed me how to tie my sandals!" She held them up proudly, and Tarkas had to restrain himself from congratulating her, so bright and charming was her smile.

"And he managed not to call me a lackwit while he did it," the mother added, snorting. "That boy will go far."

Tarkas would know all of it, and be proud of all of it, even long after his son was–Suddenly he didn't want to speak of Janosec anymore. "Are we done?"

The mother looked at him with a god's eyes. "It would seem so, young Legend. You have new powers, of course, and time to discover them, but the limits are great as well. The Deities' handbook in the library will help, now that you can read those sections, although different Legends tend to have different strengths–"

Tarkas had no need to ask which library, only the library at Mendilorn would have a copy of the handbook. And new lore!

"–And your sword will be both help and bane. The most important things I cannot tell you, but you seem to know most of them already. The price for this early knowledge will likely be heavy."

Tarkas forced a smile. "Better than ignorance."

"Very true. Better to die a Hero."

Again the room spun madly, but this time he tipped forward as well, and found himself falling. The pinks and gauzy whites of the room vanished above him, and he saw blurs of blue and green, before he came to a standing stop in the middle of a path, no doubt the *that*way trail he had originally called up. His sword was on his back, and he wondered if the whole interview hadn't been within his own mind. That could be bad, *that*way trails get a bit testy when travelers aren't traveling. *Things* come along to… encourage them.

With Irolla on the far end, he needed no encouragement. He walked, he trotted, he ran, longer and faster than he usually could, and found himself wondering if this was one of those new powers the god had mentioned. Was it just speed? It didn't feel like speed, didn't feel like anything. Something greater that he was only using for speed now? He could not run in the mortal world like this, not with his feet sinking into the ground. Would he never be able to walk there again?

On impulse, he stopped, and picked up a stone, just a pebble. Until he squeezed it between his thumb and forefinger, when it became a scattering of pulverized pebble dust. That was about right. As a Hero, he had been able to do that in the mortal world, so in some respects it looked like his powers from that period of his life had been upgraded substantially. But the words of the god played in his head, and he wondered what was a gift, and what else a trap he had yet to fall into.

Something was coming.

The birds still sang. The insects still made their various noises. So what was he–? No, he couldn't hear anything, even though it seemed like his ears were phenomenally sharp, after his long time in the mortal world. He even closed his eyes, he'd found a long time ago that sometimes his eyes distracted him, and closing them helped sharpen his other senses.

What was this?! Usually when he closed his eyes, he saw darkness, with perhaps faint copies of things he'd just seen, if he actually troubled himself to look for them, or sometimes sparkles, or bright spots. But not this! If it had been his eyes he would have called it light, and vision, but it wasn't, so he didn't.

A twig snapped.

Something apparent to his other sense blazed.

He opened his eyes, just as the angry gormoth leaped from cover, right at him, standing stupidly with his eyes shut! But his panic was premature and quickly passed. A gormoth was barely a threat to a Hero; as a Legend, he dealt with this first attack with ridiculous ease, hurling the beast through the air while he drew his sword lazily. The second attack was the last, the wondrous black sword easily cleaving the–

Death!

Ice cold winds, dimming lights, muted sounds. Dead leaves blowing on dried grass. Waterless air moving through empty skulls. The buzzing of flies. The breaking of hearts, harsh words. All were him and he was all, the flowing of his blood slowing with the beast's, the beating of his heart ceasing with the beast's, the breathing of lungs ceasing with the beast's. His body lost its strength and he fell senseless beside his victim.

Then his eyes saw, his ears heard, his body worked once more.

"I hate to say this," said a familiar voice, "But you look like me warmed over." Tarkas hated to hear it as much as the speaker hated to say it. Trust Death to make a joke like that at a time like this. At least he did not try to extend a hand, as the ex-Hero struggled to his feet clumsily. He took one look at his friend and averted his eyes.

"*Must* you?" asked Tarkas, a little put off for some reason.

"Must I what?" inquired Death innocently. Tarkas had never objected to his bad jokes before. At the expression on his friend's face he looked on himself, and the mystery cleared at once. "Oh. Sorry," amended the skeletal figure, its jawbone working obscenely as disconnected-but-somehow-still-hanging-together finger bones smoothed its black robe, emphasizing the grotesque hollow that should have been a bulge. Tarkas wasn't looking, of course, but he had his eyes on the strange curved blade at the top of death's staff when it vanished, and it became just a staff again. Only then did he dare look down, to find the normally rotund person he preferred by far.

"Much better."

"It's just an appearance, you know," Death chided him mildly.

"It's a gross appearance, you know," replied the ex-Hero.

"Baby," muttered the entity under its breath, then more loudly said, "Allow me to be the second to welcome you to your new rank." The tone seemed rather remote, as if the being had practiced the line often.

"Why second?" Tarkas asked.

"I can't be first," explained Death, "That's in the rules. The god of the Realm always gets to go first, RHIP and all that. But it is usually not very long before you guys kill something. Hurts, huh?"

Tarkas shook his head. "The exact opposite, really. You have to be alive and feel to hurt."

"Wouldn't know," said Death, heading for a convenient rock, to support his bulk for a few precious moments.

"Take my word for it," suggested Tarkas, following. "So I guess killing things is no longer one of my abilities."

"Not living things, anyway," agreed Death, accustomed to the question. "Or responsibilities, either. You lot deal more with the unliving. There aren't as many of them, but there aren't so many of you Legends either." From behind, a thing that looked like a hand tapped on Death's shoulder, but Tarkas knew better than to try to see if the tapper was a thing that looked like a man. Nor did he ask what was in the note that Death received.

Instead he rubbed a shoulder, still sore from falling to the ground. "The god could have told me."

"Some things you have to learn the hard way, if you're going to learn them at all," observed Death dispassionately. "If he had told you, maybe you would have listened and stopped killing things. But even then you wouldn't have felt it, you wouldn't have understood the significance of Death to mortals. There's only one way for a mortal to experience death. Or was." He crumpled the note ominously.

Tarkas still flinched when Death got angry, a reflex he was going to have to unlearn. "What do you mean, *was*?"

"I have just been told," said Death in a brittle voice, powdered note drifting down from his grinding fingers, "That someone doesn't seem to have appreciated my…efforts on his behalf."

Tarkas looked at the still form of the gormoth.

Death didn't bother. "Please, I see enough of that sort of thing as it is." He struggled to his feet, using his staff ably. "Look, I have to go. Something's come up, one of my clients seems to have…denied service to his account. My staff are claiming even the account is gone, which is all I need. I have to go start the wheels in motion."

"What wheels?" asked Tarkas, a little confused with his sudden inclusion into the inner circles.

"The Major Deities," Death explained, "If this guy thinks he can get away from me *and* them he's seriously mistaken. If he shows his face anywhere under any sun, *pfft*!" Death made a wiping gesture. "Say hello to Irolla for me. Good piece of work on that Querd job, by the way."

"Thank you."

"Not you, lummox, her. Putting personalities back together is no easy chore."

"I was thanking you on her behalf."

"Sure you were," sneered Death, and then they both burst out laughing, but it didn't last. "I guess I won't be seeing too much of you anymore. I'll miss you."

"And I, you," echoed Tarkas, "Don't take any wooden nickels."

"Don't do anything I would do. Now off you *–hmm*?" Just like business to interrupt an otherwise pleasant leave-taking. Once again, a little yellow hand tapped at Death's shoulder, and again Tarkas was glad he could not see the owner and never would. Death partly turned, to receive yet another of the scraps of vellum that followed him in his interminable rounds, but this one wasn't for him. "You wouldn't happen to know someone named Tomo, would you?"

Janosec sat up, almost shouting, but the reflexes of a lifetime sleeping with lots of siblings in the same room came to his rescue, even though only Mirani was in the room with him and she was too exhausted to notice. She breathed deeply, slowly, and he listened to that pleasant sound rather than to the hammering of his heart, the panting of his breath, or the rush of blood in his ears.

Something was coming! Something was attacking me-him–Uncle! Dragons!

Dragons? *What the hell are dragons?*

Janosec threw back his covers, still strongly aware of the presence of Mirani–how strange, yet wonderful, even more so than having a room to themselves–and was careful not to disturb her as he stepped away from the bed. The window, naturally, opened onto the courtyard, designed that way in the old, old days to prevent assassins from having an easy route to the Heir.

It also happened to face the Wall, that great mass of stone nearly cutting them off from the rest of the land, once a protection, now…something less. Could it be true, what Father had said, that the world was thin there and things could come through? It was hard to imagine, even though they had done it themselves. Looking back on it, it occurred to Janosec that the spot looked well trampled, and where had the notch in the hillside come from? Tarkas, perhaps? And hopefully not too much else, although Mother's story seemed to give the lie to the hope.

Tarkas was alive. He was certain of that, could practically feel it. So what had the other thing been, black and fearsome, cold and soul-consuming? Was that a–a 'dragon'? Somehow he didn't think so, it seemed like…just a word, however interesting it might be. Why would Uncle be thinking of words like that? Did he really want to know? Some things, he decided once again, should not be the subject of tales. After a while, he realized he was cold and considered going back to bed, but the needs of the body presented themselves, so he decided to do what it was going to make him do eventually anyway and went off to use the privy instead.

On the way back he made a misstep, the looser, creaking boards of the second floor still unknown to him, and betrayed himself.

"Hey!"

Inside himself, he wilted, standing stock-still on the floor in the hopes that the call would not be repeated. In vain. "I'm thirsty!"

Crap.

"I'm thirsty!"

"Yes, Denora, I'm coming," he mumbled. He pushed open the door, slowly, and saw her silhouette against the window, standing up in her bed, arms outstretched.

"Hi, Ja'sec," she called. "I'm thirsty."

"Yes," he agreed, "I heard you." He picked her up and carried her downstairs, well aware that the only way to get her, and therefore himself, back in bed, was to get her something to drink and let her decide for herself to go back to bed. It was a pain in his butt, but she was actually very good about it, much better than some other clan's children he could think of.

The kitchen was empty, of course, modestly illuminated by the banked coals of the stove. He sat his littlest sister down in a convenient chair while he went and got a cup and ladled some water into it.

"Uppie me!" she commanded, when he handed her the mug, "I want to sit with you."

Nothing for it but to pick her up, sit down, and place her carefully in his lap, her back comfortably snuggled up against his front, his arms loosely clasped around her as he sipped carefully from her mug. "Thank you, Ja'sec," she said, politely, and then continued the ritual herself, "You're welcome, D'ora." He didn't have to say a thing.

She slurped and swallowed peacefully for some time, and then said, in a tone of wondrous discovery, "Ja'sec, you home."

"Yes, I am," he agreed.

"Where you go?" she asked ungrammatically, "What are you doing?"

He shuddered around her, tremendous laughter that could not explode out of him. "Well, Denora," he said, when it was all over, "This is what happened…"

Epilogue

High above, someone waited.

The Hero must die.

He wore a long robe with a hood, so one could not see his hair; his manner suggested age, while his hands bespoke youth. He sat with the kind of preternatural stillness that usually only the undead can muster, the kind where one had to look to see if he breathed or not. He didn't.

The Hero must die.

The cowled one watched for him, his posture revealing not one whit the anxiety he felt. The young man had accomplished all, as he had expected, his own intervention undetectable. Or it should have been. Apparently he had forgotten a detail. And he had compounded that error with another, missing what should have been an easy target on the night of his return, alerting the local authorities to the presence of his goblins, if not himself. He would hate to lose them.

The Hero had to die. The goblins would kill him when next he returned. And he would come home, of that the god with no name was certain.

The Hero will come home, if I have to tumble Querdishan into the sea to do it.

Meet the Author:

Marc Vun Kannon was born in Bethpage, Long Island. After surviving his teenage years, he entered Hofstra University. Five years later, he exited with a BA in philosophy and a wife. He still has both, but the wife is more useful.

After dabbling in fulfilling pursuits such as stock boy and gas station attendant, he found his spiritual home maintaining and repairing fire extinguishers for Fire Foe. Fourteen years later he is still there. Still married to that wife, too.

For diversion, along the way, he almost accumulated a PhD in philosophy and is currently working on his second BA in Computer Science. He feels that his real job is being a father to his three children, husband to his wife, and author to his books.

He, and they, now reside in Wading River, Long Island, New York.

Visit his site at
www.marcvunkannon.com

Also available from Echelon Press Publishing

Situation Sabotage (*Global Adventure*) Graeme Johns

*Contamination…sabotage…*terms feared by food industry executives around the world. They prefer to announce the problem as a potential…*situation.* Now, Investigator Barton has been called in to solve the case before word leaks out. A frantic dash across the Pacific uncovers three murders before he discovers the mastermind behind the sabotage.

$12.99 ISBN 1-59080-477-5

Invasion of Justice (*Women's Adventure*) Regan Black

In 2096 an empath with a penchant for all things retro, Petra Neiman is making a good name for herself reading crime scenes for the judicial system. That is until a serial killer drags her into his crimes and pins a gruesome murder on her brother. Now she must sort through myriad feelings and memories to unravel a plot that began before her birth.

$12.99 ISBN 1-59080-443-0

Dangerous Affairs (*Romantic Suspense*) Kelle Z. Riley

A man fighting his past. A woman fleeing hers. When fate throws them together they form an unlikely—and temporary—alliance. Soon real passion infuses their fake marriage and they begin to dream of more. But someone has other plans. Someone who would rather see them dead than happy.

$12.99 ISBN 1-59080-468-6

Fractured Souls (*Suspense*) T.A. Ridgell

*People aren't always what they seem...*Terrifying accidents have Dr. Benita Kyser on edge. Teaming up with private investigator, Sean Turner, they work against time to identify the threat. *Cracked Minds Lead to Fractured Souls...*One man wants more from Beni. She's the reason for his success--or failure. He will have her as his own. And if he can't--then no one will...

$12.99 ISBN 1-59080-471-6